"ANYTHING I HAVE IS YOURS FOR THE TAKING . . .

"Ginny, no one forced me to give you my name. I did it of my own free will," he said. "Can you not exercise the same will and be my wife completely? Till death do us part—that was the vow."

The strong hands cupping her shoulders, and his warm breath touching her neck, snatched Ginny's thoughts from her head. A small tremor beset her body.

"Forget the past, and concentrate on the future . . . our future." He lowered his head to the nape of her neck, and the coat she'd wrapped around her shoulders slipped unnoticed to the floor.

CAPTURE THE GLOW
OF ZEBRA'S HEARTFIRES

AUTUMN ECSTASY   (3133, $4.25)
by Pamela K. Forrest

Philadelphia beauty Linsey McAdams had eluded her kidnappers but was now at the mercy of the ruggedly handsome frontiersman who owned the remote cabin where she had taken refuge. The two were snowbound until spring, and handsome Luc LeClerc soon fancied the green-eyed temptress would keep him warm through the long winter months. He said he would take her home at winter's end, but she knew that with one embrace, she might never want to leave!

BELOVED SAVAGE   (3134, $4.25)
by Sandra Bishop

Susannah Jacobs would do anything to survive — even submit to the bronze-skinned warrior who held her captive. But the beautiful maiden vowed not to let the handsome Tonnewa capture her heart as well. Soon, though, she found herself longing for the scorching kisses and tender caresses of her raven-haired BELOVED SAVAGE.

CANADIAN KISS   (3135, $4.25)
by Christine Carson

Golden-haired Sara Oliver was sent from London to Vancouver to marry a stranger three times her age — only to have her husband-to-be murdered on their wedding day. Sara vowed to track the murderer down, but he ambushed her and left her for dead. When she awoke, wounded and frightened, she was staring into the eyes of the handsome loner Tom Russel. As the rugged stranger nursed her to health, the flames of passion erupted, and their CANADIAN KISS threatened never to end!

LINDSEY HANKS
LONG VIRGINIA NIGHTS

ZEBRA BOOKS
KENSINGTON PUBLISHING CORP.

To our Mothers
With Love
Naomi *Lindsey* Boyd
Laverne *Hanks* Wilson

ZEBRA BOOKS

are published by

Kensington Publishing Corp.
475 Park Avenue South
New York, NY 10016

First printing: March, 1992

Printed in the United States of America

1

Lord Oliver Summerfield, eighth Duke of Hallsway, took a pinch of snuff and sneezed vigorously. The troubled man leaned back in his chair and studied the raindrops that splattered the multipaneled windows and rolled leisurely down the glass. The droplets reminded him of a woman's tears, of his beloved Johanna, dead these many years. He could still recall the salty taste of her tears as he had kissed them away, assuring her that he would carry out her wishes. In the evening of that same day, she had died in his arms, a tender smile on her lips. She was at peace, because she knew her lover's promises were not made in vain. He would take care of their son.

Oh, what a beautiful creature she had been. How he had loved her, from the moment he had scooped her up from the ice-laden pond. She had thanked him sweetly, and timidly admitted that it was her first try at this sport. He had been quick to offer his direction and a strong arm. After hours of a most enjoyable day, Lord Oliver and Johanna had shared hot mulled wine and quiet conversation. That moment had been the beginning of an everlasting love.

Lord Oliver was a married man, but his marriage was an arranged one, as were so many of his class—a business venture, no more, no less. The bloodlines stayed pure and amassed fortunes and titles for the joined families. More often than not, the gentlemen of these situations took a mistress. Lord Oliver had his share of women. Yet the instant his eyes beheld Johanna Cross, his heart was never truly his own again. That she loved him so boldly in return, never ceased to astonish him.

Johanna had married at a very young age, and widowed only a few years later. She managed nicely on the inheritance her late husband left her.

She had understood and accepted Lord Oliver's marriage, as she did so many things that life had dealt her. Nevertheless, she had always known that his heart belonged to her. They had lived and loved and laughed as lovers are wont to do. They shared secrets and dreams and fears, or just comforted one another when sadness crept in.

The birth of their son, Jonathan, had been a joyous occasion. Lord Oliver smiled fondly. It was clear their son had inherited the choicest qualities from each parent. He hesitated, maybe not, he thought wisely. Jonathan was endowed with a damnable temper and fierce pride.

After Johanna's death, Lord Oliver moved Jonathan, bag and baggage, into his own home. His wife had been sickly, and spent her time abed or closeted in her chamber. She never forgave Lord Oliver for foisting his illegitimate son on her. He knew Jonathan had suffered from her cutting tongue.

His legal son and heir, Geoffrey, appeared to accept Jonathan's presence. No one's fool, Lord Oliver knew of the cruel tricks played on Jonathan and the spiteful destruction of his toys. Jonathan attended the same schools as Geoffrey, soaking up knowledge like a dry sponge. Still, Lord Oliver had been aware of the stigma his son was unable to overcome. Regardless of his good works, the label haunted him.

Granted, he loved both his sons. Geoffrey, although turned like his mother, was a personable chap. Lord Oliver supposed Geoffrey could not help it if his constitution was not as strong as Jonathan's. Geoffrey absolutely abhorred hunting, and horses sent him into a twitter. He preferred to spend his time with his tailor, designing new and outrageous fashions, or entertaining ladies and lords of the realm. Dandified was the perfect word to describe his eldest son. Geoffrey would never want for anything; his birthright had seen to that. Would he ever give him grandchildren? Lord Oliver doubted it. Geoffrey was more interested in women as comrades rather than love mates.

Jonathan, on the other hand, was everything a man could ask for in a son—trustworthy, dependable, and much too handsome for his own good. He had strong shoulders that bore a heavy burden. Yet, how long would he continue to try, when the stain of his birth hampered him from attaining the respect due a son of the realm? Lord Oliver had pondered this dilemma for many years. In the last few, it had plagued him relentlessly. He didn't know the whole of the story, but something in Jonathan's life had hurt him and made him terribly bitter. Jonathan's man servant, Blue, had let slip that Jonathan had been rejected by the girl he loved. Her family was very well-heeled, and didn't want their name besmirched by a bastard. Lord Oliver's heart wept for his proud son, and he tried harder than ever to come up with a solution to help Jonathan. Some time ago he had struck upon an idea that had unlimited potential. Perhaps a bit of deceit was in order. He would use any means available. His plan would afford Jonathan the opportunity to lead a rich and fulfilling life, enable him to grow in his own right. To keep a promise he had made long ago, Lord Oliver would have to do the hardest thing he had ever had to do. He had to send his son away, a bitter powder indeed, but he had procrastinated long enough. Would his Johanna understand his tactics? The time was nigh. He sighed deeply and checked his timepiece. Jonathan would arrive soon.

"Blueblood," snorted the elderly gentleman. "I am sick to death of the term. I want grandchildren with rich red blood flowing through their veins." The muted sound of tap, slide, tap repeated itself, as the speaker shuffled to and fro, heartily abusing the fine carpeting.

"Sir, would I be out of line if I reminded you that your blood is as blue as that which you scoff?" inquired the young man.

"Humph, my point exactly, and what has it got me? My heir is a simpleminded twit, more concerned with the color of his neck cloth than the running of multiple estates. My wife, God rest her soul, was sickly from the time she conceived that twit, until her dying breath two years ago." Running aged fingers through his thick white hair, the old man sighed. "Truth to tell, I believe the blood's too blue."

A mocking brow shot up beneath unruly ebony hair.

"I don't need your sarcasm," snapped Lord Oliver. "I need your cooperation."

"Then you shall have it," came the pert reply.

Lord Oliver settled himself in a plump chair, and for several seconds studied the ornate handle of his cane before he finally spoke. "Jonathan, I did not speak in jest concerning my desire for grandchildren. It is my most heartfelt wish."

"I did not take it in jest, sir, but in the same frame, I don't know of what help I can be. Wouldn't it be better to speak with Geoffrey of your desires? After all, he is your legal son and heir."

Lord Oliver slammed his cane against the floor. "You are my son, also," he shouted.

"Your bastard son," was the soft reply.

"Nonetheless, you are my son."

"You want me to sire your grandchildren?" A hint of sarcasm laced the young man's words.

"That's correct," his father replied undaunted.

Jonathan sprang to his feet and paced the same path his father had deserted only moments before. "Do you have any idea what you ask? If I did have a wife, any children I might sire would suffer because of my illegitimacy. Could you consign your grandchildren to such a cruel fate?"

"Like you've had, Jonathan?"

"I'm not complaining."

"No, you have never complained, but I know how difficult it has been for you. Come, let us have a brandy. I have a

8

devil of a good plan lurking in here." Lord Oliver tapped his forefinger against his head.

"Jonathan, it has been a heavy burden for me to tolerate the knowledge that you can never inherit any of the estates."

The young man paused briefly before accepting the crystal glass from his father. "That in itself is the reason I must implore again, would not your desires be readily attainable through Geoffrey?"

"Humph! That poppycock has been the bane of my existence for more years than I care to admit. He dotes on a whirl of parties, routs, and his ability to lead the *ton* in the latest fashion. When called upon, he can strike a pose to lead a minuet in an instant. However, question him about the milk he pours into his tea, and I assure you he won't know from which end of the cow the milk comes." The old Duke snorted once again. "I'm convinced that when the Lord said, *Males, come this way,* Geoffrey was probably powdering his nose and thought He said *mail.* Thinking he would receive no correspondence, he ignored the summons."

Jonathan burst into laughter. He settled himself into a chair, the mate to the one his father occupied. Setting his drink aside, he steepled his fingers and studied his father with respect and admiration. He would listen to the plan, for he owed his father that much. Lord Oliver had always played straight with Jonathan. They did not always agree, and on occasion, their disagreements had rung through the airy rooms, sending the servants into shock at the unusual display. No one talked to Lord Oliver in a negative fashion, much less raised his voice in defense of an opinion. The servants had come to believe Lord Oliver relished the verbal battles as much as he did the presence of his dearly beloved son.

"It is quite well-known that you are a ladies' man, Jonathan. Indeed, a rascal in your pursuit of pleasure, racing, wenching, and gambling. I dare say the stables boast the finest horseflesh available, and you have left a string of broken hearts in your wake. Not to mention the empty pockets of those foolish enough to wager against you."

9

Jonathan shrugged his shoulders. "I fear my deeds are blatantly exaggerated."

"Humph! I would ask, do you truly enjoy your life-style?"

"It passes the time."

"I have it on very good authority that you'd be content to remain in the country working with your horses."

"I see Blue has been talking out of turn again. However, I must admit it gives me pleasure."

"Then you should not find my plan unfavorable. You are aware that I own many properties in America."

Jonathan nodded.

"Just recently I have gained a sizeable plantation in Virginia."

"Tobacco country," Jonathan supplied.

"You have always been knowledgeable about this country. Would you be adverse to living there?"

Jonathan's brow shot once more beneath his hair, and for an instant pain swept his gray eyes. "You want to send me away?"

"I want something better for you, *son*. You can have all the things in America that you are denied here, and damn it, I want grandchildren."

A twinkle danced in Jonathan's eyes. "Sir, as grand as this Virginia sounds, I am sure that you cannot pluck grandchildren from the trees, nor grow them from the fertile soil."

"No, but you can damn well find yourself a wife with rich red blood, and beget me a grandchild."

"You are being unreasonable."

Lord Oliver snorted. "You can call it unreasonable, when I want you to be the master of your destiny?"

"It appears, sir, that you have my destiny mapped out already."

"That's unfair, Jonathan. I might as well get down to the bare truth, or have you think I am no more than a cantankerous old man. I'm getting on in years, and I wish to see you happy and well settled while there is still time." Lord Oliver ran his weathered hand slowly over the area of his heart as he spoke.

Concern etched Jonathan's features as he questioned, "Are you ill, father?"

"No." He hedged for a brief instant. "Nothing other than this damnable gout. It gives me no rest and vexes my good nature." While Lord Oliver spoke, his heart hammered with pleasure. It was a rare day indeed when Jonathan addressed him as father.

"Jonathan, I'm concerned with your future. If you will bear with me, I will tell you of my plan."

"You have my undivided attention, sir."

"As I've told you, I have bought this plantation. My agent in America, Richard Denby, assures me that if managed properly, my investment will yield a hefty profit. The former owners were not wise in several ventures. Also, they continued to live beyond their means instead of tightening their belts to weather the losses. We import huge amounts of American tobacco every year. It would be wise to invest in this crop. And who more able than my own son to see the venture through?"

"My knowledge of raising tobacco would in no way enable me to raise such a taxing product. You would lose your investment in a year's time."

"I have thought of that, and have taken steps to correct the situation. Mr. Denby has hired an excellent crop master. He will teach you everything you need to know."

"This is your plan?"

"Not all of it," Lord Oliver announced with a twinkle in his eyes. "You will also find yourself a wife. On the day of your wedding, you shall receive the title to the plantation. When your first child is born, you shall receive the titles to varied other properties and shares that I own in America. My agent is aware of my wishes. Should anything happen to me, he will see them carried out as I desired."

"A very generous offer, Your Grace."

"Make of it what you will, Jonathan. It is yours to build a life around, or to lose on the turn of a card. This is my way to make up in some small degree for the grievous error I committed against you by your illegitimate birth. Last, but by no means least — I want grandchildren."

"If I should agree to your demands, does it mean I cannot return to England?"

"You may return anytime you wish, but I hope you will embrace your new country with a zest that leaves you no time to brood for England. I have heard it said that anyone can be anything they desire in this land, if they work hard enough. That is not the case in England. There are too many class distinctions."

Jonathan studied his father intently for several moments. He pondered his father's decision, wondering if Lord Oliver was shamed by his presence in England. The tentacles of disappointment and bitterness wrapped around his skeptical heart. The sadness lurking inside, he masked, as he had often done in his five and thirty years of life. He made a solemn promise that no one would ever know the pain surging through him. Once again he was being cast aside . . . this time by his father.

He extended his hand to his father. "I shall try to execute your wishes to the best of my ability."

Lord Oliver clasped his hand warmly. "I've never had any doubt that you could; it was whether or not you *would*."

Father and son's laughter brought a smile to the servants working throughout the lower floor of the mansion.

Jonathan's eyes drifted around the familiar rooms, reviving a host of memories as he walked slowly through them. These were the same rooms he had shared with his mother as a child. Lord Oliver had taken care of the town house after Johanna's death. When Jonathan finished his schooling, he had divided his time between the town house and his father's stables. Still, this was home to him. He had never been comfortable living in his father's mansion.

Jonathan had inherited from his mother and invested carefully. The profits garnered from his investments enabled him to indulge his favorite pastime. Horses. Over the years, he had gained quite a reputation for his fine horseflesh. He studied particular breeds and the qualities he admired in each animal, then crossbred until he developed a strain with stamina and strength, coupled with beauty. His horses were always in demand. At one time or another the creme de la creme of London society had traipsed through the stables, seeking to add to their own stables, or asking a multitude of questions. These dealings with his peers never for one instant diminished the tag of illegitimacy. Their condescending attitude left him feeling as though he wore a banner around his neck, proclaiming him a bastard. He came to loathe the very people who lined his pockets with coins from their purchases — thus nourishing his wild escapades.

The women especially had made a lasting impression. He was the forbidden fruit, made more desirable because of his carelessness. Once they had had a taste, they were reluctant to give him up. The one time he'd let himself care had been enough for him. Caring only brought heartache and misery. His venture into love had cured him of gentle emotions. Women of his acquaintance soon bored him to distraction, with their talk of current fashion or the latest rumors. He cared little for their clinging ways or their capricious whining. The surprise never quite deserted him that they could malign their friends one minute, and hours later receive them as though they were well-loved intimates.

He had reached a time in his life when he was ready for a change. Had Lord Oliver noted his disenchantment? Actually, Jonathan relished the new challenge. America had always fascinated him. Englishmen were quick to scoff at these adventuresome people who had taken it upon themselves to forge a new world. Jonathan admired their courage, and was eager to join their ranks. The only drawback was the notion of taking a wife. God, he needed a wife like he needed an extra foot. Why had his father taken it into his head that he wanted grandchildren? Was his father keeping something from him? Jonathan feared he was ill. Still, only time would tell, because wild horses couldn't drag information out of Lord Oliver until he was ready to share it. Should

13

he chance upon a female with *rich red blood,* he would ponder his father's wishes.

"Boss, the carriage is ready, if you've a mind to make it to the ship before it sets sail."

"I'm ready, Blue. I was just making a quick check to see that everything is in order."

"I know what you mean. I've been doin' a little wool-gatherin' myself. Who knows, we may not be passin' this way again."

"You're not regretting your decision to accompany me, are you?"

"No, it's just that this place holds a lot of memories for me, too. Still, it's time we moved on. I have a good feelin' about this place called Virginia. It's gettin' on that ship with a bunch of skittish horses that has me bothered. Still, we'll manage. Once we get them settled, they'll give us few problems, I'm sure."

Jonathan chuckled as he checked his timepiece. "You did say something about the ship hoisting anchor?"

"Bloody light, I reckon I did."

Blue hurried on his way, mumbling beneath his breath about smart-mouthed Englishmen, until he and Jonathan settled themselves in the waiting carriage.

2

America

The talebearers were in their element. A startlingly handsome face and a weighty purse grasped their attention. Every tidbit of gossip they could garner was rehashed and embellished, until the right was wrong and the wrong was right.

Jonathan Cross had indeed taken Virginia by storm. Unlike England, he became an instant success. He was introduced to the finest families and constantly pursued for every social event. Whether lounging indolently at a gaming table or in the finest parlors, his brooding good looks presented the coveted picture of the gentleman planter.

Yet, there was a darker side to Jonathan, a bitterness, a harshness, and a cold, steely directness that left one cautious. When he wasn't playing the gentleman, he was a rascal of the highest order. His business deals were whispered about behind closed doors, admiration and fear building a reputation he only scoffed at. He had no morals and not a glimmer of a conscience.

He drank and gambled, and pursued his deviltry with an untiring voracity that left his companions breathless. As far as the fairer sex went, anything in a skirt Jonathan pursued. He played a woman's body with the same fine-honed skill he dealt with everything. It was like food, it filled a need, but like food, he soon tired of the same course and sought diversion. He had no compunction about his affairs or his bedmates.

Women loved him. Aside from his dark good looks and lazy brooding smile, his jaded reputation only enhanced their desire to tame him. But he scorned their declarations of love.

Early morning sun sifted through the draperies, glancing off the toes of polished black boots. A hardy curse followed a grunt of pain. "My god, Blue, the arm is attached, if you don't mind."

"I don't," came the unruffled reply. "It makes it handy if you decide to shoot someone. What I can't figure out is why you stood there this mornin', and let Samuel Evans take potshots at you?"

"What would you have had me do? Kill the man for defending his wife's honor, as tarnished as that honor might be? Samuel saved face, and I came away with little more than a flesh wound."

"I believe he was aimin' for your black heart, but his tremblin' hand sent the bullet off the mark."

A guileless smile lifted the corners of Jonathan's mouth. "Then my good fortune lies in his frayed nerves, instead of a generous spirit. Now, if you will cease hovering over me like a mother hen and fetch me a fresh shirt, I will dress."

"If you would give up this never-endin' pursuit of pleasure and see to the runnin' of Crossroads, I wouldn't have to drag myself out of bed at such an ungodly hour to tramp through the mist, only to stand by helplessly as your second, and watch you take a man's bullet, as though you didn't bloody care, one way or the other."

"If you must know, Amanda Evans was no pleasure. She has hips like a washboard and legs like an eel," came the dry reply.

"Really?" Blue questioned before he could stop himself.

A glimmer of amusement flickered in Jonathan's eyes. "Really."

16

After donning a fresh shirt, Jonathan wandered to the window and opened the drapes. In the street below, carriages and wagons lined the busy road. Servants rushed here and there, carrying everything from baskets of flowers and vegetables to cages of chickens and rabbits. Women dressed to the nines paraded the walkways on the arms of gentlemen suited to the teeth.

What would he do today? Would a bottle of brandy to dull his boredom complete his day? Would another bottle of brandy and a willing body see him through the night, only to begin the process all over tomorrow? He hated to admit it, but he was tired of the social whirl, tired of the nightly drinking and gambling. And most of all, he was tired of the flirting, clinging women. This life of debauchery had its drawbacks. He couldn't remember the last time he'd had a full night's sleep. His eyes looked like a red spiderweb, and his body felt like hell. Where had his dreams gone? Would he give them up, just because he'd been dismissed from England like a naughty child? Hell no! he decided firmly. He needed to get his life back on track, and set his course in another direction.

Making his decision, he turned to his loyal friend. "Blue, you should be pleased to know I've decided we will go on to Crossroads. I've suddenly become anxious to discover what kind of farmer I am."

Blue smiled brightly. "I'll see to the packin', and rent a carriage to send ahead with our belongings. You want me to send word that Mr. Denby should join you?"

Jonathan nodded absently, still studying the street below.

Shaking his head ruefully, Blue added, "I just hope they ain't no skirt-tails within five miles of Crossroads. I ain't anxious to see another angry husband or father, starin' you down from the barrel of his pistol."

Jonathan hooted with laughter.

After sending his regrets to several hostesses for upcoming events, Jonathan posted an advertisement in the newspaper for a housekeeper. Denby had assured him he was in dire need of one. Denby had taken care of everything else, but so far he'd failed to find a suitable housekeeper.

Blue watched as Jonathan talked softly to the spirited animal and pressed his strong thighs against the quivering muscles of the stallion. If the fates would grant him but one wish, he would apply it to the happiness of the man sitting before him on the skittish mount. Blue knew Jonathan better than anyone. He'd watched in silence, feeling the pain the young man suffered at the hands of his peers in England. Now they had a fresh start, and he prayed the true happiness that had eluded the young devil-may-care man would somehow find him in this new setting.

Jonathan relished the warmth of the sun beating down on him, and the wind whipping across his face as he gave Beowulf his head.

The road they traveled wound its way along the river amidst the beauty of long-limbed mimosa, their delicate pink flowers and featherlike leaves quivering in the gentle breeze. Strong sturdy white oaks created an arbor of shade as they passed beneath them. Everywhere there were wild flowers, bluebottle cornflowers with their stems proudly erect, the drooping harebell, brick red scarlet pimpernel, and butter yellow dandelions. Birds abounded in the verdant surroundings. Cardinals adorned in fiery red feathers flirted with their mates of lesser coloring. Fearless sparrows darted from place to place in their search for food, and vibrant bluebirds watched over their mates, protecting all they deemed theirs. In the distance, from the lofty boughs of a dead pine, a red-tailed hawk surveyed all that lay before him.

Yet, Jonathan didn't notice the beauty spread before him, nor did he hear the call of the bobwhite or the song

18

of mockingbird, for his head was filled with plans.

As they rounded a bend in the road, he saw the coach Blue had rented, stalled before a bridge. Jonathan halted Beowulf. Stroking the animal's neck, he pondered the situation before him as Denby drew up beside him.

The driver of the coach stood in the middle of the road, shaking an angry fist at the occupants on the bridge, his voice loud and clear. "If you don't move that friggin', lop-eared mule out of my way, I'm goin' to shoot him."

"That should solve all your problems," came the gentle reply. "But tell me, if you shoot Lord Adelbert, how do you propose to cross the bridge?"

Flustered, the driver declared, "I'm not that stupid. I'd move him off the bridge, before I shot him."

"Then by all means, be my guest. Moreover, if you can coax him to move from the bridge, there won't be any reason to shoot him, will there? Unless, of course, you just have a general dislike for mules."

Lord Adelbert? Jonathan mused as mirth danced across his face. He leaned forward in the saddle, trying to get a look at the owner of the gentle voice.

After an instant's hesitation, the driver stomped onto the bridge. Jonathan raised his head to study the beast causing the dissension, and had to swallow the laughter bubbling up in his throat.

Lord Adelbert stood stone-still, his tail making a swishing sound as it slapped against his sides. Atop his head perched a straw hat, decorated with faded yellow ribbons. His ears poked through the hat, standing as though at attention, wiggling when an insect buzzed his head. As the driver approached, the mule didn't blink. When he reached for the bridle, Lord Adelbert's lips parted, revealing large yellow teeth. The man jerked his hand away and stepped back. "Maybe I got a while yet, just so's I get these things to the plantation before Mr. Cross gets there." Dropping his head sheepishly, the driver asked, "You got any suggestions, miss?"

Coming from the side of the wagon, a young woman stepped into Jonathan's view. Shuffling behind her was a large black man, grumbling with every step. His words drifted back to Jonathan. "I shore do wish they's somethin' I could do, but dat ornery varmint don't take to me a'tall. He near bit my hand clean off, just 'cause I straightened his bonnet."

"Here, let me try something," the girl volunteered.

"You be careful, Missy. Why I wouldn't trust dat hateful sack of bones in a outhouse with blinders on."

The smile that lit her face caused the breath to catch in Jonathan's chest. Simply beautiful, he thought. Her brilliant red hair was coiled neatly into a thick braid that fell across her shoulders. He couldn't make out the color of her eyes, but he noted the humor that sparkled in her face. Her dress was a simple cotton of faded jade, boasting no adornments or added frills. His gaze dropped to her full breasts and down to her small waist. It was evident she wore no corset to give her the curves she boasted.

"I'll be careful," she said, stepping toward the mule. Facing him head-on, she stared him straight in the eye, a frown creasing her smooth brow. Lord Adelbert met her gaze unflinchingly. She gripped the bridle and stood on tiptoe, until her mouth was inches from his ear. She whispered for several seconds, then stepped back, as though waiting his response.

Suddenly he snorted, then shook his large head.

"Addle-brain!" she said, pacing back and forth in front of the mule, shaking her fists at him. "I've had it with you."

Grabbing the reins, she slapped them across his rump. "No work, no food, you no-account varmint."

Lord Adelbert didn't budge an inch.

Nat threw up his hands in exasperation. "Now, what we gonna do?"

She deliberated a few moments longer, then with a last-ditch effort, she snatched the straw hat from Lord

Adelbert's head, nearly removing his ears. Giving him a sullen glare, she walked to the edge of the bridge and held his hat over the water. "Do you like your hat overly much, Your Grace?"

Lord Adelbert snorted, finally turning his head in her direction. He moved one step forward and paused, watching her warily.

She lowered the hat closer to the water. "It was such a nice hat, too."

After the threat, the reluctant mule took several halting steps.

Nat caught the reins and a wide grin split his face. "He must really like dat ole hat of his."

The driver of the coach applauded her triumph.

She plopped the straw hat on the mule's head, and lightly flicked her finger on his velvety nose. "A wise decision, Lord Adelbert."

"Remind me to call for your assistance, if I need help dealing with a stubborn animal," called a husky voice behind her.

Startled, she spun around to see two riders watching them, the one astride a majestic black horse capturing her attention.

The coachman paled when he saw the men, and lifted his hat to her in farewell. "Good day, ma'am. Mr. Cross, I'll have your belongings to the manor in no time flat." He boarded the coach and with quickly called orders rattled across the bridge.

Wide green eyes fastened on Jonathan.

He was the most handsome man she had ever seen. An ebony strand of his windblown hair partially draped a gray eye, giving him a rakish appeal. His eyebrows were thick and well-defined, his mouth full and tempting.

Untutored in coyness—where a young lady should blush and smile shyly—she boldly ran her eyes over the length of him, until she had her fill. He had draped his coat over the saddle horn, giving her an appreciative view of his broad chest and shoulders. Beneath a green satin waist-coat, he wore a white lawn shirt opened casually at the throat, showing a hint of crisp black hair below the neck-line. Doeskin breeches hugged his long, muscled legs. The sun glinted down on the highly polished surface of his black knee-length boots. Unaware of the minutes that had lapsed, she slowly retraced the path she had just followed. When her eyes returned to his face, his teeth gleamed white as he smiled. She blushed for the first time in her life.

"Allow me to introduce myself. Jonathan Cross," he said, and acknowledged his companion. "My agent, Richard Denby."

"My pleasure, miss," Denby returned.

"Ginny Lynn Sutton," she replied softly. Suddenly she felt very dowdy in her favorite dress. "And this is Nat, jack-of-all-trades."

When Ginny lifted her head, she saw Mr. Cross and Mr. Denby exchange smiles. "You ride a fine horse, sir."

Cross's gray eyes swept her, then slowly came to rest on her face. "At times, he can be as troublesome as your fine-looking mule." Though he responded graciously, his lips twitched with amusement.

After quickly glancing at Lord Adelbert, Ginny turned to Jonathan, a frown etching her brow. "Lord Adelbert? Surely you jest."

"Perhaps a little," he teased, and then continued. "I have moved here recently from England, and I'm in the process of taking up residence in the former Lyndal House."

"Oh, are you a relation?"

Denby coughed and quickly covered his mouth to hide his amusement.

"No, I am the new owner."

"I was unaware the plantation had been sold."

"Do you live around here?"

"Yes, just up the road a ways."

"Perhaps we could escort you home, since your mule

seems reluctant to do so."

"You are kind to offer, but Nat and I are on our way to the Harris plantation. That is, we were until Lord Adelbert decided otherwise."

"Lord Adelbert," Jonathan repeated. "Tell me, is so stubborn an animal worthy of bearing such a noble title?"

"As worthy as any who lay claim to it," Ginny replied in earnest.

Jonathan threw back his head and laughed at her rejoinder.

Ginny pursed her lips in a way that Jonathan thought enchanting. "Do you make sport of me, Mr. Cross?"

"No, not at all. I find your frankness quite diverting, and your placement of titles refreshing, for I have known many who boasted titles that would have better suited their livestock."

Ginny smiled and once again blushed. "If you gentlemen will excuse me, I shall try to move Lord Adelbert once more. If he has long to ponder the delay, we will never coax him from this spot."

Turning, Ginny lifted the hem of her skirt, showing a tiny foot and trim ankle as she stepped up into the wagon.

Nat took his seat and gathered the reins, while Jonathan and Denby backed their horses out of the wagon's path. As Lord Adelbert lumbered past them, Ginny nodded to the men. "It was a pleasure meeting you gentlemen."

"The pleasure is ours. And a very good day to you, Miss Sutton," Jonathan returned warmly.

Jonathan watched as the wagon disappeared around the bend, his companion forgotten as his thoughts remained on the young woman.

Denby noticed Jonathan's interest in the girl. "She is quite a comely wench."

"Yes, indeed she is."

"Sir, forgive me if I seem to be speaking out of turn, but she is nothing more than a poor farmer's daughter. I am certain your father would not look favorably—"

23

"You were not hired, Mr. Denby, to interfere in my personal life." Twisting in his saddle, Jonathan scowled at the agent. "Do I make myself clear?"

Flustered, Denby replied, "Yes, of course, sir. I only thought —"

"You thought wrong," Jonathan countered brusquely. Reining his horse in the direction of his home, Jonathan left Denby to eat his dust.

Jonathan slowed his mount on a grassy hillock and viewed the splendor before him. Lush meadows and thick stands of trees paralleled the red brick manor. The boxy look of the house was softened by a sweeping veranda and large towering columns that supported the roof. Adjoining wings on either side of the house added to the stately elegance, and outbuildings of varying sizes dotted the landscape. Yet Jonathan noticed that the lawn was overgrown, and there was an overall shabby appearance to the manor.

In the distance to the left, acre after acre of neatly planted rows of tobacco nodded in the warm sun. To the right, newly built stables and mile after mile of fencing snaked along the grassy meadows. Jonathan beamed with pride as he noted his horses grazing in the peaceful setting. A wash of contentment filled him, and he vowed silently that he would make this new venture work.

"Quite impressive, isn't it," Denby acknowledged, reining his laboring mount in beside Jonathan.

"Quite," Jonathan agreed. "And thank you for seeing to the construction of the stables and the fencing."

"Your instructions were quite detailed. I followed them to the letter."

"Tell me, through the trees I can make out a chimney. What is it?"

"That's a problem."

A dark brow lifted in question. "A problem?"

"Yes, the girl you met on the bridge. That's where she

24

and her mother live. It's a long story."

"I have all the time in the world."

"Ginny Sutton's father tutored the Lyndal children and others from nearby plantations. From what I've been able to gather, Mr. Lyndal offered a small portion of property to the Suttons, in payment for his services. Anyway, if Lyndal made such an offer, it was verbal. Nothing was in writing, and no legal property transaction ever took place."

"Are you saying the Suttons are lying about owning the property?"

"I'm saying, your deed guarantees that no claims exist against the property. The Suttons own nothing."

"Yes, we do have a problem. It's not that I mind that they live on the property, but should they decide to try to sell, it could cause all manner of problems. Let me think about it."

"As you wish."

When they drew closer to the house, Jonathan's first impressions caused his stomach to lurch. The outside was overgrown with weeds, and the paint was peeling from the columns. The inside, he found deplorable. Besides the obvious neglect, the furnishings reminded Jonathan of a cut-rate brothel. Indeed, he had his work laid out before him. Denby had used every available hand on the planting and working of the fields and the building of new stables. The house had received only a paltry amount of attention. Jonathan had not seen the first glimpse of a servant since he'd entered the house.

3

The sweeping bough of the sycamore trailed down into the gently flowing river. Ginny rested quietly within its deep arch, her drab linen shift blending with the rough bark of the tree. Closing her eyes, her thoughts drifted with the current, her mind envisioning the untouched fields laden with the lush green leaves of tobacco. Someday . . . someday . . . her mind echoed, but, as always, reality surged in. How would she and her mother ever find the means to improve their lot in life? Though her brother, Patrick, gave them a portion of his wages each month, and her mother drew a small income from the hats she made, there was never enough money left after expenses. Growing tobacco was no easy task; she and Nat couldn't do it alone.

Nat, their devoted servant and a freed slave, lived in a small cabin next to the barn. In exchange for food and lodging, he helped take care of the livestock and saw to the maintenance of their small farm. If Nat had not been here to help them, Patrick would never have stayed in Williamsburg.

Neither Ginny nor her mother regretted that Patrick sought his livelihood elsewhere. Like her father, farming had never interested Patrick. He had left home at age thirteen, to serve as an apprentice to a silversmith in Williamsburg. After her father's death three years ago, Patrick had suggested that she and her mother sell the

26

farm and move into Williamsburg. Her mother had been as stubborn as Ginny when they discussed uprooting their home. They would have problems no matter where they lived. Patrick told them he would leave his job and help them run the farm. They had insisted that he remain in Williamsburg, now that he had become a skilled tradesman. His expenses were minimal, for his proprietor had given him lodging in the apartment above the silversmith shop. Yet, they could not rely on Patrick's help forever. That thought weighed continually on Ginny's mind. Someday, he would marry and have a family of his own.

Ginny thought of all the hours her mother labored, making hats for the ladies on the surrounding plantations. She had never turned down a customer. Orders were always waiting to be filled. The ladies liked the personal touches her mother gave each hat, making certain no two women ended up with identical hats. Patrick had also found a shop in Williamsburg that agreed to sell her hats.

When Ginny considered the hard work her mother and brother did to help carry them through their hardships, she felt guilty about her own meager offerings. True, she worked in the garden, growing enough food to take care of their needs, but she never regarded it a chore, because she enjoyed it. When the tiny shoots of her labor broke through the soil on a warm spring day, she welcomed their arrival with as much joy as when a chick broke through its fragile shell. She had the God-given talent of making anything grow. It frustrated her to work only a small plot of land, when they owned acres of untilled fields that were just waiting to be planted . . . if not in tobacco, at least in something that would bring them a profit.

Hearing a noise, she opened her eyes. Directly beneath her, a doe and her fawn lapped at the cool water. Knowing any movement would frighten them away, she avoided swiping at her nose as a pesky fly buzzed around her head. For several minutes, she watched them at her leisure, as they nibbled the tender sprouts that grew near the bank. Feeling something tickling her big toe, she spied a green caterpillar crawling across it. Without thinking, she shook it from her foot. To her dismay, the doe and fawn darted into the woods.

Tucking a stray reddish gold lock behind her ear, she slowly rose to her feet. Her shift, cut full and straight for easy movement and comfort, concealed legs that were slender and resilient. Barefooted, her small, lithe body easily scaled the curved bough. Catching a branch, she swung to the ground.

Her laundry lay scattered on the bank, some items hanging from branches, others lying over sun-warmed rocks to dry. Taking a fresh bar of soap, she waded through the cool water. Glimpsing a lazy lizard sunning on the rock, she nudged it with her finger and watched it slither into a crevice. As she lifted the hem of her shift to remove it, she caught a glimpse of a horse and rider through the trees, galloping down the path.

Dashing from the water, she grabbed her musket and positioned it against her shoulder. When the horse broke through the clearing, she saw the familiar figure of her friend, Milly Vincent, astride her sorrel mare. Beneath her hat, thick, honey blond curls bounced against her shoulders, as the horse trotted Ginny's way.

Drawing her mount to a standstill, she stared at the gun. "For goodness sake, Ginny, it's just me."

Ginny lowered the gun and propped it against the tree. "Well, the next time, Milly, call out to me before you come riding in here like that. You scared me to death."

"Oh rubbish! You're much too cautious." Sliding gracefully from the sidesaddle, Milly led her horse to a tree and tethered her.

Ginny watched her with admiration. As always, Milly was dressed in the latest fashion. Today, her tall, slender figure was swathed in an indigo riding habit, and atop her head she wore a matching hat with a white plume curving gracefully from its peak.

Noticing Ginny's wet garment and the bar of soap in her hand, Milly said, "Oh, you were about to bathe?"

"How astute you are," Ginny snapped.

"My, my, you're in a beastly mood today. Did that cantankerous old mule kick you?"

Milly's remark brought a grin to Ginny's face. "No, he knows better." She cocked her head. "Isn't it a little early in the day for you to be making calls. I would have thought you'd still be abed."

Milly smoothed her skirt beneath her as she sat down on the bank. Her clear sky blue eyes twinkled with excitement. "Perhaps it is, but I have some news. Please go ahead with your bath, while I tell you."

"Thank you, I will," Ginny said, wading into the water.

As she drew her shift up over her hips, Milly said, "I declare, Ginny, do you not have a modest bone in your body?"

"Do you bathe in your clothes?" Ginny quipped.

"Of course not, but I bathe in the privacy of my room," Milly announced with a flash of dignity.

"You also have several servants to bring your water."

"Well, yes, but aren't you afraid someone might see you?"

"No. There isn't anyone around within miles of here."

"Oh? Then you haven't heard that a man by the name of Jonathan Cross has bought the Lyndal plantation."

The sound of his name brought his image before her eyes. "Yes, I know. I'll have to be more careful when I bathe." Giving up the idea of bathing in the nude, Ginny let the shift slide over her hips. "I'd almost forgotten the place was even there, since the Lyndals left for England months ago." Sitting down on a rock, she soaped her cloth and began washing her face and neck while Milly chatted.

"Edna Talbot told me Christine's grieving horribly over the sale of her family home. She also said Christine had planned to buy it back, after Mr. Iverson's estate was settled."

"Well, thank the Lord for Mr. Cross. These past several months have been the most peaceful months of my life. Now that it's sold and she's a wealthy widow, do you think she'll do me a favor and join her family in England? Who knows, she might find herself an old duke and dupe him into marrying her."

"Yes, just like she did old Mr. Iverson. Do you know what I think? When she heard they would not arrive in England in grand fashion, she grabbed Mr. Iverson and dragged him to the altar. Christine would die before she'd meet the lords and ladies of the realm in last year's fashions."

While Ginny bathed and washed her hair, Milly's thoughts remained on Christine Lyndal. Christine had been Ginny's enemy from the time they were children. She had taunted and harassed Ginny about her threadbare clothing and unruly red hair, for no other reason than to hurt her feelings. Ginny, tiny for her age, never allowed Christine to intimidate her. For every insult Christine delivered, Ginny had quickly retaliated. Milly's pity soon changed to admiration for the spunky little redhead, and they became fast friends. Christine had asked Milly why she wasted her time with a little ragamuffin who would never amount to anything. Milly always stood up for her friend, but as they grew from children into young adults, Milly worried constantly that Christine's bitter remarks might prove true.

As Ginny waded from the water, Milly pushed aside her sad thoughts and said, "Edna says Jonathan Cross is the most handsome man she's ever met. She said she positively swooned when he looked at her."

Not daring to reveal her own sudden faintness at his striking appearance, Ginny replied insouciantly, "Poor Edna would swoon if *any* man looked at her."

Milly laughed and her eyes lit up. "I overheard a conversation between Father and a gentleman from Williamsburg. Some man caught his wife with Mr. Cross in a rather compromising situation and summoned him to a duel. Mr. Cross must be a real rake."

"He might be," Ginny said, plucking a clean dry shift from a branch, "but he appears to be a gentleman."

Milly's head snapped up. "How would you know?"

"Because I met him."

"You've met him?" she exclaimed with rapturous wonder in her voice.

"Yes, last week on my way to the Harris' house."

"Is he as handsome as Edna says he is?" Milly asked anxiously.

Ginny puckered her mouth and tilted her head thoughtfully. "I suppose he's . . ." she purposely let her voice slip into a pause, "so-so."

A look of disenchantment washed over Milly's face. "Only . . . so-so?"

Ginny grinned. "I'm only teasing you, Milly. Actually, he's quite a handsome man."

Ginny stepped behind a clump of bushes to change clothing. She told Milly about Jonathan Cross and his agent coming upon them while they were trying to move the mule off the bridge.

"And there he was behind me, astride his fine horse, watching me behave like a silly goose," Ginny said, trying to conceal her excitement. "Added to that, after introductions, everything I said came out wrong, Milly. You know me, my mouth is always two steps ahead of my brain. But do you know what he said? He found my

31

frankness quite diverting."

Milly's hand flew to her throat in exasperation, as she implored, "Good Lord, Ginny, don't be diverting! Be captivating, alluring, or even coy, but never diverting. You would be wise to use your God-given beauty to snare a husband."

Ginny moved from behind the shrubbery. "Frankly, I haven't given it much thought."

"That's just an excuse. You're already twenty years old. Have a care, Ginny, or you are going to wither into an old maid. Or even worse, you'll marry some poor old widower with a house full of children. Is that what you want?"

Ginny smiled softly at Milly, as she sat down across from her. Drawing a brush through her wet hair, she said, "If there was anyway I could change my situation, I would, Milly. When have I ever had the time to entertain such thoughts?"

Milly reached out and smoothed a damp tendril from her friend's face. "Take the time, Ginny. You are pretty and intelligent. A score of men would ask you to marry them, if they knew you existed."

Ginny snorted. "Who'd want someone as poor as a church mouse, except another church mouse? I'd as soon remain unmarried, thank you."

"But I worry so about you and your mother. And Patrick, too. Sometimes I get so angry with him, and think he's selfish for leaving you with all this responsibility. Oh, Ginny, I know he hates farm life, but you need him here, not in Williamsburg."

"Milly, try to understand. Patrick makes more money working as a silversmith than he could ever make farming. We desperately need the extra money he gives us. Of course, you wouldn't understand that."

Milly stiffened her back. "That's unfair, Ginny Sutton."

Ginny smiled teasingly. "Oh, I'm sorry, Milly, you can't

help it because you're rich."

"You could be, too, if you would give yourself the chance. Jonathan Cross isn't married. Why not try to spur his interest in you?"

"That's a frivolous remark, Milly," Ginny argued. "I would no more fit in his world than he would in mine. I have nothing, Milly, absolutely nothing that would interest him."

"I disagree. When two people love one another, material things don't matter. They can find happiness just being in each other's company."

Closely scrutinizing Milly's face, Ginny said, "You couldn't talk of such emotions, unless you yourself are feeling them. Are you, Milly?"

Milly shrugged her shoulders and avoided Ginny's gaze.

"You're in love with Patrick, aren't you?"

Milly's eyes flew open and her face reddened. She started to deny the accusation, but the words died in her throat.

"I knew it," Ginny said, shrugging her shoulders in despair. "Oh, Milly, my heart goes out to you." Leaning forward, she clasped Milly's hands in her own. "Does Patrick know you love him?"

Lowering her head, Milly mumbled, "No. To him, I'm only the pesky little brat who used to follow him around. Anyway, the only time I ever see him is when he's visiting you and your mother, or when I go to Williamsburg. Even then he doesn't pay me any mind."

"Rightly so, Milly. He knows your father would never accept such a match." Gently squeezing Milly's hands, Ginny asked softly, "Are you sure you are not in love with love itself? Stop dreaming and be realistic."

"I am *not* dreaming," Milly argued, tears glistening in her eyes. "I've loved Patrick all my life, I swear I have. How can I marry someone I don't love—like my sister,

Anne—wed to a man she barely knows because of family wishes. I've lived all my life under those same conditions. My parents seldom display any affection toward each other. They go their separate ways, Mama doing one thing and Papa another."

"Well, they must have met somewhere in between, or they wouldn't have produced three children."

Milly blushed. "Ginny, you're awful."

"Maybe I am, but I know better than to dream impossible dreams."

For several moments they sat in silence, each lost in thought. Milly's voice broke the quietness. "Mother's planning a ball to celebrate my eighteenth birthday. Would you—"

"No."

"You don't even know what I was going to ask."

"Yes, I do," Ginny said. "You were going to ask me to come to your ball, and if Patrick happens to be home, he can escort me."

"Well?"

"No, Milly. You'll have to find another way to get Patrick's attention. Furthermore, he probably won't be home. His employer is ill, and he's relying on Patrick to tend to everything. He couldn't leave if he wanted to."

"By the time we have the ball, maybe his circumstances will have changed. Oh, Ginny, Patrick would do anything you asked him."

"Patrick is no more a socialite than I am."

Milly tried another approach. Somehow she would overcome Ginny's stubbornness. Plucking a twig from her skirt, she stated casually, "I'm sure mother will be sending an invitation to your new neighbor, Mr. Cross."

"Since his property joins mine, I'm certain to run into him without having to attend your ball. Besides, I have nothing to wear." She immediately regretted her hastily spoken words.

Milly's face brightened. "You can wear something of mine. We're almost the same size." She realized her remark was ridiculous, since she was at least four inches taller than her friend. Her eyes scanned Ginny's figure, then fixed on Ginny's full breasts. "Well . . . almost."

A smile tugged at Ginny's mouth as an outrageous thought popped into her mind. "Do you know the story about Cinderella?"

"Of course, I do."

"Then imagine this scene. It's the evening of the ball, and gilded coaches line the drive of your magnificent home. Somewhere in the midst of this glorious caravan is not a pumpkin and six white horses, but a rickety old cart drawn by a bony mule." Looking down at Milly's upturned face, she continued, "Now, Patrick and I might temporarily fool your friends that we are members of the upper class, but no disguise on earth can hide the fact that Lord Adelbert is an ornery mule, regardless of his impressive title."

Milly giggled in spite of herself.

Beyond the bend of the river, only a scant distance from Ginny and Milly, Jonathan rested on the bank, letting Beowulf have his fill of the cool water. He chuckled quietly after Ginny's enchanting tale, enjoying her version of Cinderella better than the original. Still, there was a sad note underlying her story. A vision of Ginny as the char-stained Cinderella turned princess, drifted across his mind. Could she be turned into a princess and retain her innocence and spirit? Or would the trappings of wealth and position soil her personality, and clutter her head with nonsense? The challenge was tempting.

He didn't know the girl called Milly, but evidently they were the best of friends, yet worlds apart in their beliefs.

Jonathan had not intentionally eavesdropped on the girls' conversation. He had been on his way to pay a call on the Suttons, and decided to break the monotony and

35

ride alongside the river. As he'd neared their home, he recognized Ginny's voice immediately and had almost approached them, until he heard his name mentioned.

So, this Milly thinks I'm a rake, he thought, surprised that news of his escapades in Williamsburg had reached the outlying plantations so swiftly. His peers in London had expected such behavior from him, but here he had clearly shocked the community with his reckless behavior. Only this time it was different; no one knew he was the bastard son of a duke. All that concerned them was his apparent wealth. His reputation as a philanderer had not mattered one whit to the families looking for a wealthy husband for their marriageable daughters. He frowned bitterly. In London, they wanted him purely for pleasuring them in bed, but as husband material he wasn't acceptable. Not only did the women here want to share his bed, they wanted to share his name also.

Shrugging aside his thoughts, Jonathan rolled to his feet and gathered Beowulf's reins. Rubbing his hand over the horse's shimmering black mane, he whispered, "I think, my friend, it's time we meet the ladies."

4

"Good morning, Miss Sutton," Jonathan called out.

Ginny and Milly turned in unison, surprised to see the handsome man approaching them, pulling his stallion behind him.

"Is that *him?*" Milly whispered.

"Yes," Ginny whispered back, feeling her heart racing in her chest.

He turned to Milly, and with a polite nod of his head, introduced himself. "We haven't met. I'm Jonathan Cross."

Milly smiled demurely, thinking he was all that Edna had said he was. Oh, how she wished Ginny would encourage him. "Milly Vincent. It's a pleasure meeting you, Mr. Cross."

He smiled lazily. "My pleasure, ladies. It's such a lovely morning, I decided to take Beowulf for a ride along the river. I was sitting on the riverbank enjoying the scenery, when I heard you two talking."

Two pair of startled eyes shot to each other, as each recalled their conversation.

"How long were you sitting there?" Ginny squeaked.

"Oh, not long," he assured them.

Their sighs of relief were audible.

After tethering his horse to a low-lying branch, he leaned against the trunk of the sycamore tree that Ginny had vacated earlier, his gray eyes taking in the laundry hanging from several branches and over the rocks. Ginny stirred restlessly, and a flood of burning shame swept through her, as he watched her underwear flap like faded banners in the breeze. She recalled seeing Milly's pretty silk chemises, petticoats, and drawers, adorned with delicate lace trim. Never had she coveted Milly's possessions, her own simple, homespun garments suitable for her needs, but at this moment, she wished . . . she wished . . .

When Jonathan shifted his attention to Ginny, she found it difficult to breathe as he gave her a slow, seductive smile. Was he picturing her in that horrid underwear? she wondered with chagrin, as his hooded gray eyes traveled leisurely over her.

She reminded him of a woodland nymph, her natural beauty blending in with her surroundings. He did not realize he was staring at her so daringly, but old habits were hard to break. Her tiny pink toes peeking out beneath the hem were a pleasurable sight, especially so, when he envisioned the shapely legs attached to them. Unabashedly, his eyes roamed over her straight-cut shift, recognizing the hint of her curves beneath it. His attention moved across her face, to meet her watching him with uncertainty. Unbraided, a canopy of dark red tresses fell in long, wet curtains on either side of her small cameo face. A desire to run his fingers through its shimmering length was almost irresistible. Had she bathed in the river? When he thought about how close he'd come to witnessing that pleasurable moment, he felt a sudden tightness in his loins.

Milly was not oblivious to Jonathan's bold-face perusal of her friend. *He is a rake,* Milly thought, enviously wishing Patrick would look at her so scandalously.

"I hope everything is going well with you in your new home, sir," Milly said, interrupting Jonathan's thoughts.

He gave a slight shrug, then chuckled. "Not as well as I had hoped, but in time I should have everything in proper order. My agent told me that three generations of Lyndals have occupied the home at one time or another. It's a shame they could not find a means to keep it."

"Mr. Lyndal was not the businessman his father was, I'm afraid," Milly said. "They used to have several balls a year, when most of the other planters only had one yearly event. When Christine, their only daughter, made her debut, it was the grandest, most lavish affair ever held in Virginia. Why, the meal alone would have fed a large family for a year. My father said it couldn't last; he was right."

"And where do you live, Milly?"

"Oh," Ginny piped in, "Milly comes from one of the finest families in the area. Her father's a very successful planter, and later this year, when Milly turns eighteen, her parents are hosting a lavish ball for her. I imagine every unmarried gentleman within a hundred miles of here will offer for her hand."

Ginny felt Milly's elbow discreetly nudge her arm.

"My friend has a tendency to be overly dramatic, Mr. Cross," she said, her teeth clenched as she smiled threateningly at Ginny.

Jonathan dragged his eyes from Milly to Ginny. "Miss Sutton, I should like to ask a favor of you."

"A favor?" she asked with surprise and sudden interest.

"Yes. As I said, we have problems at my plantation—" he chuckled, then added, "several, in fact, but the shortage of fresh vegetables is one of my biggest concerns."

"Vegetables," Milly blurted. "Why, the Lyndal gardens were huge."

"*Were*, Miss Vincent. My agent told me the old gardener died earlier this year, and no one took his place. Fortunately, the slaves have their own gardens, but the main garden is in a sad state. It's hard to distinguish the leaves of the vegetables from the weeds." He paused. "As I was riding by your place the other afternoon, Miss Sutton, I noticed you have a sizeable and quite productive garden. Do you need all you produce? If not, I should like to buy any surplus you might have."

Ginny was astounded. Here was a man who was probably the wealthiest man among all the planters, and he needed something from her—she who had nothing.

When Ginny did not respond immediately, Jonathan said, "I will pay you well."

The word *pay* jolted her attention. "Oh! We have plenty to serve your needs."

"I appreciate your generosity. I should like to send one of my servants later this afternoon to collect it."

"That will be fine, Mr. Cross."

"Is there anything I can do to help you?" Milly asked humbly.

Jonathan swept her tall, slender figure in admiration, just now noticing her loveliness. He smiled at the genuine concern marking her pretty face. "No, but you are kind to offer."

"If you will wait right here, Mr. Cross," Ginny said, her eyes beaming with excitement, "I will bring you some squash I picked last evening."

"Please, you needn't go to any bother. I can wait until later."

"No bother," Ginny announced and hastened toward the house.

Milly watched Jonathan's eyes dwell on Ginny, until she disappeared into the thick woods.

Feeling awkward at being alone with a man in such a secluded place, especially a man with a notorious reputation, Milly said, "I should be going. My groom's waiting for me."

"Please don't leave just yet, Miss Vincent. I promise to keep you only a moment."

Milly's blue eyes widened, and her heart started pounding against her chest. "Why?"

Jonathan noticed her nervousness and smiled warmly. "I assure you my intentions are quite honorable. I only wish to discuss something with you."

Milly's brow winged upward. "What?"

"I understand Miss Sutton and her mother have had a difficult time since Mr. Sutton's death."

"Well . . . yes, they have," she said hesitantly, feeling uncomfortable discussing her friend's situation with a stranger.

"I've noticed they only work a small portion of their farm." Unable to think of a less obtrusive way to phrase his question, Jonathan asked forthrightly, "I wonder . . . ah . . . if they've ever considered selling it?"

"Oh no, Ginny would never do that! She dreams of planting the fields in tobacco someday." She tilted her head askance, her brow knitted in a puzzled frown. "Do you wish to buy it?"

Expecting such a question, Jonathan answered, "No, I have enough problems trying to tend to what I have already. Still, if they sold the farm, it would solve some of their financial needs."

Milly laughed lightly. "She'd starve first. She says she isn't a dreamer, but she is when it comes to that farm."

"But what would we have, if we didn't have our dreams, Miss Vincent?"

She thought of her love for Patrick. "Oh, I have my dreams, too, Mr. Cross. But how can Ginny come up with the money to see her dream realized?"

"If she had a husband to help her, she—"

"She hasn't had time to give marriage much thought."

41

Milly smiled at his puzzled face. "I'm just repeating her words. I've told her pretty much the same thing and got nowhere with her. She's as stubborn as that mule of hers."

"Yes, Lord Adelbert. We've met."

"I know. She told me. I really need to go. My groom will wonder what has happened to me. Tell Ginny I'll see her next week, when she delivers my mother's hats."

"I will," Jonathan said. Then bringing her horse to her, he lifted her into the saddle. "I shall eagerly await an invitation to your ball."

Milly gazed down at Jonathan's handsome face. *Yes, indeed, rake that he is, he would still make Ginny a fine Prince Charming.*

As though he had read her thoughts, Jonathan remarked, "If I happen to run into a fairy godmother between now and then, shall I ask for her assistance?"

A crimson blush stained Milly's face. *He did hear our conversation.* "Please," she said, before she gently nudged her horse and galloped up the path.

Jonathan remained at the river, waiting on Ginny's return. Well, he had his answer about the property. He felt better knowing the Suttons would never try to sell the property, but the deceit he lived with did not set well with him. He was trapped between the devil and the deep blue sea, and no matter what he did, the Suttons would suffer.

Ginny returned, interrupting his musings, carrying a cloth sack filled with her offerings. She looked around for Milly. "Did Milly leave?"

"Yes, she said her groom was waiting for her, but she would see you next week."

"Oh? I must have stayed longer than I realized." She handed him the sack. "I put in some fresh butter, too."

"Thank you. How much do I owe you?"

42

She shrugged her slim shoulders. "Whatever you judge a reasonable price."

He dug in his pocket and removed several coins. Taking her hand in his, he saw the bitten nails and felt the callouses on her palm, a harsh reminder of her labor. He placed the coins in her hand, then moved to his horse, and tied the sack to his saddle.

After he mounted Beowulf, he smiled down at her. "Good day, Ginny."

His smile caused a sense of lightness to fill her head. "Good day to you, Mr. Cross, and thank you."

It wasn't until after he left, that Ginny realized he had called her by her given name. Suddenly, she felt a strange warmth wash over her.

Ginny knelt between a row of beans in her garden pulling weeds. The late afternoon heat was stifling, and rivulets of perspiration rolled down her face, neck, and between her breasts. She mopped the tail of her apron across her forehead and sat back on her haunches, looking at the cloudless blue sky. Would it never rain? She and Nat had drawn pail after pail of water from the river, painstakingly watering the vegetables. The weather could not have chosen a worst time to be so uncooperative. She could not, would not, let Mr. Cross down, regardless of the dry spell.

Jonathan Cross, she thought wistfully, her eyes shining with pride and excitement. He had needed something from her. And she was making money and saving it. Of course, she could not expect such good fortune to go on forever; no doubt he would replant his own gardens eventually.

Finished with the row of beans, she moved to the row of cabbages and checked the plants carefully. She paused

43

and smiled. Never had she met anyone like him. What did it matter if everyone thought he was a rake? She knew better. But there again, only a rake would look at her the way he had at the river. Even now she could feel the heat emanating from his eyes as they roamed over her.

"Impossible," she said, brushing the frivolous thoughts from her mind. "I was only imagining it. He was watching Milly, not me."

5

The full bloom of summer had heralded a changing diet for the Suttons. Besides a profusion of flowers, their small garden supplied fresh vegetables, while the woodland added a variety of fruits from the many fruit trees abounding in the area.

Ginny stretched her full length, her fingertips barely grazing the shiny surface of the June apple. The nicest ones always seemed to be on the highest limbs, she thought, her shoulder aching when finally she plucked one loose.

Her mother promised to make an apple pie, if Ginny picked some of the early apples, and dumplings, if Nat would supply a rabbit. She groaned as a limb slapped across her face, becoming tangled in her hair. Balancing herself and the cloth-filled sack, she worked the limb free and carefully dropped to the ground.

Jonathan leaned forward from his chair and rested his elbows on the surface of the dust-laden desk, gazing around his library. Deep mahogany bookshelves lined one wall from floor to ceiling. The Lyndals had taken their favorite books, leaving the shelves in disarray. Also, where they had removed paintings, there were large white patches on the dingy walls. The fireplace still contained thick ashes and partially burned wood from their last fire, and the smell lingered in the musty, airless room.

Sighing wearily, Jonathan glanced over the list of applicants. After interviewing a half-dozen women and finding no one suitable for the job as housekeeper, he was at his wit's end. Was he perhaps being too critical?

"Mr. Cross?" Willis summoned from the door, interrupting Jonathan's musings, "A Miss Emma Byrd to see you, sir."

"Show her in, Willis." *Please be kind,* he prayed, as Willis stepped aside for her to enter.

Tall, rail-thin, and clothed in a garb of black, Miss Emma Byrd lingered for several moments in the doorway. With her mouth compressed, her cold hazel eyes critically viewed the room from floor to ceiling, taking in the dust that settled on the floor and furnishings, the tarnished silver candlesticks on the mantel, and the cobwebs that blanketed the ceiling.

Stiffening her back, and with an authoritative, stern voice, she announced, "Shall I start now, Mr. Cross?" she asked, whipping off her gloves.

"I have yet to engage you, Miss Byrd. Please have a seat," he instructed, nodding to the chair across from the desk.

With the carriage of a soldier, Miss Byrd walked to the chair and sat down, her blue-veined hands clutching a crisp white handkerchief in her lap. She sniffed the air, her beaklike nose wrinkling in disgust at the stale odor that lingered in the room.

"Miss Byrd, are you experienced as a housekeeper?"

She lifted her head haughtily. "Yes, I come to you highly qualified." She then questioned him. "I understand you don't have children?"

"No."

"Good. They're such messy, undisciplined little hooligans, their playthings always underfoot. Servants have enough to do without spending valuable time picking up after children. Yes, one should always give the matter considerable thought before venturing into parenthood."

Raising a brow, Jonathan replied glibly, "Perhaps one should consider venturing into marriage first, Miss Byrd."

His comment wrecked her stiff composure. Miss Byrd's face turned from pasty gray to crimson.

Lowering his head, Jonathan rifled through the papers and said distinctly, "You may go now, Miss Byrd."

"But . . . but . . ." she stammered, "I haven't given you my references."

"You've given me all the information I need."

Miss Byrd rose from the chair and hastily donned her gloves. "I will await word from you, Mr. Cross. I am most certain you will not find a more suitable person to fill this position. Thank you and good day."

The instant the door closed behind Miss Byrd, Jonathan slumped back in his chair, disgust marking his features. God forbid having a woman like her in his household. She reminded him of Agatha, Lord Oliver's housekeeper. After his father took him into his home, she never missed the opportunity to sequester him in his room until everything was in proper order. Geoffrey, the real culprit, would sneak into Jonathan's room when he wasn't around, scatter his belongings, and eagerly await Agatha's tirade when she viewed the destruction. Jonathan knew she would never believe that sweet, innocent little Geoffrey could do such a thing. He kept his complaints to himself, thinking Geoffrey would get his comeuppance someday. He never had, at least not while Jonathan lived at the manor.

At the sound of the door opening, Jonathan straightened abruptly in his chair, awaiting the next applicant.

"Miss Violet Prangle to see you, sir," Willis droned, as

he rolled his eyes heavenward.

Jonathan's eyes matched those of his butler's, as the woman's immense figure filled the doorway. As she undulated into the room, she knocked against a table, sending a vase containing dead flowers shattering to the floor. As she halted in front of his desk, he noticed perspiration spewing like a geyser from the large pores on her face. Smiling affably, she declared breathlessly, "I just l-o-o-v-v-e-e your home, Mr. Cross."

Jonathan smiled weakly and asked her to take a seat . . . a mistake. He heard the chair's arms creak and groan as she made room for her hips.

Jonathan knew he could not hire Miss Prangle, but he felt he owed her the courtesy of an interview. She would collapse with exhaustion before she ever reached the second floor. Or, he mused, the second floor might collapse should she manage to make it. At the end of their discussion, Jonathan wished her well and bid her good day.

Dipping his quill into the inkwell, he drew a line through the name of each woman he had interviewed. When he came to the name, Mavis DeWitt, he paused and smiled. He recalled her teary eyes and quivering lips. Her daring decolletage had held his attention as she leaned forward from her chair, telling him that her husband, a furniture maker, had taken ill and could no longer work. She desperately needed the job, since she was now the sole support of the family. Later, Jonathan learned that Mavis had an uncontrollable temper. She had broken all the windows in her former employer's home, then chased him through the house, threatening him with a poker.

Willis entered and closed the door behind him. Jonathan looked over at him and ruefully shook his head. "Ask the others to return tomorrow, Willis. I'm calling it a day."

"Miss Prangle was the last, sir."

"Thank God."

"Will there be anything else, sir?"

"Yes, I believe a brandy is in order, Willis." Jonathan leaned back in the chair and lit a cheroot. The thick smoke circled his head, as he pondered the applicants he'd interviewed. He needed a miracle, and fast.

In the distance Ginny heard the crack of a gun. She smiled. "Sounds like Nat got a rabbit," she said to the apple, just before she sank her teeth into the crisp fruit. Deciding to meet him, she walked in the direction of the gunshot. She loved the forest and the river that skirted its banks. When time permitted, Ginny loved nothing more than sitting on the riverbank, fishing the day away. The fish taught her patience and cunning. Whereas the woodland creatures taught her about flirting and courtship, and having a mate of your very own. Sometimes in the spring of the year, as she watched the creatures and their courting rituals, she yearned for someone who would care for her just as she was. Unlike the young ladies of her acquaintance, she didn't have beautiful clothes or creamy complexion, but most of all she didn't have a dowry. She had nothing to offer a husband other than a strong back and undying loyalty.

She watched as squirrels scampered along tree limbs and barked in annoyance at squawking blue jays. Suddenly, the sound of voices raised in anger reached her ears. She shifted the sack of apples and hurried through the woods. When she entered a small clearing, the scene that met her eyes brought her to an abrupt stop. Nat was nose to nose with a man as big as himself. With arms hanging loosely from their bodies, and teeth bared, they circled each other.

"I ain't no thief," Nat growled.

"Well, you could have fooled me, mate, I caught you red-handed."

"The missus say Nat bring me a rabbit. I get a rabbit. Who are you to say Nat's a thief!"

"My boss is the new owner of these lands, and he won't stand for no poachin'."

"Nat ain't no poacher. I been huntin' these woods for years."

"Is that right? Well, I'm here to see that you don't anymore."

"The missus ain't gonna like this, nosuhree."

"Stop it, stop this instant," Ginny shouted as she rushed between the two men. "What's the meaning of this, Nat?"

Jerking his thumb toward the stranger, Nat replied, "He said I was poachin', and dat's a lie. He said dis property don't belong to you, and dat's a lie."

She eyed the stranger with a frown. "Well, forevermore. Who are you to make such an accusation?"

Blue watched the spunky girl with distaste. Her hair was disheveled and tangled with twigs, her dress rumpled and soiled with dirt. He dismissed her as no more than a peasant, and his tone implied as much. "Off with you, wench, before I decide to take you to task for trespassin'," he said, pushing her away.

Ginny was thunderstruck. The utter gall of this man!

Nat had seen all he would stand for. No one treated his mistress that way. "It ain't fittin' you shove the missus," Nat warned, as a rushing blow caught the stranger just beneath the jaw and another plunged into his midsection.

A loud grunt left the stranger as he staggered. Gaining his balance, he lowered his head and plowed into Nat. They became a commotion of swinging fists and meaty blows.

50

Ginny was helpless to stop the fight. She watched as they circled one another. Nat was a big, brawny man, his size not matched by many. But he and the stranger seemed equally paired. Their breathing came fast and hard, as each strained to gain control. Ginny could smell the sweat that glistened on their brows and sprayed the ground, as they exchanged mighty blows. In the midst of the melee, animals scurried in the background, birds continued their singing, and a careless breeze whispered in the treetops.

Ginny fumed with indignation. The stranger didn't up-set her. Noting her appearance, she could understand his dismissing her so lightly. The man's employer was the culprit. That rascal better make it clear to his employees where his property ended and hers began. And she had every intention of seeing that he did so . . . and soon. She would not have Nat abused and accused wrongly.

When it appeared that there would be no winner of the fracas, Ginny decided it was time to put it to a halt. She spied Nat's musket and picked it up. Checking the load, she replaced the cap and hoisted the cumbersome stock against her shoulder. Taking a bead on a distant limb, she squeezed the trigger. The blast was deafening, but the mound of decaying leaves that cushioned her rapid descent was soft. Her ears hummed with a vibrating roar. Two pair of shocked eyes met her surprised gaze.

"Lordy, Miz Ginny, are you all right?" Without waiting for her reply, Nat turned to his adversary. "Now look what you've gone and done."

"Don't go layin' the blame at my doorstep. It's as much your fault as mine. If you hadn't been poachin', none of this would have happened."

While the men renewed their argument in earnest, Ginny shook her ringing head and got to her feet. Plac-

51

ing her thumb and forefinger to her delicate lips, she splintered the charged air with a shrill whistle.

Two faces shot once more in her direction. One, a gleaming mahogany with a head of wiry hair, the other, a fiery red with a head that was as slick as the apple she'd coveted a short while earlier.

Ginny shifted her gaze to the stranger. "Mr. — ?"

"Just call me Blue," he answered stubbornly.

"All right, Blue, tell me why you think Nat is on your property?"

"It's not my property, but Mr. Cross's, and we are standin' smack dab in the middle of it, and that's Mr. Cross's rabbit that's headed for the cook pot."

"That's what I thought," Ginny said. "We shall get this settled once and for all. If you gentlemen will follow me, we shall see what Mr. Cross has to say about trespassers."

"Fine with me," Blue agreed, hitching up his breeches.

Nat gathered up the powder horn, musket, and the rabbit in question.

The thudding of hoofs and the snapping of branches drew the trio's attention.

Richard Denby jerked his lathered horse to a halt and dismounted. "Pray tell, what is going on here?"

"I assure you, Mr. Denby, we have everything under control."

Denby eyed Nat's bloody mouth and Blue's rapidly swelling eye. Lastly his gaze raked Ginny, from the tangled hair across her smudged face and down the length of her dirty dress. "Yes, I can see that you do," he replied sarcastically.

Ginny had had it. She'd been called a wench, and Nat a poacher. Now Richard Denby was looking down his long sloping nose at her, as though she were no more than a pesky insect. "Mr. Denby, there is only a misunderstanding over the property lines. However, if you

52

would be so kind as to point out to Mr. Blue here that we are indeed on Sutton property, then we'll have no problem."

Richard Denby wrinkled the sloping beak and shook his head slowly. "I'm afraid I can't do that, Miss Sutton."

"I beg your pardon?" she questioned.

"I'm afraid it's a moot point. This land for as far as you can see belongs to Jonathan Cross—lock, stock, and barrel."

"No! This belongs to my family. Mr. Lyndal deeded it to my father years ago."

"And do you have a deed of ownership for the property in question?"

Ginny looked at him dumbfounded.

"I thought not. You don't own anything, Miss Sutton. It's only by the grace of Mr. Cross that you remain rent free in that hovel you call a home."

A fury unlike anything Ginny had ever experienced bolted through her. She would get to the bottom of this, if it was the last thing she ever did. "We'll see about that."

6

Ginny turned angrily and walked rapidly toward Jonathan Cross's home. A multitude of questions whirled through her head; the most frightening was Richard Denby's declaration. Had Mr. Lyndal not deeded the property to her father? She'd never seen a deed, never had reason to concern herself by the absence of one. Oh please, God, don't let it be true.

As Ginny faced the steps of the mansion, she hesitated, her bravado faltering as she gazed about her at the splendor. The house was large by anyone's standard, a bit overpowering to one used to so little. The house was not new to her. As a child, she'd spent many hours here with her father, taking her lessons alongside the Lyndal children and others from neighboring plantations. And more lately, delivering hats to the Lyndal women. The home and grounds lacked the care the Lyndals had lavished on it, but Ginny was sure that Jonathan Cross would see that its luster was restored. Still, even in its present state, the sheer size of the place impressed her.

The palms of her hands were damp with perspiration. She shifted the sack of apples, swiped her hands on her homespun dress, and pushed the loosened tendrils of hair behind her ears. What a sight she must make, coming to see the lord of the manor in her threadbare dress. Her thoughts brought a frown to her brow. Why should she care? This was no social call; she was here on business.

And the sooner she got it over with, the better she would feel. She glanced over her shoulder.

Richard Denby sat his horse with a smirk of ridicule clear on his face. Blue shuffled his feet nervously and dodged her gaze, a look of misery encompassing his features, as though he regretted his part in the development. Nat stood proudly, a slight nod of his head encouraging her.

Stiffening her back and tilting her chin defiantly, she took a deep breath. With a great deal of fortitude, Ginny walked up the steps and approached the large double doors. Lifting her hand, she grasped the brass knocker and pumped it several times.

The doors swung open immediately. The butler peered down at her, as though she'd just crawled from beneath a rock.

Before she could utter a sound, he informed her, "Mr. Cross isn't interviewing any more applicants today. You'll have to come back another day, Miss."

Her face flamed with embarrassment. What was this man talking about? She would not be put off. "If you, sir, can bend your stiff neck, maybe you can read my lips." Ginny spoke very slowly, pronouncing each word very carefully. "I'm not here to be interviewed. I am here to see—"

"Willis, what is the meaning of this?" Jonathan questioned as he approached his butler. "Why haven't you invited Miss Sutton inside?"

It was the butler's turn to flush with embarrassment. "I thought, sir—"

"Thought what, Willis?"

He turned to Ginny. "Come in, Miss Sutton."

"No, this is not a social call. It is a matter of business that needs your immediate attention."

Jonathan's brow shot up.

"Is it true?" she blurted out.

"What?" he asked, joining her on the porch.

"I'm sorry, first I should explain myself. My friend has suffered the meanest of accusations, not to mention a sorely abused body." She turned to the men still waiting at the foot of the steps.

Nat met Jonathan's gaze steadily. "I ain't no thief, Mr. Cross."

Jonathan's eyes shifted to his own servant. Blue was questioning the wisdom of his actions. Just the same, he lifted his head and peered at his employer with his one good eye. The other had swollen completely shut. "I was just protectin' your property, boss."

At last he raised his gaze to Denby. "I, too, was protecting your property, sir."

"Blue, while Miss Sutton and I straighten this out, you and Nat see if Bertha won't fix you something cool to drink, and send someone to the ice house. Your eye and Nat's lip could use a cold compress. And, Denby, we will talk later."

Unwilling to leave his mistress, but wanting to give her privacy to conduct her business, Nat ignored Cross's suggestion and replied, "I'll wait for you over there by that pecan tree, Miz Ginny."

She nodded, and for a moment watched the men walk away.

"Will you join me inside, Miss Sutton? We can discuss this over something cool to drink."

"No! All I want is the truth. Is Mr. Denby right? Do you own the property we have laid claim to all these years?"

Her stance was proud and the tilt of her head arrogant, still, Jonathan could see the fear mirrored deep in her eyes. Oh, God, how he wanted to lie. Yet he knew better. Her pride would never stand for it.

56

"Please," he asked, extending his arm.

She stepped away from him and shook her head. "It's true, isn't it?"

Sadly, he nodded his head.

Trying to control the tears and swallow the lump in her throat, she replied. "I didn't know."

"I know you didn't. However, I never dreamed Denby would take it on himself to inform you."

At last Ginny's shoulders wilted, all her hopes and dreams shattered by a few words. What would they do? Where would they go? "I don't presume to know why Mr. Lyndal didn't honor his word. I do know my father worked for years to buy the land. Still, if Mr. Lyndal did not deed the property to him, it is of little consequence what arrangements they made. My father is dead, and Mr. Lyndal is in England. I will pay you what rents you deem fair up to this time, and we will vacate the property as quickly as possible." Ginny turned, afraid she would embarrass herself by crying.

Jonathan placed his hand on her arm. "Miss Sutton, you don't have to do that—we can work something out."

With angry sparks glinting in her eyes, she brushed his hand away. "I don't need your charity, Mr. Cross. And I also won't be picking your vegetables," she snapped.

Jonathan frowned. "Have I not paid you enough?"

Her eyes flashed as she looked at him keenly. Shifting the sack of apples from one arm to the other, she said, "Oh, you paid us plenty."

Ginny was on a roll, and she had no intention of stopping until she'd had her say. Pacing back and forth in front of Jonathan, her frank, expressive words tumbled one over the other. "Oh, I know what you were about, Mr. Cross. You were soothing your conscience. Well, we don't need your charity." She paused breathlessly, then added, "You needn't have paid us so richly for the vegetables. You do own the dirt they were grown in."

Jonathan flinched at her words, his eyes dark and profound. He saw the hopeless despair in her eyes and answered softly, "But you labored in it, not I, Ginny. Your time was worth something."

She laughed a hard little laugh. "Perhaps, but you deceived my mother and me. Did you plan to keep your ownership a secret, until you had paid us enough to find another place to live?"

"I'm sorry you see it in that light. Try to put yourself in my place. If I had told you I owned the property and offered to sell it to you, would you have had the means to buy it?"

"No," she said in a flat toneless voice.

"Would you have accepted it, if I gave it to you?"

She lowered her head. "Of course not."

Jonathan sighed. "I knew I would have to tell you sometime, but I didn't know how to go about it. Besides, someday you might have decided to sell it, then you would have discovered you didn't have a deed."

Her head snapped up. "I would *never* have sold it."

"You say that now, Ginny, but who can predict the future?"

"If what you say is true, and we did decide to sell, don't you think we would give you, or whoever owned the Lyndal plantation, the first opportunity to buy our property?"

"I hadn't thought of that."

"There's a lot of things you haven't thought about, Mr. Cross." Tilting a stubborn chin, she called to Nat. "Let's go, Nat."

Nat and Blue shuffled across the lawn. They appeared in deep conversation. When they reached the steps, Blue twisted his arms behind him and rocked back on his heels.

58

"Miss Sutton," he cleared his throat. "Miss Sutton, I would like to apologize for my ungentlemanly behavior, and ask your forgiveness. Being in danger of havin' my other eye blackened, I listened while Nat explained the property lines, and pointed out my failures as a gentleman."

"I'm afraid, Mr. Blue, that I am the one who owes you an apology. Nat was indeed trespassing, as was I. And if we really get down to it, the rabbit was not ours to take, nor the apples." She leaned over and placed the sack against the wall. "Although I must assure you, Nat believed he was right, as I did. I cannot fault you for doing what you thought right, and I hope you won't fault us for our mistake. I assure you it won't happen again."

In the distance, a pair of matched bays made their way smartly up the drive. Ginny recognized the passenger in the open carriage immediately. Christine Lyndal Iverson. Dread swept over her. At every opportunity Christine made a point of touting Ginny's poverty. Ginny was not ashamed of her position in life, but it galled her that Christine always chose to have an audience before she began her setdown. Oh, how Christine would love this new development.

Her posture became rigid as she turned to Jonathan. "Please let me know how much rent I owe you."

"You don't owe me anything."

"Oh, but I do, and I fully intend to pay. Come, Nat, let us be on our way."

Nat turned to Blue and quietly informed him. "I done tol' you I ain't no poacher." He eyed Blue angrily. "I don't know what your Mr. Cross has tol' to the missus, but I don't like it. She's a good woman, and they don't nobody work as hard as she does."

Shame etched Blue's face, and the eerie feeling that he'd just lost a good friend filled him with remorse. Still, before he could answer, Nat dropped the lifeless rabbit at his feet and stalked away.

Jonathan rubbed a weary hand over his face. As he removed his hand, a corner of the cloth sack caught his attention. As he watched, the sack shifted, and one by one Ginny's apples rolled from the bag and thumped down the steps, gathering in a forlorn heap on the lawn.

He cursed Richard Denby as Ginny walked away. He could feel her pain, and the shattered dreams he knew she was thinking about. *Damn Denby and his bloody interference,* Jonathan thought, as he prepared himself to meet his visitor.

Before Ginny could cut across the lawn, the carriage stopped beside her. "Well, well, Ginny Sutton," came the dripping sweet voice. "I hope you haven't led Mr. Cross to believe you are the welcoming committee. I would hate for him to think we all dress with the same flavor *you* insist on displaying."

"Christine, I can assure you that I haven't led Mr. Cross to believe I am anything. And furthermore, my labor is what accounts for my appearance. What's your excuse?"

Smarting with resentment at the setdown, Christine fluffed the skirt of her amber gown. "Ginny, this just happens to be the very latest fashion from England. Of course, I don't know why I waste my breath explaining to you. It's plain to see that it would take more than current fashion to make you presentable."

"You're probably right, Christine. Nonetheless I don't have time for your whining today." Ginny turned and walked rapidly away, blinking furiously to quell the onrush of tears.

7

"Whine, *me?* What utter nonsense." Christine grimaced, patting her flushed face with delicate gloved hands.

As Jonathan approached the carriage, he'd heard the exchange. With difficulty, he controlled the smile that threatened the corners of his mouth. Ginny Sutton was more than capable of taking care of herself. Inside, he applauded her rejoinder. It appeared this Christine was cast from the same mold as other ladies of his acquaintance. Was Ginny Sutton the exception?

Christine's pout turned to a practiced smile, and her eyes gleamed with satisfaction as she perused the length of Jonathan Cross. "Mr. Cross, I'm so happy to at last meet you."

Ginny didn't have to turn around to know that Christine was having her first glimpse of the devilishly handsome new owner of Crossroads. In her mind's eye, she could describe exactly what Christine was seeing: his rumpled ebony hair, a strong, deeply tanned face with mocking gray eyes, a snowy white shirt tucked neatly into snug black breeches, and knee boots that shone with a high gloss. The fine cut of his clothes emphasized his broad shoulders and lean waist. His silky voice only enhanced the image playing in her head.

Ginny shook her head, as though that would rid her mind of unwanted thoughts. She had more pressing matters to think about. Her dreams had disintegrated like a windswept mist. What would she and her mother do? Her carefully hoarded monies would pay the back rents. Still, what could her father have been thinking, not to have insisted on a deed? On that account, Ginny didn't have to ponder long. Her father had been a dreamer. He loved his books and the knowledge they held. He'd dedicated himself to reading and then pondering everything he read. He taught with a zeal that his students could never appreciate. Eugene Sutton hadn't worried about tomorrow or the day after, assuming everything would take care of itself. It did, but only because of Maureen's dedication to him. Many were the times Ginny had heard her mother tell him, "Go ahead with your reading, dear. Me and the children will dig the potatoes," or some other like chore. He would smile tenderly and pat her hand, and in moments be completely absorbed in the words before him. Ginny wondered for a moment what Christine Lyndal would do in her situation? It was ludicrous to even ponder such a thought. People like Christine always landed on their feet.

Christine was busy making calf eyes at Jonathan Cross, and pondering several avenues of carnality.

"And to what do I owe this pleasure?" Jonathan asked, helping her from the carriage.

"I'm Christine Iverson. It was such a lovely day, I thought I would ride out and welcome you to Virginia. I would have come sooner, but I had to meet with my seamstress. Choosing fabrics is such a hectic job. Of course, arranging for a new wardrobe is very time-consuming. Winter clothing is my absolute worst season. The colors are so drab compared to the bright fabrics of spring and summer. Don't you agree, Mr. Cross?"

Jonathan nodded his head. "Tiring, I'm sure."

When Christine stumbled and fell prettily into Jonathan's arms, she gasped. "Why, I'm so clumsy, if you hadn't been there, I fear I would have fallen. Thank you," she purred, brushing her hand across his chest. "That hateful Ginny Sutton has upset me terribly. She talked so ugly to me, and even went so far as to accuse me of whining. Me, the essence of a lady. All I can say is she better watch herself."

"And why's that, Mrs. Iverson?" Jonathan asked smoothly.

"Why, she's a disgrace, the way she works in the fields like a man. No decent man would have her." Christine wrinkled her nose.

"Have you ever thought it might be a matter of necessity instead of desire?"

"I suppose a first encounter would elicit pity for her, but when you've known her for as long as I have, her appearance becomes tiresome. She's nothing but poor white trash," Christine scorned.

Jonathan's brow shot up, and a grimace flashed across his face. Once more a jolt of compassion shot through him. He and Ginny Sutton were not so very different. The labels were different, but the hurt, he was sure, was just as painful. And doubly so for a female.

"I beg your pardon, Mrs. Iverson. I didn't hear you."

"That's perfectly all right. I was saying before my marriage and widowhood, my maiden name was Lyndal."

Oh, please God, not a widow, Jonathan beseeched silently.

Christine swept her hand in a grand flourish. "This was my home before I married. Don't you just love living here? It's so much grander than many of the river homes in this area."

"Yes, it is quite comfortable. Would you care to join me for a cup of tea, Mrs. Iverson?"

"What a marvelous idea. Maybe I can be of some small service, by telling you how we had the house decorated when I lived here. You might want to implement some of my ideas in your theme as you decorate."

"To be sure," Jonathan agreed, as he escorted her across the lawn. Oh my God, he groaned to himself. He had filled the side yard with discarded items from the house that were too garish for his taste. The servants had taken great pleasure in choosing pieces for themselves.

Christine's bejeweled hand patted his arm. "I'll be a great help, too, you'll see."

Lord, would the remainder of his day be taken up entertaining the widow Iverson?

Sending Nat on ahead, Ginny took her time going over and over Denby's cruel disclosure, then Christine's taunts. When she reached the bridge, she dropped to its planked surface. Her spirits were as low as the dark billowing clouds moving across the valley. Slipping off her shoes, she dangled her legs over the side of the bridge and let her toes skim the water. Seeing Christine in all her finery didn't help her mood. Everything around her was falling apart, and there was nothing she could do, except watch it happen. Never had she felt so completely helpless. She leaned toward the water as far as she could and examined her reflection. What she saw was not encouraging. Her hair was wild and unruly. Her features were pleasant enough, except the freckles that sprinkled her fair complexion. She lifted her hair and pulled it from side to side. Was her neck too long, her eyes too big? She held her hand out and examined its surface. Despair suddenly enveloped her as she studied her rough, chapped hands, her nails bitten to the quick. They looked like a piece of worn-out shoe leather, and felt just about as rough. Her fingernails looked like she'd run them through a sausage grinder. Her mother had tried everything, from pepper to coating the tips with turpentine, to discourage her from biting them. Nothing worked.

Anyway, there wasn't a thing she could do about her appearance. What did she care? Even if she had a wardrobe full of beautiful clothes, she would have nowhere to wear them. Ginny smiled cynically. She wondered how the dress Christine had on today would hold up behind a plow.

Dispirited, she slapped her foot against the water, sending ripples across the smooth surface. What was she doing sitting here feeling sorry for herself? She didn't need these thoughts wasting her valuable time. What foolishness, she chided herself.

It was something about Jonathan Cross that evoked these thoughts. One moment she wanted to tame her hair, cream her skin, and stop biting her nails. All to impress him. On the other hand, she wanted to despise him because he owned her land. She was just being ridiculous, she thought, cramming her wet feet into her shoes. All she wanted was to be left alone to do her work, that's all she'd ever wanted. She didn't care what people thought about her. Oh well, maybe she'd try really hard not to bite her nails, and when she was working outside, it wouldn't hurt to remember to wear a hat. One thing was for sure, she would do it for herself . . . not for Jonathan Cross, or anybody else.

Unexpectedly, a large rain drop splattered the water. Then another, until suddenly it began pouring down. She scrambled to her feet, aggravated at herself for daydreaming instead of paying attention to the clouds she had noticed earlier.

Crouching beneath the limbs of a large oak, she decided to wait out the storm. Before long, she realized her mistake. Instead of diminishing, the rain continued to pour. Very quickly, she was soaked. As she decided to make a run for it, a great black stallion streaked across the bridge.

"Jonathan Cross," she whispered. What was he doing out in this downpour? She would have thought he and Christine were cozy and comfortable in the warmth of his home.

Horse and rider turned suddenly and drew up beside her.

When she looked up at him, he was startled by the misery in her green eyes. Compassion whipped through him; it was the memory of her clear, bright green eyes that had haunted him since their first encounter—eyes with a curious mixture of innocence and fire. After her discovery today, the brightness had vanished, replaced by disappointment and pain. If it were in his power, he would put the sparkle back in her eyes. He dismounted and shrugged out of his greatcoat. "Here, take this."

Ginny pushed away the offered coat. "No, I couldn't. I'm already wet, you keep it."

"You will take it, Miss Sutton, you're shivering. You'll catch your death, if we don't get you dry," he snapped, wrapping the coat around her trembling shoulders.

"What about you, Mr. Cross? What's to keep you from becoming ill if I take your coat?" she asked through chattering teeth.

"If we continue to stand here in this downpour and argue, we'll likely both be sick. I'll take you home."

Before Ginny could protest, he laced his fingers together and bent toward her. Unable to refuse him, she placed her hand on his shoulder and her foot in his hand. A quick boost, and she was sitting atop the stallion. When Jonathan mounted, it became perfectly clear how close they were. He placed his arms around her and grasped the reins. Clicking his tongue, he alerted the horse of his wishes. Ginny would not have admitted it for anything, but she was terrified. Never in her life had she ridden a horse, nor had she ever been so close to a man.

The rain continued to fall. Not only was his vision hampered by the rain, it was difficult to take his eyes off Ginny. Bundled in his coat, with her wet hair plastered to her head, she was a vision. He couldn't deny it; she was very fetching, and she pleased him. Yes, she pleased him very much.

"What are you doing out in this mess? I thought you were busy entertaining Christine."

"At the first thunderclap, I warned her of the impending storm. She was eager to reach her home without delay. Something about damaging her gown in the weather."

Ginny felt his warm breath on her neck. "It was such a beautiful gown. I hope she made it."

"I'm sure she did. Her driver careened down the road in a cloud of dust."

Lifting his hand, he brushed a dripping strand from her shoulder. The gesture startled Ginny, and she clutched his thigh. Embarrassed by her actions, she quickly released his leg. In the process she almost tumbled from the horse. She blushed crimson.

Jonathan saved her from further embarrassment by ignoring the incident. He placed his arm around her waist, steadying her. "Tell me, Ginny, how did you get caught in the storm? It was only a sudden impulse that sent me out to make sure you had arrived home safely."

"You were looking for me?"

"Yes."

"I just let the time get away from me, I guess."

"I want you to know I'm sorry Denby took it upon himself to blurt out the situation about the property."

"Don't worry about it. We could never afford to work the land properly anyway."

Jonathan knew she was lying. He'd seen the shadows of fear she'd tried to hide while awaiting his answer.

"Maybe we can work something out."

"I don't think so." Ginny shook her head as they rode into the yard, trying to put aside the pain that gnawed her insides.

Jonathan dismounted and lifted his arms to Ginny. When she placed her hands on his shoulders, a vicious bolt of lightning ripped to the ground only yards from them. Ginny screamed and fell into his arms. Beowulf danced nervously. An ageless oak toppled to the ground, barely missing Ginny's home. She screamed again and buried her head against Jonathan's chest.

Nat appeared beside them. "I'll take care of de hoss," he shouted, pulling a skittish Beowulf behind him.

Jonathan scooped Ginny into his arms and ran to the house.

Her mother stood in the doorway, nervously twisting her apron. She moved aside as Jonathan carried Ginny inside.

"The lightning frightened her."

"I've been worried sick about her."

"You can put me down. I'm all right now, beyond being terribly ashamed of my behavior."

"Why are you ashamed? The lightning scared me, too. I thought for a moment there that Nat was going to have to carry us both," Jonathan teased as he set her on her feet.

A delicate smile trembled on her lips. Jonathan's finger tilted her chin. "Come on, you can do better than that."

Slowly, a tremendous smile spread across her face.

"Now that's more like it."

"You two need to get out of those wet clothes," her

mother announced. "There's some clothing of Patrick's in the loft, if you'd care to change into them, Mr. Cross."

"I'm sorry, my manners have deserted me," Ginny apologized, as she made the introductions.

"I assumed this was Mr. Cross," Maureen Sutton replied, as she directed Jonathan to the loft.

When Jonathan was out of earshot, Ginny whispered, "Mother! What are you doing? How could you suggest that he wear Patrick's clothes?"

Maureen picked up a towel and began drying Ginny's hair. "Ginny, there is nothing wrong with your brother's clothes. They are clean and dry. What would you have had me do?"

"I don't know. It's just that he is used to so much better."

"Well, at the moment 'his so much better' is wet. I'm sure he will be grateful for anything dry, regardless of the cut of the cloth. Now, along with you. Get yourself into dry clothes, while I get supper on the table. I believe we still have some of the cocoa Patrick brought the last time he came home. I'll heat some milk. That should chase away the chill."

"Mother," Ginny said softly. "I learned some very sad news today."

Maureen cupped Ginny's face and stroked her wet head. "I know, dear, Nat told me when he got back. Promise me you'll try not to grieve about it. We'll work something out. Haven't we always? And Ginny, it's not Mr. Cross's fault."

Reluctantly dragging her feet, Ginny approached her tiny room. As she changed clothes, she wondered at Jonathan's behavior. Why in the world had he come in search of her? Did he feel sorry for her? Her breath caught in her throat even now, as she thought of resting her body so close to his. An indelicate snort escaped her lips. That man had probably ruined her life by the news she'd learned today, and here she was mooning over him. Determined that she would pay no attention to him, she yanked up a hairbrush and left the room.

Her mother and Jonathan were sitting at the table talking quietly.

Ginny pulled a stool before the fire and sat down. Lowering her head, she swept her hair forward and began the thankless task of brushing the tangles from her damp hair.

Jonathan had been in the process of lifting a cup to his mouth. The cup poised in midair as he watched the firelight glint off her coppery mane. His eyes swept her trim figure, her breasts straining against the fabric of her dress, as she lifted her arm. He remembered her as she was, cold and wet. His memories brought a stirring to his loins that he was hard-pressed to control. He shifted uncomfortably and brought the cup to his lips.

Maureen did not miss the direction of his gaze. "Mr. Cross, will you join us for supper?"

"Please call me Jonathan. I wouldn't want to impose, but something certainly does smell good."

"Ginny, are you ready to eat?"

Ginny groaned inwardly. "Yes, mother." Casting her mother a discreet glance, she thought: *The next thing I know she'll be inviting him to stay the night.*

As they sat around the table eating fried squash, fresh green beans with new potatoes, and crisp corn-pones, Ginny noticed that Jonathan seemed to enjoy the meal. When he had polished off his second helping he rocked back in his chair and eyed Maureen Sutton. "That was delicious. That's the best meal I've had since I arrived at Crossroads."

"You jest I'm sure," Maureen replied, pleased.

Jonathan lifted his hand in the air. "No, I swear it's

the truth. I don't mean to be unkind, but everything my cook prepares tastes the same. If she makes corn, it tastes like potatoes, peas—taste like potatoes. Even the meat she prepares tastes like potatoes." He shook his head sadly. "The only thing she fixes that doesn't taste like potatoes, is potatoes."

The rain continued and a strong wind whistled around the corners of the house. Yet, inside before a crackling fire, the occupants put aside their worry and confusion and simply enjoyed each other. Their merry laughter testified to that as it lifted to the rafters and beyond.

8

Pacing the library, Jonathan massaged the taut muscles in his neck. The air was thick and sticky. He moved to the window, hoping to catch a breeze. The flowers had revived from the rain, and now poked their colorful heads through the overgrown weeds lining the edge of the walk. Jonathan closed his eyes and a feeling of nostalgia swept through him, as he remembered the beautiful gardens that surrounded his father's home in London. Would he ever succeed in bringing that same beauty to his home? There was so much to do . . . so much to do, he thought tiredly.

Willis knocked smartly on the door.

"Yes," Jonathan called.

"Mr. Denby is here. Shall I send him in?" Willis asked.

"Yes, send him in, and no interruptions please."

Jonathan's eyes narrowed as he watched Denby stroll toward him. For a moment he surveyed the tall, thin man, dressed immaculately in dark suiting. His thin black hair, intermingled with unruly gray strands, made him appear older than his years, when Jonathan knew he was only a few years older than himself. His face was long and narrow, his cheekbones hollow, his eyes resembling two small onyx beads. Jonathan had given Denby's appearance or character little thought. Now, he wondered; what kind of man would knowingly destroy the meager hopes of another?

"You wished to see me, Mr. Cross."

Jonathan scowled. "No. What I want to do is dismiss you, Denby. But because you work for my father, I fear I shall have to tolerate you in my life for a while longer." Jonathan returned to his desk and sat down. Propping his elbows on the desktop, he steepled his fingers and studied Denby.

After a moment, Jonathan questioned, "Whatever possessed you to tell Miss Sutton about the property?"

Denby stiffened. "Everything was in such an uproar, it just slipped out."

"Just slipped out? For a man of your intelligence, you must excuse me if I find that difficult to believe."

"They would have found out eventually," Denby said coolly.

Jonathan turned from Denby and clenched his teeth, the muscles at the corners of his mouth twitching with suppressed rage. "Yes," he growled, "but it was my choice, not yours, about when and how I would tell them."

"Perhaps an apology would—"

"Apology!" Jonathan spun around and stared at Denby incredulously. "It will take more than a damned apology to correct the damage you've done."

For a few moments neither spoke, until finally Jonathan waved his hand, dismissing Denby. As Denby opened the door, Jonathan said, "From now on, attend to matters I have assigned you. Namely, find me a damned housekeeper."

"But, sir, between the two of us, we've interviewed at least a dozen women. What do you propose we do?"

"Run another advertisement, raise the wages, offer them an elaborate suite of rooms, do anything to get us a decent prospect. The damned house is falling down around me," he said, raking his finger through the thick dust on his desk.

"I'll take care of it," Denby said, passing Willis on his way out.

73

"Are you ready to dine, sir?"

"Later, Willis."

"But Bertha says she's been holding breakfast for an hour, sir."

With Denby leaving him in a damnable temper, Jonathan sneered and sarcasm laced his voice as he countered, "She could hold it for a week, and it would still taste the same. Tell her to put it away. I'm not hungry."

"Yes, sir," Willis said, closing the door behind him.

Jonathan propped his feet on the desk and leaned his head back, studying the cobwebs that swung from the ceiling. Damn it, he didn't need all this guilt roiling through him. He had enough problems of his own without trying to deal with Ginny. Just the thought of her brought visions of a wet, slender body pressed against his. The pelting rain turned her hair into coils of shimmering bronze, tempting him to bury his face in the rippling mane and lick the raindrops from the curve of her brow. His heart had thumped like a mad thing against his chest. He had ached to kiss her, but he had cautioned himself that it was not the time. Regardless of their situation, she stirred more than guilt inside him.

After sitting down at the table to dine with Ginny and her mother, he had waited tensely for the dreaded subject of the property to arise. When several minutes had passed without any mention of it, Jonathan had relaxed and enjoyed the best meal he had had since coming to Crossroads. His stomach rumbled in remembrance, for that was probably the best meal he would have for a long time to come. Bertha couldn't boil water without scorching it.

During the meal, he had watched Ginny, wondering what thoughts were running through her mind. Occasionally, he would glimpse a shadow of despair and fear in her eyes, emotions she tried to mask with smiles and casual conversation. Her silent suffering made him feel like the lowest thing that had ever lived. Even now, her look

74

haunted him, the sadness of it squeezing around his heart like a giant hand.

A light tap on his door brought his mind back to the present. "Yes?"

Willis stepped inside and closed the door behind him. "Mr. Cross, Miss Sutton's servant wishes to see you."

"Nat?"

"Yes, Nat. I'd forgotten his name. Shall I tell him you are busy?"

"No, send him in," Jonathan said with a puzzled frown.

Nat lingered in the doorway momentarily before stepping inside the room, his large brown hand twisting the ends of a cloth pouch.

Jonathan rose from his chair. "Please come in, Nat. I hope you and Blue aren't in another dispute," he said with a smile, hoping to ease Nat's apparent nervousness.

"Nosuh," Nat said, ambling slowly toward the desk. Avoiding Jonathan's eyes, he placed the pouch on the desk. "The missus said to give you this."

He heard a jingling sound as he picked up the bag. "Why?"

Nat thrust his hands into the pockets of his baggy trousers and shifted restlessly. "For the rent, Mistah Cross," he mumbled.

"Rent?" he asked, stunned.

"Yassuh."

"But I didn't ask for rent," Jonathan snapped.

"I don't know nuthin' about that, Mistah Cross. She just say to give it to you, so that's what I'm doin'. Can I go now, suh?"

"Yes, thank you, Nat," Jonathan said quietly, his spirits sagging to a new low.

After Nat left, Jonathan opened the pouch and spilled the coins atop the papers on his desk. He suspected it was money they'd painstakingly saved for months.

Sliding the paper to the edge of the desk, he held the

75

bag and funneled the coins into it. As he placed the paper aside, his eyes fell on the list of applicants. An idea suddenly leaped to his mind, an idea that would benefit both parties. *So, she wants to earn her keep? Well, I have finally thought of a way for her to do it. No time like the present to put this plan into action,* he thought, as he shouted for Willis to see that Beowulf was saddled.

Swinging the milk pail, Ginny strolled toward the barn, her senses attuned to the sounds and beauty of her surroundings. Daisies, dandelions, and clover scattered the yard, and honeybees buzzed over them, drawing the sweet nectar from the blooms. She heard the ring of the ax as Nat chopped off the limbs of the huge, fallen oak, a task that might take several weeks to complete. The aged tree, with its broad trunk and thick branches, had shaded their yard on hot summer days and had shielded their home against the bitter cold winds of winter. For perhaps a century, it had withstood nature's perils. Ginny felt a common bond with the ageold oak; both had weathered many storms in their lives. She thought it uncanny that on the same day the lightning had struck and killed the tree, she experienced her own life-shattering shock with a force almost as destructive, but unlike the tree, she would survive.

Ginny had groped for a solution to their problem, other than moving in with Patrick and disrupting his life. They had nothing of value to sell, so they could establish themselves in a place of their own. No one would want their crude furnishings, or the out-dated farm equipment that Nat was continually repairing, and they would get only a piddling amount for their livestock. Without finding another alternative, Ginny finally realized that Patrick was their only choice. Her mother would continue making hats, of course, and with the additional talent of being a fine seamstress, she might find work with an established dressmaker. Ginny had racked her brain trying to think of something *she* could do to occupy the long hours during the day, but the only idea she could come up with was to hire on as a barmaid in one of the local alehouses. She shuddered at the thought.

She recalled her offhanded remark to Milly: "At least when you're poor, you have nothing to lose." Now she realized how foolish she had been to make such a statement, because she'd *had* something to lose. Maybe her family didn't have material things, but they had never depended on anyone but themselves. They had never known hunger, and they had a roof over their heads. Poor didn't mean having nothing. *Now,* they had nothing. Jonathan Cross had everything, including their last coin.

But the thought that Jonathan felt sorry for her and her mother, hurt more than the deceit. Well, he might think his action generous, but Ginny wouldn't accept charity from anyone. She had seen that he got his money back in rent money.

She picked up the cow bell and started to call in the cow, her hand pausing in midair when she heard the bees humming from their nest in the rafters. She looked up, wondering if she dare try to invade their kingdom again, recalling Nat's painful ordeal a few days ago. She and Nat had decided to raid their hive, while most of the workers were away. Nat had dressed appropriately for the task, wearing long sleeves, gloves, and a scrap of her mother's netting over his head. He had cautiously climbed the rickety ladder, while Ginny stood below him and held it. Her mouth had watered as she anticipated hot biscuits drowned with butter and honey. Nat's screams had echoed through the rafters as several bees flew inside his glove, stinging him unmercifully. Ridding himself of the bee-infested glove, he had rapidly descended the ladder, breaking two rungs in the process. Ginny had stepped aside just in time, or he would have surely crushed her. After that, he had sworn he would never try it again.

So, if honey was to be had, Ginny knew that she would have to get it. Deciding she'd milk the cow later, she set the cow bell and milk pail aside, and found the netting and gloves hanging on a peg inside the barn. She removed the ribbon from her hair, then slipped her hand into the glove, tying the ribbon snugly around the wrist for protection. After rolling down her sleeves, she screened her face with the netting. Last, she tucked the hem of her shift into the waist of her apron for easy movement. Propping the ladder against the wall, she climbed to the rafters and found the nest lodged within a hollow corner. Several bees fanned their wings around the entrance, guarding their golden honey from intruders. Holding one hand on the ladder for support, Ginny gingerly slipped her gloved hand inside the opening, and loosened a large chunk from the layers of combs. As she eased out her hand, a dollop of honey landed on the tip of her nose. Smiling victoriously, she began her descent down the ladder.

Suddenly, a bee lit on Ginny's honey-laden nose. She froze, looking cross-eyed through the netting at the insect, watching as its tongue dipped into the honey. Another bee hovered for a brief second, then joined its companion. Afraid of loosening her hold on the ladder to swipe at them, she jutted out her lower lip and tried to blow them off. Their wings fluttered, but their tiny, hairy feet remained glued to the netting. Not knowing what else to do, she continued down the ladder, carrying her passengers with her.

Jonathan stood in the entrance of the barn, watching Ginny's shift hug her rounded buttocks, as she carefully found footing on the rung beneath her. What was she doing? He held his breath, knowing that if he called out to her, she might tumble from the ladder. Walking quietly toward the ladder, he steadied it, without her knowing he was standing beneath her.

Her mind on the bees rather than her footing, Ginny had forgotten about the missing rung. Since Jonathan's eyes were on her shapely legs and buttocks, he never saw it either . . . until she slipped and began falling, carrying her precious honeycomb with her.

Stepping backwards to catch her, Jonathan tripped over the milk pail, as she landed in his arms. Falling backwards, he brought Ginny down with him. The second his back hit the ground, Ginny threw up her hand and flattened the honeycomb against his face.

Breathless and dazed from the impact, their hearts beat in rapid staccato. Finally, Jonathan wiped the back of his hand across his eyes, wondering what was causing his blurred vision. Running his tongue over his lips, he tasted the sweet substance. Then he became conscious of Ginny's soft, slender body covering his long, hard one. He gloried in the moment, knowing that as soon as she regained her senses, she would pull away from him and end this pleasure. Lifting his hands from the ground, he placed them on her back and lightly stroked her. When he raised his knees, he realized the intimacy of their position. He felt her legs between his, felt her hips nestled against him. How many times in the past had he awakened to find a woman's soft body nestled against him like this? Many times, but none so lovely as this one, he thought, clenching his teeth to quench the fires burning inside him.

What was running across her back? Ginny wondered, trying to clear the cobwebs from her mind. She remembered falling from the ladder, but this didn't feel like the ground beneath her. She moved her hand above her head.

Jonathan thought he might smother as she laid her sticky glove on his nose and mouth, then squeezed lightly.

Feeling the features of a face, Ginny's head whirled around. She jerked her hand away, shiny threads of honey came with it, still attached to the most hideous face she had ever seen. Beneath thick, spiky eyebrows and matted dark eyelashes, his eyes appeared as two wrinkles in his face. Then the mouth grinned at her.

Ginny peeled back the netting from her face. "Mr. Cross!" she shrieked.

"Yes, Ginny, fortunate for you, but not so fortunate for me. In my lifetime, I've been involved in many *sticky* situations" he stressed, "but nothing quite as sticky as this."

"You look horrible," she said with laughing green eyes.

"Maybe so, but I certainly taste good," he commented, slowly sliding his tongue across his lips.

As she removed the gloves from her hands, her gaze lingered on his lips, and pleasurable warmth surged through her as she imagined tasting his honey-laden mouth. Before she thought, she lifted her hand and touched her finger to a dollop of honey that clung to his chin. She touched her tongue to her finger, tasting the golden drop. "Hmmm . . . good," she sighed.

"You're telling me," Jonathan said, honey the last thing on his mind. Again his tongue slid slowly across his lips.

Oh, to be kissed by such a man, she thought, weakness stealing over her.

Their mouths mere inches from one another, Jonathan watched as her mouth parted, the tip of her tongue enticingly mimicking his own. Every part of his body was tormented with longing for her.

Ginny caught her breath as she felt his powerful thighs tighten around her hips, until now forgetting she was lying on top of him. Had she lost her mind? How could she be dreaming about his kisses, when he was the cause of all her problems? Pushing against his chest, she rolled off him and came abruptly to her feet.

"Just why are you here?"

Jonathan stood and slid his hand inside his coat, removing the pouch of coins. Taking her hand, he placed the pouch in it. "I never asked you for rent money."

"I can't . . . no, please," she protested, trying to return it to him.

"Yes, take it." He looked at her for a long moment, then said, "I have an idea that I hope will solve our dilemma."

She looked at him in surprise. "What?"

"Before we discuss it, would you mind if I wash this mess off my face and clothes, before the bees mistake me for their hive?"

She laughed lightly as she imagined such a scene, and examined her own honey-smeared clothing. She gasped, her face turning beet-red when she saw her bare legs, finally remembering she had tucked the hem of her dress into the waistband of her apron.

Jonathan, noticing her lowered head, followed the direction of her gaze. Though he couldn't see her face, the heat emanating from it was almost tangible. With any other woman, he would think nothing of telling her she had pretty legs, but Ginny wasn't any other woman, and he sorely doubted she would take his remark as a compliment. Jonathan raised his head and glanced around the barn, deciding to make casual conversation. "You keep your barn in good shape."

Seeing his attention elsewhere, Ginny quickly yanked the hem of her skirt from her apron and dropped it to the floor, hoping he hadn't noticed. "Yes . . . ah . . . Nat takes care of it."

"We could certainly use him around my place. My barns are in sad shape . . . as is the house," he added slyly.

A light went off in Ginny's mind. *He wants Nat!* She didn't know whether to feel pleased or angry. She had wondered what Nat would do when they moved to Williamsburg. They couldn't take him with them; there wasn't enough room for him to live at Patrick's. But Nat didn't belong to anyone; he was a free man and could make his own choices. If Jonathan wanted him, then he would have to pay him for his services. Somehow that made her feel better.

Jonathan returned his attention to Ginny, smiling to himself when he saw her dress back in proper order. "Where would be the best place for me to clean up?"

"You're welcome to come to the house."

"No, I'll just make a mess of everything."

"Well, there's the water trough outside, or there's the river, just a short distance from here."

"I'll use the trough since it's closer."

"Shall I bring you some cloths and soap? I fear the honey will be difficult to wash from your hair without soap."

"If it won't be any bother."

She smiled softly. "I don't mind. I'll go get everything and meet you out back."

After Ginny left, Jonathan removed his coat. Tossing it casually over his shoulder, he went outside, and strode toward the watering trough. After laying his coat aside, he loosened his cravat, and sat down on the end of the trough, waiting for Ginny.

Could they ever be friends, now that Denby had made such a mess of things? Friendship? he questioned, knowing it was not only her friendship he desired. She was as difficult to approach as a rose encircled by thorns. Perhaps her indifference toward him was the reason he enjoyed pursuing her. He had suffered through several incidents with women who approached him with airs of affectionate cannibals, determined to possess him. Courtesy they had mistaken for a welcome to share his bed; if he offered friendship, they took it as love.

His first meeting with Christine Iverson **ha**d alerted him to what mold she fit. He'd recognized that stalking gleam in her eyes. Avoiding her would be a full-blown task, damned near impossible.

But thoughts of seeing Ginny everyday produced the opposite effect. Each time he was with her, he looked forward to her company again.

Feeling the perspiration running down his face and neck, Jonathan stood and removed his cravat and waistcoat. Bending over the trough, he splashed water over his hair and face.

He didn't see Lord Adelbert leave the field, where he had been grazing, and amble in his direction. But Ginny saw him as she came around the corner of the barn. She stopped, her gaze riveting toward Jonathan. She saw the mule approach Jonathan from behind. For a second, Lord Adelbert stood rock still. Then suddenly, he lowered his head toward Jonathan's rear and bared his yellowed teeth.

"Jonathan, watch out!" Ginny shouted, but her warning came too late.

A sharp pain ripped through Jonathan's buttocks. As he howled, his fisted hand shot behind him, cracking against Lord Adelbert's nose. Cradling his aching hand, Jonathan jerked around, meeting his tormentor face to face.

"What the bloody hell!"

In answer, the mule positioned his nose against Jonathan's chest and pushed.

Ginny watched as Jonathan tumbled into the water, his legs making a perfect arch before he sank into the depths of the water. When Jonathan's head surfaced, he shook the water from his face, glistening droplets sprayed the ground. Gripping his hands on the wooden sides, he hoisted himself from the trough, never taking his glittering eyes from the mule.

"Oh, Jonathan, I'm so sorry," Ginny cried, running over to him. "Did he hurt you?"

"Hurt me? Hell, I'll wager he brought blood," he countered angrily. "So help me God, if I ever get my hands on him, I'll yank every damned tooth out of his head."

A thoughtful frown creased her brow. "I can't understand why he attacked you, unless he doesn't like you bathing in his drinking water."

Lord Adelbert snorted and curled his upper lip as though in agreement.

"See, that's it," Ginny announced gleefully. "I knew there had to be a reason."

"Then by all means have at it," Jonathan growled with a sweeping wave of his arm. "You should like the taste better, Lord Adelbert. I sweetened it for you."

Ginny pressed her hand over her mouth to hide her smile, but she couldn't hide the laughter twinkling in her eyes.

"So you think it's funny, do you?" Jonathan accused. "I never thought you to be the blood-thirsty kind."

"Oh no, I'm not," she quickly interjected. "I'm truly sorry he bit you on your . . . your . . . ah," she blushed furiously.

"Well, pardon me, if I don't share your amusement, I probably won't be able to sit comfortably for a week."

Picking up his clothes, he added, "If you don't mind, I shall finish cleaning up at the river, and leave Lord Adelbert to drink to his heart's content."

"I'm sure you can handle this alone," she said, handing him the towels and soap. "I'm sorry you've had such a bad day."

"What worries me the most is that it's just begun," he replied dryly.

9

Jonathan removed his wet shirt and draped it over a branch. Sitting down on the bank, he flinched as a rock pierced his wounded buttock. To have a honeycomb smashed in your face, and then be bitten by a fractious mule, all within the span of an hour, was not the makings for a productive day.

Stretching out one leg, he drew his other knee to his chest, feeling the hot rays of an unrelenting sun beat down on his back. He was not accustomed to the heat, not for days on end. Not a breath of air stirred. The stillness was interrupted by the sound of a woodpecker tapping against a tree, the oppressive heat even limiting the activities of the forest creatures.

Ginny hurried down the path, bringing Jonathan the soap that he had dropped. She came to an abrupt halt and sucked in her breath, her eyes wide with something akin to wonder. She watched as Jonathan picked up a smooth flat stone and flicked his wrist, sending the pebble skipping across the water, the thick muscles spanning his broad back and arms, rippling like the surface of the water.

He is so . . . so beautiful, she thought, her eyes scanning his sun-browned back. Is he this dark all over? she wondered, feeling a strange sensation spiraling through her.

She swallowed deeply, then walked hesitantly in his direction.

Hearing footsteps behind him, Jonathan twisted his body towards her. "So you decided to join me after all."

"No, you dropped your soap," she said, handing it to him, unable to tear her eyes from the crisp black hair that matted his chest.

"Thank you. Was Lord Adelbert in better spirits after my departure?"

"Yes, and has your mood improved?" she mumbled, feeling a peculiar heat wash over her that had nothing to do with the weather.

He leaned back on his elbows and smiled up at her. "Yes, although lately I've been short-tempered. It must be this damnable heat. I was thinking about taking a real bath, the water looks so cool and inviting."

His remark destroyed Ginny's hard-won composure. Quickly turning her head, she looked everywhere but at him. "Be my guest. I'll be on my way."

As she started to leave, he rolled to his feet and took hold of her arm. "No, please stay. You could do with a little cleaning up, too," he taunted, as he removed a piece of honeycomb that had stuck to her arm. "Besides, we haven't had our talk."

Thinking he wished her to swim with him, she jerked her arm away and stiffened her spine. "I'll bathe later, thank you. Come to the house after you've had your . . . your bath, and then we shall talk."

"Ginny," Jonathan said with a broad grin spanning his face, "you misunderstand me." He wanted to say it sounded like a wonderful idea, but held his tongue.

Ginny had no problem voicing her thoughts, so she said in her candid way, "Well, what did you expect me to think, after finding you here half-dressed."

A slow, tantalizing smile curved his mouth. "If you had arrived a moment later, I might have truly shocked you."

"Oh," she said, trying to seem nonchalant, though her heart nearly leaped out of her mouth.

He screwed up his face, feeling his skin tighten beneath the honey. "Now that we've settled the matter, I'd like to wash."

Ginny lowered her gaze and said quietly, "If you wish, I'll try to get the honey out of your clothes."

A smile softened his features. "Thank you. I would greatly appreciate it."

As Ginny gathered up his clothing, she studied him from the corner of her eye as he leaned over and picked up the soap and towel. His waist and hips were sleek and narrow, his tight fawn trousers encasing thick, powerful thighs. He reminded her of the magnificent statues she had seen in one of her father's books. Each muscle and vein in his beautiful body seemed carved from relief, conveying a subtle, yet perceptible strength.

Her thoughts unsettling her, she finally sat down beside him. Lifting his coat, she brushed the soft velvet collar over her cheek, wondering how it would feel to be clothed in a gown made of the fabric. Placing the garment in her lap, she sprinkled water on the sleeve and gently toweled off the honey. Next she plunged his satin waistcoat beneath the water and washed it gently, then laid it aside.

Jonathan turned toward her, his face as red and shiny as an apple. "Is it all off?"

"Almost." Taking the cloth from his hand, she dipped it in the water, then knelt beside him. "Close your eyes," she instructed. "You have honey in your lashes." As she dabbed his eyes with the cloth, she teased, "Did you know honey's good for the complexion?"

"Is that why you were raiding the beehive?"

"No, I had my mind on hot biscuits dripping with butter and honey."

"Ah . . ." he sighed wistfully. "You know how to make biscuits?"

"Of course. Everyone knows how to make biscuits."

Jonathan grunted sourly. "Not my cook."

"You've mentioned your cook before. Surely she isn't that bad."

"She is."

"Why don't you find another one?"

"I will, when I hire a housekeeper."

"You don't have a housekeeper? What happened to the Lyndal's housekeeper and cook?"

"They took them to England."

"What a shame."

"Yes, with everything else to do, I've—"

Before he got the words out, she ordered softly, "Close your other eye."

Jonathan complied, intently studying her face with his open eye. He noted the golden speckles in her clear green eyes, her long, thick eyelashes the color of rich coffee, the tiny freckles that spanned her delicate cheekbones. His attention settled on the sensuous curve of her mouth. *What would she do if I kissed her?*

"Finished," Ginny announced, interrupting his carnal thoughts. "You'd better wash your hair before the honey dries."

Picking up his clothing, she rose and laid them neatly over the rocks, smoothing the wrinkles from the fabrics. Behind her, she heard his muttered oaths and watched him as he tried to wash the sticky beeswax from his hair.

She approached him and asked softly. "May I help you?"

His hands paused in his hair. He looked up at her, a grateful smile on his face. "Would you please?"

Kneeling beside him, she rubbed the bar of soap gently through his hair until she produced a thin lather.

As she washed his hair, her eyes scanned his bare, tanned back down to his waist, where his trousers had ridden lower on his hips. She noticed a narrow strip of lighter flesh and blushed. No, he wasn't dark all over, she mused, then immediately berated herself for her perusal.

Jonathan very nearly melted beneath her touch. No one had washed his hair for him since his childhood, and he remembered how he had hated it. His nanny must have hated the chore, too, for she had pulled his hair until he wondered if he would have any left on his head. But Ginny's soothing ministrations produced in him a feeling of lethargy.

He has such gorgeous hair, Ginny thought wistfully, as she massaged his scalp and raked her fingers slowly through the strands. Cupping her hands, she dipped them in the water, and repeatedly poured the water over his head, until his hair shone like watered silk. Her eyes followed the narrow rivulets of water that ran over his tanned broad shoulders, becoming trapped within the dark hair on his arms.

Jonathan's shoulders and neck ached from his stooped position, but he didn't complain as she repeated the process time and again.

After combing her fingers through the tangles, she asked him to raise his head. With deft fingers, she shaped his hair to fall into its usual style, but an unruly lock continued to drop over his forehead. "I've done all I can. It feels clean."

Their eyes met and held. She watched him with a rapidly beating heart, wondering at the strange expression on his handsome face.

He tilted her small chin with a long finger, his voice husky when he said, "How lovely you are."

Her muscles went limp, and moisture broke out on her hands. She began swaying toward him involuntarily, then abruptly caught herself, the sound of her own voice breaking the spell. "I . . . I think you jest," she said quickly, but when nervous, her tongue rambled as though it had a mind of its own. "Milly scolds me for going without a hat when I work outside. She pleads with me to use all kinds of concoctions on my face, which she swears will get rid of my freckles." She sat back on her haunches. "That's why she's so pretty, I suppose."

"But you would rather keep your freckles?" he asked, humor twinkling and dancing in his eyes.

"I really don't have the time or the patience to go through such a ritual."

Stirred by some deep emotion which he could not analyze, Jonathan brushed the back of his hand across her cheekbone. "I find your freckles very appealing."

Unaccustomed to compliments, Ginny shrank away from him. "Well, I wouldn't do anything about it if you *didn't* like them." With the back of her hand, she flipped her braid from her shoulder to her back.

Jonathan gathered the thick braid in his hand, again startling her. "I also like your hair, but unbound, as it was the day I met you and Milly here."

Ginny cocked her head in his direction, a frown knitting her brow. "Why are you doing this?"

He smiled crookedly. "What am I doing?"

"Filling my head with nonsense. Do you think to beguile me with your flowery compliments?"

He dropped her braid and replied in earnest, "I assure you, Ginny, I only issue compliments where they are deserved."

Ginny stared at him, temporarily speechless. "I think the honey has seeped into your brain."

Jonathan tilted back his head and laughed heartily.

Tongue-tied and no longer able to meet the steady gaze of his gray eyes, Ginny rose to her feet and began gathering up the wet towel and soap. "If we are done, I should be leaving."

Jonathan caught her wrist. "Please, not yet. I need to talk to you."

Ginny looked at him with an expression of uncertainty, then sat down beside him. "All right, but I don't have all day, I have chores to do."

"I shall try to be brief." He gazed at her expectantly. "As I told you, I am without a housekeeper. Mr. Denby and I have interviewed at least a dozen women, finding not a single prospect among them." He chuckled. "They were either too big or too small, too meek or too temperamental, too outspoken or too reserved." He paused, dreading this moment, but he knew he could not put it off any longer. He looked her straight in the eye. "None of them would ever do the job as well as you could, Ginny."

"Me!" she shouted in disbelief.

"Yes, you."

"Never," she said tartly, twisting her hands together in her lap.

"Why not?"

"Because," she returned artfully, "I'm too small, too temperamental, and certainly too outspoken, but mainly because my experience at housekeeping has been restricted to three rooms—not three dozen."

"Thirty-four to be exact," he said unboastfully. "Thirty-four rooms that haven't had a cleaning since the Lyndals left. Of course, I will pay you well for your services."

"Yes, just like you paid me for my vegetables?"

A flicker of frustration crossed his face. "Ginny, I am giving you a chance to work and earn a salary. You want to remain in your home, I gather?"

"Yes, but—"

"You may give me what you can afford each month to

91

buy your property. We will handle it legally this time, with the proper papers and all."

It frustrated Ginny that she would even consider his proposition. Still, he knew the mere mention of the land would sway her—and besides, she needed the job. "You won't overpay me?" she challenged.

"No, I will pay you exactly what you are worth. After you see the terrible state my house is in, you will understand what I mean."

Her confidence plunged. "What if I do a poor job? Please promise me you won't feel charitable again and . . . and keep me because you feel you have to."

"I promise. Now, will you accept the job?" he ground out, his jaws aching from clenching his teeth.

"I really have no alternative, do I?"

Jonathan felt he might as well be pleading with a rock. "Yes, you have a choice," he said, biting each word. "Damnation, you are the most stubborn woman I have ever met. I don't want your bloody land. Keep it and continue as you have been."

"You know I can't do that?" she shot back.

Jonathan threw his hands into the air, the anger he had been holding in check finally surfacing. "Then tell me what the hell you *do* want."

With an impending sense of doom engulfing her, she stammered, "I . . . ah . . . suppose I could try . . . but you'll probably regret it."

"You are probably right," Jonathan mumbled beneath his breath. "Now, can you come to work tomorrow?"

"So . . . so soon?" she asked hesitantly.

"The sooner the better."

"Would you . . . would you still wish me to ah . . . supply you with vegetables?"

"We do need them, but, Ginny, I don't expect you to tend to your garden and my house. I'll have one of my

92

servants harvest them."

"Thank you. Nat can take care of the weeding, but he doesn't know much about gardening."

"We also have need of a gardener, if we ever plan to supply our own foods again."

"You wish me to clean your house and teach your cook to cook. If you are now asking me to instruct a gardener, you must understand these things will take time. I hope you are a patient man."

"Patience is one of my strongest virtues," he lied. Rising, he gathered up his clothing. "I will walk back with you. I tethered Beowulf in front of your house."

As they strode together along the shady path, Ginny asked, "Did you bring Beowulf with you from England?"

"Yes, along with several of my finest horses. Someday, I hope to find the time to do what I enjoy most, breed and raise them. I understand Virginians, like Englishmen, enjoy racing. Perhaps they need good horse-flesh."

Ginny laughed lightly. "You are talking to the wrong person about horses."

"Would you like me to teach you to ride?"

She looked at him in surprise. "Oh no, but thank you."

"They frighten you?"

"A little, yes. Milly rides beautifully, but her father taught her to ride almost before she could walk. We never had horses. Lord Adelbert serves my purpose . . . most of the time," she added jokingly.

Still feeling the pain in his buttock, Jonathan thought he would make a fine watchdog, too.

Ginny stood on the porch and bade Jonathan goodbye. The smile left her face as soon as he rode out of view. If only she had a few days before she went to work, she could ask Milly to advise her about the duties of a housekeeper. Then there was the other matter that alarmed her more than being Jonathan Cross's housekeeper. Spending time with him today had confirmed her worst suspicions. She had undeniably strong feelings for him, feelings she had no business having at all.

10

Early the following morning, Ginny made her way to Crossroads Plantation. When the manor came into view, she grimaced as she counted at least a dozen windows on the front of the house. Thirty-four rooms, she thought with a sigh, and all boasting windows to clean. From habit, she stopped on the walk that led to the house and knelt, pulling weeds from around several flowers. This is where she could really be of use, she mused, as she worked her way to the steps. Why, in a few weeks she could have the grounds looking as they had when the Lyndals lived here. Suddenly the thought of being cooped up in a house all day long did not sound appealing to her at all.

Last night, tears of relief had sprung in her mother's eyes, when Ginny had told her they wouldn't have to leave their home. Her mother had noticed her uneasiness about working as Jonathan Cross's housekeeper.

"I don't know what a housekeeper does, Mother," she had said.

"Don't worry so, Ginny. You are used to doing the same chores in your own home. This is only on a larger scale. Just try to think of one room at a time, instead of all of them. Mr. Cross has servants who will help you."

"He says I must make them work. How do you make someone work when they refuse? Already his butler doesn't like me. Is my position as a housekeeper more important than that of a butler?"

"I'm sorry, Ginny, I have no idea. Mr. Cross, I am sure, will explain all this to you."

"Oh Lord, I hope so."

Hearing the door open, Ginny looked up from her stooped position, a clump of weeds in her hand. Willis closely scrutinized her, a look of disgust on his face. Finally, he announced with an air of authority, "You're late, Miss Sutton. Mr. Cross awaits you in the library."

Now was as good a time as any to put Willis in his place, Ginny thought, tossing the handful of weeds aside and wiping her hands on her apron. Rising, she squared her shoulders and lifted her head haughtily. "Late? I'll wager, Willis, I've more taxing chores to do in a morning than turn a knob and open a door."

Her insult struck home. The thin corded muscles bulged in Willis's neck. It would not have surprised her if his starched white collar didn't lift its wings and fly like a startled bird from its resting place. With a satisfied smile on her face, she stepped upon the porch and brushed by him, entering the wide foyer.

Casting her a nasty look as he passed her, Willis opened the door to the library. "Miss Sutton has arrived, Mr. Cross."

"Please send her in, Willis, and round up all the servants."

"Yes, sir."

Stepping aside, Willis motioned her into the room and closed the door behind her. Jonathan rose from the chair behind his desk and smiled. "You did come."

"Of course, I told you I would." As she nervously twisted her apron in her hands, she glanced around the huge, unkempt room.

She looked so thoroughly wretched, that Jonathan felt

96

a sudden stab of guilt for hiring her to undertake such a task. The simple drab green shift and apron she wore were more appropriate for the rag bag. Later, he would buy her several new gowns, befitting her role as house-keeper.

Lounging against his desk, he asked, "Are you having second thoughts?"

She gave a slight shrug. "I've had a number of them since I accepted your offer yesterday. Are the rest of the rooms this terrible?"

"Some worse, I fear."

"How much time do I have?" she countered, a look of doubt and hopelessness on her face.

One eyebrow shot up. "You sound like a person who has just received the death sentence."

"I'm afraid you might expect too much from me too soon," she said in a thin voice.

"Time isn't of essence here. Anything you do, no mat-ter how long it takes, will definitely be an improvement." Pushing away from the desk, he strode toward her and pried her hands from the apron. "Are you frightened?" he asked, tilting up her chin and smiling down at her warmly.

She answered with a trembling smile. "A little."

Jonathan had a sudden urge to still her lips with a kiss, but instead, he gently brushed his thumb over her lower lip and held it there for a moment. "I'm always here if you need me. Don't ever hesitate to tell me if something is bothering you. Understand?"

"I hope that won't be necessary, but thank you all the same."

Taking her by the arm, he said, "Now, if you will come with me, Willis has assembled the servants. He will introduce you to them. If you want to know the truth, I know them little better than you."

Before she could ask him about her duties, he whisked her from the room and into the wide foyer. Several pairs of eyes looked her up and down. Ginny felt her cheeks begin to burn. Willis introduced them, and announced their duties so quickly that Ginny could remember but one name when he finished — Bertha, the cook, the only one welcoming her with a smile.

Bertha stepped forward and took Ginny's hand in her large brown one. "Welcome to Crossroads, Miz Sutton."

Ginny smiled as she picked up the odor of burned bread wafting from Bertha's clothing. "Thank you, Bertha."

Jonathan told them he expected to see results from their labors at the end of every day. They must obey Miss Sutton's orders and respect her position as housekeeper. As he talked, Ginny studied their expressions, hoping to see their acceptance of her written on their faces. Her hopes were unrewarded.

When Jonathan finished his speech, he turned to Ginny. "I have to spend most of the day at the stables. If you have any problems, send Willis down to tell me." Next, he addressed Willis. "You are to assist Miss Sutton in any way she needs you. She has a tremendous task before her."

Ginny thought she detected a hint of a threat in his order. And when Jonathan turned his back, she saw Willis cut his eyes toward her. Ecstatic to have Willis at her mercy, she gave Willis a warning look and smiled graciously.

"Do you have any questions, Ginny . . . ah . . . Miss Sutton?" he said quickly. He must remember to address her formally in front of the servants, he realized, as he noted several raised brows.

Afraid she would lose her advantage over the servants if she admitted her ignorance, she replied with a confi-

98

dence she didn't feel, "None just yet, Mr. Cross. I am sure we will do fine." Her eyes traveled from one servant to the next. "Won't we?" she asked with a smile.

A few nodded, some smiled, because their master was watching them.

"Then I shall leave you to your duties." He smiled and nodded politely as he opened the door and departed.

The room turned so deathly quiet, Ginny knew they had to hear her heart thumping wildly against her chest. *What am I supposed to do next?* She felt like a tiny mouse standing in the midst of a pack of hungry cats. Finding Bertha's smiling face among them, she drew on it for strength. After taking a deep breath, she turned to Willis and said, "Since you are the only man among us, Willis, you shall remove all the carpets to the backyard, so we can beat the dust from them."

Willis wilted, his mouth dropping open. For a moment he was speechless. "All of them?" he croaked.

"No, just the main floor today."

"But . . . but there must be a dozen of them . . . and . . . they're quite large. Also, I'll have to remove the furniture from them first."

"Then I suggest you start on it now. We must remove them before we can properly clean the rooms."

"But who's going to answer the door when someone knocks?"

"We will handle that problem should the need arise."

When Ginny turned her attention to the rest of the servants to issue instructions, she saw them nudging one another and snickering. They abruptly stopped when they saw her staring at them. Some coughed, some stared at the ceiling, and some stared at the floor. Bertha's smile engulfed her whole face. What had she done? Ginny wondered in puzzlement. Well, whatever it was, at least she got a reaction from them.

"I know each of you have had specific duties in the past, but for a while, we must all work together at cleaning the main floor first."

" 'Cuse me, ma'am?" a little voice squeaked.

Ginny directed her attention to the servant speaking. "Yes?"

"You're supposta start on the top floor first, 'cause the dust'll fall to the main floor, and then it'll have to be done all over agin."

How was she to know that? Ginny thought, mildly offended. After all, she only had a small loft in her home, not an entire floor of rooms to clean. Tossing her braid over her shoulder, an unconscious show of embarrassment, she said, "Of course. I wasn't thinking. The top floor then."

"You mean I have to lug all those carpets from upstairs to downstairs all by myself?" Willis argued.

Recalling the tales of the *Arabian Nights*, Ginny smiled at him nicely and said, "Maybe they're magic carpets and you can ride them down."

From the dumb look on everyone's face, Ginny knew they had never heard the story. She felt like a fool. Goodness, couldn't she do or say anything right?

"Well, let's get on with it," she announced, heading up the stairs. Hearing no one behind her, she paused midway and looked down at them. "Is there a problem?"

"Mr. Cross'll be mighty angry, if his clothes don't get washed."

"And ironed," another voice added.

"I do the master's needlework."

"I'm supposta spread the cloth and set the table."

"Lord a'mercy," Bertha chimed in, "I plumb forgot about the stew and I smell it burnin'. 'Cuse me, ma'am," she said, dashing from the room.

Ginny clenched the banister and gritted her teeth. "Is

100

there anyone here who actually does housecleaning?"

Everyone's eyes riveted toward Willis. He glared back at them. Placing her hands on her hips, Ginny impatiently tapped one foot. "Well, is no one able to answer my question?"

Silence hung in the room.

"Very well, in that case, we are wasting time. Please go about your usual chores while Willis and I begin upstairs. Oh, before you go, where do you keep the cleaning supplies?"

A mixture of surprise and uncertainty crossed their faces. A servant answered, "I'll get them for you, ma'am."

"Thank you," Ginny said with a smile, surprised by the offer. As she proceeded up the stairs, she heard Willis snort with a disdain as he followed her.

When Jonathan and Blue came in for lunch, Jonathan heard Ginny talking with Willis upstairs.

"You go ahead, Blue. I'll be there shortly."

Almost at the top of the stairway, Jonathan had to flatten himself against the wall as Willis began dragging a wide rug down the steps. He heard Willis's ragged breath and mild oaths as he yanked the rug this way and that way, trying to loosen the fringe that had caught on the ornate spindles.

Willis grumbled when he saw Jonathan, but otherwise didn't utter a word. Jonathan had trouble suppressing his laughter.

Seeing sweat rolling like a waterfall down Willis's face, and soaking into his limp white collar, Jonathan asked, "Why don't you change into something cooler, Willis?"

The look Willis shot him would have lit a fire. "And who'll answer the door, sir?"

"Blue can handle it. After all, we have had only a few callers."

Afraid of being demoted again, Willis said loftily, "I'm perfectly capable of handling both jobs, sir."

"Suit yourself. Where is Miss Sutton?"

"On the floor in the bedroom on the right, sir," he snapped.

On the floor? Jonathan wondered as he stepped upon the landing. Entering the bedroom, he saw Ginny on her knees, a bucket beside her. For a while he watched her as she worked her way along the wall, scrubbing then rinsing the grime from the wainscotting. With her hair secured back from her face with a kerchief and the dirt coating her face and arms, Jonathan thought she could indeed be Cinderella and just stepped out of the story book. But damn it, he had not hired her to be Cinderella.

"Miss Sutton, would you please get up off the floor," he barked.

She barely glanced at him. "I'm almost through."

"You are through."

Ginny stared up at him in bewilderment, his sharp words startling her. "Did . . . did I do something wrong?"

"Where are the servants?" he asked, his eyes darting around the room.

"Downstairs, I suppose. Why?"

"Why? *They* should be up here scrubbing these walls, not you?"

"They can't just yet. They're busy."

"Busy? Busy at doing what, pray tell?"

"Laundry, ironing, needlework, cooking, all kinds of things," she said, dropping her scrub brush and rag into the bucket. Slowly, she stood up and wiped her hands on her apron.

His anger evaporated. He should have expected as much. She did not understand her duties. Stepping toward her, he wiped a smudge of black from her cheek. "Gin . . . Miss Sutton, when I hired you as my housekeeper, I intended for you to delegate the chores, and see that they were carried out, not do them yourself."

"Oh, I don't mind, really. When they are finished with their other chores, I'm sure they will help me."

"Why should they even offer, when they know you'll do it?"

"Mr. Cross, you expect too much from them," she said tartly, feeling her own temper rising a degree. "Of course, if you don't mind wearing soiled and wrinkled clothing, sleeping on dirty sheets, cooking your own meals, and washing your dishes afterwards, I'm certain they would find the time to help me."

"Are you suggesting I need more house servants?"

"As I told you, I am not experienced in this sort of thing. I only know that if something needs to be done, you do it, or it won't get done." Seeing Willis lumbering slowly past the doorway, she said, "We only have one more carpet to remove, so if you don't mind, I'd better get back to work."

Knowing her stubborn nature, Jonathan decided to let her have her way. At least she knew what he expected of her. A few days of this kind of work, and she'd be begging for help. "Has Willis given you any problems?"

"Not really. He grumbles a bit, but he's helping. Oh, one other thing. Your bedroom is not in as bad a state as the rest of the house. Could we perhaps leave it until another day?"

"Of course. Blue keeps it picked up, and even goes so far as to dust it occasionally."

"In what room do you spend the most time?"

"The library, I suppose."

"Then would you mind if I change the usual routine of

103

cleaning the second floor first and start there in the morning?"

"*You* are the housekeeper, Ginny. Whatever you wish to do, then by all means go ahead with it. Truthfully, I would appreciate it. Would you please let the servants do it?"

"If they have the time, I'll ask for their help. But, quite honestly, I would find myself bored within minutes if I'm just standing around giving orders."

Jonathan laughed. "I can see now arguing with you is futile. All right, Ginny, do it your way. Just don't hurt yourself."

As they walked outside in the hallway, Willis came out of another room and dragged the last carpet down the stairway.

"I'll wager you, I have a stronger back than that stiff-necked butler. In fact, I would have done the work myself, if I hadn't wanted to set him down a notch or two. He's a bit uppity in my book."

"You will get no argument from me. Denby tells me the Lyndals brought Willis from the fields into the house after their old butler died. He puts himself above the rest of the servants and issues orders like a tyrant."

So, that's the problem, Ginny mused. No wonder the servants snickered when she'd assigned him the task of removing the carpets. And the reason he was snubbing her, was because she had usurped his position. How on earth would she bring peace to this household without cooperation from everyone? For a second, she considered quitting her job and moving to Williamsburg as planned. But she couldn't, she just couldn't.

"That's why I hired you, Ginny. I don't have a wife to take care of problems like this, and I just don't have the time to deal with it."

She sighed wearily. "This is worse than I thought. Do

you think I'm a miracle worker?"

"No, but if there is any woman around who can come close to working miracles, it is you."

"And just how have you come to that assumption? You barely know me."

"Anyone who can coax an ornery mule can surely coax a few stubborn servants to do their work."

She lifted a dubious brow. "Well, only time will tell. Now, if you will excuse me, I had better tell Willis he needs to beat the dust from the rugs." She smiled mischievously. "As upset as he is with me at the moment, he'll probably give them the best beating they've ever had."

After Jonathan left, Ginny's mind returned to their conversation. When he mentioned not having a wife, it had been on the tip of her tongue to ask why he didn't. Of course, she knew very little about him. Maybe he was a widower. But if he had children, they would not be old enough to live without their father. There were so many other things she wished to know about him, but was hesitant to ask. Why had he come to Virginia? Were his parents still alive and living in England? Was there a woman in England he loved? Would he bring her here after he had made his home presentable? But surely he would not have behaved so outlandishly in Williamsburg, if he were in love with someone. What worried her most was why she should care one way or the other. She must remember she was his housekeeper, no more, no less.

105

11

When Ginny arrived at the house early the next morning, Blue greeted her at the door rather than Willis. "Good mornin', Miss Sutton."

Frowning, Ginny asked, "Where is Willis?"

"He's a bit under the weather this mornin'. I had to rub him down with an ointment last night."

"Oh dear, I'm so sorry," Ginny said, trying to show concern.

Blue grinned. "Are you really?"

A faint mocking smile crossed her face. "Actually, no," she readily admitted. "I hope he found muscles he never knew he had. But I'm sorry he can't help me today."

Blue tossed back his head and laughed. "I'm afraid, Miss, he'll be out of kilter for longer than a day."

Jonathan stood on the landing, listening to the conversation, his eyes sparkling with pleasure as he looked down at Ginny. He called down to Blue. "You had better watch your laughter, Blue, for with Willis indisposed, it might be you who takes his place."

Good-naturedly, Blue returned, "Anythin' would be better than spendin' the day in those bloody hot stables."

Ginny stared at Jonathan with admiration as he descended the stairs, powerful and virile in his dark gray morning coat and black trousers. *How tall he is and how handsome,* she thought, never realizing the blush that suddenly stained her cheeks.

106

"You came earlier today, Miss Sutton," he said as he stepped to the floor. "I've yet to have breakfast."

"I'm glad," she said, handing him a small crock. "Honey for your biscuits."

"Honey?" Blue exclaimed, "We haven't had honey since we came here."

"Thank you, Gin . . . Miss Sutton. So, you were successful in raiding the hive again," Jonathan said laughingly.

"Yes, and Nat held the ladder."

He smiled. "Good. I'm glad you didn't try it alone this time. Now, would you like to join Blue and me for breakfast?" He wanted to ask her if she'd make the biscuits, knowing Bertha would surely burn them.

His question caught her by surprise. "Oh no, I've already eaten. But . . . but thank you. I want to start cleaning your library before the heat sets in."

"Then I'll ask one of the servants to help you."

"That isn't necessary, really. You two just go on and eat, and I'll see you later," she said, turning away from them.

Blue whispered to Jonathan. "What's with her anyway? Does she think no one else knows how to work in this house?"

"The servants have pulled the wool over her eyes, leading her to believe they are too busy at other chores. They picked up on her inexperience immediately."

"Well, that should be easy enough to handle," Blue said with a huff. "Just tell the servants to get off their bloody arses and help, or you'll put their arses out to pasture. There's plenty of 'em who'd like to have a position in the house."

"It may come to that. Surprisingly, she doesn't seem to have overtaxed herself."

"But she ain't no bigger than a mite, boss."

"Perhaps so, but she appears to have more stamina and perseverance than ten men put together. Also, she's the most bullheaded woman I've ever chanced to meet. You tell her she cannot or should not do something, and she takes it as a damned challenge. She will do it or die. If I order the servants to help her, believe me, she will feel insulted."

"If you let them get by with this, boss, they won't ever lift a hand around here."

"Let's just keep things as they are for a while. I have a feeling Miss Sutton will come through. Last night, I overheard two of the servants talking. Her actions are puzzling them. One even admitted she felt a little guilty. Maybe Ginny knows what she's doing after all, so we ought to give her a chance."

"Whatever you say, but it just don't seem right," Blue said, shrugging his shoulders.

Before Jonathan and Blue left for breakfast, they peeked into the library. Ginny was sliding the settee off the large Oriental carpet. Seeing the frown on Blue's face, Jonathan said, "Come on, let's see if she'll let *us* help her."

Entering the room, Jonathan said, "Let us move these things for you. We'll take the carpet outside, then go to breakfast."

Ginny didn't argue, knowing they could do the job faster. After removing all the furnishings off the carpet, they rolled it up tightly. With one on each end, they lifted the heavy rug and carried it down the hall toward the back door. Seeing a servant standing in the doorway of the dining room, watching them with an expression of disbelief, they nodded politely, then winked knowingly at one another as they went on their way.

After breakfast, Jonathan decided to return to the library and work on his ledgers, although he could put it off for another day, he wanted to make certain Ginny didn't overtax herself. Yesterday she had thoroughly cleaned one of the bedrooms, should they need the room for guests. Jonathan had insisted it wasn't necessary, because he was not expecting visitors anytime soon. At five o'clock he made her cease working, offering to take her home in his carriage, but she would have none of that either, telling him walking relaxed her at the end of a hard day.

Entering the library, Jonathan stopped abruptly, vexed to see Ginny standing near the top of the ladder, cleaning the bookshelves. As he was about to step forward to reprimand her, she reached up to the top shelf to remove the books, and the shift rose slightly, showing her slender ankles and shapely calves. Slowly his gaze moved over her, drinking in her loveliness. He had never known or seen anyone like her before, and if someone had told him that such a woman existed, he would never have believed it. He found it doubly satisfying to know he could see her as often as he wished.

Jonathan tried to drag his mind away from such thoughts, but when Ginny started unfastening the buttons of her bodice, his heart almost stopped beating. Next, she pulled a handkerchief from her apron pocket and began dabbing the cloth along the nape of her neck and into the vee of her bodice. Jonathan felt his blood rush through his veins, as he imagined his own hands caressing and kneading her full creamy breasts. *What the devil is the matter with me?* he thought, frustrated beyond belief.

After rebuttoning her bodice, she picked up her feather duster and ran it over the shelves. He saw the ladder shaking as she moved, and once again his anger returned.

With long strides, he crossed the room and gripped the ladder. "Miss Sutton, come down from there this second."

His angry voice startling her, Ginny dropped the feather duster and it slapped across Jonathan's face, the dust entering his nose and eyes. With each harsh sneeze, he inadvertently jerked the ladder. Ginny shrieked, holding fast to the rung.

When he finally stopped sneezing and looked up at her with watery eyes, she snapped, "What are you trying to do? Make me break my neck?"

"No, damn it, I'm trying to keep you from it," he countered angrily. "I don't want to see you on a ladder again, at least not in my house."

"Then how am I supposed to dust the shelves?"

Jonathan took a deep breath, the air hissing between his teeth. "Just get down, Ginny."

"No, I won't. You're being ridiculous."

"And you're being your usual stubborn self."

Blue stood in the doorway, watching and listening. *Jonathan has really met his match in this little wench,* he thought, chuckling to himself.

"If you would stop telling me what I can or cannot do, I could get some work done around here."

Jonathan threw up his hands in exasperation, then dropped them to his sides. "Yes, I tell you because you work for me. And you will not, I repeat, you will not climb ladders. You could have hurt yourself badly that day at the barn, if I hadn't been there. I won't have that happen here."

For a moment they stared angrily at one another, then Ginny obeyed him, though very reluctantly. Descending the ladder, she stood before him and placed her hands defiantly on her hips. "All right. Now, why don't you go play with your horses, so I can clean your room."

Blue heard her retort and nearly choked on his laughter.

Jonathan stared at her in bemusement. "Play? With

110

my horses? I do not play with them, Ginny, I train them."

"Then train them or whatever, but please leave me alone."

Miffed, Jonathan said, "I have to work on my ledgers this morning."

"Why didn't you tell me that yesterday?"

"You won't bother me. Go ahead and clean to your heart's content." Turning, he stomped toward his desk and sat down heavily in his chair. Flipping open his ledger, he ignored her, or pretended to ignore her, while she went about her business. Sneering at him time and again, she cleaned those shelves she could reach, wiping the dust from the books as she put them back in order.

With his quill in hand, Jonathan retraced the figures he had entered several days earlier, watching her as she got down on her knees and began washing down the walls. Since she was clearly angry with him, he expected to find bare places on the wainscotting from where she was vigorously scrubbing it.

The lunch hour arrived. Jonathan rose from his chair. "Would you care to dine now?"

"I brought my own, thank you," she said with an unladylike snort.

"Very well," he returned and departed.

Ginny sat back on her haunches, eyeing the ladder. He would never know, she thought, rising quickly and snatching the feather duster from the chair. Going to the door, she peeked around it. He was nowhere in sight. As she placed her dainty foot on the first rung, she heard **laugh**ter behind her and jerked her head around.

Blue stood just inside the doorway, his broad arms crossed over his chest. "Need some help, ma'am?"

"He sent you to spy on me, didn't he?"

Pretending he knew nothing about their argument,

Blue said, "Why should he do that?"

"He thinks I'll fall and break my neck," Ginny said, ascending the ladder. "But there is no sense cleaning the floors or the furniture, if I can't dust the bookcases first. If you want to run tell him I'm not following his orders, then do it. He may dismiss me if he wishes."

"No, he shouldn't dismiss you, he should raise your bloody salary. You've done more work in a day and a half than the servants have done in months. Of course, if you don't mind the free time you're givin' them, I'm sure they appreciate it."

As she cleaned the shelves, she said, "I have never liked the idea of slavery, Willis. These people are human beings, just like the rest of us. You treat them with respect and in turn, they will respect you. Nat was a slave for several years until his master freed him. He came to my father after his master died. All he wanted was a roof over his head and food in his belly. He worked harder than any man I have ever seen. Without him, Mother and I would have never been able to keep the farm."

"Mr. Cross doesn't believe in slavery either, Miss Sutton, but until he can find another way to make a go of the plantation, he has to rely on them. Though he doesn't pay them wages, he does provide them with a roof over their head and food for their bellies. What would happen to them if he freed them? Would life treat them this well?"

Ginny dusted off the books and replaced them on the shelf. "What you say is true. But if Mr. Cross will just be patient, I will see that they lend a hand. It will happen soon, I assure you."

"I hope you're right. He won't put up with this nonsense much longer."

Ginny looked down at him worriedly. "He wouldn't have them beaten, would he?"

112

"No, but you might force him to start lookin' for another housekeeper," Blue lied. "Well, if you'll excuse me, I think I'll get a bite to eat." Nodding politely, Blue quit the room.

Ginny descended the ladder and put it back where it had been, so Jonathan wouldn't notice. Would Blue tell him what she had done? But worse, would he find another housekeeper if she didn't suit him? It just wasn't fair. He should be giving the servants orders, not putting that responsibility on her. If she made an enemy out of them, they would never help her willingly.

"Miz Sutton?" a tiny voice summoned her.

Ginny whirled around, recognizing the laundry maid. "Yes?"

"I'm done with the laundry," she said shyly. "Maybe I can help you."

Ginny's face brightened. "Well, yes, if you have the time. I'm sorry, but Willis introduced everyone so quickly yesterday, that I can't remember your name."

"Mary's my name, ma'am." She looked around the room. "Would you like me to clean the ashes from the hearth?"

"Yes, please, and I'll start mopping the floor. Together we ought to finish the room today."

As Jonathan sliced through the slab of meat, he saw Blue lift his fork and slowly turn it, closely examining the piece of meat.

Jonathan slipped the fork into his mouth. Chewing the tasteless meat just enough to get it down, he followed it quickly with a gulp of water. "I asked her to please not burn it this time."

"She did good. The bloody thing's still quiverin'. What is it anyway?"

113

"You're probably better off not knowing."

"Could be that mangy dog I saw hangin' 'round outside the kitchen this mornin'."

Jonathan's stomach lurched. "For God's sake, Blue, I'm having a hard enough time getting it down without you making it worse."

"Sorry, boss."

He saw Blue take the crock of honey that Ginny had brought and spoon some on his plate.

Jonathan passed him the basket of burned corn bread. Blue waved it aside. After dragging the meat through the honey, he plopped it into his mouth.

Amused, Jonathan did the same thing. "Good idea, Blue. You may have just found a good use for Miss Sutton's honey."

While they continued eating, Jonathan's thoughts drifted to Ginny. Blue was right. He couldn't allow her to do the servants' work. He would let her finish out the day, but first thing in the morning, he'd have a heart-to-heart talk with her. Afterwards, he'd tell the servants that if they didn't help her, he would do as Blue suggested—he'd replace them. Jonathan had hoped it wouldn't come to this; threatening people was not his way. Still, he had no alternative if they refused to work.

After lunch Blue left for the stables, and Jonathan headed back to the library. Surprise washed over his face when he saw Ginny and three other servants cleaning the room. While Ginny polished the furniture, one cleaned the windows, another mopped the floor, and the last was scrubbing the grate in the hearth.

He smiled softly, thinking Ginny Sutton was indeed a wonder. Turning, he left the house and joined Blue at the stables.

Over the next few days, a transformation occurred at Crossroads Manor, similar to that of Cinderella exchanging her threadbare clothing for a gown of shimmering satin. Ginny had seemingly cast a magic spell over the household, her glowing charm and willingness to work alongside the servants had warmed their hearts toward her. Routines were set, and everyone joined in, with Ginny seldom having to direct them. Even Willis's cynicism had become a thing of the past. Much to her chagrin, she had learned that Willis not only received guests, but had a mountain of responsibilities to oversee. He waited upon the table at mealtimes, took care of the wine cellar, and was always at his master's beck and call any hour of the day and night.

Jonathan also fell under her spell, though he reluctantly admitted it. He found excuses to stay at the house longer hours during the day, purposely seeking her out for one reason or another. His eyes followed her every movement, noticing the graceful way she carried herself as she went about her duties. He caught himself studying her every little gesture, the peculiar little way she screwed her mouth to one side when she was in deep thought, the way she flipped her braid over her shoulder when she was nervous or embarrassed. But all Jonathan thought he felt for her was desire, an emotion he could deal with, any deeper emotions, he kept buried beneath a pain he wished to forget.

12

Ginny finished her chores and looked around the room, taking a last-minute inspection. The house sparkled invitingly, the clean smell of beeswax faintly overshadowed by the scent of the lilacs she'd cut and placed in a vase in the entrance hall.

Checking the pocket of her apron, she smiled softly. She had a surprise for Jonathan and the servants. After their initial resentment and awkwardness, the servants had accepted her. But Jonathan still complained constantly about the food. An idea had wiggled its way into Ginny's head, and today she planned to carry it out. Her mother made the most wonderful sweetened bread. It really wasn't a cake, nor was it bread, but a golden loaf of sweet bread with cinnamon swirled through the dough, and nuts baked inside. Earlier in the day Ginny had mixed the dough and put it aside to rise, and set Bertha to shelling pecans.

To avoid Christine, who had developed the habit of just dropping by to see Jonathan, Ginny began arriving at daylight, so she could get her work done in the front portion of the house and move on to something else if Christine arrived. Today, Ginny was invading the kitchen.

She'd come to despise Christine's visits, because she took delight in following Ginny around, pointing out her shortcomings, and ridiculing her clothing. But most of all she hated the time Jonathan spent with Christine. It seemed that everytime Christine showed up, Jonathan would drop whatever he was doing and take Christine on an outing of one sort or another.

Bertha watched Ginny closely as she divided the dough into several balls, kneaded them, turned them, and re-read the instructions she'd taken from her apron pocket, then applied various ingredients. After completing the loaves, she slid them into a hot oven. As the bread baked, its aroma filled the kitchen and wafted beyond, until everyone from the manor made one excuse or another to stick their head into the kitchen to ask what smelled so good. Even Jonathan, unable to believe his nose or his good fortune, made an appearance. Bertha was dumbfounded when he entered her domain. And the touch of a feather could have sent her to her knees, when he plopped down at the table and began to swirl his finger around the mixing bowl. Lifting his hand to his mouth, his tongue snaked out, capturing the creamy remains. Ginny, too, stalled as she watched him, her heart beating inordinately fast.

"Hmmm," he sighed, ringing his finger once more around the side of the bowl. "You can cook, too?"

"A little," she answered softly, pleased beyond belief that he'd noticed.

His face lit up like a beacon on a stormy night. "I'm sure Bertha wouldn't mind if you wanted to give her some pointers or even help prepare the meals around here, if you have time. Would you, Bertha?"

"No, siree. I don't mind a'tall. I never did want this job no how. I don't know who had the notion I could cook in the first place."

Me either, Jonathan thought wryly. "If Ginny will help you, maybe you'll be better satisfied."

As he talked, Ginny lifted a long-handled paddle and

117

scooped the loaves from the oven. The kitchen was sweltering even with the windows open wide, but no one seemed to notice as they watched her slice through the steaming bread. She smeared creamy butter over several pieces before she offered them to Jonathan and Bertha. Bertha watched Jonathan take a bite, before she lifted hers to her mouth. His eyes slid shut as he chewed slowly, savoring the uncommon flavor.

"Do you like it?" Ginny asked hesitantly.

He only nodded his head, and lifted the slice to his mouth again, his eyes still shut.

Ginny smiled brightly.

"This shore does taste better than anything I ever fixed," Bertha said. "Where did you learn to make this?"

"My mother's a wonderful cook."

"Does your mother need a job?" Jonathan asked hopefully, reaching for another piece of cake.

Ginny shook her head.

"Some of her talent must have rubbed off on you. This is delicious," Jonathan assured her.

Of all the things Jonathan had pondered in his life, he would have never believed a *good cook* would rank very high on his list. Strange how life dealt you these little surprises, and stranger yet was how they were solved. He left the kitchen with a lighter step, and whistling a jaunty tune. Ginny Sutton could cook, too. Damn, what a surprise she'd turned out to be. His house was turning into a home, and the kitchen smelled of good things. She'd promised to help Bertha when she had time. He couldn't wait. His thoughts had shifted somewhat from the constant perusal of her body to the complexities of her mind. She was a very smart lady. It wasn't what she said, but what she didn't say that set her apart. She was very quiet. Still, she got the job done, without demeaning or criticizing anyone. The servants did for her because she'd earned their respect. She had worked her way into their hearts by her deeds, not her words, and the sheer determination and pride she took in everything she did.

Ginny heaped the platter high with the sweet-smelling bread, and made her way through the house, offering generous slices to the servants. Each and every one enjoyed the treat, and all were touched by her thoughtfulness. With a warm feeling coursing through her, she entered the hallway just as Jonathan opened the front door. She met his welcoming smile with one of her own, and for several fleeting heartbeats they studied each other, each liking immensely what they saw in the other.

Her riotous curls draping her narrow shoulders.

His ebony hair with the stubborn curl.

Her green eyes with thick bronze lashes.

His stormy gray eyes.

Her stubborn determination.

His stubborn determination.

Before either could ponder what they were doing, each took a step toward the other, their smiles still in place.

"Jonathan, are you going to leave me standing on the porch in this heat?" Christine whined, stepping from behind him and sweeping into the house.

His smile vanished.

Ginny's shoulders wilted noticeably, and she turned away.

"Well, if it isn't little Miss Homemaker."

Ginny swirled to face her nemesis. "Not homemaker, Christine. I simply work here; I don't presume to be anything else."

"You could have fooled me," Christine snapped, eyeing the platter with the remaining sweet bread.

The joy of her treat vanished along with the luster in her eyes, leaving Ginny with a hollow pit in the region of her heart. "If you'll excuse me, I'll be going. I've finished for the day."

Jonathan wanted to follow her and apologize for Christine's rudeness, but he knew he could not repair the damage Christine had wrought. It wasn't just the things Christine said to Ginny; it was the way she looked at her, as though Ginny were nothing.

As they entered the parlor, Christine pulled off her gloves and tossed them and her reticule atop the gleaming surface of a side table. After arranging her shimmering skirt just so, she sank onto the comfort of a velvet settee, showing a perfectly trimmed ankle and a length of stockinged leg.

Jonathan knew enticement when he saw it, and being only human, he took his own sweet time viewing her leg as he poured drinks.

Christine knew exactly what she was doing; she'd seduced more than her share of handsome men. Crossing her legs, she eyed Jonathan invitingly and rocked her leg slowly. The only sound in the room was the splashing of sherry as it hit the bottom of the glasses, and the swish of Christine's stockinged legs as they rubbed together.

Jonathan let his imagination have its head as he handed Christine her drink.

Reaching for the glass, her hand brushed his and lingered. Her tongue sliced slowly across her lips.

For an instant, he wondered if it was in anticipation of the drink or him.

Swish . . . swish.

The collar of his lawn shirt became uncomfortably tight, and his loins tingled with desire. How had she managed to evoke his desire, when he didn't particularly like her at all? Then it hit him like a hammer crashing down on his thumb. Ginny. This was all her fault. He'd walked a tight rope of control since she'd begun working for him.

He moved away from the settee and stood before the window, Christine's voice droning on as she talked about a new bolt of fabric that she'd ordered from England.

Staring out into the distance, he caught a glimpse of a trim figure and glorious auburn hair. The view provoked his memory. Yes, his burning desire was all her fault. He couldn't count the times he'd yearned to take her in his arms. At least every day, and sometimes more often, when he'd see her at one job or another. Once, as she stretched to reach a dangling cobweb, the bodice of her dress pulled tightly across her breasts. He'd had to vacate the room hurriedly, before she spied the sweat beading his brow and the swelling hardness he was unable to hide. Another time, Ginny bending to adjust a crooked rug, giving him a delightful view of her air-borne bottom and shapely calves, had sent him to the river to cool his flushed body and throbbing loins. Once he'd discovered her on a ladder cleaning the bookshelves in his study, her long shapely legs disappearing beneath her skirt. As he watched, she halted her work and unbuttoned several buttons on her bodice, then plucked a handkerchief from her pocket, swathing the nape of her neck and the vee of her open bodice. That had called for a bottle of strong Virginia whiskey, which he had shared with Blue that evening. The fiery pain-killing nectar did little to assuage his lust, but it gave him a hangover he would not soon forget.

Ginny was innocent of his torment. Or was she? Sometimes he thought he saw the same longing move across her face, when she didn't know he watched her. Yet he wondered if she knew what lust was? She desired her property, and the thought of the fields swaying with rich tobacco brought a smile to her face. But did she

121

have needs? Sexual needs? He doubted it. Still, heaven help him if the opportunity presented itself, he would teach her about lust. Pure and simple.

Christine bumped his arm, drawing his attention to her. "Have you heard a word I've said?"

"Yes, you were talking about the fabric from England. Would you care for another glass of sherry?"

"I thought you'd never ask," she purred, rubbing her breast against his arm.

Jonathan had already discovered Christine's love of the fermented fruit. Sometimes he wondered if her promiscuous ways didn't lend themselves from the amount of wine she'd consumed.

"Well, I'll have to admit the little ragamuffin has made a change in your home. The place virtually sparkles. Maybe she's found her niche."

"Don't be so quick to sell her short. Someday she'll make some man a fine wife. She's—"

"Spare me, please. I have no desire to hear about her wondrous contribution with a mop and broom. You forget I've known Ginny all my life, and I can't say it's been a pleasure."

That's your misfortune, Jonathan thought irritably.

Christine settled herself once more on the settee and patted the empty space beside her. "Come sit with me, it wears me out chasing you about the room, trying to get your attention."

"I'm all yours," he lied, taking the seat beside her and wondering if Ginny had made it home yet.

Not yet, you're not. But you will be, you can count on it, Christine thought smugly.

She wanted her home back, and she would go to any means to get it. Being the wife of the handsome Jonathan Cross would only add spice to an already tempting package. All she needed to do was get that damned

Ginny Sutton out of his life, before he convinced himself he was in love with her. She'd seen the way he watched the little ragamuffin, and she also saw the way Ginny's eyes lit up when Jonathan entered a room. Something had to be done, and quickly.

Several days later, a messenger arrived at Jonathan's home with an invitation for him and one for Ginny, to attend Milly's upcoming ball. When Jonathan gave Ginny her invitation, she tucked it into her apron pocket without opening it. His curiosity got the best of him. "Aren't you even going to open it?"

"No, I know what it is. I saw George coming across the lawn. He's been with the Vincents for years."

"You don't plan to attend your best friend's ball?"

"No," she answered simply and turned away.

"Ginny."

"Yes."

"I'd be honored to escort you."

"Thanks, but no thanks. Milly knows I'm not attending."

"Could I change your mind?"

The blood sang through her veins, and the fingers trembled that she lifted to her lips. She shook her head. "I don't think so," was the soft reply.

"For God's sake, I don't know why."

"Please, I've made up my mind."

Jonathan paced the room, ramming his fingers through his hair. "So? You *can* change your mind. It's not carved in stone anywhere; that Ginny Sutton will not be attending the ball given in honor of Milly Vincent's birthday, is it?"

Again she shook her head.

"The problem is you have too much pride."

"Think whatever you must. That still doesn't change the fact that I'm not attending the ball."

"Damn," he muttered. "Damn it!" he shouted and stormed from the room.

Ginny settled herself in the shade of a sweeping mimosa and pulled the invitation from her pocket. Very carefully, she opened it. The words spilled out to her.

MR. AND MRS. CALHOUN W. VINCENT
request the pleasure of your presence
on Saturday evening,
August 4th, at eight o'clock.
Rosebriar Plantation.
Dancing at 10

Ginny smoothed her fingers over the fine paper, its creamy color so faint it was scarcely visible. The bold black script dipped and swayed, like swans gliding on the surface of a gentle swell. Images of billowing skirts, reflected in dancing candlelight as they swept across a dance floor, swam before her eyes.

What if I . . . her mind teased. "No, no, I can't," she whispered violently, sobs choking her as she crumpled the invitation in the palm of her hand.

13

Ginny watched from an upper window, as Jonathan made his way smartly down the walk. He wore his formal clothing with a flair that left no one in doubt, he knew his position in life. After reaching the waiting carriage, he lifted his head and stared pointedly at the window where Ginny stood. Before she could back away, her gaze became trapped with his, and a multitude of emotions quivered through her. When he raised his hand in farewell, she lifted hers and placed it against the cool pane of glass. She wanted to reach out and touch him, push the wayward curl from his brow, smooth the lapel of his coat, and tell him how nice he looked. *What am I doing?* she admonished. Jerking her hand down, she tucked it into her apron pocket and turned from the window.

What was happening to her? Her thoughts weren't her own anymore. At the least persuasion, images of Jonathan interrupted her thoughts. Since she'd begun working for him, her opinions had altered drastically. She'd never known a wealthy man, and only assumed they had a legion of helpers at their beck and call. Not so with Jonathan Cross. He rose at the crack of dawn to see to the running of his plantation. And when she left for home in the evenings, sometimes she would see him hard at work in the fields. Other times, she'd catch a glimpse of him at the stables with his horses, or atop the powerful Beowulf speeding across the open fields.

The house became quiet as the servants finished their duties and sought their own ease, leaving Ginny to see herself out. She wandered from the room and down the wide hallway, running her hand along the wall. Her hand came away with only a smattering of dust. The house was taking shape nicely. She had lost her initial intimidation of the sprawling manor, and had fallen in love with the large airy rooms and their sparkling beauty. Many were the times she imagined a childlike image of Jonathan, sliding down the smooth curving banister of the stairway.

Her task had been enormous, but the look of pride on Jonathan's face and that of his servants made it all worthwhile. After the removal of carpets and draperies for cleaning and airing, the floors and windows were cleaned until one could see their reflection in the gleaming surfaces. Jonathan's furniture arrived, and she polished it until the rich luster of the wood shone brightly. Then she and Willis arranged it comfortably. She'd found a chessboard and pieces packed in one of the crates. She'd put the board on a table between matching chairs, and placed the men in order. After she set up the game, the temptation to move one of the pieces into play was more than she could pass up. To her surprise, the next day as she went about her chores, she noticed someone had countered her move. She deliberated long and hard before she made her play. To her immense pleasure, it was the same the next day, and the game continued.

When she reached the master bedroom, she peeked in. Jonathan's room desperately needed a thorough cleaning, she mused, noticing cobwebs hanging from the ceiling. What better time? she thought, rolling up her sleeves. He wouldn't be home for hours. Without interruptions, she could be done in no time. Hurrying downstairs, she gathered her cleaning supplies.

She had no reason to rush home. Nat had taken her mother into Williamsburg, to deliver hats and spend a few days with Patrick. This had pleased Ginny, because her mother worked so hard and got to spend very little time with Patrick.

As she moved about the room dusting, she clasped the handle of Jonathan's hairbrush, running her fingers along the bristles. She carefully picked up a single shirt stud lying on the dresser and turned it slowly in her hand. Picking up his discarded clothes, she placed them neatly in the wardrobe. Burying her face in the rich silk fabric of his shirt, a lingering trace of his cologne sent her pulse racing. She straightened a discarded evening coat, then smoothed the lapel as she'd longed to do earlier.

On a sudden impulse, she rushed to the door, peeking out to make sure the house was silent. Quietly shutting the door, she slid her dress over her head and let it fall in a heap at her feet. Her petticoat, thin and mended many times over, she let slide to the floor also. Taking his shirt from the wardrobe, she lifted her arms and let the cool silk glide down her arms. Picking up the single shirt stud, she fastened it midway down the garment, exposing a generous amount of cleavage. The fabric moved caressingly against her bare flesh, puckering her rosebud nipples. She scooped up his evening jacket and slipped it on. Adjusting the drooping shoulders and pushing the sleeves to her elbows, she turned slowly before a cheval glass. A delicious sensation swirled through her, as she thought of what she was doing. Picking up his brush, she applied it to her hair until the heavy mane swirled about her like a shimmering banner. She struck a pretty pose before the mirror, and laughed at her antics. Shifting her stance and straightening her shoulders, she mimicked his walk, naked legs gleaming in the candlelight.

Humming a lively tune, she scooped up the broom she'd earlier used to sweep down cobwebs, and the handle became her partner as she led it in a whirl around the room, dipping and swaying to the music playing in her head. The jacket front slapped against her body, and the masculine sent of Jonathan wafted about her like the words of a poem she'd learned long ago. "Mysterious Love! uncertain treasure, Hast thou more of pain or pleasure?" The words stealing her joy, she collapsed atop his bed. Tears puddled and rolled from her eyes in to the hair that fanned the coverlet. Was it love? This pain that consumed her when she chanced a glance of him, the pleasure that flowed through her when she touched his belongings? An uncertain treasure that she could never share with the one responsible.

She remembered him as he left for the ball. Was he having a good time? Was he whirling Christine around the dance floor? Or had he found a secluded place to hold her in his arms and declare his love?

Ginny's tears came faster, and her weary body gave in to them as she wrapped his jacket closer around her, and rubbed a baggy sleeve against her damp cheek. Did he ever think of her . . .

The Vincent home was ablaze with light and laughter, the mellow strains of a waltz sending couples whirling about the gleaming dance floor. As Jonathan stared out over the glittering array of beautifully dressed women, his sole desire was to see Ginny in this setting. Her beauty would sparkle like a diamond among unpolished stones. How could he convince her to cast aside the mantle of fear and face her contemporaries on equal footing? When she was dealing with them in the light of business, she held her ground and earned their respect. Why she feared facing them across a ballroom he couldn't fathom, unless Christine Iverson had made Ginny believe she was something less because of her lack of coin. The weight of a purse didn't insure the strings were attached to the arm of a lady. He smiled ruefully. Christine was as far removed from a lady, as Lord Adelbert was from a duke.

Speak of the devil, he thought, as he saw Christine bearing down on him. Lord knows, he'd had his share of women and enjoyed their bodies to his heart's desire, but Christine's gown was stretching the limits of propriety. Beneath the tantalizing bodice of her gown, it was glowingly clear that she had rouged her nipples. The sparkle in her eyes was due to her consumption of champagne.

"Jonathan, darling," she purred. "Come along, I want to show you off. Everyone is dying to meet you."

Grabbing a fresh drink from a passing waiter, he let Christine usher him from one group to another. She clung to him like a vine, flirting, laughing, and rubbing against him at every opportunity.

To combat his boredom as Christine droned on and on, a vision of Ginny, standing at the window in her faded cornflower blue muslin signaling a silent farewell, brought a tender smile to his stern countenance. The memory created an inner warmth that Christine in all her splendor could never duplicate.

Parents of marriageable daughters who witnessed the wistful smile gave up any hope of matching their daughters to the wealthy new plantation owner, drawing the mistaken conclusion that indeed Christine Lyndal Iverson had captured his heart.

After several failed attempts to catch his attention, Milly Vincent presented herself to him with the guise of introducing him to one of her sisters. An appreciative smile gleamed in his cloudy-day eyes, as she directed him to the open french doors.

"Thank you," he replied, leaning against the railing of the veranda.

"You're welcome," Milly answered softly, having no need to question him about why he was thanking her.

For several moments they stood in the darkness, each savoring the night-black sky. A gentle breeze stirred the rose bushes bordering the porch, sending the mellow fragrance of their delicate blooms into the starry night.

"I'm sorry Ginny chose not to come. I was hoping . . ." Milly's voice trailed away, and for an instant Jonathan thought he detected a glimmer of tears in her eyes.

"What were you hoping?" he questioned softly.

Shaking her head, she vowed, "Oh, it doesn't matter, it's of little importance."

Jonathan tilted her chin, and brushed away a tear that rolled slowly down her cheek. "Oh, I think it's something very important. Does it have anything to do with Patrick Sutton?"

After a nervous laugh she studied him for several seconds, thinking about the conversation she and Ginny had had that day at the river. Indeed, he had heard more than he'd admitted. "Shame on you, Mr. Cross."

"Jonathan, please," he said smiling warmly. "Maybe if you would enlighten me, I could be of some small service."

"As you wish, Jonathan." Milly turned and placed her hands on the railing, pondering the darkness, taking a deep breath as though making a momentous decision. "It has come to my attention after much consideration, that Ginny Sutton and I are not so very different."

An ebony brow arched in the darkness. "How so?"

"Ginny is trapped by her poverty. And I? Well, I'm trapped by my wealth."

"That's quite a theory, but tell me why have you drawn

this conclusion?"

"Because of dreams that are unattainable. I have come to realize that dreams are like wispy curls of smoke. Have you ever tried to grasp a handful of smoke?"

"Not that I remember, but I know what you mean."

"Would it be unkind, if I told you I thought the Suttons were stubbornness personified?"

A deep rich chuckle filled the starlit night.

"You think it's funny, Mr. Cross?" Milly snapped.

"What I think, Milly, is that you and I are going to be great friends."

After Milly excused herself to return to her guests, Jonathan remained on the porch to enjoy a cheroot. The pungent smell of rich tobacco filled the air as he pondered the darkness. He thought of the conversation he'd overheard between Milly and Ginny. It seemed that Ginny used her poverty as a shield to protect herself. What would she do if suddenly she had no money problems? He thought once again of the Cinderella story. Could he turn Ginny into Cinderella? And if he did, would she become like other women of his acquaintance? It was something to think about, he mused, as he crushed the fire from the cheroot, something to think about indeed.

As the evening marched on, Jonathan's circumstances didn't improve. He danced and mingled, until names rolled through his head like a scroll proclaiming who's who. The more champagne Christine drank, the bolder her suggestions became. At another time in his life, he would have taken up her suggestions before she had a chance to voice them. Yet now, the innocence and charm of another sweetened his memory and dulled his appetite for Christine's daring.

The one redeeming quality of the entire evening was his developing friendship with Milly. She and she alone detected his aversion to the widow Iverson. How ironic that in his dealings with women, he'd never had one simply for a friend. It was quite unusual; still, he decided he liked the idea. The truth of the matter was, he appreciated her loyalty to Ginny.

The rosy glow of complexions and casual embraces gave testament to the waning hour. An empty punch bowl and discarded champagne bottles enforced this edict. Jonathan bid his host and hostess a good night, and once more wished Milly a happy birthday.

Blue waited for Jonathan beside the coach, a look of displeasure encompassing his face. Jonathan quirked a brow in question, and Blue jerked his head toward the waiting carriage. Still not understanding his servant's mood, he asked, "Is something troubling you, Blue?"

The servant thumbed his hand over his shoulder. "Mrs. Iverson awaits you. She requires a ride home."

Understanding dawned, and the same look of displeasure that clouded Blue's face now settled firmly on Jonathan's. "What happened to her driver?"

"Mrs. Iverson said there was some misunderstandin' about his waitin' for her."

"I'm sure," Jonathan replied sarcastically.

Blue snorted.

When Jonathan opened the door, Christine leaned forward, her breasts spilling toward him like overripe melons. She patted the space beside her. "Here, sit by me, Jonathan. I hope you don't mind the inconvenience of seeing me home. My driver must have misunderstood my instructions."

"It happens," he answered shortly, and took the seat beside her. The carriage lurched forward, jarring the passengers. Blue was not in a good mood . . . and Jonathan couldn't prevent the smile that tugged his mouth.

When the ride smoothed out and they adjusted themselves in the comfort of the carriage, Christine settled herself in the shadow of the arm he'd draped across the seat. With the daring of a well-acquainted lover, she teased him. Her long sculptured nails trailed a path from the arch of his brow, across his cheek, and around the curve of his ear. Down the length of his neck she travelled, until she splayed her hand across his chest and plucked at his shirt studs. She tilted her head and eyed him with a seductive pose. "The night is still young, if you would care to explore the possibilities of seeing it through."

"I fear the night has grown old, and my consumption of brandy would hamper any exploration I might undertake," he lied smoothly, as he lolled against the plump cushions and closed his eyes.

As the carriage rocked along through the darkness, the dim light of the lantern cast a cozy glow over the occupants. Christine studied Jonathan, piqued by his apparent disinterest. She searched her mind for some topic that would amuse him, and at the same time remind him of her beauty and status in the community. The spirits she'd consumed clouded her judgment, and she bore fullfledged into the one subject she should have avoided at all cost.

"I see your little ragamuffin housekeeper chose not to show her face tonight."

Jonathan's eyes snapped open, and the muscles jerked in his cheek as his jaw tightened.

Pleased that she had his attention, she plunged ahead. "I understand she received an invitation. Personally, it escapes me why Milly would want her there anyway."

"Maybe the pleasure of her company would have added to the excitement of the party."

"Humph, she'd have only been an embarrassment."

"I would think she'd be a pleasant addition to any

gathering."

Rankled by his defense of the little baggage, Christine dug herself in deeper. "How? By her sterling ability to quote the price of eggs or the values of manure? I think not, Jonathan. It appears your pity for the chit has clouded your judgment."

Jonathan could have bellowed with laughter, but cautioned himself. It would only add more bitterness to Christine's ire, if he extolled Ginny's beauty. Pity! What a lark. It wasn't pity that sent a fire raging through his belly to settle like hot coals in his loins, when he saw her at one task or another. It wasn't pity that sent him prowling his home in the wee hours of the night, with a need that would give him no rest. Indeed he wished it was, then he could assuage his pity with a hefty coin.

Relief swept through him when he bid Christine a hasty good night, and was able to escape her clinging arms with the promise of seeing her at a later date. He joined Blue on the coachman's bench, hoping the night air would clear his head, then defeated his purpose by sharing a bottle of rich dark whiskey with his trusted friend.

"It's a bloody shame, ain't it?"

"What?"

"Women, you can't live with 'em, and ya can't live without 'em. It boils down to a friggin' pain in the arse."

As they weaved their way through the darkness, Blue's logic buzzed through Jonathan's head. "You're right, it's a bloody shame."

Blue lifted the bottle in salute. "To the friggin' fairer sex."

Jonathan pitched through the darkened house like a drunken sailor on the deck of a storm-tossed ship, his mumbled curses drifting in the silence of the mansion. By the time he engineered the stairs and approached his room, he'd already begun removing his clothes. Without aid of light, he found the bathing closet and splashed tepid water on his face and rinsed his mouth. Stripping off his remaining clothes, he felt his way to the bed and collapsed. As the fringes of sleep teased him, he rolled to his side, reaching for the other pillow. His hand brushed warm flesh and became tangled in silken hair.

He reared up in bed, a violent curse shattering the silence. Wondering how Christine could have possibly managed to beat him to his own bed, he reached for the bedside table to light a candle. The candle had burned, leaving nothing but a mound of warm wax. After several seconds of fumbling, he found a new one and lit it. Turning in the bed ready to give Christine what-for, his mouth opened in shock, and his eyes narrowed in astonishment, as he viewed Ginny's slender body curled up in his bed. Instant hardness rocked through his loins. Hesitantly, he moved toward her, watching the dim light dance in her coppery mane. Lifting a cautious hand, he brushed the tangled strands from her face and stroked the delicate lines of her cheek.

She shifted restlessly.

Almost paralyzed with fear that he might wake her and send her flying from his bed, he removed his hand. As his eyes drifted over her, a well of tenderness poured through him, when he recognized his coat draping her slender shoulders. His tenderness quickly escalated to burning passion, as he viewed his shirt gaping open to reveal a creamy breast and a hint of her darkened nipple. He caught his breath and edged closer. Like a child opening a much-yearned-for gift, he took his leisure viewing her, prolonging the pleasure. She was a vision swathed in a veil of copper tresses. He ran his eyes over his garments, and for an instant envied their good fortune. The gentle rise and fall of her breasts assured him she slept deeply. Unable to resist the temptation, he stroked her stubborn chin and the column of her slender neck. Daringly, he continued his journey across her breastbone, discovering a tiny mole on the fullness of the exposed breast. He soaked up the vision like one deprived of water for a long period of time. His loins pulsed with need and damp perspiration beaded his brow.

The silk fabric caught the light and glimmered against her fair skin. A single shirt stud halted his progress, and he was quick to loosen it and cast it aside. Her stomach was flat and soft and quivered beneath his hand. Threadbare pantalets left nothing to the imagination as he skimmed his eyes over them, clenching his jaws to keep from groaning aloud. Her legs were long and firm, teasing him to stroke their length.

Unable to bear it a second longer, he lowered his head and buried it in the sweet-smelling sleep-tossed hair. He nudged his head until his lips found the sweeping curve of her neck. The warmth emanating from her sent his ardor spiraling. Carefully he stretched out beside her, drawing her into his arms. Endless moments passed as he lay quietly just holding her, savoring her in his arms. From somewhere deep in the shadows of his cold heart, a spark of warmth ignited, slowly melting the icy wall of skepticism, filling him with an untold amount of comfort and security. Was this the feeling poets put verse to? Had he at last found something that would give his life meaning? He didn't know, honest to God he didn't, but given the opportunity, he planned to find out.

14

Jonathan's deep thinking wilted when Ginny snuggled against him and placed her hand across his chest. Her warm breath whispered against his ear, and he was loath to control the desire rampaging through his body. Lowering his head, he placed a string of kisses down her face and across her lips. Her soft mewling and bone-melting stretch dissolved any attempt he had of abandoning his ardor. When she threw a naked leg over his, he groaned hoarsely and placed his hand along the sweep of her leg, drawing her closer. His lips covered hers, gently probing until he felt a welcoming response. He touched and stroked, whispering words of encouragement as she moved to the rhythm of his voice.

At first Ginny thought she was dreaming, his words coming to her like a gentle breeze sighing through the trees. She blinked her eyes until they focused on the face hovering above her. For one single heartbeat she was frightened, then his identity became clear. What was he doing in her bed? Realization suddenly dawned as she recalled her play. Embarrassment flooded her, and tears sparkled in her eyes as she turned her face from him. "I'm so ashamed," she whispered.

"There's no need for shame, only for understanding, as we try to sort out our feelings and accept what's happening to us."

"Is it that simple?" she whispered.

"It can be, if we'll trust one another," he replied softly, skimming his knuckles over her chin and the back of his fingers over the fullness of her lips.

"I apologize for taking such liberties with your clothing; it was childish play."

"You do things for these garments I never dreamed possible," he said hoarsely, running his finger lightly down the gaping shirt front.

Her breath caught in her chest, and she closed her eyes in wonder, enjoying the hot-white heat flowing through her.

"As for childish play," he lowered his head and kissed her stomach, his tongue darting out to scorch her quivering flesh. "Far be it from me to discourage play in any form."

He cupped her bottom and worked his face over her stomach, between her breasts and up her neck, burning a path to her slightly parted mouth. Settling his lips on hers, he teased until he elicited a trembling response. She lifted her arms, wrapping them about his neck, and lost her fingers in the thickness of his ebony hair.

For a fleeting second he raised his head and peered deeply into her questioning eyes. "Oh God, Ginny," he whispered, seeking her lips once more. As he deepened the kiss, their fire and passion combined, exploding frissons of desire that shot through them like bolts of spring lightning.

Any thought of denial, Ginny sustained quickly, lost its fervor as Jonathan taught her desires of the flesh. With his coaching and gentle encouragement, she blossomed.

"Am I allowed to play by the same rules you are?" she asked hesitantly.

A hoarse groan accompanied his strained reply.

Taking him at his word, she applied every touch and stroke to his firm, naked body that he'd applied to hers,

138

quickly turning the tables on this master of sensual delights.

Her unskilled play stroked a fire in Jonathan he'd never encountered. He wanted to plunge inside her and delve deeply, until he'd quenched this raging inferno. Yet, he wanted more. He wanted her to want him with the same fierce passion that consumed him. He wanted to take his time and teach her all the marvels of this wondrous thing called lovemaking. And maybe with him she'd want to explore this thing called love, this peculiar pain or pleasure he felt when he thought of her. And just maybe they could make this love together.

A rush of lust consumed him as he captured her mouth in a kiss that stole her breath and robbed her senses. He caressed her breasts, until the taut peaks throbbed against his hand. He pulled her to a sitting position and removed his coat from her thin shoulders. Splaying his hands across the silken shirt front, he let his hands slide slowly over her breasts. Her darkened nipples stood like shadows beneath the cool fabric. His tongue licked across the tempting morsels, until the wet silk clung with a life of its own. Unable to bear it a moment longer, he settled her against the pillows. While his mouth explored hers, his hand loosened the tie holding her pantalets. He cupped her femininity and began to stroke the heat of pleasure. She writhed beneath him, seeking more.

She was carried along the abyss of pleasure as a white hot heat built in her, then melted and spread through her loins and down her legs. She arched against his hand and cried out his name.

His mouth smothered her cry as his lips moved over hers, and his tongue plied her with urgent strokes. He lifted himself above her and guided his swollen manhood home. Her hot, wet passage tightened around him, and it was several seconds before he could catch his breath. Taking care to make their joining as painless for her as possible, he moved slowly. When he reached her maidenhead, he clasped her tightly, moving deeply inside her.

The burning pain startled her, and she dug her heels into the mattress trying to push away from him.

He quietened her struggles with gentle words, assuring her the pain was gone. For a time he didn't move, other than brushing the tangled hair from her face and stroking the curve of her cheek.

She could feel his arms trembling, and hear the ragged rush of his breath. The pain diminished, and a slow heat began to build inside her, surrounding his fullness. Hesitantly, she moved against him, savoring the pleasure that escalated. He joined her movements, and very soon they were lost to everything but wondrous ecstasy.

They lay entwined, absorbing the nearness of one another, unaware of the storm clouds that rolled across the horizon.

Ginny felt a growing shyness that robbed her of her pleasure and made her doubt his claims. She needed the reassurance of his whispered words. On sudden impulse, she cupped his face and whispered softly into the dim shadow of his neck. "Jonathan," she waited.

The late hour, his consumption of alcohol, and the ardor of lovemaking, had taken its toll. Jonathan slept peacefully.

"Jonathan," she whispered again.

He clasped her tightly and mumbled.

"What?" she asked, placing her ear against his mouth. His warm breath fanned her face, and instead of reassuring her, his garbled words sent a sharp biting pain coursing through her.

"Oh Christ . . . you're good." He drifted back to sleep. Ginny slapped his hand away and kicked blindly until she was free. "Christine! Oh God, how could he lay with me one minute and call me by another's name the next? Oh God," she whispered stumbling from the bed. Clutching her stomach, she eyed him with hatred. She wanted to tear into him and rip his handsome body into bloody shreds. As she watched, he turned over on his stomach and reached absently toward the other pillow. She ripped the silk shirt from her shoulders and flung it across the bed, where it slapped him neatly on the buttocks. He slept on, never knowing the pain and frustration brewing in the room.

Ginny picked up her discarded clothes and dressed quickly, anxious to be away from Jonathan Cross. All the things Milly had told her about him rang true. He was a womanizer of the worse sort, for he peppered his seduction with vows he knew women wanted to hear. Never mind that she had placed herself in his bed, he was still a scoundrel of the highest rank. For an instant her conscience flared. Was she being completely fair? Her anger rode high, refusing to be tempered. If he had a shred of decency about him, he would have sent her home. With the devil of unreason stalking her, she approached the bed. Picking up his shirt, she tore it into four wide strips. She might not be able to do him bodily harm, but she could make him uncomfortable for awhile. Carefully, she wrapped a strip around his ankle and secured it to the foot of the bed. Her body very nearly went into shock when she clasped his hairy ankle. The other ankle proved more difficult when she had to pull it across the bed, scared that he would awaken at any second. But the alcohol had done its job. He slept on. She quickly bound his wrists with no problem. A painful smile lifted the corners of her mouth as she viewed her handiwork. He lay spread-eagle upon the bed, bound like a Christmas goose. The candlelight danced merrily down his sun-

141

darkened back, and along the lighter flesh of his trim buttocks and strong hairy legs. Had she gone too far? her conscience pricked. She didn't care. As far as she was concerned, she hoped she never saw Jonathan Cross again. She would return home to gather her belongings, and at first light, she would make her way to Williamsburg to join her mother and Patrick. Maybe Milly would have one of their servants take her. The only thing this place held for her was pain, and she'd had enough of that to last a very long time.

The moon was barely visible beneath roiling clouds, as Ginny traipsed through the darkness. With her head drooping in dejection, she didn't see the flames shooting beyond the treetops, or hear the owl that followed her progress with gentle hoots. Her mind was filled with recriminations for every word, every touch, she and Jonathan had shared.

When the acrid smell of smoke assaulted her nose, she stopped and gazed around in fear. The night sky was bright with an unholy glow that came from the direction of Ginny's home. Ashes drifted through the air like a fine mist of falling snow, and smoke thick and strong draped the trees like a dense fog.

"Oh no," she cried and sped through the night. She knew what she would find before she entered the clearing. She only hoped it wouldn't be as bad as the licking flames indicated. It was worse. As she stood in the dancing shadows of the fire, a creaking, groaning sound overrode the noise of the voracious flames, and the once-strong oak rafters of her home collapsed into the belly of the fiery monster. Tears spilled from her eyes, and her shoulders shook with the burden of her pain. It was gone, her home, her dreams. The decision was made for her and her mother. They would have to stay with Patrick. Her one consolation was that her mother

142

wouldn't have to view the destruction. She wouldn't have to witness the work of a lifetime diminished to ash-filled rubble.

In the din, a single raindrop fell from the smoky sky, and hissed and jumped when it hit the hot coals.

After the siege of tears and the acceptance of her loss, all she wanted to do was seek the comfort of her family. She turned away and began the long walk to Milly's. Her friend would help Ginny get to Patrick and her mother. Someone would come from Milly's to care for the animals in the morning. There was nothing—not even the destruction of her home—that would make her seek help from Jonathan. Nothing!

Blue stumbled up the stairs in the darkness, his heart pounding with fright. He rushed into Jonathan's room and came to a shuddering halt at the sight that greeted him. Had the situation not been so serious, Blue would have bellowed with laughter. "Bloody light, boss, how'd you get bound up like that?" He couldn't prevent the chuckle that escaped.

A frown marred the stubbled face and bleary eyes searched the dim room questioningly. He shifted his head on the pillow. When he would have lifted his arm, he found it bound to the bedpost. He became more confused than ever.

"Boss, a terrible thing has happened," Blue informed him as he began loosening the knots.

"What?" Jonathan asked, peering into the darkened corners as though he expected someone to step from the shadows. Had Ginny tied him like this? And where the hell was she? He rubbed his wrists until the stinging of the blood rushing into his hands subsided. "What are you doing here, Blue?"

"I come to wake you, to tell you the Sutton place is burnin'."

"What?"

"The Sutton's—"

"Damn it, I heard you. I just don't know why you took your sweet time telling me. Is Ginny all right?"

"Ain't nobody seen her. I just seen it myself, when I got up to relieve myself. I thought you'd want to know." His voice trailed away as he watched Jonathan whip on his clothes. He left the room, tugging on his boots.

"I sent to the stables to have horses saddled for us."

"Thanks," Jonathan said absently.

The smoking rubble that greeted Jonathan sent his heart plunging to his toes. The pouring rain that had accompanied him on his wild ride to reach her home developed into a terrible storm. Still he stayed and blindly searched the charred remains, looking for some sign of Ginny. He suffered burns on his hands and arms as he dug in the rubble.

Blue stayed by Jonathan's side. He was fearful of the emotions he detected in the young man's face. And truth to tell, he wondered if some of the wetness on Jonathan's face wasn't tears. Blue'd had no idea that there was anything going on between Jonathan and the Sutton girl. But Blue also recognized the pain on his young friend's face. He'd seen it once before. And now this. Was Jonathan destined to suffer heartache when he felt anything other than lust for the fairer sex?

The burned-out home yielded nothing. Jonathan's servants formed a search party and scoured the countryside in the downpour.

Nothing. Ginny was gone . . . Dead?

15

Ginny stumbled through the downpour, her spirits at a new low. The rain plastered her hair to her head, and her dress clung like a second skin. She trembled and shook with cold, yet her discomfort never entered her mind. All of her thoughts were centered on the destruction of her hopes and dreams, and the shame she'd brought on herself by her scandalous behavior. How could she have ever fancied herself falling in love with Jonathan Cross? And even worse, what made her think he might return her feelings? To add insult to injury, she'd put his clothes on her body, and had then settled herself in his bed at his disposal. Oh, the shame of it. What had she expected?

If she'd been at home where she belonged, maybe she could have put the fire out before it had gotten out of control. How had it started? She'd left no fire in the fireplace, not even a hot coal. Since her mother had been gone, she'd had no reason to cook. Her mother had cooked enough food to see Ginny through the days she'd be in Williamsburg. A cold biscuit had taken care of her morning hunger, and she'd carried a biscuit sandwich of salt-cured ham and an apple for her dinner. In the evening she'd eaten whatever Bertha had prepared. She didn't remember any thunder or lightning preceding the rain. She couldn't figure it out. Where had the fire started?

As she approached the bridge, she could hear the rushing of water. Never had she seen the river flood its banks, but that possibility loomed closer and closer, as she watched the churning water rise under the bridge, carrying all matter of debris. When she stepped onto the bridge, she could feel the planks shifting. The fear of having to face Jonathan was the only thing that spurred her to put one foot in front of the other to continue on her way. She had to get away. About halfway across the bridge, the roaring picked up volume. The pouring rain blurred her vision; still, no one could miss the sight that met her eyes. An uprooted tree slapped the water from side to side as it wallowed the muddy river, its tangled limbs sweeping up anything in its path. Ginny screamed and ran for the safety of the other side. She felt the impact as the huge tree root met the weakened braces of the bridge. The planks rose with a great heaving thrust, then settled like a house of cards in the foaming water. Ginny felt herself falling, felt the smooth surface of the wood as her head cracked against the boards. Her last thought as the water closed over her, was how surprisingly warm the water was.

The river rolled and foamed like a mad dog, but when Ginny's feet touched its muddy bottom, it spit her back up like a baby that had overeaten. Her body came up just as the giant tree swept by, its limbs seizing her in strong arms, and carrying her along the turbulent waters, until it beached itself miles downstream.

A hot sun rode the blue sky, drying and healing the soaked earth. The light of day revealed the true destruction of the Sutton place. Jonathan's servants sifted through the wet rubble for some sign of Ginny. Jonathan continued to search every foot the others had already gone over, praying he would find something they had overlooked. The washed-out bridge raised new questions for him, and for some reason he was drawn to its remains time and again. Any sign that she might have made it to the bridge, the

146

rain had washed away. Still, he rode the banks looking.

Guilt ate at him, giving him no peace. Something had happened to cause Ginny to leave his side, and tie him up like shocked hay. What? Had he said something to drive her away? He racked his mind, trying to solve the puzzle. He couldn't remember anything other than her warm, tempting body and the pleasure they'd shared. Memories of her green eyes studying him, and thick, sweet-smelling auburn hair curling around his hand, plagued him.

He'd sworn long ago never to let his heart get involved in another relationship. He didn't need the emotional upheaval of falling in love, but somewhere along the line, he'd forgotten his vow. Ginny Sutton had been so different. She was like leaving a smoke-filled room and stepping out into fresh air and sunshine. His admiration and respect for her had quickly lent itself to far more serious matters of the heart.

At last admitting defeat, he turned his thoughts to more urgent matters. He couldn't let Ginny's mother return home to learn the truth. She would need the comfort of her son when she learned the news. But before he rode to Williamsburg, he had to tell Milly, Ginny's beloved friend.

Jonathan and Milly sat quietly in the carriage, gazing with tear-filled eyes at the blackened timbers surrounding the remains of the Sutton home. They had just returned from delivering the tragic news of Ginny's death to her mother and brother. Until his dying breath, Jonathan would never forget the pain he'd had to inflict on Maureen and Patrick Sutton, by telling them of Ginny's death.

Patrick had so little room in his small apartment, that Jonathan had agreed to let Nat live at Crossroads and work for him. He would also have Nat move the Suttons' livestock to Crossroads. Jonathan had made a generous offer for their few animals, including Lord Adelbert.

They'd all laughed over that, and warned him that no one except Ginny had ever been able to intimidate that ornery old mule. Their laughter had soon turned to tears, and promises of staying in touch saw them parting.

At last Milly turned to Jonathan and placed her hand over his. A gentle tightening of her hand conveyed her understanding.

"Thank you for going with me, Milly. I couldn't have made it through the ordeal without you."

"It was something I had to do. She was my best friend," she replied softly.

"I know this is going to sound strange, Milly, but I can't convince myself that she's dead."

"No, it's not strange. Truly I understand. I can't believe it either."

"It's more than that. It's a gut feeling that won't go away. I don't know, I can't explain."

Milly watched the struggle he was going through, and her heart went out to him. She'd been right. If Ginny had lived, this man would have made her the perfect husband.

A whining voice penetrated the fog that swirled through Ginny's head, its irritating pitch grating on her nerves. She wanted to ask its owner to be quiet. But when she swallowed, she felt like a rock was lodged in her throat. The pain was terrible, her throat was raw and scratchy. When she tried to open her eyes, they felt like weights were on them, and when she would have lifted her hand to her burning face, her muscles screamed in pain. What was wrong with her? Where was she?

"Ain't she pretty, Ma?" asked a gentle voice.

"She's right fair-lookin', son."

"I think she's a skinny beanpole, and all that red hair and freckles are ugly," came the whining voice.

"Well, it don't matter what you think, 'cause I'm the one what found her. She's mine, ain't she, Ma?"

"She ain't one of them ol' strays you're always fetchin' home, Darryl," snapped the whiner.

"I've been takin' care of her since I brung her home. She's gonna get well, ain't she, Ma?"

"Well, if you like her so much, maybe you ought to marry her when she's up and about," came the taunting voice of the whiner.

"Can I, Ma? Can I marry her?"

"We'll see, son. If nobody comes to claim her, I don't see why not. Savin' her ain't gonna line our pockets, that's for sure. Her clothes is as poorly as me own, and her hands is hands that's known hard work. She'll more'n likely be mighty obliged to marry you. Her lot in life would undoubtedly improve as your wife, Darryl."

Ginny lay very still, fearful that she would alert them that she was awake. She no longer wanted to open her eyes. She couldn't bear to put faces to the voices she'd heard, because then they would be real. She prayed fervidly that she was dreaming, yet she knew her situation was no dream—a nightmare, yes. Her mind was like a dark cloud, with an occasional glimmer of sunshine skirting the darkness. She struggled to penetrate the haze and sort out the confusion. As the pieces began to fall in place, the voices became dimmer and her memory sharper. She saw herself standing before a window. She could feel the pride that bubbled through her, as she watched the man standing before the carriage. He lifted his hand in farewell. She lifted hers, resting it against cool glass. When he lowered his hand, it was to skim over her naked body. They lay entwined in each other's arms exploring, caressing, learning.

Ginny's mind continued its journey, her face angry and confused. She was ripping a fine silken shirt, and binding his arms and legs to the bedpost. The hair on his ankles touched the palms of her hands and teased her fingers, as she pulled and tugged on his legs. Her face was swathed in

149

pain and tears, as she fled through the darkness. Suddenly dense smoke and leaping flames jarred her memory, consuming her with more tears and pain. Her journey ended at the river, as she fell into the murky depths.

"Jonathan," she whispered, as a single tear slipped from the corner of her eye.

"She said somethin', Ma. I heard her. She's cryin', see the tear?"

A rough finger sliding gently over her face was the last thing Ginny remembered, as she slipped into a restless sleep.

The gloom that settled over Jonathan's home was oppressive, Ginny's death weighing heavily on everyone's mind. The servants went about their chores as though she was directing them. Even dour-faced Willis offered a willing hand to anyone who asked.

Blue watched over Jonathan, the young man's moods unsettling him. He wished he could help him deal with his loss, but knew only time would heal Jonathan's wounds. Blue had never brought up how he had found Jonathan tied to the bed. He knew for a fact it was not Christine, and Jonathan would never have bedded a slave. Also, a slave would never test her master in such a way. Only one person would have done such a thing . . . Ginny Sutton.

Blue knew Jonathan had had too much to drink the night he'd come home from the ball. Somehow, he'd gotten Ginny into his bed. Why she had still been at the house at such a late hour, Blue didn't know. But undoubtedly something had happened between them, and Blue knew pretty much what that something was. He'd sensed the sexual tension building between them, since she'd first stepped foot into the house. Had Jonathan forced the girl into his bed? Blue had never known a woman to refuse Jonathan. But perhaps this one had, and Jonathan had let his desires override his common sense. Whatever, Jonathan's odd behavior could mean only one thing. He'd felt more than just lust for the young woman.

Jonathan held himself aloof, the gulf of isolation dividing him from his friends and servants widening. He responded to nothing . . . to no one. He sought to deaden his remorse by shutting every door of escape, punishing himself for Ginny's death. Over and over, he berated himself for taking her innocence. The thought that she had died feeling anger toward him, was almost more than he could bear. He would never have a chance to make amends with her, tell her all she had meant to him. As the days passed, he groped in mental darkness for a light that would lead him from this pit.

Christine did not help Jonathan's mood by constantly invading his privacy. Nearly every day she'd come to Crossroads, and if Jonathan happened to be away, she'd wait on his return. Her constant chattering sorely tested his nerves, yet he ignored her, hoping his rudeness was hint enough that he wanted nothing to do with her. This woman had hated Ginny, and had ridiculed her at every turn. He knew her condolences were false, issued only in hopes of gaining favor in his eyes.

One late afternoon as Christine was riding her horse to Crossroads, she saw Jonathan astride Beowulf and discreetly followed him. He paused at the rise that overlooked the Suttons' homestead, then veered his mount toward the river that ran behind their property.

Several moments later he disappeared into the woods. Christine followed, determined to force this insane grief from his heart. She had more to offer him than that Ginny Sutton ever had, and she was going to offer it *now*. No longer would she be kind, humble, and sympathetic toward him, which went against her nature anyway. That method had gained her naught. Crossroads belonged to her, and by God, she was going to have it back.

Tethering her horse a short distance from the river, Christine stepped quietly along the well-trodden path, hoping to find Jonathan at its end. She saw him standing near the river's edge, aimlessly tossing one smooth rock after another into the water, as though he had not a care in the world.

"Do you mind if I join you?" she asked huskily.

Jonathan turned sharply toward her. His dark eyes, crinkled at the corners, had a look of unspeakable distance, yet as he stared at her, their intensity seemed to pierce her through and through.

"Yes, I mind. If I'd wanted your company, I would have asked for it." This had been Ginny's private haven, and the idea that this woman—of all women—should intrude upon it, was an insult to her memory.

"Is this where you come, when I don't find you at home?"

"Where I go is none of your business, Christine."

Christine approached him. "I don't like seeing you this way, Jonathan. No amount of grieving will bring Ginny back. She's dead. Life is for the living." There was no marked sympathy in the tone of her voice.

His eyes burned. "Ginny isn't dead."

Christine stomped her foot. "For God's sake, stop it! She's dead! As dead as that rock sitting there," she emphasized, pointing to a rock on the bank.

"You wouldn't understand, Christine. You disliked her, found fault with everything she did. Why, I don't know, and quite frankly, I don't care to know. But I do know that some people leave their mark upon this world, when they leave it. Ginny did. Yes, I grieve for her."

"Tell me, Jonathan, had she lived, would you have asked her to be your wife?"

"What I would have asked Ginny is of no consequence now."

"Yes, and that's why you need to get on with your life."

"You're tiring me, Christine." He turned from her and picked up another stone, and with a flick of his wrist, sent it skipping across the water.

"Tiring you! I care for you." She gripped his shoulder and turned him toward her. "You need me, Jonathan. I can help you, if only you'll let me."

"How? By offering yourself to me?" he asked bitterly.

"If that is your wish."

"And after that, what could you offer me, Christine?"

"Why . . . I—"

He chuckled, a sarcastic sneer curling his lip. "A warm body I can find anytime . . . anywhere. What I want, you can't give me. You're a selfish, cold-hearted bitch, taking pleasure in your own pleasures."

"I've never seen this side of you, Jonathan," she said, noticeably upset. And then she let her wrath flow. "If Ginny had lived and you'd married her, you would've been the laughingstock of all Virginia. It's only in fairy tales where there's a happy-ever-after ending. Your life would've been pure hell."

Jonathan stared at her coldly for a moment. "Even in death, she's succeeding in taunting you. Ginny always did have the last word, didn't she, Christine?"

His remark was like a splash of cold water on her face. Walking from her, he untethered his horse and mounted. "Good day, Christine." Reining Beowulf toward the path, he galloped off, leaving an angry Christine standing alone.

She raised her fist to the heavens. "Damn you, Ginny Sutton, I'll win, just you wait and see. Then we'll see who's had the last laugh."

Christine still visited, behaving as though that day at the river had never happened. Like a deeply rooted tree, she stood steadfast and lofty. Nothing Jonathan said or did to

153

her moved her. And god, he'd worn himself out trying.

Unable to tolerate Christine's visits, Jonathan began staying away from the house more and more. He'd mount Beowulf and just ride the plantation, going no place in particular. No slaves worked in the fields during this time; it was covered with brush piles. The big thin leaves had been cut in August, and had hung by their slit stems in the barn to cure slowly. He'd visited the tobacco barns and watched the slaves stripping the leaves and then tying them together, packing them in hogsheads for shipment. On some dry November or December day, they'd set fire to the brush and rake off any remaining unburned wood or charcoal. And then the cycle would start all over, and they'd plant the powdery seeds before Christmas, then transplant them in May.

When Jonathan had first arrived at Crossroads, he'd watched the slaves remove the suckers, a nasty job, because of the painful sting of the green tobacco worms. At tobacco-topping time, they'd pinch the flower buds when they appeared, so the plant wouldn't go to seed.

While the men worked with the tobacco, the women were no less busy, preserving all the produce and meats to feed their families through the winter.

Nat had taken over the care of the main garden, and had also tended Ginny's garden, which had already been planted with the fall vegetables before her death. Nat told Jonathan that he'd learned enough from Ginny to get them started. Jonathan had told him to get any help he needed to maintain the gardens. The fall harvest to date was impressive, gaining Nat a wage increase.

On his rides, Jonathan had watched the slaves' children playing in chestnut trees, shaking the limbs and sending the prickly burrs to the ground. Making a game of their chore, they'd scramble around in the fallen leaves to see who gathered the most. Also, he'd find them in the orchard picking apples. Then they'd take home sack after sack to their mothers, who pared and dried them on trays in the sun.

Occasionally, he'd also check on Lord Adelbert. As much as he disliked the ornery beast, he felt he owed it to Ginny. He'd heard the mule was not adjusting well to his new home or his new acquaintances (the other mules that shared his quarters). He was always easy to spot, standing apart from the others . . . so like his Ginny, he thought sadly. One of the slaves assigned to tend to the mules told him Lord Adelbert had been taking nips at the other mules' rumps, when they'd ventured too close to him. Jonathan had witnessed one such scene. One brave mule had the gall to bite into Lord Adelbert's straw hat, and try to yank it from his head. The poor mule had suffered dearly for his naughty deed. Lord Adelbert had made it clear that no one, man or beast, messed around with his precious hat.

As with his Ginny, the mule boasted an abundance of pride.

16

Ginny became stronger every day. The past was just that, and she was determined not to dwell there. Except thinking of her mother and Patrick, she had kept her vow. But she worried that her mother would think she had met with foul play, or had died in the fire. She had to reach her mother and let her know she was all right.

When she knew she was alone, she opened her eyes and studied her surroundings. The room was small and poorly furnished. She occupied a small bed in the corner of the room. A table and chairs took up most of the space. Spices and beans strung for drying dotted the naked rafters. Nailed to the walls were skins of various animals. There was an opening for a window, but it had no curtains or glass, only a skin to pull back during the day. By comparison, she and her mother had been wealthy.

Sometimes when she woke up, someone would be brushing her hair and talking softly to her, pleading with her to get well. Darryl—she'd come to recognize his gentle voice. He was big and strong and kind and slow. She lay as still as possible. It didn't take her long to match the other voices to the proper face. Darryl had a brother, Harold; they were twins. But Harold wasn't kind or slow. And his wife was the whiner. She was fat, and Ginny noticed that she liked to give orders. Her name was Evelyn, and she was never satisfied. She wanted everything, but she didn't want to work. If she wasn't complaining about her lot in life, she was bemoaning the injustices of having a husband who wanted no more than a full belly and a jug of fine Virginny whiskey. From Ginny's conclusion, the latter was his preference.

Then there was Ma, a thin, wiry woman who could silence the words on Evelyn's lips with one quelling look, when she was of a mind to do it. She tolerated Harold's failures, vowing he was just like his father before him. But when she looked at Darryl, there was a love and tenderness that nothing could hide. While the others scoffed at his stories of the animals he saved from one disaster or another, his mother would sit for hours and listen to him. Sometimes she helped him splint an injured animal's leg, or tear strips from her own petticoat to bandage one of his creatures. Ma's care of Ginny stemmed from Darryl's concern.

Evelyn's cruel treatment was the catalyst that got Ginny out of bed.

One afternoon she lay very still, listening to Evelyn prowl around the room, when suddenly shards of pain ripped up her arm. Her eyes shot open, and she grabbed her throbbing arm.

Evelyn's fingers were digging into her flesh. "I knew you was playin' possum. Ain't nobody can sleep that long. Now get off your lazy arse and help with the work around here. It's time you earned your keep."

Like you, Ginny wanted to say, but she didn't dare. She lacked the courage.

From that day on, her life became a living hell. Ginny was no stranger to work, but the endless criticism was almost her undoing. Her body was a network of bruises, where Evelyn pinched her when Ginny didn't move fast enough. She became jumpy and frightened of her own shadow.

It became apparent that they weren't going to let her leave. When she told them she was well enough to go home, Harold and Evelyn laughed, and told her she wasn't going anywhere, and watched her even closer. Ginny worked and plotted and hoped for some way to escape. But to make matters worse, she began each day with a delicate stomach. She couldn't figure it out. Bathing was not a priority of her bene-factors, and she wondered if their smell was upsetting her stomach. Still, that didn't make any sense, because it didn't take the sickness long to pass.

Another fear she'd developed was the attention Harold showed her. His leering gaze sent her blood running coldly through her veins. Under no condition would she let herself be left alone with him. Even when everyone was present, he found one excuse or another to touch her or sit next to her. His attention only incensed Evelyn and made Ginny's life more miserable.

The only sense of freedom she felt was when she was with Darryl. She helped him take care of his animals and encour-aged him to clean their cages. She listened to his stories, and tried to discourage him when he talked of marrying her. But she knew he truly didn't understand the meaning of mar-riage. Little by little she tried to help him understand the joys of freedom.

One afternoon as she fed kernels of corn to an injured raccoon, she watched Darryl. The animals accepted him. He talked very softly and handled them with utmost care. They rewarded his attention by letting him pet and coddle them.

"When your animals are well, do you set them free?" Ginny asked hopefully.

"Oh yes, they wouldn't like it if they had to stay caged up. Ma says they need their freedom to grow. Besides, if I kept them all, I'd soon run out of room. Harold won't build me no more cages. He thinks I'm stupid to care for the animals."

"I think you're very smart to be able to take care of so many different animals. How do you know what each one needs to make it well?"

"I don't know. Somethin' in here just tells me." He tapped a finger to his head.

"Sort of like me, huh? You found me and I was hurt. If you hadn't helped me, I would have died."

"Yeah, I guess. Only I'd never found a real person before.

You know what?"

"What?"

"It really scared me when I found you. I was lookin' to see what the storm washed ashore, when I saw this big tree that had washed up on the bank." He spread his arms as wide as they would go. "I climbed over the limbs to see what I could find. The first thing I saw was your hair. It was drapin' the limbs like moss. I reached out to touch it, and there you were. You looked like you was sleepin'. When you wouldn't wake up, I thought you was dead."

She placed her hand on his arm. "Thank you for rescuing me, Darryl. I owe you my life."

"Do you want to marry me then?"

"Marriage is a big step, Darryl. It's not something you do out of gratitude. You marry someone because you love them, and you want to spend the rest of your life with them. Do you understand?"

"No, but I could take care of you."

"I don't mean to sound ungrateful, but I can take care of myself. If you keep me here when I don't want to stay, I'll be like one of your animals that never got set free."

"But why wouldn't you want to stay? I can protect you from Harold."

"What do you mean?" she asked, startled by his disclosure.

"I seen the way he looks at you. I know what he wants to do to you."

"What?" she asked, before she could stop herself.

"He wants to breed you."

Before her face turned deathly pale, it flamed with heat. She wasn't an innocent anymore, but her one night with Jonathan hadn't made her an expert on sins of the flesh. Still, she knew in her heart that Darryl was right. If he'd picked up on his brother's intentions, then it was more urgent than ever that she get away. "You have to help me," she pleaded, tears sparkling in her eyes.

"How?"

"I must get away. I have to get to my family."

"You have a family?"

"Yes, and I know they are worried sick about me."

"If I helped you get home, would they give me some money?"

"Money?"

"My Ma really likes money, so does Evelyn. I know when I first brung you home, they was hopin' we could make a lot of money for savin' you. Then when Evelyn seen how you was dressed, she said we was wastin' our time."

"My family doesn't have a lot of money, but I'm sure they would pay you something for all your trouble."

"Oh, it wouldn't be for me. It would keep them from bein' mad at me for lettin' you go."

"Darryl, my family would be deeply indebted to you for anything you can do for me."

"Let me think on it a spell. You won't tell though, will you?"

"No, I won't tell, I promise."

When the first hard frost covered the ground and winter was indeed upon them, it was the season for hog-killing. Ginny was familiar with the back-breaking chore and didn't look forward to it at all.

She put water on to heat for a sponge bath, then took her time cleaning the platters from the morning meal.

When Evelyn came for her, the slaughtering was done, and the bleeding had slowed. They had begun heating large kettles of water very early that morning. The hog was dipped in the water and rolled over to loosen the hair, hauled out, scraped with a dull knife, immersed again immediately, and the process repeated until most of the hair was off the hide. Ginny's stomach heaved as she scraped, and she swallowed rapidly, trying to dispel the rolling in her stomach.

After they'd scraped the hide, the hog was strung up on a stout pole, and they'd completely cleaned the inside of the carcass. Two pots were started, a sausage pot for the trimmings of lean meat, and a lard pot for the trimmings of fat.

After they had taken down the hog, Ma and Harold made quick work of cutting it up. Ginny was in charge of the lard pot. She added a small amount of water and cut the fat into small pieces. She was confident she had conquered her queasy stomach, until the smell of the greasy fat sent her in search of privacy.

"Well, ain't you a pretty thing retchin' your guts out?" Evelyn taunted, as she stood over Ginny.

"Leave me alone. I'll be all right in a little while. The smell just got to me."

"It was more than the smell that got to you. I seen you before, when you were sick like this. I'd say some man has gifted you with his babe."

"What?" Ginny croaked, wiping the perspiration from her brow.

"You're goin' to have a baby."

"That's impossible."

"If you've been with a man, it ain't impossible."

"Oh my God, what will I do?"

"I've heard of a woman that can get rid of it. But you'd need money." Evelyn watched her closely.

"I don't have any money. I don't have anything," Ginny cried.

That was not the response Evelyn wanted. She'd hoped all along that there was some way they could make some money for taking care of the girl. Something about Ginny bothered Evelyn. She acted like she should have money. And she talked proper, like those that had money, although she'd known hard work and her clothes were mere rags. "Then I guess you'll be havin' the babe. Of course, you can marry Darryl and give it a name."

Ginny slumped on the cold ground and watched Evelyn walk away. What would she do? She had to get to her mother. Oh, the shame of what she'd done. How could she return to her mother with such a burden? How could she not? She couldn't bear to remain here with these filthy people. What kind of chance would a baby have in these sur-

161

roundings? And she would never do anything *to get rid of it,* as Evelyn had suggested.

Then her dismay turned to anger when she remembered Jonathan. Why couldn't he have loved her just a little? If he'd cared for her enough to at least call her by the right name, she would have stayed with him forever. "You bastard, I hate you, and I hate what you've done to me. And I'll never love this baby," she said, sobbing bitterly.

She cried a waterfall of tears, all the while bemoaning the fates that had placed her on the bridge that fateful day Jonathan Cross had come to Crossroads to claim his home. As she suffered, her greasy hand cradled her abdomen, disclaiming any vow she'd made toward Jonathan's baby.

Ginny overcame her sickness and continued with her chores, stirring the lard throughout the day as it cooked down, and helped Evelyn make sausage. As in everything else, the Marlows lacked the cleanliness Ginny was accustomed to. She hoped the meat wouldn't become tainted by their haphazard methods, because they truly needed it. Hams, shoulders, and middlin' meat were taken to the smokehouse, thoroughly salted, and put on shelves to "take the salt" through the winter months as they cured.

Evelyn hadn't wasted any time telling the others what was wrong with Ginny. They watched her closely, as though she would sprout horns anytime.

Harold was determined to have her now . . . he'd waited long enough. He planned their encounter with the anticipation of a long-awaited journey.

Ginny was exhausted long before the day's end, and looked as if any moment she would be sick again. Ma took pity on her and sent her to the house to rest.

That night as she slept restlessly, she roused the household with her pitiful weeping. Her tears settled on Darryl's heart like an injured animal, and he could no longer deny his help.

17

It was a ragged pair that set out the next morning on the pretext of finding a preacher. Darryl had never lied before, and it didn't set easy with him. Yet when he'd started to confide in his mother, she'd shook her head, looked at him with that tender smile she reserved solely for him, and assured him, "You go 'bout what you got to do. It's all right. I 'spect you'll be gone a spell, and I'll take care of your critters while you're gone."

The piebald swayback pitched and plodded, taking his own sweet time, as he rambled along the rutted roads and across streams crusted with ice. Ginny bounced and banged against the sides of the cart Darryl had hitched to the horse. Yet nothing would make her complain. She was too grateful to be on her way to her family. Imagine their surprise when she turned up on their doorstep. Suddenly it hit her. How could she make her appearance less shocking? What would they think? They had no idea what had happened to her. She knew her mother would be at Patrick's, because she would have had no other place to go after the fire had destroyed their home. Ginny was filled with remorse for all the pain she'd caused her family, not to mention the pain she was yet to cause them. She didn't know exactly how long she'd been gone. She had been sick for weeks, and when she'd recovered, she had worked like a horse day in and day out. On that fateful summer night, her life had been changed forever, and now it was winter, and she was in for more changes.

Darryl had no concept of time nor of her eagerness to get to Williamsburg. One would think he was on a Sunday outing. He stopped the swayback time and again to marvel at some discovery. The length of an icicle formed by water dripping from a rock; a cardinal perched in the boughs of a pine tree delighted and excited him. Ginny, in all her eagerness, took the time to enjoy the sights with him. After all, if not for him, she would have remained at the Marlows until an escape plan presented itself, or she was too large with child to travel. And the thought of facing Evelyn's torment and her smirk, now that she knew Ginny was going to have a baby, and Harold's leer, was more than she could endure.

They spent the night in a copse of trees, their fire little more than a sizzling, hissing blaze. Ginny stayed in the cart, shivering beneath heavy skins. Darryl slept like a baby, draped in a skin and hunched against the trunk of a tree. The night was bright with stars and damp with cold, the feel of snow in the air. As she lay there pondering her future and the future of her baby, she made up her mind that under no condition would she ever let Jonathan know about the baby. Some way she would keep her secret, even if she had to go away. He had no right to know. If he ever found out, he might try to take the babe from her. No, she would see to it that he never knew.

The air was crisp and the morning clear, as the uncommon pair made their way down Jamestown Road and onto Duke of Gloucester through the muddy street. Even now, tired as she was, Ginny couldn't help recalling the history her father had brought to life for her and Patrick. He had put great store in teaching his children the price that had been paid for the freedoms they took for granted. He'd enacted Patrick Henry's oratorical thunder on that memorable day in May 1765, during the Stamp Act crisis: "Caesar had his Brutus—Charles the First, his Cromwell—and

George the Third—may profit by their example. If this be treason, make the most of it." The Virginia Assembly declared that the act was illegal and unjust, and therefore passed resolutions against taxation by the British Parliament.

The *Boston Gazette* printed the resolutions on July 1. When the hated stamps arrived in America that fall, angry mobs wrecked the homes of the distributors and stoned the law officers who tried to stop them.

The day was hastening when Williamsburg's Capitol and its Hall of the House of Burgesses would witness events that were to shake not only Virginia, but the world. Eugene Sutton revered Patrick Henry above all politicians of his time. And for his children, Eugene brought to life the history of their homeland, and encouraged them never to lose sight of its importance.

They passed beautiful homes, the frosted panes reflecting the early morning light. Owners of businesses not yet open for trade were sweeping walkways, and studying the sky to predict the day's weather. A young boy, his arms loaded with firewood, stopped to watch the swayback for a moment, before he hurried through the early morning to stoke the fires in King's Arms Tavern.

Nestled between an apothecary shop and a wig-maker was the silversmith shop. The shop looked like a neat box with windows and flower boxes. As with many of the merchants, the living quarters were above the business. Since Patrick's employer had been in ill health, he'd moved into his sister's home, leaving the apartment for Patrick.

Darryl hitched the horse before the house and helped Ginny from the cart, neither saying anything as she led the way. Her legs were stiff and sore, but frightened that someone would see her, she hastened her pace. Her heart pounded, and she twisted the fabric of her dress in her nervous hands. She drew a shuddering breath and lifted her hand to the door. After knocking several times, she waited, Darryl standing behind her quiet as a mouse.

The door swung wide and the handsome face of her brother greeted her. "Patrick!"

"Ginny? Is it you?"

The mop of auburn hair swung wildly as she nodded her head.

"Oh my God, it is you!" He dragged her into his strong arms and hugged her tightly, rocking her gently. "Oh my God," he mumbled into her hair, "we thought you were dead."

She began to sob quietly.

"Come in out of the cold." He didn't release her, but kept his arms tightly around her as he led her into the room.

"This is Darryl. He brought me home," she said, turning in her brother's arms.

When they looked at Darryl, he was suspiciously mopping his coat sleeve over his eyes.

"Come in, Darryl."

The warmth of the room embraced her; familiar things of Patrick's around the work area soothed her frayed nerves. Ribbons and lace for the makings of a hat rested on a table next to a shoo-fly chair. Her mother's things. Ginny's eyes teared anew as she touched the delicate lace.

"Here, sit down while I get mother. This news can't wait." He pointed out chairs as he rushed from the room.

A teary reunion followed. There was much hugging and squeezing and kissing going on for some time.

Darryl surprised everyone when he announced, "I don't blame Ginny for wantin' to get home so bad."

They laughed and hugged him in turn. And when Ginny's mother placed hot bread and molasses before them, Ginny's stomach didn't as much as quiver. She was starving, and the food went down easily. Darryl ate his fair share and kept bragging on the lightness of the loaves, until Maureen Sutton blushed with pride, and made a special point to see that Darryl had plenty of the bread to take home with him.

Ginny explained that Darryl had saved her, and he and his mother had nursed her back to health. Patrick dug deeply into his savings for Darryl, and Maureen added a jar of molasses to his growing bundle. Ginny saw him out and thanked him again for all he'd done for her.

"You have a nice family," he offered.

"I know. If you're ever this way, stop and say hello."

"This is where you live?" he questioned in his gentle voice.

"It is now. My home burned to the ground."

"Can't you rebuild it?"

"We lack the funds."

Darryl dragged out his purse. "I'll give you the money your brother gave me. Maybe that will help."

She placed her hand over his. "No, you take that to your family. It wouldn't help. We didn't own the place; it belonged to someone else."

Her voice had taken on a sadness that Darryl recognized immediately. "That makes you sad?" he asked.

"It's a long story, but truly I'm better off here with my brother."

"Well, maybe I'll come see you sometime."

"I'd like that very much. Goodbye, and take care."

"I will."

She stood on the stoop and watched as Darryl and the piebald meandered through the muddy streets. She knew he was taking in everything he saw and talking quietly to the horse, because he kept pointing out various things. She marveled at the joy he received from the sights around him. It didn't matter that he was going the wrong way, and she wouldn't point it out to him. He'd find his way home, and in the meantime he would experience an abundance of discoveries—discoveries that only Darryl would appreciate.

Ginny returned inside to the comfort of the cozy shop and the love of her family. She related all the things that had happened to her since the fire, not mentioning that she'd spent the night in Jonathan's bed.

"We'll have to send word to Milly and Jonathan that you're all right."

"No! Please, I don't want to see them yet."

"But, dear, they were so concerned. Jonathan is the one who brought us the news of your death. He was distraught, as was Milly. She came with him."

"I can't help it. I don't want to see anyone yet. Where's Nat?"

"Jonathan has given him a home at Crossroads. He seems happy enough. He misses you, and when they come to Williamsburg, they stop to visit."

If Ginny's face could turn any paler, it did. "Why would Jonathan visit here?"

"He and Patrick have become friends, and you know I always thought a lot of Jonathan."

You won't when you hear the rest of my news, Ginny vowed.

"Jonathan is very concerned about our welfare. He always wants to know if we need anything. In addition to his visits, he has become a good customer. He's bought several pieces from Patrick and ordered other selections. At first Patrick questioned him about his sudden interest in his work. Jonathan assured him that until only recently, he'd been too busy getting his home in order to think of anything else. Now that he has the time, he is adding things to his home when he discovers something that catches his fancy."

"I'm sure that's the case," Ginny replied lamely.

Maureen watched her daughter closely. Something was wrong, something besides her ordeal with the Marlows. Maybe a good rest and proper food would put the sparkle back in her daughter's eyes. "I've water heating. How about a nice hot bath?"

"That sounds heavenly to me. You can't imagine the simple comforts that I've missed so desperately."

Ginny and her mother moved the tub before the hearth and filled it with water. She bathed slowly, savoring the warmth and the peace of her surroundings. She leaned back in the tub and shut her eyes. Why couldn't this contentment last? The ticking of the clock, logs crackling in the fire, and Chaser, Patrick's cat, purring from his pillow in the rocker, soothed her, and before she knew it, her head tilted in sleep.

Ginny sat before the fire, brushing the tangles from her hair. Her mother stood at a small table, wielding her scissors with the expertise of a seasoned dressmaker. She'd put aside her hats for a while, to make Ginny a dress. Her daughter was entirely too thin and too sad. Oh, she smiled at the proper places and had responded to her brother's teasing. He'd been quick to point out that when she'd knocked on the door, if her hair had been covered, he would have turned her away. But there was no denying that mop of red hair, and that it was his sister beneath the mane. She'd jabbed him in the ribs and warned him that he'd do well to watch his manners, lest some night while he slept, she'd shear his own auburn locks. It had been an ongoing battle since they were small children, this argument over the color of her hair. Actually, Patrick's hair wasn't very different from hers. Instead of the shimmering red highlights that Ginny's hair boasted, his hair was a deep brown. And nothing delighted him more than calling his sister *Red*. Simply because she hated it, and he knew it. Even his teasing hadn't lightened her mood.

Maureen was her mother, sure, but also she was a woman, and she remembered the pain and confusion of first love. Was Ginny in love? And was Jonathan Cross that love? Had he spurned her affection? It was a delicate subject indeed, and Maureen was at a loss as to how to deal with it. Yet love for her daughter urged her forward

169

cautiously. "The holidays are quickly approaching, Ginny. Wouldn't you like to share them with some of your friends?"

"Who, Mother?"

"Maybe we could have a small dinner party and invite Milly and Jonathan. It's really unfair not to let them know you are safe."

"I can't. If Milly knows, she'll tell Jonathan."

"Would that be so terrible? He seems to care a great deal for you."

Ginny took a shuddering breath and tears filled her eyes. "I just can't," she sobbed.

Maureen took her daughter in her arms and tried to soothe her. "Shh . . . shh . . . Everything will be all right. Please don't cry."

"Nothing will ever be all right again," she sobbed.

"Now, now, nothing can be that bad. We'll work it out, no matter what it is."

"Not this time, Mother. I've done a shameful thing. Everything Christine said about me is true. I'm nothing. I've brought disgrace on my family."

"Do you want to tell me what you think this shameful thing is?" She wiped the tears from Ginny's face, and brushed the damp hair from her brow.

The words rushed from Ginny before she lost her courage. "I'm going to have a baby."

"I see." Cold fear swept through Maureen. Young girls—unwed girls—did not have babies.

"And he doesn't love me." Her words were barely audible.

"Jonathan?" Maureen asked softly.

Ginny nodded.

"We'll see, darling. I'm sure if he knew about the baby, things would be different."

"It wouldn't make him love me."

"Babies make people do peculiar things. I'm sure he

would insist that you marry him."

"No, I don't want him, and I don't want this baby. His baby."

"You can't mean that, Ginny. Babies are gifts from God to be treasured."

"Who gives a gift then wraps it in sickness and pain? I'm sick all the time."

"That will pass."

"I'm so ashamed. What will Patrick think of me?"

"He'll love you as he always has. But right now, I think you need to learn to love yourself. You made a mistake, but it's not the end of the world."

"I love you, Mother, and I'm so sorry I've disappointed you."

"I'm not disappointed, Ginny. My pain is for you. Yet I can't help wondering how sweet would be our victories, if we never experienced defeat."

"I have no idea. I've known so few victories. Mother, will you tell Patrick? I can't bear to face him."

"Don't fret about Patrick. He'll huff and puff and stomp and shout, but he'll respect your wishes. Now lie down and rest. I'll go talk to your brother."

Ginny felt as though someone had braided her insides into a tight coil, then turned them loose to unwind. She heaved into the chamber pot until she was too weak to move. Patrick's bellow of rage reached her.

"I'll kill the bloody bastard. You just see if I don't," he shouted. Immediately she heard his booted feet pounding up the stairs. The door swung wide, rebounding off the wall.

The sight that met Patrick's eyes broke his heart, and sent his Irish temper vaulting anew. His beautiful sister, her frail body cloaked in his mother's wrapper, her face ghostly white, and her fiery hair tangled around her body as she knelt before the chamber pot, filled his eyes with tears. As he stormed across the room, he blinked them

171

away and tried to contain the rage roiling through him.

He picked Ginny up in his arms and carried her to the bed. Sitting down with her in his arms, he rocked her gently. When he began to whisper softly, his tone was soothing, but his words harsh. "I'll the kill the bastard if you wish."

"I don't want you to kill him," she pleaded.

"Then I'll make him marry you," he vowed.

"I don't want you to do that either."

"For God's sake, look what he's done to you. You look like you're at death's door."

"Mother says that will pass."

"Then let me kill him," he urged.

"No, it wasn't his fault."

"I've heard about his reputation with women. I can understand how he swept you off your feet."

"It wasn't his fault."

"How can you defend him, after what he did to you? If it wasn't his fault, then how in God's name do you find yourself in this situation?"

"It was my fault." She began to sob quietly.

He could feel her body trembling in his arms. "I find that hard to believe."

"It's true."

"How?"

To her shame and mortification, she had to tell him what had happened. She didn't make herself out as a martyr, nor Jonathan as a villain. Yet what she shared was the telling of a gentle growing love that bloomed despite the class differences. Her sadness when she discovered her love wasn't returned, and following that, the immediate destruction of her home, coupled with her experience with the Marlows, sent her brother's rage again into full bloom.

"Are you sure you don't want me to kill him?" Patrick asked, after exhausting all other possibilities.

"I don't want you to do or say anything, *please*. I made a

172

mistake, and I have to live with it. And the sorrow I have to bear will be shared by you and mother, and that, I deeply regret."

"Ginny, if I'm to be completely honest, I must admit that I believe Jonathan is a fine man. And his grief over your death is real. His suffering was genuine, and still is. Are you sure you don't want to tell him that you're alive, and about the baby?"

"No." Her shoulders began shaking, and her weeping started anew. "I couldn't bear the humiliation of his rejection. As horrible as it is, it's better this way."

"What about Milly? She's your best friend. Doesn't she deserve to know that you're alive?"

"I love Milly, but right now, I don't want anyone to know. Maybe later, when I'm feeling better. I know I can't hide here forever."

Patrick tucked her in bed and brushed the tears from her face. Wrapping a strand of auburn hair around his fist, he whispered, "As you wish, Red. I'll keep your secret." He kissed her brow before turning away.

He turned the lamp down and stoked the fire, then quietly left the room. He would keep his promise. He wouldn't like it, but he would do it . . . for now.

Ginny turned on her side and snuggled beneath the quilts. Being in ill health was something new to her. She'd always been healthy as a horse.

For a moment she let her mind wander. How wonderful this event would be, if she were sharing it with a loving husband! Before she could change her train of thought, a miraculous thing happened. A gentle fluttering winged through her abdomen. Her breath caught in her throat. She lay very still, afraid to move lest it happen again and she'd miss it. She cradled her stomach and waited expectantly. Nothing happened. A tear slipped from her eye, then another and another. She began to pray fervently, to ask forgiveness for the things she'd said about the baby.

173

Regardless of the situation and the shame of being un-married, it wasn't her baby's fault. She promised God if he would forgive her for her sin, she would be the best mother possible, and she would protect her baby.

With her resolutions settled in her heart, she was filled with peace. She didn't understand the things she'd been forced to endure, but she'd accept them and do the best she could.

As her body relaxed and her eyes became heavy with sleep, the fluttering began anew. For the first time in a long time, a real smile lifted the corners of her mouth. It wouldn't be easy. But being in love never was . . . and she loved her baby.

18

Blue would no longer keep silent. Jonathan's disposition wasn't improving. Denby had said there were several matters he needed to discuss with Jonathan, but he'd dismissed him, saying he'd deal with it later. Later could mean months, if Blue didn't approach Jonathan and convince him that he had a plantation to run.

He found Jonathan in the library, his feet propped on his desk, his head resting against the back of his chair, staring at the ceiling. The room reminded Blue of a vault, dark and airless. Blue opened the curtains, feeling Jonathan's eyes on him as he completed the task.

Splaying his large hands on the desk, Blue's eyes locked with Jonathan's dull ones. "It's time me and you had a heart-to-heart talk, boss."

"About what? " Jonathan asked drolly.

"About whether you're goin' to make a go of this place, or go back to England as a failure. Your father put a lot of faith in you. You goin' to let him down?"

"Things seem to be running smoothly."

"How the bloody hell would *you* know? You ain't even glimpsed at your books, and if you ain't goin' to the stables to get on your horse and go runnin' off to God-knows-where, you're sittin' in here and wallowin' in self-pity."

His monologue brought him a piercing glare from his friend. "Wouldn't you run off, too, if you had Christine Iverson constantly breathing down your neck? Besides, I've

175

been going to Williamsburg occasionally to visit the Suttons." Jonathan removed his feet from his desk and lit a cheroot. "How about fixing us a brandy?"

Blue stalked off to the cabinet and opened the door. "Your stock's runnin' low. You've been hittin' the bottle pretty heavy."

"It helps me sleep." Jonathan sighed, then said softly, "I loved her, Blue."

Blue paused, his hand gripping the bottle. *Good. He's ready to talk about it.* "I know, Jonathan. I'm sorry."

Blue fixed them a drink, then sat down on the corner of the desk, watching as Jonathan downed his drink. Leaning back in his chair, he again settled his feet on the desk, crossing them at the ankles. He took a long drag on his cheroot and exhaled. "I took Ginny's virginity."

"I know."

"Damn, Blue, is there anything you *don't* know?"

"Not much. You don't live with a man as long as I've lived with you, and not know him." He hesitated before he asked, "Did you force her?"

"No. She'd fallen asleep in my bed. She was there when I returned from the ball." He leaned forward and tapped his ashes into the ashtray, then explained the circumstances that brought them together that night. He laughed sadly. "Over and over, I've asked myself what I did or said that upset her. I'll never know, Blue. I sent her to her death."

Blue drained his glass and poured himself another drink. "No, the fire wasn't your fault. Knowin' Ginny, she would've left your bed afterwards anyway. She wouldn't have wanted anyone findin' her in your room the next mornin'."

Jonathan felt a moment of relief. Blue was right. Still, her actions weren't just playful antics. Maybe Ginny felt guilty after their lovemaking, and the only way she knew to vent her spleen was to blame him. Hell, it *was* his fault. He could not use the excuse that he'd had too much to drink, for he'd remembered every wonderful moment of their shared bliss. He should've put a stop to it, even though she had been willing. For the first time, he was seeing things more clearly. Recalling her sad version of Cinderella, he could only believe that Ginny felt insecure, thinking no good would ever come from such a union. Like Christine, Ginny also didn't believe in fairy tales with happy endings. Were he and Milly the only foolish dreamers?

Jonathan rose from his chair. He took a deep, fortifying breath, then said, "I'm going to the stables. When you see Denby, tell him I'm ready to plow into the books."

A broad smile erupted on Blue's face. "It's good to have you back, boss."

"Thanks," he said, sliding his arms into the sleeves of his jacket. "Blue, as you said earlier, my father has faith in me to succeed in this venture. I can. His other request I might never fulfill."

"What's that?"

"Finding a wife with rich red blood and giving him grandchildren. I can look for the rest of my life, but I'll never find another Ginny," he said as he quit the room.

The grief Jonathan still bore, but he expressed it in a new form. He threw himself into his work, beginning his day at dawn. It was the evenings that he found disturbing, darkness coming too early, the hours dragging by at a snail's pace. These were the times his mind dwelt on Ginny. He spent restless, sleepless nights consumed in watching and listening, sometimes actually believing his beloved Ginny's spirit was in his bedroom.

In November, a winter storm moved in. Snow dusted the meadows, evergreens, and mountains. Most days were bitterly cold, but Jonathan bundled up in his heaviest clothing and headed for the stables. Though he had stable boys to help him, he trusted no one but himself in seeing that his horses were properly cared for. They were too valuable to chance losing because of someone's carelessness.

He looked forward to spring, the season of rebirth. Several of his prime mares would foal. Already, several men had been by to see him, interested in his thoroughbreds. Since fox hunting and horse racing were favorite pastimes of Virginians, Jonathan wanted to make certain he could supply them with quality stock. Also, should something ever happen to the tobacco crop, because of unfavorable weather conditions or disease, Jonathan would have another income to supplement their needs.

Thanksgiving Day arrived. The kitchen buzzed with preparation of the feast. Without Ginny around to offer Bertha a helping hand with the menu, Blue and Jonathan regarded it as just another indigestible meal. Their only hope was that the slaves Willis had asked to assist Bertha were more skillful and imaginative than she.

Jonathan was in the library with Denby, when an excited Blue barged inside. "You got to see this, boss. Bertha and Nat are almost lockin' horns in the kitchen."

"What!"

"Oh, they're just slappin' words at each other. Nat's on a rampage."

Jonathan and Denby grabbed their coats and followed Blue outside to the kitchen. The door was partially opened, to let the cold air in and lessen the heat in the room.

"It ain't right," Nat snapped. "I worked hard at growin' these vegetables, and you don't know a sweet tater from a white tater. Sugar don't go in white taters. You plumb messed 'em up."

Bertha squared her large shoulders. "They cook jest alike." She looked toward the other cooks for support. "Don't they?"

No one commented.

"No, they don't, I'm here to tell ya," Nat put in. "And look at this. Dat poor old turkey done died once, and by the looks of him, you done killed him again."

Bertha put her hands on her wide hips and asked petulantly, "You think you ken do it better, huh?"

"Better'n this, I can," he boasted. "I've eaten Miz Sutton's and Miz Ginny's vittles, and they ain't never served anythin' dat looked like this."

Outside, the threesome heard someone lifting pot lids, then slamming them back down. Then they heard Nat comment, "Who cooked the oyster stew?"

A wee voice piped in. "I did."

"Now dat looks mighty tasty-lookin'."

"Thank you," she returned demurely.

After commenting on several other dishes that looked edible, Nat said to Bertha, "Why didn't you let *her* do the cookin'?"

Bertha squared her shoulders and her nose shot into the air. " 'Cause I's head cook, dat's why!"

"Humph!" Nat snorted. "You won't be after Mistah Cross eats this."

Afraid someone would catch them eavesdropping, the men moved quickly back into the house. That night after Thanksgiving dinner, Jonathan approached Nat and asked if he would help Bertha in the kitchen, at least for the winter. While the meals improved considerably, the atmosphere in the kitchen did not.

One afternoon, while Jonathan and Blue were walking to the stables, Blue asked slyly, "Why don't me and you go into Williamsburg tonight?"

"I'm going at the end of the week to see the Suttons."

"That isn't exactly what I had in mind, boss. I've been seein' this servin' wench at Raleigh Tavern. She has a

179

pretty friend who'd be glad—"

"Thank you, Blue," he interrupted, "but frankly, I'm not interested."

Blue stopped abruptly. "Well, bloody hell, when are you goin' to get interested?"

"In time," Jonathan answered, leaving his friend behind.

"In time," Blue mimicked, hurrying to catch up with him. "You've been living like a bloody monk. Ain't you afraid it'll shrivel up from lack of activity?"

Jonathan chuckled. "I'm sure when the need arises, he will leap to the cause."

"Bloody unlikely," Blue said with a snort.

"So, you've been sneaking off to Williamsburg and wenching, have you?"

" 'Course. You ought to try it sometime. It does worlds for the disposition," Blue hinted.

"Is something wrong with my disposition?"

"Yeah, boss, there is. God's truth, the only difference 'twixt you and Lord Adelbert is, he wears a straw hat."

"I'm sorry, Blue. I'll try to do better."

"Well, workin' yourself to death won't do it. Everybody walks on eggshells when they're around you."

Jonathan stopped and threw up his hands in frustration. "First, you complain that I'm doing nothing, and when I start doing something, you complain that I'm doing too much. Hell, Blue, what do you want me to do?"

"Find yourself a woman, that's what!" he countered, his arms akimbo. "And there's plenty around, I'm here to tell you. Plenty who'd cure what ails you. Even that woman with the washboard legs and thighs like eels."

"Washboard hips and legs like eels, Blue," Jonathan corrected. "Have you forgotten I fought her husband in a duel?"

Blue glared at him. "Hell, I'd stand guard outside her door, or better yet, maybe a bullet in your bloody arse would put some life back in you."

Jonathan threw back his head and laughed . . . it was the first time in months.

The Christmas holiday was quickly approaching, but Jonathan paid little attention to activities going on around him. He longed to be away from the scene of tiresome gaiety. Had Ginny lived, he could have spent it with her. He might even have convinced her to marry him, and they would have brought in the New Year together. Instead, he had no one, and the joyful season only reminded him of his loneliness.

He recalled the Christmases past with his mother and father. One particular Christmas Jonathan held close to his heart, the one that had shaped his destiny. Lord Oliver had taken Jonathan, then only six years old to his stables, and presented him with an English thoroughbred pony of Arabian blood. Afterwards, he'd arranged for his young son to take riding lessons. Jonathan had devoted all his time to his beautiful animal, and early on he knew what he wanted to do with his life—breed and raise horses.

That Christmas had been the last Christmas he had spent with his mother. She had died two weeks before Christmas the following year, with his father and himself by her bedside. Then his father had taken him to live with him.

In thinking back over the years he'd spent with his half brother, Geoffrey, the month before Christmas was the only time Geoffrey had behaved halfway decent to him during the year. After Father Christmas had filled their stockings, the little tyrant would let go with a vengeance, subtly destroying Jonathan's gifts. Still, Jonathan had had his father, and the hours they spent together during the holidays were the most cherished moments of his life. His whole past seemed to flash before his eyes, as he recalled the fox hunts, the horse races, the leisurely rides through

181

the countryside, and the light banter they exchanged on their outings.

A wave of homesickness washed over him. Would he ever see his father again? Or like his Ginny, would he lose him before he could tell him face-to-face how much he loved him?

It was only in the early mornings or late in the evenings that Ginny ventured downstairs. She'd taken on the task of keeping the books for Patrick. Otherwise she remained upstairs in the small apartment, stitching tiny garments for her baby. Sewing had never been her strong suit, yet she tackled the task with determination. At first her stitches were as crooked as a dog's leg, and loose enough to cause the garment to gather if the thread was pulled. But she stayed with it until her stitches became straight and small. She made tiny gowns and blankets, edging them with discarded lace her mother gave her.

For the most part she was alone during the day. Her mother spent long hours at the milliner's shop. Business was brisk, as people shopped for the coming holiday. Sometimes she just sat for hours before the fire, and stared into the flames. Other times she pulled her chair to the window and watched children playing in the street below. She discovered she was tired and sleepy all the time. Other times she had this abundance of energy, and she cleaned and cooked, oftentimes trying new receipts. Occasionally she wondered if Bertha, Jonathan's cook, had ever mastered the fundamentals of preparing a meal.

Ginny had to admit that she noticed that their financial situation had improved without the drain of the farm. Now that Patrick was in charge of the shop, his salary had increased, and word of his unique work had spread. Her mother's hats were selling better than ever. The people of Williamsburg recognized quality work when they saw it.

Ginny did her share, and if not for her condition, this would have been a time of peace in addition to prosperity. But she feared it wouldn't last long, this time of financial growth. When people discovered she was indeed alive and with child—without the benefit of marriage—they would shun Patrick's fine work and her mother's beautiful hats, regardless of the quality.

If there was anywhere she could go to save her family this shame, she would leave. Dreaming and pretending did little good to ease her guilty conscience.

She straightened in the chair and rubbed the stiffness from her neck. Picking up the dress lying in her lap, she examined the neat stitches. This was her finest work to date. Her mother had given her scraps of material from a fine cambric fabric. Ginny had cut and sewn the infant dress, meticulously adding tiny rows of delicate cording and an eyelet ruffle. Ringing her fingers around the tiny armholes, she smiled. She couldn't imagine a baby wearing the gown, not her baby.

Folding the dress, she stacked it with the other things she'd made, and let her hand drift over the tiny garments.

A shouted "Whoa, you lop-eared varmints" caught her attention, and sent the blood rushing through her body. She would recognize that voice anywhere. Rushing to the window, she stood aside and watched as Nat set the brake and jumped down from his perch atop the coach. Ginny wanted to call out to him. He looked well, and his clothes were of a finer quality and warmer-looking than those he'd worn when he worked for her.

The carriage door swung open. She held her breath. A hand grasped the door and the top of a beaver hat emerged, a shiny-booted foot touched the ground, then another. Ginny's breathing became ragged as Jonathan straightened to his full height. His greatcoat, with a deep cape, swirled around his body from the movement, before settling quietly around his body. She couldn't take her eyes

183

off him. As was his custom, his dress was impeccable and the height of fashion. He turned back to the coach and leaned inside. When he turned around, he was holding a bottle of wine.

Nat seemed very comfortable with his new boss as they talked. A smile broke across his face, and Ginny wondered what Jonathan had said.

She watched as Jonathan started toward the shop, and Nat turned back to the finely matched bays.

Ginny rushed to the door and eased it open, her palms suddenly damp and hands trembling. *Oh, Patrick, please be nice,* she prayed. She placed her ear to the opening and listened. The sight of Jonathan had unnerved her, but the sound of his voice was more than she could bear.

Tears slipped from her eyes, when she heard Jonathan ask, "How are you, Patrick?" His voice was as smooth as velvet against a cold hand. How she'd missed hearing it.

"I'll do," came Patrick's brusque reply.

"If the black clouds continue to roll in, I'm afraid we're in for a big snow. I wanted to come into town to invite you and your mother out to dinner."

"Don't put yourself out on our account."

Ginny could feel the silence, and knew Jonathan was puzzled by Patrick's tone.

"It wasn't an inconvenience. I wanted to see you."

"Well, you've seen me, and you've invited us to dinner. Is there anything else you want?"

"As a matter of fact, there is. Is your mother here? I wanted to see her."

"Let me get something straight, Cross. We don't want, nor do we need—"

A sudden crash from above halted Patrick's speech. And for an instant there was the most peculiar look on his face. He downed his head sheepishly, and plowed his fingers through his hair. "Chaser must have fallen out of his chair. Why I ever thought he would make a good mouser is a mystery to me. He does little more than sleep the clock around."

Jonathan was amazed. Only moments earlier Patrick had snapped at him in short clipped sentences. Now this long narrative was rolling from his lips like limp taffy. What was going on?

"Mother's working. I'll give her the message, but we are really busy, and I doubt we could make it for dinner." Patrick's tone bordered on friendly, yet his anger was apparent.

"I'm sorry you can't make it. I'll stop by and see Maureen, anyway. How is she doing?"

"How do you think she's doing, considering the situation? But she's busy and that helps."

"I know the season will be difficult for the two of you. Holidays are the hardest when you've lost a loved one."

Patrick was consumed with a coughing fit.

Jonathan pounded him on the back.

"I'm fine, really."

"Well, if I don't see you again before the holidays, I wish you a merry Christmas and the best of the new year." Jonathan handed him the bottle of wine.

"You didn't have to do this." Patrick turned the bottle in his hands.

"I hope you enjoy it. I brought a supply from England."

When Jonathan opened the door, an eager Chaser darted inside between his legs. He didn't say a word, only stepped outside and closed the door behind him. Something wasn't right. Why had Patrick lied about the cat? And why was he so angry? It just didn't make sense. He thought he and the Suttons had become good friends. But after Patrick's behavior, he could only assume he was wrong.

He walked to the shop where Maureen worked, intent on asking her what was wrong. Yet when he entered the shop, Maureen treated him as though he were no more

185

than a customer. Oh she was pleasant enough, but the warmth was absent, and she was very nervous. When he mentioned that he'd already seen Patrick, she turned deathly pale. What the devil was going on?

When he returned to the carriage, Nat was waiting. A closed sign was posted on the door of the silversmith shop.

Sure enough, on the ride home the heavens opened up, and large sparkling snowflakes soon covered the ground. Jonathan was aware of the falling snow, but he was too involved in his own thoughts to appreciate the beauty around him.

He couldn't shake the nagging feeling that he'd missed something. The more he thought about it, the clearer it became. Maureen and Patrick were no longer grieving. The shadows and pain were absent from their eyes. Neither one of them had mentioned Ginny. Even when he'd mentioned their loss, Patrick hadn't commented on it. On his previous visits, much of their conversation had been about Ginny. He'd shared their laughter, as they reminisced about her and some of her antics. Once he'd told the story of their first meeting and the ornery Lord Adelbert and his prized hat. He'd shared their pain when they acknowledged there would be no more times like those.

Could they have forgotten her? No. He didn't believe that for one moment. Maybe it was the season. After he'd lost his mother, Christmas had never been the same. His father had tried to make it a joyful occasion, but she was missed. She was there, but she wasn't there. Memories. It was like an empty chair at the table. Everyone knew who belonged there, and no one sat in her place, although they knew she wouldn't be coming back. Well, he for one would not accept the fact that Ginny wasn't coming back.

19

Snow ornamented the trees, and the morning sun shed its brightest beams on the sloping branches of the evergreens, and sparkled like several strands of diamonds on an empress's necklace. Not a breath of air stirred, and nothing broke the deep silence save the rolling of the carriage wheels over the frosty earth.

Jonathan and Blue were setting out on an unexpected trip to Williamsburg. Jonathan was to meet with other planters who were assembling at the Raleigh Tavern, to discuss the prices for the coming year's tobacco crop and coordinate ship sailings.

Before Jonathan had arrived in Williamsburg, he had studied its history, learning that the capital had moved from Williamsburg to Richmond in 1780, after the revolution. During the "Publick Times"—when the General Assembly and the General Court met in the spring and fall—wealthy planters would come into town and stay in their town houses, and the taverns would overflow with travelers, politicians, and lawyers. They'd gather at Raleigh Tavern—once called the second capitol of the colony—and have heated debates concerning taxes and despotism.

Though no longer the center of trade, Williamsburg retained its love for entertainment on a grand scale. The affluent still hosted balls and elegant dinner parties, of which Jonathan had taken an active part. A grimace stole across his face as he recalled his recklessness when he'd first arrived. Since taking up residence at Crossroads, he'd avoided his old haunts when he ventured into Williamsburg. He had no desire to resort to his former habits.

The carriage drew to a halt in front of the silversmith shop. The purpose of Jonathan's visit was twofold. He was determined to find out why the Suttons had changed their attitude toward him. He vowed that before he left, he would discover the reason why. Dismissing Blue, Jonathan told him he would meet him later at the Raleigh Tavern.

As he entered the shop, the song of a hammer mingled with the tingling of the bell above the door. Patrick, his back to him, had not heard the bell. "Good morning, Patrick."

Patrick turned. As with Jonathan's last visit, the welcoming smile faded, a scowl in its place.

Patrick wiped his hands on his apron and walked toward the counter. There was a forced friendliness in his manner, as he replied, "Hello, Jonathan. Is there something I can help you with?" he asked, glimpsing uneasily over his shoulder to the closed door behind him.

"Actually, there is. You can explain why my last visit caused you and your mother such discomfort."

"I don't know what you mean," Patrick said, turning back to his work.

"I thought we were friends, but it's quite obvious you are not happy to see me."

The door behind Patrick opened and Chaser streaked through it, leaping up on the counter.

"Patrick, can you come back here a moment and look at these books? There's—" Ginny's words stopped suddenly, the blood roaring through her ears, as her heart started pumping furiously.

Jonathan's own heart nearly stopped. "My god, you're . . . you're alive," he whispered.

Uttering not a word, Ginny drew her shawl over her

slightly swollen belly, and, lifting the hem of her skirt, ran toward a narrow staircase at the end of the room. Never looking behind her, she scaled the steps two at a time until she reached the landing. Opening the door, she darted into the room and slammed it shut. Breathing heavily, she rested her back against it and closed her eyes, trying to gather her composure. How long had he been there? Had Patrick told him she was carrying his child? Oh merciful God, she prayed not. Surely, he could not have seen her condition after such a brief encounter. Any moment she expected him to knock on her door . . . unless Patrick could prevent it, which she doubted.

Jonathan started to go after her, but Patrick's angry voice stopped him. "Leave her alone. Can't you see she wants nothing to do with you?"

"Yes, and I want to know why," Jonathan growled, his temper rising now that he was over the initial shock of seeing her alive. "How long has she been here?"

"Awhile," he said evasively.

"Awhile! What do you mean awhile? I've visited you on numerous occasions, and you didn't have the decency to inform me?"

"Decency?" Patrick asked with a bitter laugh. "Where was your decency the night you forced yourself on her?"

It took a moment for Jonathan to react to Patrick's statement. The idea that Ginny had even confessed she had lain with him bewildered him. Then suddenly, his thundering voice echoed off the walls of the room. "Forced! Is that what she told you?"

"No, but I know my sister, and I also know of your rakish reputation, Jonathan. I heard that one of our most respectable citizens caught you in bed with his wife, and even called you out."

"Ah . . . yes, Amanda Evans," Jonathan countered between clenched teeth. "Her husband might be respectable, but I dare say that half the men in Williamsburg have lain

189

between her legs."

"Even so, you showed yourself to be a man with unscrupulous morals. You took my sister's innocence, and because of that, she never leaves this place, for fear of being scorned and ostracized by the people of this town."

That remark really rankled him. "Excuse me, and I don't intend to sound insolent, Patrick, but I doubt anyone would know by looking at Ginny that she has lain with a man." Jonathan had no idea how he had just baited Patrick.

Patrick swallowed it, hook, line and sinker, blurting, "Well, they will in a few more weeks. She's carrying your child, Cross."

The blood drained from Jonathan's face. Finding his tongue, Jonathan warned, "I'm going upstairs to see her, and don't try to stop me, Patrick. I need to talk to her, understand?"

"She won't talk to you. She hates you, Cross."

"If so, then I want to hear those words from her own mouth."

"Then go ahead," Patrick said with a sneer.

An angry Jonathan stomped up the stairs, and, raising his fist, he pounded on the door. "Ginny, open up."

Her hand flew to her heart, and the last vestige of color drained from her cheeks. "No, go away."

"Open up, or by God, I'll break down the bloody door."

Knowing he would do just that, Ginny pulled back the latch and opened the door. Immediately turning her back on him, she scurried across the room and plopped down in the chair in front of the hearth. The fire was cheery and warm, yet it did not penetrate her icy flesh. Drawing her shawl tightly around her shoulders, she heard the boards creak beneath his feet, as he moved in behind her.

"Did you plan to keep my child a secret from me, Ginny?" he asked, grasping the back of her chair.

"Yes," she said quietly, her shoulders trembling. "I . . . I didn't want you to . . . to feel indebted to us."

"My God," he sighed. "Don't you think I should have a say-so in its future? No one is going to call *my* child a bastard. We will marry as soon as possible, and you'll return to Crossroads as my wife," he ordered, staring down at the crown of her head.

Just then the fire snapped a lusty red coal onto the hearth. Ginny jumped from her chair and grabbed the poker, pushing the coal back into the fireplace. At length, she turned toward him. For a moment, they curiously studied one another. Ginny noted he was as handsome as he'd always been, yet his dark eyes were now flat and unsmiling, and the planes of his face were hard and unyielding.

Jonathan swept her slender figure from head to toe. Her shawl had opened, and his eyes lingered on her softly rounded belly. Then his gaze moved upward to her face. She had lost weight. Her cheekbones were more pronounced, and dark shadows of fatigue ran beneath her eyes. Still, she was the most beautiful woman he had ever seen.

With a calmness that belied the trembling that shook her body, Ginny said, "No, Jonathan. After my baby's born and I'm able to travel, I'm leaving Williamsburg and starting anew. No one need ever know our child's a bastard. I can always say I am a widow."

"And might I ask how you plan to support yourself and my child?"

"There are mills up North that are always in need of—"

"No, damn it!" he roared at last, and with a few brisk strides, came to stand before her. His hands gripped her shoulders, his fingers biting into her tender flesh. "I want my own flesh and blood with me. Of course, I could take the child and raise it myself, and say its mother died during delivery."

Ginny jerked away from him. A quiver of pain shot

191

through her voice. "No! You can't do that to me."

A cynical smile etched his mouth. "The idea doesn't sound quite as appealing when the shoe's on the other foot, does it? Don't you know that one day the child will ask questions about his father? Could you lie and say I'm dead? I for damned sure couldn't do that to you. Such a secret would haunt you the rest of your life, Ginny. Wouldn't marriage to me be better to endure—than living a lie?"

Pain whipped through her. He cared naught for her, only the child she carried. Her hands moved to her belly, protecting and cherishing the precious life inside her. Yet, he spoke the truth. Still, could she also live the lie that she cared naught for her husband, for the sake of their child? Could she deny her child a future with his father, a father who could give him everything she could not? She did not belong in Jonathan's world, but this tiny life inside her was part of him and *did* belong. Things could be worse, she supposed. He could have offered to take her as his mistress, and supported her and his child instead of marrying her. Also, he could have ignored his responsibilities altogether, and left them to fend for themselves.

"Please . . . I . . . I need time to think, Jonathan."

"There isn't any time left for thinking, Ginny. According to my calculations, you are four months along."

"Yes, and everyone will know the baby was conceived out of wedlock," she cried, grasping to find any excuse she could.

"We have our child to think about now, and should not concern ourselves with a few wagging tongues." Jonathan was not being completely truthful when he made that remark. He wanted the community to accept his family. In years to come, he didn't want his child ridiculed by his or her playmates. A seed of an idea started growing in his mind. Maybe it would work. He had to try it.

Her shoulders slumping dejectedly, she consented, "Very

192

MORE PASSION AND ADVENTURE AWAIT... YOUR TRIP TO A BIG ADVENTUROUS WORLD BEGINS WHEN YOU ACCEPT YOUR FIRST 4 NOVELS ABSOLUTELY *FREE* (AN $18.00 VALUE)

Accept your Free gift and start to experience more of the passion and adventure you like in a historical romance novel. Each Zebra novel is filled with proud men, spirited women and tempetuous love that you'll remember long after you turn the last page.

Zebra Historical Romances are the finest novels of their kind. They are written by authors who really know how to weave tales of romance and adventure in the historical settings you love. You'll feel like you've actually gone back in time with the thrilling stories that each Zebra novel offers.

GET YOUR FREE GIFT WITH THE START OF YOUR HOME SUBSCRIPTION

Our readers tell us that these books sell out very fast in book stores and often they miss the newest titles. So Zebra has made arrangements for you to receive the four newest novels published each month.

You'll be guaranteed that you'll never miss a title, and home delivery is so convenient. And to show you just how easy it is to get Zebra Historical Romances, we'll send you your first 4 books absolutely FREE! Our gift to you just for trying our home subscription service.

BIG SAVINGS AND FREE HOME DELIVERY

Each month, you'll receive the four newest titles as soon as they are published. You'll probably receive them even before the bookstores do. What's more, you may preview these exciting novels free for 10 days. If you like them as much as we think you will, just pay the low preferred subscriber's price of just $3.75 each. *You'll save $3.00 each month off the publisher's price.* AND, your savings are even greater because there are never any shipping, handling or other hidden charges—FREE Home Delivery. Of course you can return any shipment within 10 days for full credit, no questions asked. There is no minimum number of books you must buy.

4 FREE BOOKS

TO GET YOUR 4 FREE BOOKS WORTH $18.00 — MAIL IN THE FREE BOOK CERTIFICATE T O D A Y

Fill in the Free Book Certificate below, and we'll send your FREE BOOKS to you as soon as we receive it.

If the certificate is missing below, write to: Zebra Home Subscription Service, Inc., P.O. Box 5214, 120 Brighton Road, Clifton, New Jersey 07015-5214.

FREE BOOK CERTIFICATE

4 FREE BOOKS

ZEBRA HOME SUBSCRIPTION SERVICE, INC.

YES! Please start my subscription to Zebra Historical Romances and send me my first 4 books absolutely FREE. I understand that each month I may preview four new Zebra Historical Romances free for 10 days. If I'm not satisfied with them, I may return the four books within 10 days and owe nothing. Otherwise, I will pay the low preferred subscriber's price of just $3.75 each; a total of $15.00, a savings off the publisher's price of $3.00. I may return any shipment and I may cancel this subscription at any time. There is no obligation to buy any shipment and there are no shipping, handling or other hidden charges. Regardless of what I decide, the four free books are mine to keep.

NAME

ADDRESS _____ APT

CITY _____ STATE ____ ZIP

( )
TELEPHONE

SIGNATURE _____ (if under 18, parent or guardian must sign)

Terms, offer and prices subject to change without notice. Subscription subject to acceptance by Zebra Books. Zebra Books reserves the right to reject any order or cancel any subscription.

GET
FOUR
FREE
BOOKS
(AN $18.00 VALUE)

well, Jonathan, I will marry you. But you must promise me, you will never touch me again."

"No, this won't be a marriage in name only."

"You would force me?"

"I didn't force you before, did I?"

"No," she admitted, lowering her head in shame.

His voice softened, yet the pain seeped through. "Why did you leave me that night, Ginny? All these months I've puzzled over the cause, feeling guilty that something I said or did sent you to your death."

She would never tell him what sent her flying from his bed that night—never. He could have called her any name but Christine, and she might have forgiven him. "If I recall correctly, you were drunk, Jonathan. Any woman would have sufficed that night. I just happened to have conveniently fallen asleep in your bed, while you were at the ball."

"I wasn't that drunk, Ginny. I damn well knew it was you in my bed. It was heaven we shared, not hell."

He saw her back stiffen and stressed, "Yes, shared. You had every chance to refuse me, but you did not."

"I know, and we are paying dearly for that one heavenly night."

"By bringing a new life into this world? In truth, Ginny, I cannot say that the idea of being a father devastates me. Rather, it brings me joy. I only wish you could see it in that same light."

I could feel joy, too, if I had the love of its father.

A soft knock on the door interrupted their conversation. "Ginny, Jonathan, may I come in?" called Mrs. Sutton.

Ginny drew in a deep breath and exhaled slowly. "Yes, of course, Mother."

Maureen entered and closed the door behind her. With a worried expression on her face, her eyes went from Jonathan to Ginny. "Are you all right, dear?"

"I'm fine, Mother."

Maureen looked at Jonathan uneasily. "Now that you know, what are you going to do?"

"What I would have done in the first place, if you and Patrick had told me she was here," he said rather irately. "Ginny has agreed to marry me."

His announcement brought a soft smile to Maureen's mouth. "I knew you would do the honorable thing."

"Was Ginny here the day I brought you the news of her death?"

Jonathan saw where Ginny had inherited her temper, when her mother snapped, "How can you even suggest such a thing? For weeks we mourned; we even held a private memorial service for her at our church. The day she straggled in here with that boy, sent us both into shock."

"What boy?" Jonathan asked, puzzled.

"Ginny, haven't you told him what happened to you before you arrived here?"

"No, I'd rather not go into all that, Mother. Please," she pleaded.

"He has to know, dear. He is to be your husband."

Jonathan shifted his weight to his other foot and demanded brusquely, "Out with it, Ginny."

"Oh, all right. I can see you won't leave me in peace until I do."

Ginny told him about being swept from the bridge during the storm and waking up in the Marlows' house, omitting the fears and the cruelty she suffered at Harold and Evelyn's hands. "They wouldn't let me leave, but Darryl— one of the brothers—brought me to Williamsburg."

"Where do they live?"

"I don't know. I could never find it again. Please, it doesn't matter now."

Her story seemed to placate him. "Very well, Ginny."

"When do you plan to marry?" Mrs. Sutton asked excitedly.

"Tonight, as soon as I find a preacher."

194

Ginny was mortified. "You can't get a preacher to marry us that quickly."

"Maybe not, but it's worth a try. When he learns of our problem, I am certain he will agree to a hasty marriage."

"You . . . you mean to tell him I am with child?"

"If I have to, yes."

Maureen went to her daughter's side and took her hand. "It's all right, dear, the reverend will keep it confidential."

"We'll marry here after Patrick closes the shop," Jonathan suggested.

"Jonathan, would delaying the marriage for three days matter that much? Then I can make Ginny a pretty gown for her wedding day."

Jonathan smiled. "No, we've waited too long as it is. Now, if you'll excuse me, ladies, I'll begin making the arrangements."

Jonathan descended the stairs. Noticing a customer just leaving, he stalled until the man closed the door. Patrick glanced his way with a sullen expression on his face. "Well, did I tell you right?"

Pushing his coat aside, Jonathan rested his hands on his hips and replied, "Partly. She was not too eager to see me."

"I warned you."

"Still, she has consented to marry me, with or without your blessings, Patrick."

Patrick's face turned a blistering red. "She did?"

"Yes. Patrick, we are to be brothers-in-law, and I want us to be friends again. Those times I spent with you and your mother helped me deal with my own grief. I only wish I had known the truth earlier, and we wouldn't have found ourselves in such a mess."

"Would you have married her, if you had not got her with child?" Patrick asked, studying Jonathan closely.

"The question is, would she have married me, if I had asked her?" he countered. "But that is neither here nor there now, Patrick. My responsibility now is to my unborn

195

child, and I will not have him or her labeled a bastard. You don't know what it's like—" he stopped, took a deep painful breath, and exhaled slowly, grateful he'd caught himself before he spilled the truth of his own lineage. "Please think about what I've said, and try to see that this is the only way we can settle the matter."

He stopped at the door, his hand pausing on the knob. "You might not believe me, but I do care for Ginny."

Jonathan used the walk to Raleigh Tavern to sort out his thoughts. He loved her, so why hadn't he confessed to Patrick his true feelings? But no, he'd said he cared for her. God's blood, there was a difference between caring and loving. He cared for a lot of things, his horses, his slaves, his home. But to say those three simple words, *I love her*—he had not permitted his tongue to speak. No, Ginny would not have married him under any other circumstances. She thought herself beneath him. He laughed softly. If she only knew . . .

He walked with long, brisk strides, his eyes on the steeple of Bruton Parish Church several blocks away. He wished he could give Ginny a church wedding with all the trimmings, but her deceit had made it impossible. Why had she done this to him? At least his own mother, aware that she could never marry his father, had allowed her son the advantage of knowing and being with his father. If he had forced Ginny that night, he might have understood her reasons for deceiving him and could forgive her. But her excuse that he had been so drunk that any woman would have satisfied him, was a damned poor excuse in his book.

In all those months they had known one another, he had hoped she had come to trust him. He had done everything possible to allow her to keep her home, without feeling as though he were giving her a handout. Of course, he had to admit he was the one who reaped most of the benefits. While she worked, he got to see her every day. That had

196

been his downfall. God, he remembered how much he had wanted to pull her into his arms and kiss her, yet had held back for fear of frightening her.

And then, as though someone had slammed a hard snowball against the back of his head, a thought burst in his head. *My God, I'd never even kissed her until the night I took her!* A wave of guilt washed over him. He had not even nourished their relationship with tender kisses or by holding her hands, but had taken all she had to offer him in one fell swoop. No wonder she didn't want him to touch her again.

Jonathan worried and mulled over that thought, until he reached Raleigh Tavern. He opened the door of the taproom and entered. Boisterous laughter along with loud conversation filled the room. Men eager to escape the winter doldrums had come here to pass the hours, playing cards or drinking with their friends. After the noon repast, they would all move upstairs to discuss business. Jonathan searched for Blue through the haze of tobacco smoke, and saw him sitting at a corner table with a pretty serving wench standing beside him.

Reaching the table, Jonathan tapped Blue's shoulder from behind. "I hate to bother you, friend, but—"

"Hey there, boss," Blue interrupted, smiling at him over his shoulder. "Have a seat."

"Blue, I need to—"

"This is Mavis," he interjected, winking at the girl. "Mavis, my boss, Jonathan Cross."

"Pleased to meet you, sir," she said, her eyes sweeping his figure admiringly. "Blue has told me much about you. He said you might be interested in meetin' Nola, my friend."

Jonathan gritted his teeth. "Blue, may I have a word with you . . . in private?"

"Sure, boss. Mavis, go get Nola and bring her to our table," he said, nodding toward a young woman bending

197

over a table and serving drinks.

As she turned to leave, Jonathan gently took her arm. "I think not, Mavis. I'm getting married tonight."

"What!" Blue shouted.

"You didn't tell me he was gittin' married, Blue," Mavis snapped. Pivoting on her heel, she angrily cut a path through the crowd.

"Bloody light, boss, if you didn't want the wench, you could've come up with a better story than that. Now Mavis thinks I'm a liar, and probably won't be speakin' to me again."

Jonathan took a chair across from Blue. He clasped his hands together on the table and leaned forward. "I was not lying, Blue."

"Humph!" Blue snorted. "You ain't even seen a woman, 'cept that Christine, and you're sayin' you're gettin' married. If that ain't a friggin' lie, then I don't know what one is."

Jonathan was enjoying the moment and couldn't help taunting Blue further. "Also, I am going to be a father."

Blue's face lost its color. "You ain't lyin, are you?"

Jonathan nodded slowly.

"How? I mean . . . Damn me, boss, this don't make one bit of sense."

"It will when I explain."

Blue listened intently as Jonathan spilled out his story about finding Ginny, alive and carrying his child.

"So, you see, we aren't exactly marrying under the most pleasant circumstances, Blue," Jonathan finished.

"It'll work out, I'm sure. You've got to admit, the months ahead of you can't possibly be any worse than the ones you've just spent."

Jonathan smiled grimly. "I hope you're right."

"Bloody light," Blue said, shaking his head in amazement, "gettin' married and findin' out you're goin' to be a father all in an afternoon!"

"Shocking, isn't it?"

"Damned right, it is," Blue said, beaming from ear to ear. "But how do you expect to marry so soon?"

"That's where you come in, Blue. When we were here at one time or another, I remember some man talking about a preacher in town who wasn't above taking a drink on occasion. The man said he always showed up on Sunday and preached a good sermon, so they ignored his habit." Jonathan withdrew a pouch from his pocket, spilling several coins on the table. "Now, this is what I want you to do, Blue . . ."

20

When Jonathan returned to the silversmith shop, he recognized Milly's voice as he opened the door.

"I like this one best, don't you, Patrick?" she asked, turning as she heard the tingling of the bell above the door. Her blue eyes lit up in surprise. "Why, Jonathan, how nice to see you!"

"My pleasure, Milly," he returned with a smile, then closed the door behind him.

He saw that Patrick's face had turned a sickly gray. For a moment, Jonathan thought the young man might drop to the floor in a dead faint.

"I've missed seeing you at the various festivities this winter. You did receive our invitation to come to the house and bring in the New Year with us, didn't you?"

"Yes, thank you for thinking of me."

"Are you coming?"

He didn't know how to answer her just yet. "I will try, Milly." Changing the subject, he asked, "What brings you into town on this snowy day anyway?"

"Mother's birthday is tomorrow. Father brought me into town to select a gift for her." She picked up the brooch she had been examining earlier and held it out for him. "Do you think she would like this?"

Jonathan took the heavy pin and turned it over in the palm of his hand. "Ah . . . diamonds and rubies. What woman would not appreciate such a gift?"

"Patrick made it," she supplied with a proud smile. "These are some of his other pieces."

Jonathan looked down at the small velvet-lined display case, filled with elegant jeweled brooches and pendants, both gold- and silver-mounted. "These are quite beautiful, Patrick. I thought you only lent your talent to silver crafting."

"In the past few years, Mr. Reynolds has been teaching me to make jewelry. His sight is failing, and he says he has always made good money from the sale of his jewelry."

"Do you also make rings?" Jonathan asked with a twinkle in his eyes.

Patrick's mouth went dry. *Oh god, he's wanting a wedding ring for Ginny. Why, oh why, did Milly pick today to come to the shop? She'll hate me for keeping Ginny's secret.* He glanced sideways at Milly as she picked up another brooch. "Yes, I have rings," he said, with a warning look in his eyes.

"May I see them?" Jonathan urged, knowing why Patrick was acting nervous. No one had informed Milly that her best friend was alive . . . among other things. *Yes, I would be nervous, too, Patrick.*

Patrick brought out another case, set it on the counter, and opened it. Jonathan's attention was drawn to an exquisite wide gold band, with a single magnificent pearl embedded in its center.

Withdrawing the ring from the tray, Jonathan held it toward the light that streamed in through the window. He visualized the lustrous pearl on Ginny's slender finger.

"It's lovely, Patrick," Milly sighed.

"It isn't an imitation, is it?" Jonathan asked, studying it closely.

"No. Mr. Reynolds has had the pearl in his possession for many years. Just recently, he asked me to mount it.

He jokingly said he had been saving it for someone special, but had never found her. He's still a bachelor."

"Yes, only someone very special would deserve to wear such loveliness," Jonathan said slyly, gazing at Patrick and noticing his face suddenly flushing. "I should like to buy it, Patrick."

Patrick coughed, then cleared his throat. "It is quite valuable, Jonathan."

"So is the person I intend giving it to . . . *soon*, very soon," he emphasized with a smile.

Milly jerked her head toward Jonathan and blurted, "Who?"

Patrick groaned audibly and, whipping a cloth from his apron, wiped his sweat-laden brow as he paced back and forth behind the counter.

"All right, just what is going on here?" she demanded. Crossing her arms over her chest, she tapped her dainty foot, her eyes shifting from Patrick's frantic pacing to Jonathan's amused face.

"I'm getting married, Milly."

"To whom?" Her hand flew to her throat. "Oh no, surely you aren't marrying that horrible snob, Christine Iverson. I will never forgive you, I promise I won't."

"No, not if she was the last woman on earth," Jonathan said laughingly.

"Well, what was I supposed to think? Several people have said they've seen her carriage coming and going from your home."

"They haven't seen me going toward *her* home, have they?" he teased. "After my marriage, her visits will surely cease."

"I doubt it. She'll probably pester your wife to death. Now, who is she? I'm dying of curiosity."

He glanced at Patrick. "Patrick will tell you. I want to talk to Mrs. Sutton a moment, then I have a few more

202

errands to run. If all goes accordingly, we will marry sometime this evening. And, Milly, I do hope you can attend on such short notice."

"Yes, I'll tell Father to wait for me. By the way, where is the wedding to take place?"

"Here," Jonathan said with a slow grin.

Milly cocked her head in puzzlement. "This . . . this is all rather . . . odd."

Jonathan chuckled as he walked up the steps. *Well, Jonathan Cross, you really are a bastard.* But if there was ever a time a woman needed her best friend, it was now. Patrick was as bullheaded as his sister, and would have put it off until it was too late. Milly would feel hurt that they had kept Ginny's survival a secret, but the pain would have been greater had she heard the news of their marriage through the grapevine. Yes, he had done the right thing, but he didn't envy Patrick the task of informing her.

He managed to get Mrs. Sutton aside for a moment, get Ginny's measurements from her, and learn the name of a good seamstress in town. Milly wanted him at her ball. He would go to her ball . . . with his wife on his arm.

When Jonathan went downstairs, Patrick was busy with another customer, while Milly was waiting anxiously for an explanation. She caught Jonathan before he left. "Why don't you just tell me, Jonathan?" she pleaded.

"No, Milly. Patrick wants to do it," he said. Tipping his hat, he smiled and opened the door, closing it behind him.

"Why should it be up to Patrick to tell me?" Milly wondered out loud, impatiently tapping her foot.

"I've upset you. I'm sorry, Milly."

203

"Yes, I'm upset. In a matter of seconds, I've just learned my best friend is alive and plans to marry this evening! Of course, I'm ecstatic after hearing such wonderful news, but to leave me in the dark is inexcusable, Patrick Sutton. We've seen each other at least a dozen times, and who have we talked about? Ginny," Milly said, sniffing and wiping her teary eyes with her handkerchief.

Patrick ached to put his arms around her, but he couldn't risk someone coming into the shop. They had already taken too many chances, seeing each other secretly. After Milly and Jonathan had come to tell him and his mother about Ginny's death, their grief over losing a dear friend and a sister began drawing them together, as they had consoled one another. Then their relationship had started taking a different turn, and though Patrick had tried to fight it every inch of the way, Milly had won the struggle. No matter how much he had argued with her that she deserved a better life than he could ever hope to give her, she said material things meant nothing to her. All she wanted was his love. Love, he could give her plenty of, but would that be enough when all was said and done?

"Milly, love, believe me, I didn't want to keep this from you, but Ginny made me promise."

"*Why,* for goodness sake? Why on earth would she want people to believe she's dead, then turn around and marry Jonathan? I'm angry with him, too. How long has *he* known she was alive?"

"Like you, he found out today."

"Today! And he's asked her to marry him already? Impossible! Doesn't he know banns must be posted before they can marry? Surely the Reverend wouldn't grant him a license until then?"

"One would think so, but money talks."

Milly stared at him in bewilderment. "You really are

204

telling me the truth."

"Yes." *Wait until you hear the rest, my dearest Milly.*

"Well, I must go talk some sense into both of them. Ginny deserves a proper wedding. There are invitations they must send, preparations for the reception after the wedding, and so many other things they have to do, I can't even begin to mention them all. I know Jonathan is delighted she's alive — as I am — but this is ridiculous." She turned and headed for the stairway.

Patrick intercepted her, taking hold of her elbow as she started up the steps. "Wait, Milly, maybe it won't sound as ridiculous, after I tell you the rest."

"The rest?"

"She's . . . she's . . . ah . . . going to—"

"Going to what, Patrick?"

"Have . . . Jonathan's b-baby."

Suddenly weak-kneed, Milly clutched the banister for support. For a moment she couldn't say anything. "Oh, Patrick, why did she keep this from me? Doesn't she know I would never abandon her?"

"Yes, Milly. That's why she didn't want you to know she was alive. It worried her that your friends would condemn you along with her, if you came to her succor."

"Well, if I should have friends that would behave so ruthlessly, then I don't want them anyway. If the situation was reversed, Ginny would have never let *me* down."

Patrick could no longer keep from touching her. He pulled her around the stairway to a secluded dark corner. "Milly, if I *ever* take advantage of you, please be strong enough to stop me. Sometimes it's so hard for me to hold and kiss you, then let you go. I could never forgive myself, if I put you in the same situation that Ginny's in now. I hate Cross for ruining my sister's life."

Milly lifted her hand and pressed her fingertips against his lips. "Patrick, love has a way of weakening our

205

strength. You blame Jonathan for all that has happened to Ginny. Please don't judge him too hastily. Ginny might have had her moment of weakness, too."

"Maybe so, Milly, but he knew better."

"Would it lessen your hate for Jonathan, if I told you he loves Ginny?"

Patrick arched his brow in question. "He told you this?"

"He didn't need to tell me. You saw his grief, as I did. It was the grief of a man who'd lost the most precious person in the world to him. And, Patrick, Ginny loves him, too, though she would never admit it. Only once did I see them together, but the attraction between them would have set the woods afire."

"There's a difference between desire and love, Milly."

Milly smiled impishly. "Oh rubbish. You're contradicting yourself, Patrick. Just seconds ago, you admitted you had difficulty in letting me go after kissing me. And even I know what comes after kissing."

"My god, Milly, don't say things like that," Patrick admonished, perspiration popping out on his brow.

Tweaking his nose, she grinned, "Oops, I hit a nerve, didn't I, love?"

"Indeed you did, Milly. You needn't elaborate."

"Oh, but I think I will," she teased. "Imagine you and I being together every day, as Ginny and Jonathan were when she worked at his house. We have only a few stolen moments together. What might happen to us if we had such a freedom?"

At that moment, the bell above the door tingled as a customer entered.

Milly pushed away from Patrick, and with a saucy tilt of her head said, "Think about that awhile, hmmm . . ."

With that, she turned and headed toward the stairs, leaving Patrick in an embarrassing state. *Thank God, I'm wearing an apron,* he thought as he went to greet his customer.

Shortly after Patrick closed the shop, Blue arrived with the preacher and knocked on the door.

Jonathan had been anxiously pacing the floor, worrying that Blue wouldn't find a suitable preacher. When he opened the door and saw Blue and another man, he sighed with relief.

"We here?" the man slurred, trying to focus his blood red eyes on Blue, as Blue steadied him.

"Yeah, Reverend Huxley, we're here," Blue announced breathlessly. "Reverend Huxley, Jonathan Cross."

The reverend tipped his hat. "Pleashed ta meetcha," he said, reeling back a step and then righting himself.

"A little coffee'll sober him up," Blue said, taking the arm of the heavyset preacher and maneuvering him into the room.

Jonathan groaned. "A wide-awake drunk is just what we need."

Jonathan briefly assessed the man. That he was a frequent imbiber of the spirits, was evident. Thready blue veins skated across his button nose, and his blue eyes, red-rimmed and waxy, bulged like a frog's. But even in his drunken state, he seemed to be a likeable man. Jonathan hoped he was trustworthy, too.

"Wheresa bride?"

"She'll be here shortly," Jonathan said. "Get the Reverend a chair, Patrick."

Patrick stood behind the counter as though in a trance, his mouth gaping wide. "Surely, you aren't going to let *him* marry you."

"Get us a chair, Patrick," Jonathan repeated, closing the door.

207

Patrick handed him a chair from over the counter, which Jonathan placed directly behind the drunk preacher. "Have a seat, Reverend Huxley."

"Thanks," he said, sitting down heavily.

"Put on a pot of strong coffee, Patrick."

"The women aren't going to like this," Patrick said, going to the fireplace. After mixing the coffee and water in the kettle, he moved it over the hot coals to boil.

"Whensa weddin'?" the preacher asked, his head lolling on his shoulders. Seconds later, he was snoring.

Jonathan rolled his eyes toward the ceiling, before they came to light on Blue's bemused face. "Tell me something about him."

"As far as Mavis knows, he's a good man. He's also a teacher, and the people around here say he's good with their children. He lives in a house on the street behind a tavern. He may or may not be the man you were talking about, but from what Mavis says, there's plenty of them around who take a nip or two."

Jonathan chuckled. "Are you sure he doesn't live *in* the tavern, Blue?"

"Don't worry, he'll come around shortly."

Jonathan asked Patrick to keep the ladies upstairs, using the excuse that the preacher had not arrived yet. They poured cup after cup of strong coffee down his throat, and afterwards walked him outside in the cold air, so he could relieve himself. A few times he hadn't made it in time, and a wet stain darkened the front of his pants. Now they were holding him in front of the fireplace, trying to dry his pants so he wouldn't embarrass the ladies.

Upstairs in their room, Ginny, Milly, and Mrs. Sutton anxiously awaited their summons. Ginny still felt ashamed that she had not let Milly know she was alive. When Milly had first entered their apartment that after-

208

noon, she had felt tense and awkward at seeing her best friend. Then Milly had crossed the room and hugged her; together they had cried a bucket of tears. Next they'd kicked off their shoes and sat cross-legged on the bed. Ginny then had related to Milly the story of her rescue and how she had made it back to her family.

Milly had had the good grace not to ask questions regarding the circumstances that had brought on her pregnancy. Instead, they'd talked about the pending birth of the child, and Ginny could not keep her voice from quivering, when she told Milly that everyone would know soon that Jonathan married her because she carried his child.

Milly tried to ease Ginny's mind. Taking her friend's hands in her own, she'd held them tightly. "Try not to think of that now, Ginny. Just be happy that Jonathan is an honorable man and wants his child. And he loves you—I know he does."

Ginny couldn't bring herself to mention Christine, so she didn't acknowledge Milly's remark.

For the occasion, Mrs. Sutton had given Ginny one of her better gowns to wear, her Sunday best, a dark blue wool with leg-o'-mutton sleeves. Though her mother was a size larger, the waist fit perfectly, due to the changes in Ginny's body. Ginny did not need fashionable clothing. She had not been to church, nor had she left the shop since her arrival, afraid that someone who knew her would see her.

"I have your hat ready, dear," Mrs. Sutton said, leaving her work table.

Milly had already fixed Ginny's hair, sweeping it up atop her head, in a cluster of soft curls that formed a halo around her small face.

Mrs. Sutton carefully placed the leghorn hat on her head. Trimmed with white ribbon, the brim was cut

209

away at the back and drawn up to the crown, with large bow strings and a rosette overriding her right ear. She'd added a touch of lace beneath the brim, as a bridal veil.

"You're sure you'll have time to make your customer another one?" Ginny asked.

"She isn't picking it up until next week, so I have plenty of time." Her mother handed her a small nosegay with white ribbon streamers. "Fortunately, I had some flowers left over from other hats I've completed."

Tears glistened in Ginny's eyes. "You've done so much for me already."

A soft smile touched her mother's mouth. "It isn't every day I have a daughter getting married."

"I have something for you too," Milly chimed in. She withdrew a wide blue ribbon from her bonnet and gave it to Ginny. "Something blue . . . for good luck. You can tie it around the stems of your bouquet."

"Thank you, Milly," she said, squeezing her friend's hand. "With you as my friend, I am already lucky. I am so happy you could be with me today."

"Me, too."

Mrs. Sutton added the ribbon to the bouquet and handed it back to Ginny. "Well, we're ready. I wonder what's taking so long?"

"Maybe the preacher changed his mind," Ginny said worriedly. Now that she had accepted the idea of marriage, she wanted to get it over with. She wound the blue ribbon around her finger. Yes, she needed all the luck she could get to make it through this ceremony . . . and through the rest of her life, she added grimly.

21

"Dear-hic-ly beloved—hic—" Reverend Huxley's head snapped back from the force of his spasm. His small black book slipped from his hands and dropped in front of Jonathan's feet.

Blue, standing beside the teetering preacher, bent down retrieved the book, and returned it to him. Reverend Huxley thumbed through it, hiccupping with each page he turned. He cleared his throat and began anew. "Friends, hic—today ish a sa-a-ad day for ush all. We have losht a fine Christian man and—hic—he will be sorely mished—" he coughed, "by hish family and friends."

Milly, Mrs. Sutton, and Patrick gasped in shock. Ginny's body turned as stiff as an iron poker, and the hackles rose on the back of her neck.

"Excuse me, Reverend Huxley," Jonathan interrupted in an unassuming manner, "I believe you are reading the wrong rites."

"What zat?"

"This is a wedding, not a funeral."

"Wedding? Y' don't shay. Hmmm . . ." Reeling slightly, he fumbled through his book for the correct page.

Ginny nudged Jonathan's arm to get his attention. He looked down at her upturned face, and beneath her transparent veil, he saw the deep frown creasing her forehead. "How could you do this to me and my family? I refuse to marry you under these conditions." She thrust out her lower lip petulantly.

"These conditions suit me perfectly." Jonathan took her hand and squeezed it. "Sh-h-h, trust me, Ginny."

"Trust you? Ha!" she said in a huff, and switched her attention to the minister as he continued searching through his book.

"Blue, find the page for him," Jonathan ordered impatiently.

"You know I can't read, boss."

Patrick had had all he could take. Marching toward the preacher, he jerked the book from his hand and found the marriage rites. Jabbing the passage with a pointed finger, he barked, "Here it is, Reverend—Dearly beloved . . ." He shot Jonathan an *I told you so* look before he rejoined Milly and his mother.

The reverend dragged the back of his hand over his watery, bloodshot eyes and resumed reading. "Dearly beloved . . ."

Time dragged by unmercifully. Ginny fidgeted, shifting her weight from one foot to the other. She didn't think her legs would hold her up much longer. She tried to fill her mind with pleasant thoughts to drown out the hiccuping, coughing, and drunken voice of the preacher, but Jonathan's mockery of their wedding day worked its way into her mind. What would another week have mattered anyway? Even three weeks? There was no way on earth that people wouldn't know he'd had to marry her.

Jonathan passed the time pondering their wedding night, unable to keep his eyes from lowering to the swell of her breasts beneath her plain gown. Could he even hope she would come to him willingly tonight? He had his unborn child to consider. Could he control his desperate urges, and slip inside her womanly softness gently? Even now, his body was reacting to her nearness, her clean sweet scent calling up passions that he had hoarded in his body for these long, lonely months. *Please, love, don't fight me,* he prayed.

The reverend finally reached the part of the rites where they would say their vows. After stumbling through the passage, he asked Jonathan to repeat it.

Jonathan's voice rose strong and clear. "I, Jonathan, take thee, Ginny . . ."

Her mind lingered on the words, to love and to cherish. How long would it be, before he returned to Christine's bed?

Ginny's voice was soft and quiet. "I, Ginny, take thee, Jonathan . . ."

The words, to love and to cherish, stood out in his mind. Would she ever feel those emotions for him?

Jonathan took her trembling hand and loosened her fingers from around the stems of her nosegay, then handed it to Milly.

He retrieved a small box from his pocket and opened it, removing the wedding ring. As he slowly slid the ring over her slender finger, she stared at him, her eyes marked with the look of a trapped animal.

He gently squeezed her cold hand in his warm palm. Ginny lowered her eyes, stunned to see the beautiful pearl ring encircling her slender finger. Then she heard him speaking as though from afar . . ."With this ring I thee wed . . ."

She looked up at him, her heartbeat quickening as she saw the hard planes of his face soften. Yet his eyes had turned dark and cloudy, as though . . . he desired her? Suddenly, a tremor rocked through her body as she thought of the night to come. She recalled his threat. *This will not be a marriage in name only.* Surely he would give her time to adjust, wouldn't he?

Ginny never heard the preacher's voice again, until he

213

slurred, "I pronounsh y'—hic—man and wife."

Reverend Huxley smiled like an idiot, the right side of his mouth drooping, his glazed eyes rolling like marbles in their sockets. Blue leaned in close to him. "Is it time for him to kiss his bride?"

"Orright," he boomed, "y' can kish—hic—the bride."

Sighs of relief swept through the small gathering. Ginny wondered if their sighs came from knowing the ceremony was finally over, or that Jonathan was about to seal their vow.

She tried to look everywhere but at him, as he lifted her veil and settled it over the brim of her hat. He cupped her chin and turned her head towards him, holding her steadfast.

In a low, husky voice, he said, "Never turn away from me again, Ginny." He fixed his eyes upon her in a commanding gaze, as he coiled his arm around her waist and drew her close to him.

A dizzy sensation swept over her as those same emotions she'd felt the night she'd lain with him began stirring inside her. The room seemed to close in around her, as she stared anxiously at his full sensual mouth nearing her own. Her mouth parted slightly and her tongue slid across her suddenly dry lips, leaving them glistening like dew on a red rosebud.

With a gentleness that belied the fire burning wildly inside him, Jonathan kissed her softly parted lips, and watched the glow of passion enter her eyes before she closed them. Caring naught that an audience was watching them, he pressed her head closer to him, and kissed her with such an urgency that it left her breathless in its aftermath. For a long moment their eyes held, and then they turned towards her family and Milly.

Ginny walked into her mother's arms, while Patrick offered his hand to Jonathan and wished them well. Afterwards, Milly embraced Ginny and whispered teasingly, "You're blushing, Ginny. No wonder!"

After they had put their signature on the marriage bond, Jonathan placed several coins in the preacher's hand and bid him farewell, hoping he was sober enough to get home. He then approached Ginny and, taking her hand, asked for everyone's attention.

"Before Ginny and I leave, I feel I owe you an explanation about my actions tonight." He paused, his eyes searching each one them. "The marriage bond that Reverend Huxley carries in his pocket is not dated today, but a week before Ginny's disappearance."

Mouths dropped open, eyes widened, yet no one said a word.

Feeling Ginny's slender body suddenly lean heavily against him, he wrapped his arm around her waist to support her. He gazed down on her startled face, and, his eyes locking tenderly with her own, he continued, "I apologize for putting all of you through this ordeal, especially my bride. But—any preacher in his right mind would have never agreed to conduct a marriage ceremony in this fashion. Reverend Huxley is not only a preacher, but also a teacher in this community. I am sure he knows that if he ever utters a word about this . . . ah . . . unusual wedding, his ethics would be questioned, and most likely, he'd lose his teaching position. I didn't like placing him in this situation, but *my* family's future means more to me than his welfare. Who knows, we may have even cured his drinking habit," he added with a chuckle.

"I admire your ingenuity, Jonathan," Patrick said with sincerity, "but people will still wonder, why Ginny left her husband so quickly after their marriage."

"They can speculate all they want. Should any doubter wish to investigate the matter further, he can not ques-

215

tion the date he finds recorded."

"Well, they won't learn anything different from me," Milly quipped.

"Thank you, Jonathan," Mrs. Sutton said, stepping forward and taking his hand. "Welcome to our family, my son."

Milly and Patrick smiled wistfully at one another, their minds traveling along the same avenue. If Jonathan and Ginny could make a future together, wasn't there hope for them, too?

After teary farewells and promises to visit one another soon, they all stepped outside to watch the bride and groom step into the waiting carriage.

Blue sat atop the coach. Jonathan drew a lap robe over them, and then the carriage lurched forward into the night.

Ginny's hands, one atop the other, laid in her lap. The lap robe covering her was warm, as was the inside of the carriage, yet she was cold through and through. Her thumb idly stroked the large pearl encircling her slender finger. The weight of the ring felt strange. Mrs. Jonathan Cross, mistress of Crossroads, its presence announced. Ginny Cross, she thought wistfully. *Hmmm . . . it has a nice ring to it.*

She still couldn't believe the turn of events. In the span of a few hours, her life had once again changed dramatically. In her lifetime she'd conquered a lot of things, but she feared this new event would be her hardest hurdle yet.

Suddenly, a strange calm washed over her, the anguish flowing from her as relief filled her being. For months she had not drawn a breath that had not been painful. But now, she no longer had to make decisions about her child's future. Jonathan had made those decisions for her. Their child would have the love of both parents. Jonathan might not ever come to love her, but he would never find fault with her as the mother of his child. Her hand moved beneath the lap robe where it rested on her stomach; she smiled softly.

Jonathan watched her, not missing a thing. He wondered about the smile. What was she thinking? During the wedding ceremony, she had stood stiffly beside him, her face a picture of despair and uncertainty. He supposed his features had been likewise. He recalled the awed expression on her face when he had slipped the ring on her finger. Had it been yearning he'd seen beneath the sorrow in her eyes? If so, could he exorcise this feeling of betrayal from his heart, and bring peace to their union?

He'd truly forgotten just how beautiful she was, and how headstrong. It was only a stroke of luck that he'd found her at all. Even then, if he hadn't stormed in and told her in no uncertain terms what they were going to do and what they weren't going to do, she would have refused him. Thank God, he was a seasoned gambler and his bluff had paid off. In truth, if he'd given her any time at all to think the matter through, she might have refused him. There was no way on God's earth that he could have truly forced her, had she set her mind against him. But there was the baby to consider, and babies belonged with their mothers and their fathers. He was truly ashamed of threatening her with taking the baby from her. Still, even as he'd voiced the thought, it was only a tool to force her to marry him. He would make her happy, he vowed to himself. After all, she was his Cinderella, and Cinderella had lived happily ever after, hadn't she? Oh God, if only it could be so simple.

He leaned over and took her hand in his. "You're freezing. Here, give me your hands. I'll get you warm."

Ginny didn't say anything, just did as he asked. His

warmth flowed into her. "I'm not really cold, I'm just scared," she admitted.

"You have no reason to be scared, Ginny. The servants all know and respect you. Even Willis grieved your disappearance."

"That old reprobate? You're kidding?"

"No, truly. He has moped around like he lost his best friend. All the servants have. You'll be a welcome addition in my household."

"Have they kept up their chores?"

"They have. And believe it or not, Nat has taken a hand in the preparation of meals. Thank God," he chuckled.

"You always did worry about your stomach. It's good to see that hasn't changed." She smiled.

"Can you blame me? Nobody else worried about it. On occasion I thought I was losing my mind. When Bertha's gravy began to taste good, I knew I was in trouble. You had to slice the damn stuff before you could eat it."

Ginny looked at him with an arched brow.

"God's truth, ask Blue. He cracked a tooth on her plum pudding."

She couldn't control her hoot of laughter. "Plum pudding? How do you crack a tooth eating plum pudding?"

Jonathan rolled his eyes. "Bertha failed to remove the pits from the plums."

Their joined laughter spilled through the carriage like sweet music. And for a little while, there was no mistrust or confusion stirring their thoughts.

Ginny felt Jonathan gently moving the ring around on her finger. "The ring is lovely, Jonathan, thank you. I recall seeing Patrick mount it."

"Do you know what a pearl symbolizes, Ginny?" he asked in an unusually tender tone.

218

"No, what?"

"Purity."

"Purity," she repeated with a sad little laugh. "Surely you mock me, Jonathan. I'm a far cry from being pure."

"No, Ginny, regardless that you are with child on this, our wedding day, on the night our child was conceived, you came to me an innocent."

"Please, I would rather put that night from my mind."

"Can you? I can't, nor will I even try," he said with finality.

His remark sent her heart racing. If only she could think it was love that had sparked their union, then she would not try to forget that night. She pulled her hands from his and cupped them in her lap. They were warm now, and there was no reason for Jonathan to continue to hold them, although she missed his warmth immediately.

The wheel hit a rut and the carriage swayed, knocking them against one another. Jonathan lifted her onto his lap.

"What . . . what are you doing?" she asked alarmed.

"Keeping you warm, both of you," he added, as he enclosed her in his arms and held her tightly against him.

Ginny closed her eyes and tried to relax, but her efforts proved futile. She pictured her child in her mind. Would he or she have Jonathan's beautiful black hair and dark skin, or her unruly auburn hair and freckled face? Oh, Jonathan was so handsome, and she was so plain. Please God, let our babe look like its father.

Jonathan fixed an intense and longing gaze upon her tranquil, lovely face. He hoped his child looked just like its mother. He could see the child now, snapping glittering green eyes and shaking a head full of reddish gold ringlets at him defiantly when he scolded him—or her— for some misdeed.

Ginny let out a little gasp. "Oh my," she said, pressing her hands against her stomach.

"Is something the matter?" he asked, his brows knitting with worry.

"No, I felt that little fluttering again."

"You've felt it before?"

"Just lately."

Ginny saw the hunger in his eyes. This is his child, too, she reminded herself. Then all her love for him leaped up in her heart and spread through her being like a flame. "I . . . I doubt you can feel it, but would you . . . like to see if you can?"

"You don't mind?"

"No, of course not," she lied, knowing full well his touch sent the blood singing wildly through her veins. She folded back the blanket and unbuttoned her coat. Taking his hand, she placed it on her abdomen, feeling the warmth of his skin through her gown.

"I don't feel anything."

"I don't either. I guess it's too soon anyway."

As he waited, he stared down into her green eyes. "He's probably tired from all his mother's activity today."

"You call it a he. What if it's a she?" she asked with concern.

"He or she, it's a Cross . . . that's all that matters."

Yes, Ginny thought sadly, that's all that matters . . . to you, Jonathan.

They were on the last leg of their journey. Ginny scooted from his lap and, sighing deeply, brushed the curtain aside. The darkness was brightened by a blanket of snow that covered everything. In the distance she could see the hill that she and Patrick had sledded every snowfall as children. Oh, the fun they'd had, then traipsing home frozen, not a care in the world. Maybe someday her child would sled that same hill. She'd have to be sure and warn him of the deep gulch at the foot of the hill.

The carriage stopped and Blue opened the door, extending his hand to help her down. "You're home, Missy."

Home, she thought. Would it ever be?

When her feet touched the snow-packed earth, she lifted her head to the mansion. It was as imposing as she remembered. The brightness of the night silhouetted the house. Wreaths of holly ringed the windows in holiday cheer, and candles burning in every window lent a welcoming warmth. *Am I home? Will you accept me and my child . . . shield us from the elements, and warm us by your hearths? Will we be loved and cherished in your bosom? Will joy and laughter supersede tears and pain?* These questions tormented her as she pondered her future in the beautiful mansion.

22

Willis opened the door and peered out into the darkness. He hesitated and rubbed his eyes, then peered again. "Miss Sutton, is that you?"

"Yes, Willis, it's me."

"Well, I do declare. Will wonders never cease? Now you be careful, these steps is as slick as a greased pig. I shoveled them earlier, but they just freeze over again right quick."

Jonathan took her arm and guided her to the door. Blue unloaded a small trunk and hefted it upon his shoulder.

Willis eyed the trunk, then eyed Ginny again. "It looks like you'll be staying a spell?"

"Yes," she answered simply.

"She's staying permanently, Willis. She's my wife."

"She's your—" The words registered, and he snapped to attention. "Yes sir." His mouth snapped shut, and even in the dim light Ginny could see his Adam's apple bobbing.

By the time they entered the house, several servants had gathered in the entry. Shouts of disbelief echoed through the rooms, followed by hugs and cries of joy that she was safe. Once more Jonathan's announcement that she was his wife garnered its share of shock and amazement. On the hills of that, Bertha and Nat came to see what the commotion was about. Nat took one look at

Ginny, and a whoop left him that shook the rafters. His eyes pooled with tears, and he enveloped Ginny in a bear hug. Her own eyes sparkled with tears as she buried her face in his shirt.

"My, my, you shore are a sight for these weary old eyes," he admitted, his voice cracking and his rough, weathered hands swiping his eyes.

"You look wonderful, Nat."

"Well, the same right back to you."

Jonathan put his arm around Ginny and drew her close to his side. "Ginny is the new mistress of Crossroads. She's my wife."

"Well, if that ain't the icin' on the cake," Bertha sighed.

Everyone glanced quickly at Bertha. Had she just insulted their new mistress? Anyone who had been at Crossroads any length of time, knew that Bertha didn't know anymore about icing than she did gravy.

"It's true," Bertha announced. "First of all, she ain't dead—that's the cake—and now she's Mr. Cross's wife. Yeah, she's the icin' on the cake."

Their collective sighs of relief could be heard around the room, when Jonathan patted her on the back and said, "Very well put, Bertha. I couldn't have said it better myself."

He turned to the other servants. "Your mistress is tired and hungry. While you put her things away, we will have dinner."

Ginny wasn't accustomed to anyone waiting on her. Several times she had to force herself not to get up. She didn't want to embarrass the servants. They seemed so proud to serve her. Nor did she want Jonathan to be ashamed of her. This new position would take some getting used to. She nibbled at the mutton chops, the spoon bread crumbled in her hand, and the rich rum cream pie stuck in her throat.

223

Jonathan watched her and finally commented, "Nat must have been at hand, when Bertha prepared the meal."

She couldn't help smiling. "It's delicious."

"You have barely touched your food."

"I'm not really hungry."

"Are you still frightened?"

"A little." She smiled weakly.

He wanted to ask her to give him a chance, to trust him. He wanted their marriage to work. But her deceit was still a sore spot, and he had his own healing to do.

"If you'll excuse me, I'd like to lie down."

"Fine, I'll be along in a while."

As she left the room, he watched the gentle curve of her back. The sway of her skirts tempted him to follow her and take her in his arms. But the proud tilt of her head reminded him that she probably wouldn't appreciate the attention. He soothed his nerves with a hefty glass of brandy and planned his next move. His wife's wardrobe was sadly lacking. Thankfully, he'd already employed a seamstress to see to Ginny's new wardrobe.

Word of her safety and their marriage would soon reach every corner of the community. He knew skepticism would lift the brows of many when they heard the marriage had taken place months ago. But with Milly's help, the lie should take fruit. No one would have the nerve to question the date of their marriage to his face, except perhaps Denby and Christine.

Ginny took note of the polished tables and the bright arrangement of holly and magnolia leaves that would remain in place until after the new year. Her hands trailed the gleaming handrail as her feet tread softly up the stairs. No one would ever know the courage it took for her to mount the stairs. Her mind was a whirlwind of the last time she'd used these steps. Heartbreak and shame her companions as she'd fled, knowing the man she loved, loved another. What would she do when faced with Christine?

As she passed the baluster, a servant was just pulling the door shut on one of the rooms down the hall from the master bedroom. "Your room is ready, Mrs. Cross. Willis laid a fire, and it's nice and warm now. Do you need me to help you with your gown?"

For just an instant her heart felt as though something pierced it. So Jonathan didn't want her to share his room. Well, that was just fine with her. Still, the moment she thought it, she knew in her heart it wasn't true.

The young servant questioned again, "Ma'am, do you need help with your gown?"

"No, thank you. I'll be fine."

Word of the sleeping arrangement of the master and his wife spread faster than a grass fire. There was a lot of tsk . . . tsk tsk . . . and tisk . . . tisk . . . tisk . . . going on below stairs.

Ginny removed her hat and laid it on the dresser, then kicked off her shoes and pulled off her stockings. Her room was sparkling clean. It was apparent that Jonathan had purchased new furnishings for the room since her departure. She could remember that this was one of the first rooms she'd cleaned, scrubbing the floor on her hands and knees. Now the floor boasted a fine carpet in gray blue, the windows were dressed in a deep shirred blue fabric that matched the counterpane on the bed, and the cushions were plumped in matching chairs that sat before the hearth. It was a comfortable room, nicer than anything she'd ever had.

She worked the buttons free and stepped out of her dress; smoothing it out, she laid it on the bed. After removing her petticoats, she turned before the mirror. Her pregnancy was beginning to show. Her stomach was a little mound, reminding her that was the reason her dress had fit so snugly.

She saw her hairbrush and mirror resting neatly on the dresser, and loosened her hair. Moving to the dresser, she picked up the brush and began the task of brushing her heavy hair. The chore was almost complete when a bellow of rage reached her ears. With hairbrush paused in midair, she rushed to the door to see what the ruckus was.

Just as she peeped around the door frame, Jonathan came storming from the master bedroom. "Ginny," he shouted, rattling the panes in the windows, his face black with rage.

"Jonathan, I'm right here."

"What the hell do you mean, *I'm right here?* You belong in my room, in my bed, and I'll have it no other way."

Without further adieu, he slammed the door back on its hinges and grabbed her arm. With Ginny in tow, he marched unceremoniously down the hall. He, in his rage, and Ginny, in no more than her camisole and pantalets.

His high-handed attitude struck pay dirt, sparking her anger and the stubbornness he'd so foolishly forgotten. She shook off his hand and dug her heels in. With arms akimbo, and her green eyes thunderous with indignation, she took a step toward him. Her hand shot out and a steely finger landed against his breast bone. "You, husband, are way out of line. If you can't make up your mind where you want me, that is your problem. But your manhandling of my person is my problem, and I will not stand for it. Do you understand?"

His anger evaporated like a mist. He couldn't prevent the smile that tilted the corners of his mouth. This was the Ginny he remembered, stubborn to a fault, with a quicksilver temper he would not forget anytime soon. As though just becoming aware of her scanty attire, he felt his knees weakening and hot embers of desire exploding in his loins. Her breasts pushed against the tight camisole, as her chest heaved with indignation.

"You're right and I apologize."

"This indecision of yours is becoming quite tedious," she offered, mollified by his apology. As she preceded him into the master chamber, he was hard-pressed to keep his hands to himself. At that moment his greatest desire was to stroke the roundness of her buttocks, and skim his hand down her shapely thighs. Yet he girded his passion and allowed himself only the pleasure of his well-trodden imagination.

When the master's door closed firmly behind him, it was no small measure of smiles that passed among the servants. Indeed, Jonathan Cross had met his match.

Jonathan leaned against the door and watched his wife, as her eyes darted around the room. What was she thinking? Was she remembering—as he was—the pleasure they'd shared?

She picked up the jacket he had tossed aside and covered herself with it.

His brow arched upward, and his eyes flared with passion. Little did she know it only enhanced her desirability.

She smoothed the rich fabric and cast her husband a furtive glance. "It seems I have a penchant for your clothes. I will return your coat, as soon as my clothes are brought from the other room."

"Anything I have is yours for the taking. Don't you know that?"

"If you desire the truth?" she questioned quietly.

He nodded slightly.

"Everything that I held dear, other than my mother and brother, has been taken from me. Still, I will do my best to make you a good wife. Even though it might have

227

been your wish to marry another, I will honor and respect your name." The last she said turning away from him, so he wouldn't see the tears in her eyes.

She didn't know he'd moved, until she felt his hands on her shoulders. "Ginny, I wished to marry no other. No one forced me to give you my name. I did it of my own free will."

Yes, but only for the babe, she thought sadly.

"Can you not exercise the same will and be my wife completely? Till death do we part—that was the vow. This is our wedding night, a lasting memory, no matter how we treat it."

"But . . . but what—" she questioned.

"Only good thoughts for tonight, promise?"

The strong hands cupping her shoulders and his warm breath touching her neck, snatched her thoughts from her head. A small tremor beset her body.

"Forget the past, and concentrate only on the future . . . our future." He lowered his head to the nape of her neck, and the coat she'd wrapped around her shoulders slipped unnoticed to the floor.

From the moment he'd discovered her in the silversmith shop, she'd vowed to be strong. She had learned a hard lesson, and she wouldn't need the same lesson twice. Yet the moment his lips touched her, her good sense sprouted wings and took flight. Whether she wanted to believe it not, she loved the feel of this man, his smell, his touch. Everything about him set her blood to boiling.

He wrapped his arms beneath her breasts and pulled her back against his hard body. He kissed his way along the column of her neck and the sleek line of her jaw. When he'd explored this avenue to his satisfaction, he turned her in his arms. Cupping the back of her head, for one long unsettling moment he probed the depths of her eyes. He saw passion and desire coupled with shadows of something he didn't quite understand. He would let nothing stand in his way. She was his wife, and he, her husband. There would be time later to clear the air of misunderstandings. He had his own shadows to deal with, but not tonight. Tonight was theirs and theirs alone. He wouldn't share it with unpleasant memories. They would make new memories, sweeter, stronger, and dearer than any intrusion from the past.

His mouth settled over hers, seeking, demanding her response. She didn't disappoint him. She twined her arms around him and nestled against him. They kissed with wild abandon, renewing the passion they'd shared that night so long ago.

He scooped her up in his arms and carried her to his bed. After pulling back the cover, he lay her down and began removing his shirt. Stepping to the bootjack, he removed his boots, then shucked off his pants.

She watched him, marveling at his handsome body. How could she have forgotten what a beautiful man he was? Even in the dead of winter, his body was dark.

He eyed her with a long passionate caress, and a smile closely resembling a leer tilted his lips. She laughed nervously and reached for the covers.

He shook his head, tossed the covers aside, and joined her on the bed. With the tips of his fingers, he began at her lips and traced a lingering path down her body. On his journey he loosened the ribbon and the tiny buttons on her camisole. Her breasts spilled into his hands. After caressing each one in turn, he moved on and flicked the tapes loose from her pantalets. Her body was silky and firm and quivered beneath his touch. He lowered his head and placed soft, wet kisses across her slightly raised stomach. She caught her breath and tried to lie very still, savoring every touch.

He retraced his journey and sought the welcoming

warmth of her mouth. He whispered words of passion and matched his movements to his declarations, bringing moans of pleasure from his mate. Her breasts were swollen and tender, yet his gentle handling of them sent her writhing beneath him. He plucked her nipples with his tongue, the hot moisture of his mouth sending chills over her belly and pleas from her soul. His utmost intention was to take his time, to fulfill his bride's every need. Yet her touch and gentle urging spun a cloud over his good intentions. It had been so long, and she felt so good.

She was hot, so very hot—he was hard, so very hard. They came together like two points of light in darkness, blending together, becoming stronger because of it. He plunged deeply, and she answered his thrust with equal ardor. They didn't think, nor speak—they felt, they moved in passion's fiery breath, until the winds of that same passion carried them to release.

With arms clasping her tightly, he rolled to his side. They lay in silence, each marveling at the depth of their union.

He smoothed strands of damp hair from her face and placed a chaste kiss on her brow. Still they were quiet, each fearful of breaking the spell they'd woven.

He took her hand, linked his fingers through hers, and rested it against his chest.

She could feel the strong beat of his heart and the gentle rise and fall of his breathing. Should she be ashamed of her behavior? Well, she certainly wasn't. They had a life to build together. Regardless of the shaky foundation, she was determined to strengthen it. Maybe time would be her ally, and her love for Jonathan, her strength. He'd told her they would make new memories. Did he mean to forget Christine? She meant to use every means at her disposal to speed the process along, if that were his intention. A deep sigh lifted her shoulders and she squeezed her husband's hand. *Her husband,* she thought as she drifted off to sleep.

The tiny smile that creased her face, caused Jonathan to puzzle over its presence when he leaned over her and blew out the light.

His joy was dimmed when the truth reared its honorable head and nagged him. What would she say, when she found out he was a bastard? Would she turn from him in disgust? He'd spouted his anger at her deceit, when in the same moment his lineage bellowed up to haunt him. He'd played her falsely and denied the truth, when he should have given her the opportunity to decide if she wanted to be married to a bastard. Could he honestly claim he was blinded by the knowledge that she was to have his babe? He thought not. It wasn't the telling of a lie that bothered him — it was the living of a lie that tore at his soul.

He felt Ginny shiver at his side and put his tormenting thoughts away. He pulled the covers over them and took her in his arms. She snuggled against him and settled in his warmth. His hand was resting on her stomach, and he felt a tiny movement beneath his fingers. A peace settled over him as he vowed to his unborn child — to love and cherish and to protect from those that would defame his honorable name. He sighed deeply as he lay with his wife in his arms, and their child growing beneath his hand. Twice in one day he'd taken vows, and he meant to keep them, come what may. Suddenly a tiny smile creased his mouth, as he thought of the things he'd said to Ginny about making memories. He'd do well to heed his own advice.

23

Jonathan was gone when Ginny woke up. She studied his rumpled pillow and a blush stained her cheeks. How could she . . . oh my . . . how could she be so, so *free* with him? It wasn't like their marriage was a match made in heaven. Yet when he took her in his arms, it felt that way.

A clatter in the hall disrupted her thoughts, and the door rocked back on its hinges. "Mornin', Miz Ginny, I brought your breakfast."

Ginny pulled the covers to her neck, as a fiery blaze whipped across her face. She didn't have a stitch on. What would Bertha think?

"Here, let me help you," Bertha said, unconcerned, as she set the tray down and hustled around the bed, picking up Jonathan's robe. "You can put this on." She helped Ginny into the robe and fluffed the pillows behind her head.

"This is too much trouble for you, Bertha. I could have come downstairs for breakfast."

"Now I don't want to hear it. You ain't no trouble a'tall. Anythin' is worth the smile on Mistah Jonathan's face this mornin'." For a moment Bertha became retrospective, then shrugged her ample breasts. "I'll be the first to tell you, it's been a long time comin'."

"What?"

"Dat smile on his face. But I figure it's there to stay,

232

now dat he's found you and brought you home."

I hope you're right, Ginny thought, straightening against the pillows.

Bertha placed the tray gently on Ginny's lap and busied herself straightening the room. "Water's a'heatin' for your bath when you're ready, and I'll see dat your clothes are brought in here."

"Thank you, Bertha."

"It shore is good to have you back."

"It's good to be back."

"I'll see to your bath. You eat all your breakfast. You've lost weight. We'll have to see if we can't fatten you up a little."

As Ginny sipped her morning tea, she thought it strange that the morning sickness was absent. Not even a twinge of discomfort affected her. It was the first morning in a long time that her stomach hadn't rolled and protested at the thought of nourishment. In fact, she was famished, and felt wonderfully good.

Ginny didn't know what awaited her downstairs as the new mistress of Crossroads. She was hesitant to assume her new position, but never one to put off until tomorrow what needed to be done today, she forged ahead.

It was open arms that welcomed her. The night before, the servants had been joyful that she was alive and well, not to mention married to their handsome master.

This bright crisp day was a new beginning, and Ginny had decided to model herself after Milly's mother—such a lady. At first she'd thought to emulate Christine, but decided very quickly that was not the kind of person she sought to be. As far as Ginny was concerned, Christine Iverson was no lady. She used her wealth and social standing solely for her own promotion.

Her own mother was a lady of the highest order, but had always lacked the funds to dress the way other ladies of Ginny's acquaintance did. She knew in her heart it didn't take wealth or social standing to be a lady. It was like the color of one's eyes—a person was born with the traits.

Putting her best foot forward, Ginny would try to control her temper and her impulsiveness. She moved through the mansion, straightening this, or repositioning a chair, or moving a vase.

She directed the servants with gentle encouragement and a helping hand. Willis seemed always to be at hand. They'd gotten off to a rocky start long ago, yet now Ginny wanted his approval. She was quick to ask his opinion, or for his suggestions on various household duties. She won his heart and his undying devotion.

Her main goal was the kitchen. Jonathan loved good food and Ginny meant to see that he got it, and plenty of it . . . especially sweets. With her best armor of gentleness and persuasion, she tackled Bertha's domain. Bertha didn't enjoy cooking, and lacked the knack for culinary imagination. As Ginny watched the preparation of various dishes, she spotted one of Bertha's helpers that could whip an egg white until it peaked and stood firmly in the bowl without touching the sides.

Amazed, Bertha questioned the girl, "Now how'd you do dat?"

When Bertha tried it, what she didn't send flying out of the bowl, was speckled with the yolk she'd broken when she tried to separate the egg. Her whites didn't peak, but laid limp and yellowish in the bottom of the bowl.

Laine was the girl's name, and she bubbled with enthusiasm, *and* had the gift of knowing invariably how a pinch of this and a pinch of that would enhance flavor.

Ginny took Bertha aside and asked her to join her at the table for tea. Bertha's face beamed with happiness,

234

because of all the attention from the mistress.

When they were seated, Ginny asked, "Bertha, do you like children?"

"Oh, yes, but I like babies the best."

Ginny had her solution. Bertha would be the first person she confided in about the baby, although she knew without a doubt that the news would soon be all over the manor.

"Bertha, I'm going to have a baby."

Bertha's hands shot to her mouth, and her eyes quickly became filled with tears. "Dat's 'bout the happiest thing dat could happen."

"Would you help me take care of the babe?"

"Nothin' would please me more. But what 'bout the meals?"

"Do you think Laine could take over your position, if we found her some help?"

"Well, I know one thing for sure, she surely does get a kick out of cookin'. Me, I never did want the job. It just sort of fell in my lap."

"It would be a lot of responsibility, this new job. We'll need to prepare a nursery for the baby. And a hundred other things I haven't thought of yet."

"I ain't scared of hard work. It's just with dat infernal cookin', I never could tell when somethin' was done. And I either burnt it to a crisp, or brought it to the table still kickin'," she said with a good measure of disgust.

Ginny laughed and placed her hand over Bertha's. "Everything will work out fine. You'll be happier in the nursery, and Laine can cook to her heart's content."

"Well, I know Mistah Cross puts a lot of store in his food. I'm afraid I've been a terrible disappointment to him."

"You've been no such thing. Don't you know I need a very special person to take care of my baby? I wouldn't

235

want just anybody."

"Well, since you put it dat way, I'll feel better turnin' over the apron strings to Laine. But here lately I've been doin' better with my cookin'. Your Nat's been helpin' me. He sure does holler a lot, though."

Ginny could never remember the gentle Nat raising his voice to anyone except to Blue, when he accused Nat of poaching. Still, she'd already heard about the squabbles he and Bertha had.

When Jonathan came in for supper, Ginny didn't say anything about the change in the kitchen. She wanted to see what his reaction to the food was first.

Laine had prepared a succulent roast of beef with a thick rich sauce. Green peas and carrots, a bowl of whole potatoes cooked and then fried a golden brown, and bread as light as a new fallen snow made up the main course. Ginny watched as Jonathan filled his plate with a look of dread. When he lifted his fork to his mouth for the first taste, she couldn't take her eyes off him.

His eyes slid shut, and a sigh of pure undiluted pleasure escaped him. He chewed slowly.

"Good?" Ginny asked.

"Hmmm, delicious."

Jonathan forked one of the potatoes and put it in his mouth. His taste buds exploded with pure pleasure, and the potato tasted just like a potato should. He eyed Ginny with disbelief. "You didn't prepare this meal, did you?"

She smiled and shook her head.

"What did you do, stand over Bertha the entire day?"

Again she smiled and shook her head.

"I know Nat didn't do the cooking. He was with me the entire afternoon."

"I've arranged for a new cook, if she meets with your expectations."

236

"What did you do with Bertha? I couldn't bring myself to hurt her feelings."

"If you approve, I've found Bertha another position. One she's more suited to."

"God, I don't care what it is, as long as she's out of the kitchen."

"I thought she could help me set up the nursery, and when the baby comes, she'll make a wonderful nurse."

Jonathan eyed her with a warmth that caused her heart to swell with pride. "You are very clever, Ginny Cross."

"Not really, it's just that I also have given a lot of consideration to your stomach," she said, her eyes twinkling merrily.

"Let me assure you, I'll be eternally grateful."

Laine cleared away his empty plate, and placed before him a large slice of feather-light Sally Lunn teacake, smothered with a thick cherry sauce.

Again Ginny enjoyed his reaction. After the first bite, he lifted his gaze once more to her. He tapped the spoon against his plate and pondered aloud, "I wonder if anyone has ever said the way to a man's heart is through his stomach?"

"If they did, I'm sure they wouldn't admit it," Ginny said, cocking a brow at Jonathan before she tasted the cake.

"What is the way to your heart, Ginny?"

His question caught her off guard. Her eyes shot to his, and for a moment neither moved. "I don't know what you mean," she answered softly.

"Yes, you do. Tell me what I can do to make you trust me."

"I can't give you something that I don't have."

"You mean you don't trust anybody?"

"I didn't say that. Trust is something that is earned. Maybe small children have blind trust. But as an adult, I

237

think it is something that grows little by little, somewhat like a seed."

"Didn't you trust me at one time, before the fire?"

"Perhaps it was misplaced trust, I don't know."

"We'll see."

Several days later Ginny had barely finished dressing, when a caravan of women were ushered into the bedroom. A tiny little woman with hair like corkscrews whirled into the room, commanding the entourage with short, clipped demands.

All Ginny could do was watch in openmouthed amazement as they took over the room, tossing bolts of fabric in every color imaginable onto the bed.

"Mrs. Tims is my name, and these are my assistants," she announced, swinging her arm to encompass the group. "Your husband has told me that everything you owned was destroyed in a fire, except what you were wearing at the time. I've come to replenish your wardrobe. And I might add that it's to be done in record time."

What Mrs. Tims didn't tell her was that Jonathan had doubled the price, to see that it was done quickly. Mrs. Tims had had to drop everything she was doing to take the job. But she couldn't pass up the opportunity for such a profit, even if she had to work day and night. To serve someone as wealthy as Jonathan Cross was a boon to her ability. Her reputation as a couturiere was well established in Williamsburg. Still, it didn't hurt to stretch one's self to the outlying areas, especially this wealthy plantation owner, for his wife's new wardrobe would only garner more business, when her friends saw the beautiful gowns. Every bolt of fabric she'd brought had been chosen by the young lady's husband, when he came into her shop to order a gown for the coming New Year celebration. She had to admit that he had an eye for detail and color. She could see by looking at his wife that his selection would only enhance the beauty of the gown, for she was truly beautiful.

"Mr. Cross brought your measurements when he selected the fabric for your New Year's gown. If you'll slip this on, it won't take me anytime at all to add the finishing touches."

Ginny nodded dumbly. She had no idea Jonathan had ordered anything for her. What was going on?

Mrs. Tims opened a large box, and removed the most beautiful gown Ginny had ever seen. She spread the garment across a chair, then helped Ginny remove the dress she was wearing.

Ginny held her breath as she stepped into the dress. Yards and yards of shimmering blue green taffeta swept her body. It was like looking into the deepest, clearest lake one could imagine. The fabric was cool as it settled against her flushed skin. The sleeves were tucked and gathered at her elbows. The dress fit perfectly. The bodice was cut simply, yet enticingly, and her breasts swelled above the fabric. No other ornaments cluttered the gown, and the simplicity only enhanced the beauty of the wearer.

Mrs. Tims turned Ginny toward the mirror. Lifting Ginny's hair, she coiled it around her hand, and held it so this vision of loveliness could be appreciated.

Ginny couldn't believe it was her own reflection in the glass. Her green eyes sparkled with something she couldn't describe. Was it Jonathan's fierce lovemaking of the night before, or was it the beauty of the gown? Suddenly the story of Cinderella came to her mind. It was true Jonathan had turned her life around, given her a reason to hope. He was her prince—if only he would

239

love her as Cinderella's prince had loved her. Yet, she had to be reasonable. He was a wealthy man, and she was his wife. He expected nothing short of the best for her. Even though she lived in a beautiful home and would wear beautiful clothes, it didn't make her Cinderella, because she lacked the vital ingredient to happiness. Love. She could pretend and play the wife to the hilt, yet like Lord Adelbert, no one could disguise the fact that she was just plain Ginny Sutton.

The bedroom door opened, and Ginny shifted her gaze from her reflection to the intruder. Jonathan leaned against the door, his eyes sweeping the vision before him. His breath caught in his throat. "Beautiful," he whispered.

"Yes, it's lovely," Ginny agreed, smoothing her hand over the glimmering fabric.

Mrs. Tims loosened Ginny's hair and moved away, busying herself with sorting through the bolts of fabric.

The dress was the last thing Jonathan had in mind. His wife was beautiful, and her beauty made the dress. The cut of the gown showed off the creamy column of her neck, and more breasts than he'd anticipated when he'd ordered the gown. The green of her eyes rivaled the coloring of the fabric, and yes, her lips were slightly swollen from his kisses. She was everything he'd dreamed and more.

"Thank you, Jonathan."

"You're very welcome, my love." He pushed away from the door and moved behind her. He lifted a heavy coil of her tawny hair, and watched as it curled around his finger. When he raised his head, his eyes locked with hers in the mirror. "Then you like the dress?" he questioned softly.

"Yes, very much."

"It needs something more, don't you think?" His hand

skimmed her bare shoulder and lightly played over the scoop of her neckline.

"Maybe if I had a piece of the fabric, I could make a ribbon for my neck. Is that what you mean?"

"Something like that. Let me think about it."

Ginny thought Jonathan would leave. Instead he made himself comfortable in a chair. "Did you bring the sketches, Mrs. Tims?"

"I did," she replied, handing him a stack of various drawings.

He flipped through the sketches, handing Mrs. Tims the ones he approved and tossing the others aside. One of the assistants helped Ginny out of the dress, and she scrambled into Jonathan's robe. Taking her place on the foot of the bed, she watched as he and Mrs. Tims selected the bolts of fabric for her new wardrobe.

Mrs. Tims's assistants couldn't take their eyes off Jonathan. They bumped into each other, stumbled against the foot of the bed, and became tangled in a bolt of fabric. Ginny was sure they would swoon at any moment. But she could understand. It was difficult for her to take her eyes off her handsome husband, too.

He lounged back in the chair with the greatest of ease, one leg propped across his knee. A white linen shirt spanned his wide chest, and a single ruffle crisply decorated the front. His dark brown kerseymere breeches fit his body like a second skin, and Hessian boots polished to a sheen hugged his muscular calves.

With an experienced eye, he chose delicate lawn and soft India cotton for undergarments, nightgowns and wrappers. He selected slippers of every color in the rainbow, reticules, muffs, gloves, handkerchiefs, and silk stockings. Mrs. Tims agreed to purchase only the best, if she herself couldn't supply something he'd chosen.

When Mrs. Tims reminded him that he hadn't ordered

any hats, he was quick to tell her they had their own source. Then he'd turned to Ginny and winked boldly. She'd blushed furiously and smiled softly.

After Jonathan left the room, Mrs. Tims measured Ginny from head to foot. When Ginny told her about the baby, the seamstress assured her she would make the dresses with allowances for the growing babe.

Mrs. Tims and her assistants left the same way they had arrived, in a whirl, leaving not so much as a thread in their wake. Ginny was exhausted. They'd pulled and tugged on her, and stretched and pulled her some more. The only thing Mrs. Tims hadn't measured was the girth of Ginny's belly.

24

The week preceding Christmas was one of the most peaceful times of Ginny's life. She kept thoughts of Christine and the doubts and suspicions of Jonathan's reasons for marrying her locked away. She determined to make this holiday season bright and happy for everyone. She brought the house to life, Ginny did. As she worked throughout the manor, humming a medley of Christmas carols, it wasn't long before the servants were humming also. Some even burst out in song. Jonathan himself wasn't immune, and caught himself humming as he worked. And laughter, what a wonderful gift, she also brought to Crossroads Manor.

Before he'd found Ginny, Jonathan had dreaded the holiday season in the worst way. The tragedy of losing her, then spending his first Christmas in America alone, was not conducive to a joyful spirit. What a shift his life had taken, when he brought her to Crossroads! Now he couldn't wait to return home from his chores at the stables. Something nice always awaited him, whether it be a garland-draped banister or the smell of some tantalizing dessert. Other times, it was Ginny sitting before the fire, stitching tiny baby garments.

He examined the gowns with interest and trailed his fingers along the delicate lace decorating the soft blankets, impressed with her skill. "I didn't know you could sew," he'd commented once.

She'd laughed and assured him, "I didn't either."

He and Willis had made much ceremony over the huge yule log they'd wrestled into the house. Willis never once uttered a complaint. Ginny was delighted, and immediately bundled up to go in search of holly to decorate it. Jonathan joined her, and they traipsed through fields and forest to find a holly tree Ginny thought she'd seen. She just had trouble remembering exactly where it was. They found a tree filled with mistletoe, that was a favorite nesting place for birds. She teased him that he could never climb the tree as well as she. Jonathan forbade her to even think about climbing trees in her delicate condition, and set out to prove he could get her mistletoe. His grunts of exertion drifted back to her as she danced around the tree, pointing out the cluster she desired. And for just a moment, she had to pinch herself to confirm that she wasn't dreaming. Could this man hanging precariously from the branches be the rake she'd heard so much about, the notorious gambler and womanizer that had sparked the gossips' interest for so long? Her husband?

When he dropped to the ground with his offering of mistletoe, it was a proud smile that he bestowed on Ginny. A fine line of perspiration beaded his brow, and his hair was littered with twigs.

He bowed deeply and presented her with the greenery. "Now, are there any dragons my lady would like for me to slay? I'm in a very generous mood today."

She curtsied deeply, taking up the game. "Not any that come to mind," she replied, accepting the mistletoe. "But the day is still young. It might come to me later."

"Let me know, if it does. Slaying dragons for my lovely bride can't be any more dangerous than procuring mistletoe."

244

She lifted her hand and placed it on his cheek, smoothing her fingers across a small scratch. "Thank you."

"And what does my lady have in mind for the mistletoe?"

She turned away as a blush stained her cheeks, and said softly, "A kissing ball."

"I'm sorry, I couldn't hear you."

"I shall make a kissing ball."

As she walked away, he scanned the length of her back and her trim buttocks, and followed in hot pursuit. The leer that encompassed his face would have given credit to any rake of his caliber.

"Do you have anyone in mind that you'd like to kiss?"

If he hadn't been on his toes, he would have mowed her to the ground when she stopped suddenly and turned to him.

"Could be," she answered boldly, then resumed her journey.

He rubbed his hands together in anticipation and followed. Just the thought that Ginny would initiate something as simple as a kiss sent his pulse racing. She bent to his will when he took her in his arms, responding to his lovemaking with abandon. Still, just once he wished she would turn to him and put her arms around him, and seek his attention without any coaching.

After they found the holly tree, they returned to the house, their faces were red with cold, but their spirits as bright as a summer day.

After supper, Jonathan relaxed before the fire in his favorite chair with a glass of brandy, and read. Ginny decorated the yule log they'd placed to the side of the hearth with the bright holly, then turned her attention to making the kissing ball. Jonathan couldn't concentrate on his reading for admiring his bride as she cut and arranged the stems of shiny mistletoe. Giving up any pretense of reading, he tossed the book aside and volunteered his services to his wife.

The smells and sounds that permeated his home in this Christmas season would remain in his memory as long as he lived. He saw everything in a new light, and developed an understanding of what the holiday truly meant. It was all about love, and the sharing of that love, and the giving of one's self.

He didn't miss England or the grand festivities that dominated his homeland. His father was the only thing he missed of England, and he had a deep need for Lord Oliver to meet Ginny. They didn't attend any of the balls he'd received invitations to. Instead they remained at home, peaceful and content, developing a bond neither was aware of.

Denby was the only blot on their contentment. He'd come by to get Jonathan's signature on various papers, and to relay the news that Jonathan's tobacco had been loaded aboard a ship bound for England and the London factors.

Ginny didn't know what Denby's reaction was to their marriage, and didn't want to know. He'd always treated her with contempt. Well, if the truth were told, she didn't think too much of him either.

To her utter amazement and delight, Nat and Blue assured everyone that they were going to provide a plump turkey for the holiday fare. As they went out of sight, they were arguing about who was the better marksman, and wagering everything from Blue's fine-soled leather boots to the tightly knit cap atop Nat's head. Ginny knew Blue had a special interest in the cap her mother had made Nat, for it would keep his bald pate toasty warm.

Jonathan had sworn that Blue would argue with a fence post, if it struck his mood. It was the Irish ancestry Blue claimed so fervently that caused the flaw, although to his knowledge Blue's feet had never touched Irish soil.

Ginny was quick to point out that it was no flaw, but instead, a matter of pride. And she also had Irish blood flowing in her veins. Nor had she ever set foot on Ireland's shores.

On Christmas day, her mother and Patrick came to have dinner with them. Jonathan and Patrick revived their flagging friendship and talked and laughed comfortably. When Jonathan took Patrick off to the stables, Ginny showed her mother the classroom that she and Bertha were planning to turn into the nursery.

Maureen wasn't displeased with the way her daughter looked. She was more beautiful now than she'd ever been. The shadows had disappeared from her face, and a rosy glow lit her cheeks. Everything would work out fine for Ginny and Jonathan—Maureen knew in her heart that this was so. Couldn't Ginny see the love shining from Jonathan's eyes when he looked at her? And Jonathan? Surely someone as worldly as he, only had to watch his wife to see the love she put into everything she did for him. Truly, love must be blind. But eventually, as their hearts came to recognize the feelings their heads wouldn't let them admit, their eyes would open.

Ginny had never seen so much food in her life. Slowly but surely, it was dawning on her that her husband was a wealthy man. She'd always known it, but Ginny had no concept of wealth. Yet every day she experienced his wealth in some new form. He wasn't boastful. He just accepted it. And he was generous to a fault. Everyone around him benefited from his riches, especially Ginny. But for someone like her, who had never had more than just the bare necessities, he appeared extravagant at every turn.

The holiday meal was only one indication. The table groaned with the bounty. Nat had indeed provided a plump turkey, that Laine had roasted until just the smell of it was mouth-watering. She'd also created a crusty game pie with the pheasant Blue had provided. And for the delight of any true Englishman, she'd cooked Jonathan a sirloin of beef. There was a fragrant baked ham and sweet potatoes baked in their jackets, dripping with butter, fresh mushroom, celery laced with a white wine sauce, creamy peanut soup, succulent scalloped oysters, acorn squash, cranberry relish, and golden loaves of crusty bread. And the desserts—Jonathan's taste buds were in high hopes as he waited expectantly to sample each one—Tipsy Square, plum pudding, spicy mince pies, and fruit cake studded with jewels of candied fruit.

They ate until they were miserable, enjoying every bite and the company they shared. After the meal, they settled in comfortable chairs before the fire. When it began to snow, they stood at the window and watched the gently falling flakes. As they stood there, Nat and Blue started across the yard. Ginny burst out laughing when she saw the pair. It didn't take Jonathan long to figure out her merriment and join the laughter. Nat was fairly floating across the lawn in Blue's fine-soled leather boots with his knitted cap still intact, Blue slouching along behind him.

Ginny told her family of the wager they'd overheard Nat and Blue making, about who would bag a turkey. Nat had wagered his cap and Blue his boots. True to his word, Blue had paid his debt, and Nat was the new owner of the fine boots.

Jonathan and Patrick enjoyed a game of chess, while Maureen and Ginny talked quietly. Always conscious of Ginny's presence, Jonathan noticed immediately when the conversation ceased. He turned to see what she was doing. Sitting in the chair, her head was nodding one way, then the other, as she slept. He pushed back his chair and scooped her up in his arms. "I'll be right back," he whispered, "after I put sleepyhead to bed."

Patrick and Maureen watched as he carried his sleeping wife from the room. They'd noticed also how Ginny had snuggled against his chest, and sighed peacefully.

As they stood in the doorway and waved goodbye to Ginny's family, she was overcome with happiness and couldn't help the tears that rolled from her eyes. She lifted her tear-filled eyes to Jonathan. "Thank you for a wonderful holiday."

"And thank you for sharing your family with me. Now, no more tears." He brushed the droplets from her face, and she smiled brightly.

The catch in his chest had nothing to do with her tears. He shut the door and prepared to follow his wife, when he noted where she was standing. "Wait."

She stopped abruptly, wondering what was wrong.

He moved toward her slowly. "I can't let all your work be in vain, not to mention my wonderful abilities at scaling trees. Something I've developed since coming to Virginia, I might add."

She laughed and followed his gaze to the kissing ball, hanging above her head.

"Mustn't let it go to waste," he said, cupping her face in his hands.

His kiss was light and gentle. Ginny responded in kind, as his hand slid through her hair until he was cupping the back of her head. The groan that escaped his lips told of his need, and the urgency of his mouth dictated that she join him in his quest.

Wild horses would have had trouble parting the lovers when they became absorbed in one another. They made good use of the kissing ball, until Jonathan decided he had more than kisses in mind.

For the second time that day, he scooped Ginny up in his arms and mounted the stairs. As before, she snuggled against him and sighed deeply.

Long after the lights were snuffed and the lovers' re-plete, a teasing voice vowed that anytime his wife wanted to go in search of mistletoe, he would be her willing companion.

25

Ginny heard the clock chime the midnight hour, and turned on her side to face her sleeping husband. The moonlight silhouetted the strong lines of his face, and his rumpled hair draped his brow in its customary position. Ginny couldn't ever remember seeing anyone as handsome as her husband, nor as persistent.

She'd made it through the first few weeks as mistress of Crossroads and wife to Jonathan Cross. How the days had flown by. The servants hadn't blinked twice, when they learned she and Jonathan had been married months before. It was really odd. They actually believed the lie. Now they could put reason to their master's devastation when Ginny had disappeared. That was Nat's answer. He'd told her in depth how Jonathan had searched for her and mourned her, never believing that she was dead.

So much had happened in such a short period of time. She was trying to adjust to the upheaval of emotions taking place inside her, and the daily changes in her body, and assume her position as wife to such a strong husband.

One setback that had hurt her deeply was when she overheard some of the servants talking about Christine. Apparently, Christine had been a frequent visitor at Crossroads in Ginny's absence. Oh, what had Ginny done? She'd made it impossible for Jonathan to be with the woman he loved. Now she had to attend a party where all the prominent families of Williamsburg and outlying areas would be in attendance. How she dreaded the party! That was the reason for her sleeplessness.

Mrs. Tims had delivered the gown. It was breathtaking. Ginny still couldn't believe she would be wearing something so rich. She only wished she could be a credit to the lady's beautiful work.

Milly was her best friend, and she would do everything in her power to make Ginny feel at home. And Jonathan played the part of the adoring husband to the hilt. But how would he react when faced with Christine? Could he still play his role? It was the thought of seeing Christine that caused her anxiety. What would Christine say? How would she treat her?

Please God, help me make Jonathan proud. I promise I'll love him enough to make up for the loss of Christine.

She sighed deeply and shifted in the bed. A warm arm encircled her waist, and a husky voice whispered, "Don't worry, it will be all right. You'll be the most beautiful creature there."

"How did you know I was worried?"

"I know you better than you think I do. Now go to sleep. Tomorrow is going to be a long day and night. I don't want you falling asleep on me, when we're seeing the old year out and the new one in." He pulled her into his arms. "I can't wait to show you off."

Ginny had taken a long leisurely bath and pampered herself sinfully. She'd learned early in their marriage that Jonathan had no compunction about interrupting her bath. He'd paraded through their chamber as though it were a public thoroughfare.

She'd often wondered how he knew when she was bathing. At first she had placed a screen before the tub. He moved it. She put it right back. Several days later it was gone from the room. She was self-conscious about her nudity and her growing figure. Jonathan wasn't self-conscious about anything. Once when she walked in on his bath, it had embarrassed her to death. But he'd been quick to ask her if she would shampoo his hair. What could she say? He was her husband, and she loved the task. She came to relish these times, nude or not. They developed a closeness that otherwise would have taken months or years to develop.

She sat before the mirror trying to tame her unruly hair. It was the bane of her existence. She'd washed it early in the day, so it would have plenty of time to dry. As she pondered her dilemma, she remembered pictures she'd seen of women who cut their hair short. She was sorely tempted to apply the scissors to her own mane. But she didn't know what Jonathan would think about the idea, and she didn't have the nerve to tell him what she was contemplating. After brushing out the tangles, she pulled it atop her head and studied her reflection. Maybe if she only cut several inches, no one would ever know. She took the scissors from her sewing kit and tested various lengths, to see how much she should cut. Deciding to cut the strands that always worked themselves free from her pins, she snipped the hair in front of her ears. Immediately she was sick. How had she gotten it so short? When she lifted the scissors again, a bellow of rage scared her to death and the scissors dropped from her hand.

"What the hell do you think you're doing?" Jonathan's face was black with rage.

"I'm trying to do something with my hair. It looks terrible."

He tossed the box he was holding onto the bed, and knelt beside Ginny's chair. "Don't you know how beautiful your hair is?"

Tears sparkled in her eyes, and she shook her head.

"Then I'll tell you," he pronounced, picking up the shorn locks from the carpet. He rubbed them in his hand and watched as they curled around his fingers. "When you were missing, I used to dream about you. In my dreams you were very much alive, and I could always see your hair; I could smell it and feel it. Sometimes you would be running across a field, and your hair would be blowing behind you like a banner. I thought you were running away from me, but I knew if I could just put my hands in your hair, you would be mine. I would have caught you."

Touched by his story, she placed her hand on his and watched as he wrapped a long reddish gold strand around their joined hands, binding them together. "Did you ever catch me?"

He shook his head.

She broke the melancholy mood by patting her stomach and laughing. "Well, you have now."

"Yes, but I had to catch you first. You wouldn't come to me of your own free will.

"I didn't think you wanted me," she added softly.

A soft knock on the door shattered the moment. "Do you need any help with your dress?" Bertha asked, opening the door.

"I'll help her with the dress," Jonathan offered.

Bertha smiled brightly and closed the door behind her.

"What about my hair? How am I going to fix it?"

"I've never fancied myself a lady's maid, but I have an idea that I can help you with your hair, if you will promise me never to take the scissors to it again."

"I promise."

"I would like for you to wear it down. But I know that wouldn't please you." Ginny sat very still as Jonathan brushed and brushed, then pinned and pinned until he was satisfied.

When he was finished, she examined his coiffure very carefully. He'd pulled part of her hair atop her head and pinned it. The rest he brushed until it lay in thick curls on her neck and down her back. Where she'd cut her hair, he coiled it around his fingers until springy curls bounced before her ears. He truly did a good job, and she was very pleased with the results.

While he bathed, she finished her toilette, then helped him with his evening clothes. He held her gown for her as she stepped into it, and fastened the tiny buttons that scaled the back. "You are very beautiful, Ginny, and nothing should detract from that. Your beauty is so great, it will only enhance the brilliance of jewels."

She looked at him with a puzzled brow. "I don't have on any jewels, Jonathan."

"You do now, my love."

He placed a diamond and emerald necklace around her neck.

"Oh, Jonathan, it's beautiful!"

"I believe this will work much better than a ribbon, don't you?"

The emerald sparkled against her skin, and the diamonds glimmered like an icicle in the light. Ginny couldn't believe it.

"Now hold still, I've never done this before," he cautioned, placing matching earrings on the lobe of her ears. With every turn of her head, the jewels sparkled.

Jonathan couldn't take his eyes off her. She was truly magnificent and a fascinating creature.

"But I don't understand. Why would you gift me with something so valuable?"

"The jewels belonged to my mother. Who more fitting to wear them than my wife? Besides, I'm sure it would please her to know that you're wearing them."

"Belonged?" Ginny questioned.

"Yes, she died when I was a boy."

"I'm sorry."

"It was a long time ago."

Ginny fingered the necklace and turned before the mirror, admiring the glittering jewels and her shimmering gown. "Oh Jonathan, you have outdone yourself with all my finery! What will people think?"

"That I'm a very lucky man."

She in turn was as enthralled with him. He was the

most handsome man she'd ever seen. The black evening wear enhanced his dark coloring, and the ruffles on his crisp white shirt stood firmly and neatly, a white satin waistcoat trimmed with silver threads hugged his beautiful body. The only jewelry he wore was a gold ring on his little finger. When she lifted his hand to study the ring, she asked about the unusual mounting.

"My father gave it to me. It has been in his family for generations. It's the family crest."

"It's very beautiful."

He dismissed the ring with no more than a shrug.

When they presented themselves downstairs, the servants were breathless with praise. Willis lent his arm to his mistress, and warned of the cold night. As if on cue, Jonathan produced a beautiful cloak for Ginny. It was a rich brown and lined with ivory-colored velvet, the hood lined with the same velvet and trimmed with a dark brown fur. There was also a matching muff, and once she'd placed her hands in the warm muff, Ginny couldn't resist burying her face in the soft fur.

"You'll spoil me terribly, if you're not careful," she whispered, as they stepped out into the clear cold darkness.

"It's about time someone did," Jonathan assured her, just before he placed a quick kiss on her lips.

Blue was waiting for them with the coach. He helped Ginny inside, before he turned to Jonathan for his instructions.

When Jonathan joined her inside the coach, he couldn't help noticing her smile in the lantern's soft light.

"What are you smiling about?" he asked, drawing her close.

"I just hope that at midnight this coach doesn't turn into a pumpkin," she said softly.

A train of carriages rocked slowly up the winding drive. The Vincents' brick, two-story home was situated on the summit of a wooded hill that overlooked the James River. Yellow candlelight gleamed from the windows, splashing over the long, sloping lawn.

Ginny perched on the edge of her seat, her hands fisted tightly in the folds of her gown as their carriage neared, and her stomach tightened into a hard knot. Many times over the years, she had visited Milly in her beautiful home. Yet this time she was arriving in a gown and jewels befitting a princess, instead of a faded threadbare shift. But even her clothes could not hide her origin. The people she would be with tonight had known her when she had labored in the fields, her body cloaked with dirt and perspiration, rather than scented soaps and fine perfumes. Also, most of them had pretty daughters they had hoped would become the next mistress of Crossroads, and that she had won Jonathan's hand in marriage would not sit well with them.

Their marriage would also unleash a wealth of demons in Christine Iverson. Ginny did not doubt the gossip she'd overheard between the servants. But she would not dare question them about her other nagging suspicions, for fear that word would get back to Jonathan. During those months, had Christine shared his bed? The same bed *she* now shared with him? That thought hurt her worst of all.

Jonathan took her hand in his and tried to ease her tension. "You'll do fine, Ginny."

A nervous little laugh escaped her mouth. "This has to be the most horrifying time of my life."

"Even more horrifying than our wedding day?" he asked teasingly.

"Yes, I'd rather face a drunken preacher any day than face these people."

"Ginny, Ginny," he said with a long sigh, "these people have known you for most of your life."

"Yes, known me as Ginny Sutton, the farm girl, the last person on earth they'd ever think would become your wife. If you'd married any one of the daughters who'll be here tonight, you would have received a dowry, more land, and . . . and . . . respect from your neighbors. When you married me, you gained nothing."

"I gained you and the babe, did I not?" he asked with the same seriousness.

"Yes. I just hope you don't regret it someday."

At that moment the carriage drew to a halt in the circular drive in front of the house. The Vincents' footman opened the door, and Jonathan stepped out, assisting her from the carriage.

"Have a nice evenin'," Blue said from his seat atop the carriage. "You look mighty fetchin' tonight, Mrs. Cross."

She smiled up at him nervously. "Thank you, Blue."

Taking her gently by the arm, Jonathan escorted her along the torchlit path that led to the house. Thick columns supported the narrow porch, standing like sentinels guarding the door. On the left side of the house was the ballroom that ran from front to back, and through the sheer curtains that draped the long windows, Ginny could see the people moving around inside.

The closer they came to the entrance, the faster Ginny's heart pumped. Her legs felt like lead weights, as she walked up the steps. The butler, Jonas, was already at the door, waiting for them. Ginny had known Jonas for years. In the times she had come to deliver hats and visit with Milly, they had always carried on a lengthy conversation before she'd gone to see her friend. It took a moment for the old butler to recognize her, then his brown face broke into a wide smile. "Why, good evenin', Miss Sutton, I mean Mrs. Cross and . . . Mr. Cross. Please come in."

"Well, everybody knows we're married," Ginny said uneasily to Jonathan, as they stepped into the foyer.

26

When they entered the foyer, a wide central staircase was the first thing that met their eyes. Resting on the landing was a long case clock, the brass pendulum catching the light from the heavy brass chandelier as it swung to and fro. Exquisite paintings with gilded frames and pale green damask adorned the walls. In the past, Ginny had paid little attention to the splendor of Milly's home, but now she noticed, for she lived in a house that was just as grand.

Ginny saw Milly and her parents standing outside the door that led into the ballroom, welcoming their guests. As she started toward them, Jonathan took her arm. "Your cloak, Ginny."

Her hand gripped the front of it, as she turned to him in alarm. "Do I have to? The . . . gown is so . . . revealing."

"No, it isn't," he scolded lightly. "You will see far more skin than what you are displaying now. Besides, you'll draw more attention wearing it. People will wonder what you are hiding, my love."

Reluctantly she released her death grip. Jonathan drew the cloak from her bare shoulders and handed it to the servant. Ginny glanced down at the full crescents of her breasts, and wanted to fold her arms over them.

If only she realized just how lovely she is, Jonathan thought, proud to call her his wife.

They approached the Vincents. Milly's face brightened the moment her eyes came to rest on them. As with Jonas, the Vincents greeted them as husband and wife. Milly excused herself from her parents, and took Ginny and Jonathan aside.

"Where on earth did you get such a beautiful gown on such short notice? And your jewelry is exquisite. You will be the envy of every woman here."

"Jonathan took care of everything, and the jewelry belonged to his mother," she added, smiling up softly at him.

Milly leaned in closer to them and whispered conspiringly, "I hope you don't mind, but I took it upon myself to spread the word of your marriage, and I *accidentally* let it slip to Edna Talbot that I attended your wedding before Ginny disappeared. And so no one will ever know that you'd been staying with your mother and Patrick, I also told her about the people that found you and nursed you back to health, until you were able to return to Jonathan."

Jonathan couldn't help chuckling. "You've been a very busy young lady, Milly."

"No, not really. One only needs to tell Edna, and word spreads like wildfire!"

"But your father surely knows otherwise, since he waited on you while you attended our wedding," Ginny said worriedly.

"No, he thinks I stayed late and dined with Patrick and your mother." She paused and her brow knitted into a frown. "I'd better warn you. Christine's here." Seeing Ginny's face suddenly grow pale, she added quickly, "Mr. Iverson's sister, Margaret, is a good friend of Mother's, and when she asked that Christine accompany her, there was nothing we could do."

"Don't worry, Milly, I will take care of Christine," Jonathan interjected.

"A man escorted them here, so maybe she won't behave like her usual self."

"Do you know him?" Jonathan asked, wondering at the identity of Christine's newest victim.

"No, I've never seen him before, and I was talking to someone else, so I didn't hear his name." Then she clasped her hands together and said excitedly, "But I do have some good news. Patrick's here. I doubt he would have come, if he hadn't thought the two of you might be here."

"Did Mother come?"

"No, Patrick said she appreciated the invitation, but she was behind on several orders and planned to work tonight."

Ginny knew that was only a polite excuse. Her mother would not have a gown suitable to wear for such an occasion.

"Well, shall we go in and find your brother, Ginny?" Jonathan asked, lacing her arm with his.

"I'll be along soon," Milly said. "We aren't having a large crowd tonight, only our closest friends, and almost everyone has arrived. Dinner will be shortly."

Milly took her position in line again, as Jonathan and Ginny entered the ballroom.

Ginny wanted to turn and run from the house. Every head turned in their direction. She heard conversations buzzing from behind several of the ladies' fans. Then she saw Christine standing with a group of men, and even from a distance, she clearly saw the contempt flashing in the woman's eyes. Ginny held her head a degree higher and squared her shoulders. There was about her a sudden air of jaunty, unconscious dignity, associated with a lady of quality. Yet, Ginny was not aware of this change in herself. Her most secret desire was to make it clear to Christine Iverson that she was no longer Ginny Sutton, but Mrs. Jonathan Cross. If she expected Ginny to be meek and just hand her husband over to her, she was in for a rude awakening.

His arm linked with hers, Jonathan led her through the immense room, lighted by dozens of candles and chandeliers. The room was full of beautiful costumes, velvets, silks, satins, and brocades, the rich deep colors of rare jewels. Ginny felt eyes following her and heard their whispers. They could not find fault with her gown, for truly she thought it more beautiful than any she saw. And Jonathan was right; in comparing her low-neck bodice with the others, she was not displaying half as much flesh. This raised her confidence a notch higher, and she beamed with pride.

Men stopped them as they walked through the room, and congratulated them on their marriage. Jonathan smiled to himself, as he saw the admiring glances his wife was receiving from men young and old. The wives were friendly to Ginny, but their daughters were cool and remote.

Ginny became extremely conscious of the gulf which separated her from the social positions of these people. As Jonathan's wife, she would attend more of these functions in the future. Her father had tutored most of these young women, and they had been friendly toward her then. She knew that if they were to become friends again, she would have to take the initiative. Overcoming her shyness and feeling of inferiority, she struck up conversations with them, her charming and sincere manner melting their resistance. She played on their vanity, complimenting their beautiful gowns and their stylish coiffures. Jonathan's eyes glistened with amusement, as he noticed some of the young ladies were not worthy of her flattery.

Ginny saw Patrick standing with Edna Talbot in front of the fireplace. He wore a helpless expression on his face. Edna had undoubtedly latched onto him the moment he'd arrived, trying to find discrepancies in the information Milly had given her. Edna was a plain-looking, plump girl with fleshy pink arms. Her large bosom bulged from her low-necked gown, and partially lost within her deep cleavage was a diamond necklace.

Catching Patrick's attention, Ginny waved at him.

"Well, well, will wonders never cease?" came Christine's

haughty voice from behind them. "Ginny Sutton and Jonathan Cross married."

Jonathan and Ginny turned in unison, surprised to see Richard Denby's arm linked intimately with Christine's.

"Christine, Mr. Denby," Jonathan said, acknowledging them with a slight nod. "I had no idea you knew one another."

Christine leaned into Denby and clutched his arm tightly against her side. "Oh yes, we know each other quite well, don't we, dear?"

Denby, noticeably flushed, replied, "Yes, of course."

Christine slowly swept Ginny's figure from head to toe, as though measuring her with a yardstick, then she turned her attention to Jonathan. "So, you've been married for several months. Why did you keep it a secret?" Christine asked, toying with a blond curl that fell over her breast. "Could it be you needed time to acquaint your wife with the social graces befitting a lady, before you broke the news?"

The blood froze in Ginny's veins. Jonathan, sensing her temper about to flare, pressed his hand against the small of her back and urged her forward. "Excuse us, Christine, Ginny would like to visit with her brother," he said, as though he never heard the comment leave her mouth.

"Don't let her rile you, Ginny. It's she who isn't the lady."

"You should know," Ginny muttered beneath her breath.

"What?"

"Nothing," she returned, and quickened her pace.

When they joined Patrick, Milly was with him instead of Edna.

Patrick smiled as his eyes traveled over his sister. "You look absolutely stunning, Ginny, like a princess who has just stepped out of a fairy tale."

Ginny glanced at Milly and saw the smile wreathing her face. She was also remembering their conversation at the river that day so long ago. "Thank you. You're quite handsome, too, Patrick."

"What did Christine say to you?" Milly asked. "From the expression on your face, it could not have been kind."

"It wasn't, but is it ever?"

Before they could visit, Jonas called the gathering to dinner. The Vincent dining room was large enough to seat their guests at one sitting. A damask tablecloth and beautiful embroidered napkins of excellent quality graced the long table. Ginny tried not to gawk, as she sat down and viewed the table from one end to the other. In the center of the table was an elegant epergne filled with sweetmeats. Placed symmetrically about the table were silver platters piled high with roast beef, goose, ham, and fish, along with an assortment of vegetables. Located at appropriate places were silver candelabras, their flickering flames mirrored in the silver dinner plates. She wondered vaguely if any of the silver pieces came from Patrick's shop.

Patrick and Jonathan sat on either side of her, at the end of the table with Milly's family. When everyone had taken their seat, Mr. Vincent gave a short blessing. Afterwards, Mrs. Vincent rang a small silver bell, and two servants entered and made their way along the length of the table, filling the crystal goblets with deep red wine.

Mr. Vincent rose, and when the conversation at the table ceased, he held up his wineglass. "Ladies and gentlemen, I would like to propose a toast to our newlyweds, Mr. and Mrs. Jonathan Cross." He smiled down at the couple. "May the years ahead of you be blessed with health, happiness, and prosperity."

Again all eyes were upon them, as the guests clinked their wineglasses against those of their neighbors. Ginny could not help looking at Christine. Proper etiquette required Christine to join in the toast, but as she raised her glass, she directed a venomous glance toward Ginny. She could imagine the toast Christine was repeating in her own mind. *May the years ahead of you be blessed with sickness, unhappiness, and failure.*

The men ate with hearty appetites, while the women ate

sparingly. Milly sat across from them, and Ginny watched her friend carefully, so she would learn the proper etiquette in formal dining. She needed to prepare herself for the day Jonathan might want to entertain his friends in such a fashion.

Christine, Margaret Iverson, and Mr. Denby were seated at the opposite end of the table. During the meal, Ginny would occasionally glimpse Christine watching her, probably trying to find fault with her manners. No doubt, Christine's upbringing would have made her a better mistress of Crossroads, but Ginny was determined to show Christine and everyone else at the Vincents that she would not prove to be an embarrassment to her husband.

After dinner some couples went into the drawing room to play cards, while Jonathan and Ginny joined the others in the ballroom. At the far end of the room, the musicians picked up their violins and flutes and began playing a minuet. Jonathan led Ginny to a settee. "I'll be back in just a moment."

He returned with two drinks and handed her one, then sat down beside her.

"What is it?" she asked.

"Rum punch."

She took a sip and screwed her face in distaste.

"Would you like some more wine instead?"

"Oh no, I'll . . . I'll get used to it." This time she took a deep drink. She coughed and her eyes watered, as the liquor burned a fiery path to her stomach.

"Careful, it's very intoxicating," Jonathan warned.

After noticing most of the women enjoying their drinks, Ginny was determined to learn to like it. She finished it and asked Jonathan to get her another one, but he refused her, telling her that Mr. Vincent would serve champagne near midnight.

She saw Christine hanging onto Denby, rubbing her breasts against him. Christine had definitely had too much to drink. Ginny was glad that Jonathan had refused her another one. No, she didn't want to be like Christine at all.

Yet her wine at dinner and then the rum, made Ginny become more daring with her words. She leaned into Jonathan and whispered, "Does it bother you that Mr. Denby and Christine are seeing one another?"

"No, quite frankly, they're two of a kind and deserve one another."

Ginny was struggling with herself to refrain from speaking of what was on her mind. He certainly wasn't behaving like a man who'd just lost his mistress. "You speak as though you don't like Denby, and he works for you."

"He advises me on business matters. He is intelligent and knowledgeable on many things . . . except his choice in women, it would seem. But someday I won't need him, and I gladly await the day I can release him."

"Christine likes money. Is he a wealthy man?"

"I pay him good wages, but not enough to support Christine in the manner she is accustomed to." The orchestra changed from the minuet to the lively tune of "Turkey in the Straw." Everyone lined up for the Virginia reel. Wanting to change the topic of conversation to something other than Christine, he said, "Patrick and Milly seem to be enjoying themselves."

Amazement struck her face. "I didn't know he knew how to dance," she blurted.

"He does it quite well."

"They look like they've danced together all their life."

Jonathan leaned down and whispered, "Do you think perchance, she has been giving him lessons?"

Ginny tilted her head in thought, and a sly smile curved one corner of her mouth. "I believe you're right, Jonathan. Now that I think about it, Milly came quite frequently to see Patrick while I lived with him. Also, there were nights when he came in late, saying he had been to one place or another. He always had this sheepish smile on his face."

"I noticed them making eyes at each other across the

table tonight. Do you suppose Patrick loves her?"

"I don't know, but I've known for sometime that Milly loves him. I hope he has more sense than to become involved with her."

"She's your best friend, Ginny. Wouldn't you like to have her as your sister-in-law?"

"Nothing would make me happier, but her parents will never allow it. Did you notice the man sitting next to her tonight?"

"Yes, William Braden. I've met him. He and his father came by my stables in the fall, interested in purchasing some horses this spring."

"He's the man Mr. Vincent wants as a son-in-law, not Patrick. His family is quite wealthy, and they've been friends of the Vincents for years. Milly thinks the world of William, but it's more of a brotherly affection. Her parents have always liked Patrick, but they've thought that he and Ginny were just good friends."

Jonathan was remembering the conversation he'd overheard between Milly and Ginny. In essence, it was the same conversation he and Ginny were having now. He had his Cinderella, yet she was still clinging to her old beliefs. How long would it take for her to realize that he wanted her as a part of his life? Would it make her transition any easier if he told her that he was an outsider himself, that he was deceiving everyone in this room by allowing them to think he was a person he wasn't? He wanted so much to tell her the truth, but the painful memories of another woman's rejection returned to haunt him.

Jonathan rose and took her hand. "Come, dance with me."

"I don't know how," she replied, alarmed.

"I'll teach you."

"No, Jonathan, I won't make a fool of myself and you. Besides, not everyone is dancing."

At that moment, Mr. Vincent came over to them. "Jonathan, William Braden and Rufus King are trying to get a table together for whist. Could I interest you in joining them?"

Jonathan turned to Ginny. "Would you mind?"

"Of course not. I know how to play whist, but do the ladies play, Mr. Vincent?" Ginny asked excitedly. Finally there was something she could do, and do well. Her father had taught her and Patrick at an early age how to play the game, and on many a winter's evening, they had played well into the night.

"Yes. In fact, several are playing now." He glanced at Milly as she danced with Patrick. His eyes suddenly narrowed, and a slight frown etched his forehead. "I'll ask Milly to join you, and you can get two other ladies to play."

It was then that Ginny realized Mr. Vincent suspected more than a friendship going on between his daughter and Patrick. When Mr. Vincent strode across the room to get Milly, Ginny saw the crestfallen expression on her brother's face as Mr. Vincent drew his daughter from the young man's side.

After Milly and Ginny took their seat at a table in the drawing room, Christine and Edna entered, their gaze coming to rest on their table. From the maliciousness Jonathan saw glittering in Christine's eyes, he knew the purpose of her mission.

27

Jonathan leaned down and whispered to them. "I'm sure they will insist on joining you. If you'd like, I'll get Patrick, and *we'll* play whist with you."

Ginny smiled devilishly. "No, let her join us, Jonathan. I will enjoy the challenge. Milly, it's been a while since we've played together. Do you remember how we used to beat Patrick and my father, when they played against us?"

"Of course, I remember," Milly said with a cheeky grin.

Mr. Vincent looked from Milly to Ginny. "Now, girls, Christine will know if you cheat. She's an excellent whist player. I've seen men and women leave the table empty-handed after gambling with her."

"For goodness sake, father, we don't cheat! We're just familiar with how the other plays. Hush, here they come."

Christine and plump Edna approached their table. "May we join you, or are you playing with them?" Christine asked Jonathan.

"No," Jonathan said, "I'm joining another table."

"I'm afraid, Christine, Milly should find herself another partner," Ginny put in. "It's been years since I've played."

"Don't worry, Ginny," Milly said, following her friend's lead, "I'm sure Christine and Edna won't mind playing a couple of practice hands first."

"Do you . . . ah . . . play for stakes?" Ginny asked hesitantly, a frown creasing her brow.

"Yes," Edna said. "Otherwise, why even play?"

"Then I think I'd best not participate." Ginny started to rise from her chair, when Jonathan placed his hand on her shoulder.

"Rest assured, ladies, I will cover my wife's debts." Jonathan opened his pouch and spilled several coins on the table in front of Ginny. "Now enjoy yourself, love."

Oh, I will . . . immensely, she thought gleefully. "Don't say I didn't warn you, Jonathan," she added laughingly.

Christine and Edna sat down, and Milly dealt the cards. The last card she turned up was a spade, so spades were trumps. Ginny had only three low spades, and her other suits were sadly lacking in face cards. The two practice hands they played, Ginny and Milly lost. Ginny insisted again that she shouldn't play. Milly and her opponents urged her to continue, assuring her that her luck would change.

Edna won the deal, and now they were gambling instead of playing for fun. Suddenly Ginny wasn't so sure of her or Milly's skill. It was obvious that Christine and Edna were expert players, and had played together often. Ginny planned her strategy, knowing Milly would realize what she was doing. She purposely played her cards wrong and appeared embarrassed afterwards, apologizing to her partner when the game was over. They lost several games in this manner, increasing Christine's confidence that she was playing with amateurs. Ginny cringed each time Christine and Edna raked in their winnings, hoping she could regain her losses as the game progressed.

After several hands, Ginny and Milly exchanged faint, mischievous smiles. They'd finally decided it was time to stop with the nonsense, and get down to serious business. Of course, Christine wanted to raise the stakes; she was winning. Ginny turned to Jonathan, who was playing at the table next to them, and apologized for losing all his money.

"When you reach the point where we'll have to wager Crossroads, let me know," he said with apparent disinterest.

Jonathan and the men at his table stopped playing, find-

270

ing the ladies' game much more interesting. Jonathan suspected Ginny and Milly were up to something devious. Ginny would never gamble away his money, without having a game plan in mind.

And he was right. From that point on, it was they who held the winning hands. Christine and Edna glimpsed worriedly at each other, but felt sure that their opponents' luck could not go on forever.

They were wrong.

By now, several people in the ballroom had heard about the intense card game going on in the drawing room, and left to watch the game. Patrick stood behind Milly and, catching Jonathan's attention, smiled knowingly.

Christine's and Edna's nerves were stretched to the limit. They became more determined than ever to beat their opponents. Jonathan noticed Denby moving casually behind Ginny, so that he had a good view of her cards. When Christine and Edna won that particular hand, Jonathan knew Denby was somehow signaling Christine.

He rose from his chair and positioned himself beside Denby. "I found out today that the price of tobacco is dropping," he lied. "I'd like to talk to you about what we should do."

"Now?" Denby asked, anxiously glancing at Christine.

"Yes, now. Let's step over here, where we can talk privately." As they walked away, Jonathan noticed Denby glimpse at Christine over his shoulder.

It was Ginny's deal. She turned over the last card; diamonds were trumps. Her heart pounding, she looked at her cards. Four mediocre diamonds with ace high. She glanced at the player's faces. Milly had a secretive smile on her face, as she casually stroked her chin in deep thought. Edna wore a glum expression, while a tiny frown line etched Christine's forehead and the vein at her temple pulsed rapidly.

Christine asked someone to tell Denby that she needed to see him. Leaving Jonathan, he approached the table. He leaned down, and Christine whispered in his ear. Christine had already resorted to borrowing heavily from Denby to cover her wagers, and from appearances he'd finally called a halt to it. She glared at Denby's back, as he returned to continue his discussion with Jonathan. She would die before admitting defeat, especially to Ginny Sutton Cross. Unhooking the clasp of her ruby and diamond necklace, she laid it on the table.

Mortified, Edna looked on, her hand moving to the strand of diamonds she wore around her own neck, and clutched it tightly. She saw her father standing nearby, his face marked with a threatening scowl.

"We both know this necklace is worth more than the money you've won, Ginny," Christine boasted. She eyed Ginny's necklace and earrings, and estimating they were worth far more than her own necklace, suggested, "Perhaps you would like to wager your pearl ring."

"No, this is my wedding ring," Ginny snapped. "Why don't you give up, Christine? Truthfully, I'm growing quite bored with the game."

The insult was Christine's undoing. "You have to give me a chance to reclaim my winnings."

Jonathan came to the table. "Ginny, I'll match the value of Christine's necklace."

There was a gasp of astonishment from the spectators.

"But," he added, "it isn't fair to draw Milly or Edna into your wager."

Edna nearly fainted with relief. "I . . . I don't mind being your partner, Christine," she said hurriedly. "But I . . . I can't wager my necklace. Father gave it to me on my last birthday."

"I'll play, too," Milly piped in triumphantly. She fairly itched to see Ginny win Christine's necklace.

Mrs. Iverson came to the table, a worried expression on her face. "Christine, dear, my brother gave you that necklace. It belonged to my beloved mother. Surely you have something else to wager."

"I am going to win, Martha," Christine hissed between clenched teeth.

From her show of confidence, Ginny and Milly both knew

she held a good hand, but her partner must be sorely lacking.

Jonathan made sure Denby could not see any of the players' hands.

The game was on. Christine did have two high trumps and won a couple of tricks, but Milly held length in trumps. Christine was banking on her long heart suit, but in the end she never got to play even the first card in the suit. Because of their experience in playing together, Milly and Ginny raked in one trick after another, draining Christine's hand of all her winning cards.

The game finished, Ginny casually reached across the table and took the necklace. Christine eyed her malevolently, before she slid back her chair, grabbed Denby by the arm, and stomped from the room.

Ginny rose from her chair and walked over to Martha Iverson, who was wiping her teary eyes with her handkerchief. "Mrs. Iverson?"

"Yes," she sniffed.

Ginny took the old lady's hand and turned it palm up, dropping the necklace into it. "I believe this belongs to you."

A deathly silence fell over the room, as the guests looked from one to the other. Ginny had won the necklace fairly and no one had expected her to give it up, regardless of the fact that it was a family heirloom.

"You . . . you needn't do this, Mrs. Cross."

"Yes, I do," she said with a soft smile. "My victory will suffice."

Cheers and applause broke out among the guests. Jonathan thought his heart would burst with pride and joy, as he watched one person after another approach his wife and commend her for her kindness. Beating Christine was not her true victory. She had won something much more valuable, respect and admiration from the people she had thought would never accept her in their world. From the confused expression on her face, he knew she had not intentionally set out to gain their approval, but had only done what her heart had told her to do.

He made his way to her side as a young woman was congratulating her. "It does my heart good to see Christine get her comeuppance, Ginny. I doubt we will see her gambling again for a long time."

"Hey," someone called out. "We're only ten minutes from the stroke of midnight."

The drawing room emptied quickly, as everyone moved toward the ballroom. Alone, Jonathan drew Ginny into his arms. "You are the most wonderful woman I have ever known."

Lowering his head, he kissed her gently, passionately, the moist, warm tip of his tongue finding passage into her mouth. Ginny melted in his arms and sagged against him. His kiss became bolder, as did his hand as it moved over her breast, his finger slipping beneath the bodice to toy with her hardened nipple. Ginny moaned in pleasure, her body arching against him, oblivious to the sounds of music and laughter drifting from the ballroom.

Milly came into the room, finding them embracing. Her face turned a fiery red when she noticed Jonathan's hand on Ginny's breast. Jonathan saw her, as she turned and darted from the room. Breaking the kiss, Jonathan chuckled huskily. "We'd better go, before we get caught doing our own private celebrating." He would never tell her that her best friend had already caught them.

When they entered the noisy ballroom, a footman passed them, and Jonathan whisked two glasses of bubbling champagne from his tray. As they joined Milly, Patrick, and William Braden, the music stopped, and they listened to the chimes ringing from the tall case clock in the foyer, announcing the new year almost upon them. Excitement filled the room as the people began shouting in unison, "Ten . . . nine . . . eight . . . seven . . . six . . ."

The great clock at last rang the hour of midnight, and the musicians began playing "Auld Lang Syne," and everyone sang along with it, welcoming in the New Year.

When Ginny looked up at Jonathan, her eyes sparkled in merriment as she lifted her glass, and together they drained their glasses of the bubbly champagne. Afterwards, he picked her up and held her against him, kissing her soundly as he whirled her in his arms.

All around the room, people were hugging and kissing and passing bottles of champagne from one to another, refilling their goblets again and again.

They witnessed Patrick kissing Milly, and William Braden kissing another pretty girl. Neither men's kisses were casual, as they held the young ladies in their arms, their lips lingering longer than propriety would allow.

"Oh no." Ginny nudged Jonathan. "Mr. Vincent's watching them. Poor Milly is going to have to do a lot of explaining after the ball's over."

Jonathan chuckled. "So is William Braden. Mr. Vincent and William's father had better forget the match they've planned all these years."

"Would you mind if I leave you a moment and freshen up a bit? Maybe Milly will see me leave and follow. I need to warn her."

"Of course. We'll leave as soon as you return. I know you must be tired."

"Strangely enough, I'm not."

"Good, because I have other plans for you when I get you home," he said brazenly, his eyes fixing on her breasts.

When he lifted his gaze, the heat in his eyes sent the blood rushing to her face. Her hand unconsciously moved to her chest, and she stammered, "I . . . ex-excuse me." She turned in embarrassment and walked quickly from the room.

As Ginny made her way down the hall to the powder room, she thought she heard someone speak her name and stopped abruptly. The voices seemed to be coming from the alcove beyond the powder room. She moved quietly along the wall, and stopped as their whispered voices became clearer.

"I'll tell you why Jonathan married that little ragamuffin, Richard. Because he's illegitimate, and thinks he's unworthy of a decent woman."

"Christine, it matters little what you think. He married

her, and there's not a damned thing you, I, or anyone else can do about it."

Ginny's face turned deathly pale. She looked quickly down the hall, making sure no one else was listening.

"Don't be so sure about that. I am sure Jonathan's father won't deed Crossroads to his son, when he discovers his wife is nothing but trash. In fact, he might make Jonathan seek an annulment, if he wishes to have the deed to his estate."

"Lord Oliver did not specify whom he wanted Jonathan to marry, only that he marry, Christine. And if he should happen to meet his daughter-in-law in the future, she would in no way resemble the Ginny I described to him in my letter before she disappeared."

"Well, all he has to do is ask any family around here, and they can tell him."

Denby chuckled. "After tonight, my dear, I doubt anyone would criticize Ginny Cross. And you have yourself to thank for that. What did you expect to gain by your foolishness anyway? Crossroads, perhaps?"

Between clenched teeth, she hissed, "I'm beginning to wonder where your allegiance lies, Richard, with me or with Ginny."

"Of course, with you, Christine, but I fear we are fighting a losing cause. Jonathan has already posted a missive to his father, informing him of his marriage. We will just have to wait and see what comes of it. Maybe you will get your wish, and Ginny will be out on her nose."

"Yes, and then Jonathan will ask me to marry him, which he would have done in the beginning, if Ginny hadn't cuckolded him into marrying her. There's still a mystery behind this farcical marriage, and I plan to find out what it is. From what Milly told Edna, a family found her washed ashore miles away from home and nursed her back to health. What I want to know is *why,* on the night of the fire, Ginny was at her house in the middle of the night, rather than in her husband's bed?"

"Christine, I saw the marriage bond. They didn't lie about the date."

"I still don't believe that for an instant." She paused. "I dread returning to the ballroom, but we must make an appearance . . ."

Ginny slipped inside the powder room and waited for Denby and Christine to pass. Jonathan . . . illegitimate . . . had to marry before he received the deed to Crossroads. No wonder he wanted this child to have his name! He was a bastard himself, and knew the hardships his child would suffer. A well of compassion sprang up inside her. She felt ashamed for ever considering keeping his child a secret from him. From Christine and Denby's conversation, she assumed Jonathan's father was nobility. But was it true, as Christine stated, that Jonathan felt he didn't deserve a proper lady as his wife?

No wonder Christine was in such a rage. From the gist of their conversation, she had known about his illegitimacy all along. She had wanted to reclaim her beloved home, regardless of his blemish. And Ginny, her archenemy, had unexpectedly ruined all her plans, when he showed an interest in her.

In the beginning when they'd first met, had he known then that he wanted her as his wife, simply because she wasn't a lady of quality? An avalanche of thoughts tumbled through her mind, everything seemed to become so much clearer. He'd kept it a secret that he owned her home, because he knew in the end he would have her as his wife, and she'd never know. He'd lured her into his house on the pretense of needing her as a housekeeper, when he could have found someone else better qualified. When she'd foolishly fallen asleep in his bed, he had had his way with her. If he had not mistakenly called her Christine, she would have probably continued sharing his bed, because she had loved him so much.

And she still loved him. Could his father have their marriage annulled? Surely he couldn't request such a thing from his son, when she was carrying his child? Now more than ever, Ginny firmly resolved to make her marriage work. She would prove to Jonathan's father—and to everyone who knew them—that she would be an asset to her husband, not a liability. Tonight, she would begin her mission. She vowed that in time she would also make him love her as passionately, as deeply, as she loved him.

28

Though January was a monotonous month, the cold weather keeping everyone inside, Ginny found plenty to do to occupy her time. During the day, she spent most of her hours in the nursery. The servants had moved the school furnishings to the attic, and had scrubbed the walls and floor. One of the servants had made new curtains with tiny blue flowers and dainty ruffles. Bertha was furnished with a bed and wardrobe, since she would be taking care of the baby. The only item the room needed was a carpet, that Jonathan had said he would order.

Jonathan ventured into the nursery frequently. Ginny knew he was checking up on her, making certain she wasn't overtaxing herself. One day he surprised her, by bringing in a cradle he'd bought from a shop in Williamsburg.

Also while in Williamsburg, Jonathan had asked around and found the name of a good, reputable doctor, and had sent for him to come to Crossroads and examine Ginny. Doctor Pritchet told them her pregnancy was progressing favorably, and gave them a list of do's and don'ts and what they should expect in the following months. If Jonathan should need him at any time, he said to send for him, but because of the doctor's frequent calls, Jonathan could not depend on him to be around to deliver his child. He gave Jonathan the name of a midwife, Mabel Wagner, who lived nearby, and suggested he contact her.

Shortly after the Vincents' ball, several young ladies Ginny'd seen there visited her at Crossroads, Edna Talbot among them. Ginny knew Edna was Christine's eyes and ears. Still, she gathered her courage and told the girls she was expecting her baby in early May, knowing they were probably counting the months in their minds, to see if the date coincided with their marriage.

Milly also visited frequently, and finally confessed to Ginny that she and Patrick were seeing one another secretly. She and William Braden had discussed their dilemma. The two families were considering a fall wedding. Somehow they had to convince their families that they did not belong with one another, because they each loved someone else.

When Patrick and her mother had come to dine with them one evening, she'd talked privately with Patrick. She didn't try to discourage him from marrying Milly, knowing her love for her own husband had changed her mind. Actually, she envied the young couple their deep love for one another. It wasn't a one-sided love, as it was with her and Jonathan.

Ginny discovered that loving Jonathan was easy, his treatment of her unselfish and gentle. Yet making him love *her* required more effort. He still kept a part of himself distant from her, and sensing its source was his illegitimacy, she sought to transform his pain into happiness and lighten his burden. Since the night of the ball, she no longer feared Christine's interference in their lives. Jonathan had supported his wife during the card game, and had appeared to take as much delight as herself in the woman's defeat. She assumed this was his way of telling Christine that their relationship was over.

Though Jonathan had not yet confessed he loved her, Ginny knew without a doubt he desired her. He made her feel beautiful, stroking her swollen belly and breasts with such tenderness, her heart overflowed with joy. Every night they made love, and sometimes during the day he would drag her from the nursery, telling her it was time for her nap. Ginny looked forward to these times, for he always left her so exhausted and satisfied, she sometimes slept the afternoon away.

Ginny forgot her own quest for happiness and merged her whole existence into giving unselfishly to her husband, hoping that in time he would gain dignity and self-respect in his own eyes, therefore strengthening the foundation of their marriage.

Jonathan, tired and distraught, stroked the mare's neck. She whinnied softly and nudged his shoulder. Earlier, his stable boy had rushed to the house in a panic, telling him one of his pregnant mares had started acting peculiar as he tended to her. Jonathan had grabbed his coat and gone to the stable, arriving shortly after the mare had aborted twins.

"I'm real sorry I couldn't git to de house sooner, Mr. Cross," Toby said.

"It wouldn't have mattered, Toby."

The boy sighed deeply. "I thought maybe I brushed her too hard or sumpin'."

"No. When a mare carries twins, there's always the likelihood of her losing one or both. She ought to be fine in a few days." Adjusting the blanket on the mare's back, he said, "I'm going to stay with her awhile. Would you please go to the house, and tell my wife to dine without me?"

"Sure, Mr. Cross."

After Toby left, Jonathan fed the mare and sat down in the corner of the stall. Drawing one knee to his chest, he laid his arm over it and rested his head against the wall. As he thought about the loss of his foals, his thoughts turned to his wife and unborn child. No man should ever take for granted that the seed he planted would bear healthy fruit. Yet, whenever he had allowed himself to think otherwise, he had brushed the doubts aside, not wanting to think of the possibility that such a thing could happen to Ginny and him. He knew that Ginny was stronger and better fit than most women, but that did not mean she could not have complications before or during delivery. She was approaching her sixth month, and looked the picture of health. Though Jonathan knew everything about the breeding and delivery of horses, he doubted his knowledge would help him if complications should arise.

Last week he had ridden out to the midwife's farm. Mrs. Wagner was a big, rawboned German woman with seven children, ranging in ages from ten to twenty. That in itself gave Jonathan reason to trust her skills. She was also a big talker, boasting about all the babies she'd delivered over the years. Jonathan asked her if she had ever stayed in a home when the time of birth was drawing near. Noticing his concern, Mrs. Wagner had smiled affably, and told him Ginny would know when to send for her. And yes, if it required staying with the mistress a few days, she would oblige. So Jonathan had left, feeling assured he had hired a good, dependable woman.

Almost overnight, Ginny had blossomed, the new clothes he'd bought her already becoming too small. Yesterday, Mrs. Tims had returned to redo the clothing. He'd overheard the dressmaker telling Ginny she must have miscalculated her due date. Knowing there was no way the date could be wrong, Jonathan worried that perhaps the babe she carried was too big for her to deliver without complications.

Immediately, he'd sought Bertha, and asked her if he ought to send for Doctor Pritchet. Right off, Bertha had set the matter straight.

"You don't have nuthin' to worry 'bout, Mistah Cross. Miz Ginny was jest late showin', dat's all. She had some catchin' up to do, so did it real quick-like. Lots of women-folks do dat."

"You don't think her small size will cause her to have a difficult time during delivery."

282

Bertha had not immediately answered. "It's true she's small, Mistah Cross, but even big women can have problems. Miss Milly tole me dat midwife, Mrs. Wagner, is as good as they come. She'll know what to do, if Miz Ginny has a hard time of it. Now, quit yore worryin'," she'd insisted.

But he did worry. He thought of the many times they had made love since their wedding night. Had he penetrated her too deeply? When she'd cried out, were her cries from pleasure or pain? He decided then and there, he would no longer jeopardize his wife's or child's life to satisfy his own needs.

Jonathan stood up, and seeing that the mare had plenty of oats and water, left to check another mare that was due to foal in the spring.

When he stepped outside to the corridor, he heard a familiar voice say, "Oh, there you are."

Jonathan felt the hair rising to salute on the back of his neck. He turned to see Christine standing just inside the door of the stable. He had not seen her since the Vincents' ball. He'd thought she'd finally given up her pursuit of him, but here she was again.

"What are you doing here?" he asked with an exasperated sigh.

"Now, Jonathan," she crooned, "is that any way to greet your visitor? But in answer to your question, I was making a call on your wife. Willis said she was indisposed at the moment, and as I was leaving, the stable boy arrived and delivered your message."

"I don't have time to visit with you either, Christine," he snapped, and entered one of the stalls.

She followed him. He knew she would. He glanced behind him before he knelt beside the mare. She had removed her fur hat and unpinned her wealth of blond hair, until it cascaded like a rippling waterfall over her shoulders. *Bloody light, she's the most brazen bitch I've ever chanced to meet.*

Jonathan turned to the mare and gently massaged her udders, to prevent resentment when the foal first nuzzled to obtain sustenance. The horse snorted and turned her head toward him, then tried to take a nip out of his shoulder.

"I suppose pregnant horses are like pregnant women. They don't like you touching them."

He ignored her and rubbed the mare's belly, whispering soothingly.

After several moments of silence, Christine stepped in closer and leaned over, lightly raking her long nails through his hair. "I wouldn't mind at all if you touched me, Jonathan," she purred.

Shivers ran along his spine, not shivers of passion, but of anger. He stood up and turned to face her. "Damn it, I don't want you. What do I have to do to convince you?"

"Perhaps it is *I* who should convince you." She leaned into him and whispered, "I heard Ginny's expecting a baby."

"You state that fact as though it's a deep dark secret. It isn't. Our baby's due in a couple of months."

"*Our* baby, Jonathan?" she asked, one eyebrow winging up askance. "Are you sure it's yours?"

A red-hot fury whipped through him. He felt his hands drawing into tight fists at his sides, as he fought the raging desire to wrap them around her neck and choke the very life from her. "Christine, get out!" he snapped, baring his teeth like a mad dog.

"Jonathan," Ginny called out from the corridor. "I brought you something to eat."

"Oh God," he groaned.

Christine quickly turned from him and brushed her cloak aside, loosening the buttons of her bodice. Placing her hands on her hips, she anchored the cloak behind her.

Ginny pushed open the gate of the stall. She froze. Her heart stopped beating, and she bit the inside of her lip until she tasted blood, as she viewed Christine's wanton dishevelment. Her bodice was unbuttoned to her waist, her hair unbound and mussed. One long strand draped one breast, while the other breast spilled over the top of her undergarment. Her dark, taut nipples were clearly defined beneath the fine lace.

"Well, what a pleasant surprise," Christine said, buttoning the neck of her cloak. She swept Ginny's plump figure. "You poor dear, you must be miserably uncomfortable."

Ginny's eyes shot up to Christine's face, and saw victory magnified in the depths of her eyes. Then she riveted her gaze toward Jonathan. The look she cast him cut through him like a thousand knives. All the happiness they had shared faded into nothingness before his eyes.

Ginny scorned Christine. Though she was falling apart inside, she managed to keep her voice from shaking as she said to Jonathan, "Willis said your mare lost her twins. I'm sorry." Walking past Christine, her head held high, she gave him the cloth sack. "Since you are unable to join me for dinner, I brought it to you . . . *dear*," she stressed, her green eyes snapping dangerously.

Turning on her heel, she strode toward the gate, then paused and glanced at Christine. "Before you leave, Christine, perhaps you would like to come to the house and see the changes I've made . . . since you were last here," she added subtly.

"Changes?" Christine asked uneasily.

"Yes, I've completely redecorated the master bedroom. We've bought new furnishings and rid it of those heavy, dark drapes. The rug didn't match the new curtains or bedcoverings, so I removed it and gave it to Bertha."

"That's an Aubusson carpet! My parents paid a fortune for it."

"Oh?" Ginny shrugged her shoulders. "Well, I'll tell Bertha. She'll take good care of it, I'm sure."

Jonathan stared at his wife in amazement. Revenge, her goal, she had delivered it as swift and true as an arrow, hitting the mark right on target.

"If you two will excuse me, Laine is holding dinner for me."

After Ginny left, Christine turned angrily to Jonathan. "How can you let her do this, Jonathan? She knows nothing about decorating and will ruin my—your home," she quickly corrected.

"It's her home, too, Christine, and she can do anything she wants to it. You'd be amazed at what she can do with sack cloth and straw mats—a touch of ribbon here and a little fringe there. Why, it looks wonderful."

"Oh God, she didn't," Christine muttered.

"Would you like to go up with me and see her efforts?"

Christine had completely forgotten her purpose for seeking him out, her thoughts only on the disastrous state of her home. "No, I couldn't bear it. Good day, Jonathan," she said and hurriedly left the stable.

Jonathan stepped outside to the corridor and heard her carriage leaving. He stayed at the stable for another hour, not to tend to his animals, but to give Ginny time to cool her temper. Surely she couldn't blame him for Christine barging in on him. Didn't she realize Christine was grasping at straws in trying to find a way to drive a wedge between them? The absurd remark she'd made about the child not belonging to him had really riled him.

The instant Jonathan entered the house, he knew something was wrong. He cocked his head and listened to the sounds going on upstairs. He heard Willis ask, "Where do you want this, Mrs. Cross?"

Another servant said, "You don't need to be pullin' that trunk, ma'am. I ken get it."

Jonathan took the steps three at a time and ran toward the master suite, weaving his way through the furniture that cluttered the hall. At the same instant he reached the door, a servant backed out, and he fell on top of her.

Ginny's hand flew to her mouth when she heard the whoosh of air leave the girl's mouth, as Jonathan flattened her against the trunk.

Jonathan righted himself and helped the poor servant to her feet. Blood dripped from her chin.

"Oh goodness," Ginny said, running toward the girl. She pulled her handkerchief from her pocket and wiped away the blood. "Tansy, you've cut your chin. Do you hurt anywhere else?"

"All over," she groaned, "but ain't nothin' broken, I don't reckon."

"Willis, take her downstairs and have Laine tend to her."

Bertha could see the rage in her master's eyes, and knew she wanted to be anywhere besides where she was now. She saw several servants lingering in the hall, waiting to be told what to do next. Bertha cleared her throat. "Uh . . . you want us to . . . uh . . . work in the guest room awhile, Miz Ginny?"

"Yes, please do," Jonathan growled, his mouth tightened into a thin, white line.

Bertha quit the room quicker than a hiccup.

Jonathan closed the door and turned toward his wife, glaring at her.

Ginny glared back at him.

Finally he spoke. "That could've been you I just smashed."

"But it wasn't," she countered, raising to her full height.

He looked around the room. All that remained was the bed, and it was missing its mattress and canopy. His eyes cut toward Ginny. "Did you think you could move two rooms of furniture, before Christine took up your invitation?"

"Yes," she said, seething. "I thought I would have *plenty* of time to do it."

He didn't appear to notice her implication. "Well, you needn't have bothered. She isn't coming."

"Oh? Poor dear, she must have been miserably uncomfortable," she countered, using the phrase that Christine had taunted her with earlier. Her arms akimbo, her eyes flashing, she continued with her tirade, "I hated that bed anyway." *Because Christine slept in it,* she finished in her mind. "In fact, I hate everything about this entire room. Why didn't you redo the master suite instead of the guest room?"

He folded his arms across his chest. "Because at the time, I didn't have a wife to tell me she didn't like it."

"Well, now you know," she bit back.

Jonathan threw up his hands in exasperation. "We could have moved to the guest bedroom, instead of switching everything."

"No," she argued, "I told Christine I had redecorated this room, and I'm making good my lie."

He walked toward her. She stepped backwards until her legs rested against the bed frame. He came to stand before her and placed his hands on her shoulders.

She swiped his hands away. "Don't touch me!"

"I will touch you, Ginny, anytime I want."

"No, not after you've touched her."

"When did I touch her?" he persisted.

"Before I got there," she snapped.

He chuckled. "You do have an imagination, don't you?"

"It doesn't take much imagination, when the evidence stares you right in the face."

He frowned. "What evidence?"

The temptation to tell him was on the tip of her tongue, but that was just what Christine would want her to do. Besides, he knew already. He'd unbuttoned her bodice and had had his hands all over her. No, she wouldn't let him know how much he had hurt her.

"Forget it." She moved around him and walked briskly to the door. "I have work to do . . . if we plan to have a bed to sleep in tonight."

"Ginny, I didn't touch Christine," he said softly. "I can't prevent her from coming here. If I could post guards completely around the plantation to keep her out, I would."

Ginny turned and lifted her chin. "Let her come. I don't care," she lied. "Perhaps I'll even invite her to dine with us

288

one evening." With that parting remark, she left the room.

Jonathan followed her into the guest bedroom. The servants had moved the master bedroom furnishings from the hall into the room, and were hanging the drapes. She instructed them to leave the room until tomorrow and work in the master suite.

They looked at Jonathan for approval, as he leaned casually against the wall beside the door. When he made no comment, they filed from the room. Ginny didn't even glance his way as she followed them. Before Jonathan left, he heard Ginny instruct Willis to place the Aubusson rug in the nursery. He smiled. Bertha would get her rug after all.

Late that night after everyone had retired, Jonathan, unable to sleep, leaned over and brushed his lips across Ginny's cheek. She was sleeping soundly, her back to him and curled up in a ball. He quietly eased from the bed and tossed another log on the fire, watching the sparks flash and fly up the chimney. He propped his arm on the mantel and rested his forehead on it.

Since the New Year's ball, he had thought their marriage was moving along smoothly. She had appeared more self-confident and had tried to please him in any way she could—in the bedroom and in the kitchen. And she had succeeded. For the first time, his home felt as a home should feel, pulsing and breathing as though it were a living thing, exuding warmth and contentment into the corners of every room. Ginny's presence within it had made it that way. Now he sensed a return of the loneliness, as though a door had been left open, letting in the cold.

Tonight, he would have made love to her and saved his vow for another night, but she had shunned him. When they had climbed into bed, neither had spoken. Though she would never have admitted it to him, she had needed reassurance from him that he didn't care one whit about

Christine. He also had needed reassurance that she still wanted him. Now he wondered if she would ever allow him to touch her again.

"Damn," he muttered softly. Doctor Pritchet had warned him that sometimes pregnant women behaved strangely, and the least little thing could upset them. But Jonathan had to admit that Ginny would not consider finding him with Christine a little thing.

Still, where had she come up with the notion that he and Christine were having an affair? One would have thought she had caught them making love. He could not make sense of her remark, *It doesn't take much imagination when the evidence is staring you right in the face.* What evidence? He wasn't even touching the bitch. If he had been choking her—which had been his inclination at the time—it wouldn't have taken much imagination on Ginny's part to know what he was doing to Christine. God, until today, he would not have believed the limits Christine would go to hurt someone. Suggesting that there was a possibility that the child did not belong to him, was a cruel and vicious act. Christine would think nothing of planting that seed of doubt in everyone's minds, and that was what bothered him now. He'd always admired his wife for her strong constitution, but everyone had a limit to how much pain they could endure. If Ginny ever got wind of such gossip, could she find the strength to withstand it?

He climbed back into bed. Drawing the blankets over him, he snuggled against her back, absorbing her warmth. As he lightly caressed her side, she turned slightly to her back and his hand came to rest on her stomach. His heart lurched against his chest as he felt a movement beneath his hand, nothing momentous, but proof that within this woman he cherished, was a child they had created.

And not for a moment did he doubt it belonged to him.

29

On the first warm day in March, Ginny opened the windows in the bedroom and a fragrant breeze caught her hair, blowing it about her face. The gloom of winter had passed, and the songs of the birds broke the stillness. Green grass had broken through the winter-browned landscape, and lush new buds were opening on the bare branches of the trees, while tiny purple violets and dandelions dotted the yard.

Ginny washed quickly and donned her oldest gown, eager to escape the confines of the house. She picked up her brush, and as she arranged her hair, the sunlight flashed on her pearl ring, creating its own ring of pain around her heart.

Her husband didn't want her. Ginny viewed herself in the mirror. Though it was she who had avoided his touch since Christine's visit, she could understand why *he* had not enforced his husbandly rights. She was nearing her eighth month, and her body looked hideous. She recalled wishing her breasts were as voluptuous as Christine's, but now she wished a pox on them. She was embarrassed for even the servants to see her. There was nothing pretty about her. Her face was sallow, and deep shadows ran beneath her eyes.

She'd had difficulty sleeping. She would awaken several times during the night with leg cramps, or to use the chamber pot. If that weren't bad enough, she had a recurring nightmare that was so real, she dreaded falling asleep. In her dream, Jonathan snatched their baby from her arms, immediately after it was born. "Our marriage has been annulled, Ginny," he said. She could hear Christine's laughter outside their window, as he stepped into her waiting carriage and carried off Ginny's baby.

Jonathan would always shake her awake while she was chasing the carriage. "Ginny, it's all right. You're having a nightmare." He'd brush the tangles from her eyes. One time he'd asked, "What did you mean when you screamed, *You can't do this to me!*"

She'd never explain. He would only tell her it was her obsession with Christine that was causing her nightmares. Some nights she would slip quietly from their room and sleep in the nursery, so she wouldn't disturb her husband's sleep.

She hated to admit it, but she missed Jonathan's company. He was staying longer hours at the stables, using the excuse that he wanted to keep close attention on a couple of mares that could go into labor at any time. She'd wanted to shout at him, "What about *me?* Are your precious horses more important than your wife?"

She needed her husband now more than ever, yet she had only herself to blame for his inattentiveness. Time and again he'd tried to convince her Christine was purposely trying to drive them apart. But she wouldn't believe him. She recalled those days he and Christine had spent together while she'd worked as his housekeeper, and then the night he had called her Christine. Sometimes she wondered if he had joined forces with Christine to drive her to insanity. Often she'd thought they had already succeeded. She hated herself for thinking these terrible thoughts about her husband, but she could not prevent them.

The day too beautiful to think sad thoughts, Ginny

292

shrugged aside her despair. After braiding her hair to keep it out of her face, she hurried downstairs and ate a quick breakfast, then left to ask Willis where they kept the gardening tools.

He frowned and gave her a quick once-over. With a skeptical eye, he said, "You sure you ought to be gardening, Mrs. Cross?"

"I only want to pull some weeds, Willis. My goodness, I used to do it all the time."

"Yes madam, I know, but—" he stopped abruptly. A servant wasn't supposed to scold his mistress, or call attention to her condition. "Be careful, please?"

Ginny smiled. "I appreciate your concern, Willis, but really, I'll be fine. Anyway, I've been cooped up in this house so long, I fear I've been difficult to live with lately."

Willis wouldn't comment on that remark. He and the servants had noticed her depression. They'd also noticed the lack of affection between their master and his wife. Know-it-all Bertha had told them some couples reacted strangely when the mistress was with child. They'd wondered where Bertha had gained such knowledge, when she'd never been married or had a child.

"Well, the tools are in the shed on the right side of the house. Now, don't go digging. Nat will do all that."

"I won't," she said laughingly and hurried outside. Retrieving a small spade, basket, and a worn pair of gloves, she decided to tackle the weeds along the walkway first. It took her a while to lower her cumbersome body to the ground, but she finally managed a kneeling position. When she leaned forward to pull a weed, she thought she might suffocate as her stomach and breasts pushed upward. She leaned back on her haunches and took a deep fortifying breath. Looking around to make sure no one was watching, she dropped to all fours, her stomach scant inches from the ground. Little rocks dug into her knees, but at least she could breathe.

Returning from the stables, Jonathan saw her. He paused at the fence and watched her. She was truly a comical sight, but God forbid that he should tell her. At first, he started to reprimand her, but changed his mind. He knew how much she loved digging around in the dirt. Maybe it would improve her mood. God's blood, nothing he'd said or done for the past two months had helped it.

Anytime he was near her, she ignored him, so he decided it was best for both of them if he stayed out of her way. If this was an example of a woman's behavior when she was expecting a child, he didn't think he could go through it again. He'd thought that after her confrontation with Christine, she would soon see how foolish her beliefs were, but he was sorely mistaken. If anything, their marriage had gone from bad to worse. Each time he'd approached her to air their differences, she'd left the room.

Nights were his worst times. Her nightmares disturbed him. He wanted so much to comfort her, yet she wouldn't allow him to touch her. Also her legs cramped, and she'd ease from the bed and try to walk out the pain. He'd asked if he could massage them. No, she'd deal with it herself.

Sometimes he'd wake up and she wouldn't be in bed. He'd find her asleep in the nursery and carry her back to their room. He'd thought very seriously about telling Bertha she could go ahead and occupy the room, but Ginny would only find another room to sleep in. At least, this way he didn't have to go from room to room in the middle of the night searching for her.

Her grunts and groans interrupted his thoughts. After watching her several more moments as she inched her way down the path, he decided she was not overexerting herself by just pulling weeds. Her greatest difficulty was to come. He wondered how she would ever get back on her feet. Rather than go to the house and work on his books as he had planned, he turned and retraced his steps back to the stables. It wouldn't do for her to know he had been watching her.

As Ginny weeded, she gathered the dandelions, placing them in her basket to take to Laine to cook for dinner. Ginny had learned at a very early age to identify the edible wild greens that flourished in the spring. Her mother used dandelions in many ways, either boiled or as a seasoning. In the late fall, when the roots were near their strongest, she would slowly roast them all afternoon until they were crisp and resembled coffee beans. After grinding the roots, they would substitute it for coffee, or mix the two to extend their supply. Later, when the clover appeared, she would make tea, or they would eat the young leaves and flowers raw. She wondered vaguely if Jonathan had ever eaten scrambled eggs with dandelions. She would tell Laine to fix it for him one morning.

She heard a carriage stop out front. "Oh no," she wailed. Looking over her shoulder, she saw an unfamiliar man step down from the carriage.

While the coachman removed his trunk, the gentleman turned his attention toward the magnificent house. His gaze swept it from side to side, then from roof to ground, where his eyes came to rest on a woman's buttocks. She was up on all fours, one hand reaching behind her and tugging on the skirt tail that had become trapped around her shoe. With a loud grunt, she jerked it free.

Ginny wished the ground would open up and swallow her, her embarrassment was so great. She managed to get back to her knees, but there was nothing nearby to hold onto for support. Leaning to the side, one hand on the ground, she tried to drag one foot from beneath her to set it firmly on the ground. Her large belly stopped her progress. She panted and grunted with her efforts, and stifled her scream as an infernal cramp struck her hip.

She heard a tapping sound, and glimpsed a cane and a pair of shiny-booted feet heading her way. He stopped beside her. She slowly lifted her head with chagrin. His attire was more fashionable than that of the planters. He was an older gentleman, tall and stout, with white unruly eyebrows, his eyes a bluish gray. A tall hat covered his head, but she noted the thick hair that framed his ears and neck was as white as the clouds floating above him. He looked strangely familiar, but she knew she had never seen him.

The gentleman studied her curiously for a moment. She looked like a servant, but then she didn't. Her face was smeared with dirt, the streak running beneath her nose resembling a mustache. She wore her hair in a long braid that traveled the length of her back. Wisps of reddish gold hair curled around her small face, and the prettiest green eyes he'd ever seen stared up at him. And she was obviously expecting a child. Now that rankled him.

"Might I assist you, miss?" he asked pleasantly.

"Yes, please," Ginny gasped.

Bending, he gently wrapped one arm around her shoulder, and with his other hand gripped her arm and lifted her upright. Her hip aching, Ginny fell against him.

He held her, balancing his weight on his cane. "What in bloody light were you doing down there in your delicate condition?"

Ginny's head shot up at the tone of his harsh voice. "Weeding, sir."

"Weeding! Poppycock! Is there no one else available to do that back-breaking chore?"

Embarrassed that someone as dignified as this gentleman had caught her looking her worst, Ginny decided

296

that since he didn't know her, she'd pretend she was a servant. Lord help her should he ever discover she was the mistress. And Jonathan would be furious. "No, I'm the only one around here who knows the first thing about gardening."

"Humph! Then I'll see to it someone else learns," he barked. "Is Jonathan at home?"

Jonathan? she wondered. The man must know her husband well to be addressing him by his given name. Then a disastrous thought suddenly leaped to her mind. *Oh no, what if Jonathan asks him to stay for dinner? He will expect me to join them.*

The color drained from her face.

Jonathan couldn't work for worrying about his wife. She had no business weeding the damned gardens, when he was paying Nat to do it. He headed toward the house and stopped abruptly at the end of the walkway. A man, his back to him, had his arm around his wife.

He heard a familiar voice ask gruffly, "Are you certain you're all right? You look like you're about to swoon."

Jonathan almost swooned himself. "Father?"

Lord Oliver Summerfield, eighth Duke of Hallsway, turned to his son. "Well, it's about time you got here. This young woman needs attention."

"No, I'm fine . . . really I am." Ginny turned woodenly in the man's arms and faced her husband.

"I thought I had reared you a gentleman. This servant has no business toiling in the hot sun," he snapped.

Jonathan stiffened. In all his dreams of seeing his father again, he had never imagined such a stern, uncaring greeting. "Sir, she isn't a servant. She happens to be my wife," he bit back.

"Your wife?" Lord Oliver asked, surprised, and glanced down at the girl he held against his side. She smiled weakly.

Lord Oliver removed his hat, showing off an abundance of thick, curly white hair. "Please excuse me, dear, for my misconception."

"No, I should apologize. I don't exactly fit the ideal image of a mistress. Do forgive me, sir."

"You," he said with a pleasant smile, "I could forgive anything, but my son?" He cut his eyes toward Jonathan. "How could you allow your wife to overtax herself when she is carrying *my* grandchild?" he demanded.

"Oh, he didn't allow it, sir," Ginny put in quickly.

He frowned at her. "So, you were sneaking behind his back?"

"No," she replied calmly though her nerves were becoming frayed. "I never bothered to ask him. He wasn't here." *He's never here,* she wanted to scream.

Lord Oliver's whole expression changed, as did Jonathan's. "Oh, then I owe my son an apology."

Both broke into smiles as they greeted each other in a warm bear hug.

Stepping back, Lord Oliver rested his hands on his son's shoulders. "Just like old times, isn't it, Jonathan? We never seem to start off on the right foot together."

Jonathan chuckled. "And we probably never will. But, damn, it's good to see you. I never expected you to come."

"We have many things to discuss, or I wouldn't be here. That damnable trip over here was almost my undoing. I was sick almost the minute the ship left port."

As they turned toward Ginny, she relaxed when she saw the anger gone from their faces.

Lord Oliver stopped in front of her and lightly scolded, "Young lady, while I am a guest in your lovely home, I forbid you to so much as lift a hand to see to my comfort. Now, go inside and wash your face. I know that somewhere beneath that grime is the prettiest face in all of Virginia."

298

A broad smile flashed across Ginny's face. Immediately she loved the stately, gruff old gentleman. "Thank you, Lord Oliver, I will. Only I hope you won't be disappointed," she said over her shoulder, as she lifted her skirt and hurried up the steps.

"And slow down," he bellowed.

She answered his order with tinkling laughter and entered the house.

Lord Oliver looked over at his son and frowned. "Is she always that . . . ah . . . full of energy?"

Jonathan laughed. "Her condition has slowed her down a bit."

Lord Oliver clucked his tongue and winked at his son. "Well, you always did like spirited fillies. This one, I am thinking, will be your biggest challenge yet."

"How well I know. Let's go inside. I'll have Willis get your trunk."

It was after the door closed behind them that Jonathan realized he had never formally introduced them.

Jonathan met Willis in the foyer and asked him to tell Laine to fix them some tea, then tend to his father's trunk. They entered the drawing room, and Jonathan closed the door behind them.

Lord Oliver looked around the impressive room, noting familiar items that had belonged to Jonathan's mother: the pastoral painting of a fox hunt on the wall over the mantel, a pair of matching Oriental vases, and the Persian rug that had covered her parlor floor. He noted the chessboard sitting on the table, the game pieces moved strategically on the board, as though a game were already in progress. He recalled the times he'd spent with his son, teaching him the game on this same board.

"Still playing chess, I see."

"Occasionally Blue and I share a game."

"Where is he?"

"He spends a lot of time in Williamsburg with a serving wench. It wouldn't surprise me if he doesn't marry her one day."

Lord Oliver chuckled. "Blue, marrying? I doubt it. But there again, I had my doubts about you, too. Tell me, son, when did you meet her?"

Jonathan frowned. "I explained all that in my letter. I mailed it shortly after Christmas. Didn't you get it?"

"No, it must have come after I left London. Before I boarded the ship to come here, I spent a month traveling."

"Traveling? You've never had the desire to travel."

"It wasn't for pleasure. I'll explain later." He waved his hand, dismissing the subject. Settling himself in a plump chair, he asked, "What I wish to discuss now is your new wife. I don't even know her name."

Jonathan sat on the edge of the desk, one foot on the floor. "I know. Everything happened so fast, I didn't realize I'd failed to introduce you until she'd already left. Her name is Ginny. I met her a year ago."

At this, Lord Oliver asked casually, "Ginny Sutton?"

"Yes. How did you know her maiden name?"

"Denby told me. But he also said she had died."

Jonathan felt his anger rising close to the surface. "Did you pay him to spy on me?"

"No, Jonathan, calm down. In the business letters Denby sent me, he hinted that you were falling in love with a poor farm girl. The last letter I received from him, he said she had died in a fire. I'd wanted to write you, but knew I wasn't supposed to know, and I didn't want to cause problems between you and Denby. Now it doesn't matter, because my mission here is to dismiss him."

"Now that's cause for a celebration. I never did like that man."

300

Laine knocked, then entered the room, carrying a tray with hot tea. She set it on the table and poured two cups. "Will that be all, sir?"

He nodded. "Yes, Laine, thank you."

Handing his father the cup of tea, Jonathan took his seat in the chair behind his desk. "Sir, does the idea of me marrying a poor farm girl displease you?"

Lord Oliver replied softly, "No, Jonathan. Did I ever state who you were to marry?"

"No," Jonathan said, sighing with relief. All his life he had wanted approval from his father. It was no different now. He eyed his father carefully. "I had thought that perhaps you expected me to marry a wealthy planter's daughter. But Ginny is so different from any woman I have ever known. She has had so little in life, yet she is so giving of herself." *At least she was until a few months ago, when their world had fallen to pieces.* But he could not tell his father his disappointments, and shatter the dreams he'd had for him. Somehow, he would have to mask his pain and show Lord Oliver he was living in bliss. Could Ginny do the same? If not, his father would leave Crossroads a very unhappy man.

Lord Oliver said wistfully, "I envy you, my son. For the better part of my life, I was married to a woman I didn't love. I count my blessings everyday that your mother came into my life and taught me the meaning of love, or I fear I would have left this life without experiencing the emotion. And you will have another benefit that I missed, the chance to be with your child every day, and watch him grow from a baby into an adult."

"You do have Geoffrey," Jonathan reminded him.

"Who?" Lord Oliver asked with a slight shrug of his shoulders. "That remark was uncalled for, I know. Geoffrey is my son, yet he isn't. He loves what I can give him, but that is all. This brings me around to another matter, Jonathan. I petitioned the court. You

301

are now legally my son."

Jonathan stared at him in bewilderment. "You didn't have to do it. No one here knows I'm a bastard."

"No, that's where you're wrong. Denby knows. I trusted him to keep my secret, even called him my friend. He isn't. Jonathan, he's been skimming off a portion of the money we've made on the tobacco."

"How did you discover this?"

Lord Oliver rose and paced the length of the room, then turned. "I became suspicious when in your letters you remarked how well the crop was going, telling me I should be happy with the profits. Denby's letters stated just the opposite. When he sent me an account of the business, I became worried. You see, he didn't think I would believe you—you who had no knowledge of tobacco. As I said earlier, I spent a month traveling. I contacted other clients of his and found a few who had let him go, because they suspected he was doing the same thing to them. I've brought with me the account he sent me, and I think that when we compare it with *your* entries, we'll find a gross discrepancy in the figures."

Jonathan raked his hand through his hair. "There was always something about him that bothered me. You aren't hiring another agent?"

"No, I've learned a valuable lesson in all this. I trust you can handle it?"

Jonathan smiled. "Actually, I've been handling the books since the beginning. Denby only looked them over and approved them. Now, I'm wondering if I did it right," Jonathan said with a worried frown. "Well, we'll find out first thing in the morning, won't we?"

"Yes, but I wish I'd had your insight, and we would never have found ourselves in this mess. That was the reason why I made the trip here." He smiled broadly. "And thank goodness I did. My son's married, and already about to start a family. Since you've kept your end of the bargain, I'll sign Crossroads over to you as soon as possible."

"That's not why I married Ginny, sir."

"I'm pleased to hear that, son."

A short rap on the door interrupted their conversation. "May I come in?" Ginny called.

"Yes," Lord Oliver returned anxiously.

Ginny entered and paused just inside the door. Her eyes sought Jonathan's first, looking for approval. She had tried so hard to make herself look pretty, not wishing to cause him further embarrassment. Oh, if only Lord Oliver had met her when she wasn't as big as a cow, she would feel more confident in pleasing him.

Jonathan thought she looked beautiful. Her pale green gown enhanced her sparkling green eyes. She had un-braided her hair and swept it into a soft coil atop her head, allowing a few curls to fall gently onto the nape of her neck. His eyes expressed his appreciation, as he nodded and smiled. "Father, now *this* is my wife, Ginny," he teased. "Ginny, Lord Oliver Summerfield, my father." Jonathan studied her closely, to see if she noticed the difference in their surnames.

Lord Oliver strode across the room toward his daughter-in-law. Taking Ginny's hand, he drew her into the room and closed the door behind her. He placed his hands on her shoulders and critically studied her face.

She held her breath.

"Well, forevermore! My daughter has freckles!"

30

Ginny jumped, her face turning beet red. "I'm sorry, but they won't wash off."

Lord Oliver laughed outright. "I wouldn't want you to wash them off, if you could," he countered reproachfully. "I see why my son married you."

"Because of my freckles?" Ginny asked blankly.

He laughed and tried to hug her to him, but her protruding belly got in his way. Stepping back from her, he said to Jonathan, "You have chosen well, son."

Oh Lord Oliver, if you knew the truth, what would you think of me then? Ginny wondered. But he liked her. What a relief. All the time she was getting ready, she kept remembering what Christine had said about Jonathan's father asking him to have the marriage annulled. And she wouldn't have blamed him at all, especially if first appearances had anything to do with his decision.

"Now, when is my grandchild due?" he asked.

"In a month or so," Jonathan answered. "Can you stay until it's born?"

"You couldn't move me out of this house, if you tried," he said. "That is, if my daughter can put up with a cantankerous old man for that long."

"Oh, we should do fine, Lord Oliver," Ginny quipped saucily. "You couldn't be half as cantankerous as Lord Adelbert."

304

Jonathan coughed.

"Lord Adelbert? Hmmm . . . his name isn't familiar." He turned to Jonathan. "Is he your houseguest?"

"No, he stays in the barn," Jonathan answered matter-of-factly.

"You house your guest in a barn?" Lord Oliver asked, aghast.

"Oh yes," Ginny said, enjoying the game. "He has a horrid temperament. Sometimes he'll take a bite out of you for no reason at all. Ask Jonathan. He could hardly sit for a week."

"A man of nobility behaves in such an unethical manner? Why don't you send him on his way?"

Ginny's sides were hurting from holding in her laughter.

"Lord Adelbert is Ginny's mule," Jonathan announced.

Lord Oliver's face lit up in astonishment, and then his booming laughter filled the house.

After dinner, Jonathan took his father to the stables to see his horses. He soon discovered his father was more interested in discussing Ginny than the horses. Lord Oliver wanted to know everything about her. Jonathan did his damnedest to explain their history without lying, but his father was very perceptive and the questions he asked could either lead to lies or the truth, depending on the route Jonathan chose. Never in his life had he lied to his father. Jonathan elected to tell him the truth.

"Well, you *are* a chip off the old block," Lord Oliver sighed. "But unlike me, at least you were able to do the honorable thing and marry the mother of your child, the woman you love. I am glad you have found happiness with one another."

Jonathan never mentioned Christine and Ginny's belief

he was having an affair. His father needn't know everything that was happening in their marriage.

When they returned from the stables, he and Ginny took him on a tour of the house and showed him to his room.

That night, Ginny retired early, while Jonathan and his father played a game of chess in the library. It was late when Jonathan entered the bedroom. He quietly removed his clothing and climbed into bed next to his sleeping wife.

"Jonathan?" she asked softly.

"I'm sorry I woke you."

"You didn't. I haven't been asleep." She turned on her side and faced him in the darkness. "I like your father."

I wish you liked me, he wanted to say. "He likes you, too."

"You really think so?"

"Yes, Ginny. Didn't you hear him say I had chosen well?"

"Yes, but he wasn't just being nice, was he?"

"You will learn in time, my father isn't nice just for the sake of being nice. You would have known immediately if he didn't like you."

"I was worried that I might have offended him when I—" she giggled, "pretended Lord Adelbert was nobility. He must think I'm a silly goose."

"No, he likes your humor." He paused for a moment, his voice serious when he asked, "Ginny, could I ask a favor of you?"

"Of course. What?"

"I fear my father is in bad health, but he would never tell me if he was. He thinks we have a good marriage, Ginny, and I would like for him to go on believing it. I know this might prove a difficult task for you, but could you at least *pretend* you love me?"

306

"Pretend?" she asked chokingly. "Yes, but can you?"

"Yes. He's not easily fooled, but we seemed to have convinced him today without any effort."

Ginny bolted upright in bed.

Jonathan joined her. "The baby?" he asked anxiously.

"No," she groaned, "cramps in my foot and leg."

"Lie down," he ordered.

"I can't. I have to get up and walk around," she countered.

"Damn it, no! It's because of me you're having them, so let me help you."

"What do you mean, it's because of you?"

"Because *I* got you with child. Now, don't argue with me. Just lie there and *pretend* you're enjoying it."

He moved to the foot of the bed and pulled the cover down, tossing her the blanket to wrap around her. Kneeling, he asked, "Which foot?"

"The left one," she said, groaning with pain.

Picking up her foot, he placed it on his thigh. She flinched as he began working her toes, pressing his fingers into the tight muscles.

"Oh, that hurts worse than the cramp," she cried.

"It won't in a minute, I promise."

He deeply massaged the sole, then cupping her heel in his palm, he raised her foot to his mouth and stroked her big toe with his tongue.

Ginny jerked her foot. "Jonathan, that isn't necessary!"

Ignoring her, he held her foot tightly as she tried to pull it away, drawing her toe into his mouth and lightly sucking it. Ginny felt a sudden warmth begin to radiate in her foot, then spread up her leg and settle in her groin.

After kissing each tiny toe, he lowered her leg to his lap. "Is your foot still hurting?"

"No," she moaned. Where she ached, he had no busi-

307

ness knowing—no, not at all.

Pushing her nightgown to her knees, he worked his way up to her calf. She nearly came off the bed when he hit the hard painful muscle, but she didn't complain. Instead, she *pretended* she enjoyed the feel of his hands on her, wishing that she had not been so stubborn on all those other painful nights and had allowed him to work his magic on her.

He felt the muscle slacken, a sign that the cramp was fading. "Better?"

"Yes, but I'm afraid it will happen again."

"It won't as long as you stay relaxed." He continued massaging her leg and Ginny sighed, a peaceful calm settling over her.

But when he shoved her gown over her belly and started pressing and kneading her thigh, her calm evaporated. "I don't hurt there."

"Not yet, you don't. I'm just making sure you won't."

Remembering the cramp she'd experienced in her hip earlier in the day, she didn't argue.

"You overdid it today, didn't you?" he asked softly as he worked.

"No," she protested.

"Yes, you did. That's the first real exercise you've had in months. You aren't able to do what you used to do, Ginny."

"After the baby's born, I can."

"I pay Nat to do it," he lightly scolded.

She raised up on her elbows. "Jonathan, I love gardening. That is one thing I won't give up. Now I'm trying my best to be a good mistress, but you can't expect to change *everything* about me."

"I don't want you to change," he said, surprising her by placing a warm kiss on her swollen belly. "Ever." He brushed his mouth over her belly.

"Stop that," she cried out, as ripples of pleasure shot through her.

"Pretend, Ginny, pretend you're enjoying it," he groaned hoarsely.

Pretend? she wondered. Her whole being was on fire for him. Strange. He didn't seem displeased with her ugliness, but seemed to revere it. Of course, he couldn't see her in the dark, she reminded herself.

At that moment, the baby changed positions.

"There's nothing like getting a foot in your mouth," he said, chuckling.

"The foot's not in your mouth, it's in *my* ribs."

"Maybe it was a fist. Whatever, our child certainly packs a whollop. Almost knocked out my teeth," he teased, continuing his exploration of her belly.

"Pretend you enjoyed it," she returned cajolingly.

Ginny was enjoying their teasing and light banter. Jonathan knew that, and was taking advantage of her recklessness. All he wanted was to have her near him, hold him, tell him she wanted him, regardless that they could do nothing to bring them complete fulfillment. It had been so long since he'd felt this closeness. He wished the night would go on forever.

Jonathan turned his head and rested his cheek on her stomach, his hand stroking and gently kneading her upper thigh and hip. Ginny stared into the darkness, tenderly combing her fingers through his hair.

"God, that feels wonderful," he said softly. "You feel wonderful."

"Wouldn't it be more wonderful, if we weren't pretending?" she returned, her heart in her throat.

He slid his body up in the bed and braced his hands on either side of her, his face mere inches from her own. "We aren't pretending, Ginny. We could spend more nights like this, if only you would let it happen. Do

309

you realize this is first time we've talked in ages?"

"Yes, but—" she let her remark hang in the air.

"But you still don't trust me," he finished with a sigh. Lightly kissing her forehead, he rolled to his back.

"Do you still believe I'm seeing Christine?"

"I have no idea what you do with your time when you're not here, besides spending hours at the stables."

"She hasn't come to the stables again, Ginny."

"Maybe not, but she'll come again, you can count on it."

Jonathan knew she was right, so gave up the argument. Today when he'd heard they had a visitor, he thought Christine had come to torment them. For some reason, she was laying low now, but he sensed it wouldn't be long before she set her evil mind to its tricks again.

But Jonathan was determined that this woman would not destroy his marriage. Somehow, he would find a way to wash away the poison of mistrust she had left festering in his wife's heart and mind.

Ginny slept late the following morning, after having spent most of the night awake, thinking about her husband. *Was* she imagining these horrible things about Jonathan and Christine? It was not her imagination that Christine's bodice was unbuttoned that day, yet . . . Christine could have purposely made it look as though they had been making love. *Oh Jonathan, I do want to believe you.* Yet, he had never said, *Ginny, I love you, only you.* She would not beg those words from him; her pride wouldn't allow it.

He had asked her to pretend she loved him, for the sake of his father. She smiled sadly. Pretend? *What an easy task it will be to pretend I love you, my husband.*

With that thought in her mind, Ginny dressed and

went downstairs. Willis told her Jonathan and his father had spent an hour or so in the drawing room earlier that morning, then had left for Williamsburg. They planned to return by mid-afternoon.

Though Ginny knew this would be the perfect opportunity to resume her chore of weeding the beds beside the walk, she controlled her urge. Instead, she went to the barn and visited with Lord Adelbert. As usual, he kept to himself.

After her noon meal, she told Willis she was taking a walk to her old homeplace. He insisted someone go with her, but she said she wished to go alone. As she strolled through the meadow, pain wrenched her heart when she saw the lonely chimney rising from the charred remains. She came to stand in front of it, noting a maze of several thin paths weaving through the rubble, evidence that Jonathan had made a thorough search to find her remains. Lifting her skirt tail high above her ankles, she took one of the paths, trying to find at least one memento to carry home with her. She went from one path to another, tears building up in her eyes when she discovered everything was gone except iron pots and tarnished metal. As she turned to leave, she saw the sunlight reflecting off something partially buried beneath the ashes. With a great effort, she lowered herself and picked it up. Her heart pounded with happiness.

"Ginny! For god's sake, what are you doing now?"

Recognizing Jonathan's voice, she called back to him excitedly, "Oh Jonathan, you're back earlier than I expected. Come see what I've found!"

Jonathan approached her. She looked up at him with tears sparkling in her eyes. In the palm of her hand was a silver chain, holding a small silver heart. "Patrick made it for me," she whispered.

The scolding he'd planned to give her completely left

his mind, as he saw the happiness that brightened her eyes like a thousand suns. He smiled warmly. "I'm surprised you were able to find anything in this mess. Here, let me help you up."

She gave him her hand, and he pulled her to her feet. "He gave it to me on my sixteenth birthday." She laughed chokingly. "I remember him apologizing to me because it wasn't perfectly formed. It was his first attempt."

"Let me put it on you."

Ginny gave him her back and swept her hair up from her neck. Jonathan fastened the chain. When she turned around, they both gazed down at the locket resting between her full breasts.

"It's still beautiful, even though it is misshapen, isn't it?" she quipped lightly.

"Yes, as beautifully misshapen as the woman wearing it," he said hoarsely.

Her head shot up and she gave him a startled glance. He'd actually said he thought her beautiful, and here it was broad daylight?

He smiled and took her by the arm. "Come on. Father's waiting for us at the house."

Jonathan had been doing some heavy soul-searching since his father's arrival. He figured she must have overheard his father's name through conversations with Denby, though he could not remember ever mentioning Lord Oliver's name. It hadn't been necessary. He had almost broached the subject of his illegitimacy last night in bed, but he just couldn't bring himself to discuss it. She had probably already figured it out anyway. Anyone with an ounce of sense would notice the difference in his and his father's last names. Still, he feared the repercussions that might befall him when he actually told her. It would undoubtedly widen the estrangement between them, and she might completely lose her faith in him.

He took her arm and stopped in the meadow. "Ginny, you're probably—" His mouth suddenly went dry. He cleared his throat, unable to look at her, and studied the blue sky. "You're . . . ah . . . probably wondering why my father and I have different last names."

Ginny's heart tripped several beats. Before she could reply, he said, "He couldn't marry my mother." That was so much easier to say than admit his illegitimacy. He waited for the explosion. It didn't come.

Instead, she said softly, "I'm sure he had a good reason."

"Yes, he was already married."

"Still, he must love you very much, to come such a long distance to see you."

"Yes, I never realized just how much until yesterday." He lowered his gaze toward her upturned face. "Does it bother you, Ginny?"

"Does what bother me?"

"That you're married to a . . . a bastard?"

"Jonathan, that's such a ridiculous question it doesn't merit an answer. Surely, you haven't forgotten I could very well have found myself in the same situation as your mother. But thank goodness, you were free to marry me."

"Ginny, you have every reason in the world to be angry with me for not telling you."

"Oh, I'm a bit miffed, but not because you're illegitimate, but because you didn't tell me when you discovered I was carrying your child. Then I could have understood why you were so determined to marry me." She was purposely baiting him, hoping he would admit he was starting to care for her, at least just a little.

"I would have wanted the child to have my name, regardless of my circumstances."

She was right back where she started. If anything, his confession had only reinforced his purpose for marrying her. *Pretend, Ginny, pretend you don't care,* her mind screamed.

"Father did give me some good news, although it might be a little difficult to explain to our acquaintances. He petitioned the courts and legally claimed me as his son. No longer am I Jonathan Cross, but Jonathan Cross Summerfield."

"Jonathan, how wonderful!" Suddenly, the happy glow flew from her face. "Oh dear."

"What's the matter?"

"What does that make me?" she asked.

"Why, Ginny Sutton Summerfield, I'd assume."

"But . . . but are we legally married, since the names aren't right on the marriage bond?"

"We can easily have it changed, Ginny. Unless—" he arched a questioning eyebrow.

"Unless what?" she asked fearfully.

"Unless you want to change your mind," he teased.

She cocked her head and seemed to be giving the matter some deep thought. "I ought to, you know," she said pertly, then turned and walked toward the house.

The teasing smile left his face. Could she change her mind and renege on their vows? God, he'd never thought about the legalities that might be involved in this delicate matter!

When they entered the drawing room, Lord Oliver was seated in Jonathan's chair behind the desk, studying the ledger. He looked up and smiled when he saw Ginny. She didn't realize it, but during her exploration, she'd raked the hem of her blue gown through the ashes and had also soiled the front of it.

"Caught her digging around in the dirt again, I see?" he asked, arching an unruly brow.

Ginny reddened as she saw the smudges on her gown. "She was going through the rubble at her homeplace.

314

This is the first time she's been there since it burned."

Lord Oliver's face turned sympathetic. "You lost everything, Jonathan tells me. I am truly sorry, Ginny."

"No, not all was lost. I found the locket my brother gave me on my sixteenth birthday. I'd forgotten all about it." She turned to Jonathan. "Do you think after the baby's born, we could clean up the site? I might find some things that belonged to my father."

"That's a good idea. When we searched through it, we weren't looking for things like that, we were looking for—" he turned his head sharply, "you."

Ginny's heart leaped to her throat. She had seen the pain that suddenly gripped his features before he'd turned from her. He *had* grieved over her death! Everyone had told her this, yet it had taken that particular look on his face to make a believer of her.

Forgetting Lord Oliver was even in the room with them, she went to Jonathan and placed her hand on his arm. "I'm sorry, Jonathan."

He continued to stare ahead. "It's all right, Ginny."

"No, it isn't all right. I did you a terrible wrong. I ask your forgiveness, but if you don't wish to accept it, I'll understand."

"Ginny, we can't discuss this now. My father's with us. Remember our discussion last night?"

"Yes, I remember. Pretend, right?"

Her hand still on his arm, Jonathan covered it with his own and squeezed it lightly. "Right."

They both turned to see Lord Oliver quickly lower his head to the ledger. Ginny wondered if he had heard their conversation.

Jonathan cleared his throat. "Have you found any other discrepancies?"

"Yes. From the looks of things, he's been at this since day one."

"Can you tell me what your problem is?" Ginny asked.

Lord Oliver looked up. "We dismissed Denby this morning."

"You mean he doesn't work for Jonathan anymore?"

"Humph!" Lord Oliver snorted. "He won't be working for anyone, when I get through with him."

"Ginny, he's been stealing from us. And not just from us, but from several people."

"Are you going to report him?"

"Yes, after we discuss it with his other clients. We want to get enough evidence to put him in prison for a long time," Jonathan said.

"But what's to keep him from running?"

"We didn't tell him what we've found, only that we didn't require his services any longer. Of course, Denby could suspect we're wise to his crime and leave, but he has other clients in the area, and we hope he's greedy enough to hang around awhile."

"Are you going to hire someone else to help you manage?"

"No, I'm going to keep the books myself," Jonathan said. "I've been doing them anyway."

Ginny didn't say anything for a moment. Finally, she said, "I kept the accounts for the silversmith shop, Jonathan. Would you let me help you? I'm good with my numbers."

He grinned. "I know."

She lifted a questioning brow. "How?"

"I've seen you play cards. But, Ginny, it's very involved. Everything that comes in or goes out of the plantation must be accounted for."

"Yes, just like Patrick's accounts, except on a larger scale. I can do it, Jonathan, I know I can," she announced with confidence.

Lord Oliver's interest perked. He rose from his chair.

"Why don't we give her a chance, Jonathan? In fact, my eyes are already weary from looking over these figures. Maybe she'll see something we've missed." He chuckled. "Also, it will give her something to do, and we won't have to worry about her doing things she ought not be doing."

Ginny looked up at her husband pleadingly.

"All right, Ginny, the job is yours."

"You won't be sorry, I promise." Raising on her toes, she put her hands around his neck and, pulling down his head, kissed him soundly on his mouth.

Yes, this was indeed a very good idea, Jonathan thought to himself with a smile.

And Ginny kept her promise. She tackled the books immediately, and by the end of her third day had found other conflicting entries in the accounts Denby had listed. She had laughed with delight when she reviewed the enormous food expense, and had affectionately patted her husband's tummy. "One would think, Jonathan, you are feeding two, instead of your wife."

31

Ginny adored Lord Oliver, and he in turn doted on her. They were a common sight around the plantation, walking or talking together. She swore she didn't walk any longer, but waddled everywhere she went. Some days she was so swollen that she didn't waddle at all. She vowed her legs looked like hams and felt as though someone was pricking her with a thousand needles, and she couldn't begin to get her swollen feet into her shoes. Ginny abandoned wearing her pearl ring, because her hands swelled so badly the ring cut into her finger. And to her utter astonishment, when she sat down—and that was a feat in itself—she couldn't get up without help. Mrs. Wagner assured her that her condition was normal. But even she was concerned about Ginny's size. She'd never seen anyone blossom the way Ginny had. When Bertha told her she ate like a bird, Ginny was quick to point to her bulging stomach and comment dryly, *Yes, like a vulture!* But in comparison to her girth, she didn't eat much at all, even though some of her combinations of food were very unusual.

As the weeks progressed, her burden settled itself lower, making it nearly impossible for Ginny to get comfortable in any position. Yet, on this particular sunny day, she woke with an abundance of energy.

Jonathan kept a close eye on her at all times, but with his father in attendance, he felt comfortable leaving her for short periods. It did his heart good to see the two together. Ginny put on a good front, but Jonathan knew her well enough to know that something troubled her deeply. Sometimes he glimpsed the shadows of pain, when she thought no one observed her.

Something Christine had said that day in the stables had set his mind to full speed. She acted as though it were only a matter of time before she resumed the position as mistress of Crossroads. As he pondered the possibilities, it became clearer and clearer that Christine's interest was in the house, rather than him. When she thought Ginny was going to make any changes in her former home, she had been livid and unable to hide it. And on several occasions, she'd made the error of calling Crossroads hers. Jonathan knew he was Christine's link to Crossroads. He was relieved at once to realize that, and distressed in the next moment, to think what she might do to reclaim her home. The woman was completely daft, or Jonathan had missed the mark completely.

Beowulf pawed the ground and snorted the air, trying to get Jonathan's attention. Jonathan rubbed the velvety nose, and asked the stallion if he was pleased with all the mares Jonathan had sent him? The horse's eyes sparkled, and Jonathan would have sworn the beast knew exactly what he was talking about. Jonathan himself could do with a little female companionship, but the only female he had any desire for was presently waddling through the field with his father, gathering wildflowers.

He propped his arm on the fence and watched the pair. Indeed, what a sight they were, Ginny burdened with his child, and his father burdened with an armload of flowers. But Jonathan would have been willing to bet that Ginny outshone any blossom that scattered the fields. Her laughter floated back to him, tingling on the gentle breeze.

Unable to concentrate on anything else, he left his position at the fence and started across the field. "Do you need an extra set of arms?"

"Maybe I did overdo it just a bit," she admitted, laying another bouquet of flowers in Lord Oliver's arms. "There are so many, and they are so beautiful, I couldn't resist."

"No more beautiful than the one gathering them," he commented softly.

"You jest, I'm sure. I'm as big and lumbering as that cow in yon field," she replied, then pondered the cow for several seconds before she added, "On second thought, that cow has a way to go before she's quite as large as I am."

Lord Oliver and Jonathan couldn't control their laughter, as they spied the cow as though measuring its girth.

The trio that returned to the manor with their spirits as buoyant as the spring day was a sight to behold. Ginny wasn't as light on her feet as the men, but with their helping hands it didn't matter. As Ginny collected an array of vases for her flowers, Jonathan found a comfortable chair for her. Lord Oliver took himself off to take a nap, which Jonathan thought strange, for his father never napped during the day. Then it hit him that his father wanted them to have time together, alone.

When Ginny returned, she questioned the smile on Jonathan's face. "I was thinking about my father the matchmaker, and his subtle disappearance."

"So that's what it was. I wondered why he was taking a nap, because to my knowledge he hasn't taken a nap since he's been here."

Jonathan cut the stems as she arranged the flowers, and placed the overflowing vases where she asked. They were unaware of a rickety old wagon pulling to the front of the manor.

320

For no reason at all a chill swept Ginny, and she shivered slightly. She was reminded of what Patrick used to say when they were children. A shiver meant someone had just walked over your grave. She shivered again.

Willis came into the room, his composure completely absent. "Sir." He twisted his hands before him.

"Yes, Willis."

The servant cleared his throat and began again. "Sir, there is a man at the door, claiming that he has come for his wife."

"Are you sure he has the right residence?"

"It's Mrs. Ginny the man wants."

"What?" Jonathan bellowed.

"It's Mrs. Ginny—"

"For God's sake, I'm not deaf. I heard you. I just can't make any sense of what you said."

Ginny turned a deathly pale and clutched the edge of the table for support.

"I didn't understand the request myself, sir. I'm just passing on what he said."

"Then he better damn well tell me himself what he wants. Where is he?"

"He's still on the porch. I didn't deem it necessary to let him in. He has a foul odor about him."

"Oh no," Ginny whispered.

"What is it, Ginny? Do you know who this man is?"

"It sounds like Darryl, the man who found me when I fell in the river. He and his family never put much store in bathing. But I don't understand why he would say I was his wife. He's the one who took me to Williamsburg on the pretext of finding a preacher."

"Well, I'll find out what's going on, that's for damn sure."

Ginny loosened her death grip on the edge of the table and placed her hand on Jonathan's arm. "Be careful, Jonathan. His family will do anything to get money. They would have ransomed me, but they knew by my clothing that I didn't have money."

"I wonder how they found out where you were?"

"I have no idea."

He smoothed his hand over her cheek and brushed her hair from her face, noting the worry in her eyes. "Don't worry, my love. I'll let nothing—*nothing*—take you away from me."

He turned and left the room, a nervous Willis following in his wake.

When Jonathan reached the foyer, the man had stepped inside and his greedy eyes were pursuing the riches he saw around him.

"What's this all about?" Jonathan asked, taking the man's measure.

"I've come to fetch Ginny. She belongs to my brother, and it's his babe she carries."

Jonathan let the man's declaration flow over him like water off a duck's back. He would not give the man the satisfaction of seeing his shock. "How did you know where to find Ginny?"

"I have my ways," the man answered.

"I'll just bet you do." Jonathan wanted nothing more than to slam his fist into the filthy man's face. Ginny was right. He definitely had no penchant for bathing.

"Ginny is my wife, and I protect what belongs to me. I'll not turn her over to the likes of you."

"Now just a minute—"

Ginny entered the foyer and stopped stone still. Willis, who stood shifting his weight from one foot to the other nervously, and Jonathan and the stranger heard her gasp. They turned their attention to her.

322

"Well, well, it looks like you done real good for yourself, Ginny."

The way he said her name and looked at her with hooded, beady eyes made chills run up her spine. He acted as though he had known her intimately, and that was very far from the truth. She'd been unable to tolerate him when she was with his family.

"Harold," she whispered.

"You have really blossomed since I last laid eyes on you."

"Where is Darryl?"

"Oh, he's takin' care of his varmints. He really misses you, Ginny, and he wants you to hurry home with his babe."

Ginny placed her hand against the wall to steady herself.

Jonathan rushed to her side and draped his arm around her. "My wife needs to sit down. Willis, will you show our guest into the drawing room?"

"Just a minute, let me get Evelyn. She's anxious to see you, Ginny." Harold turned to the door and bellowed to the woman in the wagon.

"If he says my name one more time, I'm going to throw up," Ginny warned Jonathan, as he helped her from the room and settled her in a comfortable chair.

Evelyn sashayed into the room as though she were a frequent guest, her bulk undulating like raw dough beneath the faded dress. But like her husband, nothing could conceal the glitter of greed that sparkled in her eyes. She dropped herself into a richly upholstered chair. Ginny held her breath, hoping the chair wouldn't splinter beneath her weight.

Riches was their motive, Ginny knew this as well as she knew they were up to no good. They wanted to ruin her in front of her husband. But why? It made no sense.

323

How had they known where to find her? If they wanted money for taking care of her, that was one thing, but the lie that the child belonged to Darryl was ludicrous. Jonathan wouldn't believe that for a second . . . would he?

"You poor thing, you'll probably never be your old skinny self again," Evelyn intoned with pleasure.

"How many children do you have?" Jonathan was quick to ask, noting the rings of fat that encircled her body.

"None," she retorted and snapped her mouth closed.

He'd made his point and saw no need to pursue the matter. He sat down beside Ginny and draped his arm around her shoulder.

Ginny felt compelled to introduce the pair as distasteful as the chore was.

After the introductions were made, Jonathan frowned. "And Darryl is your brother—the one who actually rescued Ginny?"

"Yes, my twin brother, but we all helped take care of Ginny. She was very sick for a long time, and for a while, we didn't think she would live. She ran a high fever for days, and I remember Ma sayin' if she couldn't get the girl's fever to break, there weren't much hope of savin' her."

"I thank you for taking such good care of my wife. I don't suppose she told you she was married?"

"Never breathed a word about bein' married. The only talk of marriage that I rightly remember was her and Darryl plannin' their own weddin'."

"Maybe she had a memory lapse brought on by the high fever."

Harold looked at Jonathan as though he'd sprouted horns. "They wasn't nothin' wrong with her memory, if yore hankerin' to excuse her behavior with my brother. She was hot for him, and that's all there was to it. Now look at her."

"You're lying," Ginny said. "I don't know why you're doing this, but you know as well as anyone that your entire family knew I was with child before Darryl returned me to my family."

Evelyn snorted.

"Evelyn is the very one who told me I was going to have a baby. The day you slaughtered the hog, I prepared the fat for lard and helped make sausage. I became deathly sick. Evelyn followed me. Do you remember what you said to me, Evelyn?"

Evelyn shook her head.

"I do, word for word." Ginny mimicked Evelyn's whining voice as she repeated, "Well, ain't you a pretty thing retchin' your guts out?" She hesitated. "You even told me that you knew of a woman who could get rid of the babe, if I had money." Ginny placed her hand protectively over her stomach.

"Yeah, and you told me you didn't have any money," Evelyn said, before she could control herself. "You lied."

"So I did," Ginny lied, because at the time she didn't have any money or a husband, but she'd never admit it to these vile people.

Jonathan was having trouble controlling the rage roiling through him. Yet he was very proud of Ginny. She'd faced the issue head on and had had her say. He placed his hand over Ginny's and squeezed it. "I believe any business you thought we had is concluded. I would have been very generous and paid you handsomely for the care you bestowed on my wife in her time of need, if you had but asked. Instead, you storm into *our* home and flay my wife's good name for God only knows what reason, only to be found out instantly that you are nothing but liars. Please remove yourself from *our* home and *our* presence. You have sorely abused *our* hospitality."

Harold stomped across the fine carpet and jerked his

wife to her feet. When they reached the door, Harold turned with a triumphant challenge. "Should you ever wonder, ask your wife what she and Darryl did all those days when they were alone together. Tell me why my brother would sit for hours and brush her hair . . . if there was nothin' goin' on between them. A man doesn't perform such intimate duties for a woman just for the sake of doin' it. Think about it, Mr. Cross, when you see the babe and wonder if it's really yours."

"Get out!" Jonathan bellowed.

Ginny could no longer control the tears she'd held at bay. They seeped from her eyes like crystal droplets from an emerald lake, and her shoulders shook with sorrow.

Jonathan took her in his arms and lent what comfort he could, while inside he raged with fury. The scene that had just played out before him had Christine Iverson's name all over it. That was the only way the people could have known where to find Ginny. Someway Christine had found out about them, and induced them to call on him. He had no way of proving his theory, but his instincts screamed that it was her handiwork. And he'd always paid attention to his instincts. She was a bitch of the highest order, and she couldn't bear to see Ginny Sutton happy. And God forbid that Ginny was now the mistress of Crossroads. That was the most bitter of powders for Christine to swallow.

"Jonathan, Harold was lying," she said between sobs.

"I know that, Ginny. Don't you think I have more faith in you than that?"

"Can I tell you about Darryl? He's not at all like Harold."

"Yes, I'd like to hear about him."

"They are twins, that's true. But Darryl reminded me of a gentle giant. He cares for hurt or abandoned animals, sort of like I was. And it was Darryl and his

326

mother who cared for me, not Harold and Evelyn. He did brush my hair. I think the color fascinated him. Still, that was when I was sick. Sometimes when I'd wake up, he would be sitting by the bed brushing my hair. And the time I spent alone with him was when I helped him take care of his animals, and to get away from Harold. I was afraid of Harold. Darryl would never have done anything like Harold just implied. There wasn't anything wrong with Darryl that you could put your finger on, but still he was slow. Do you know what I mean?"

"Yes," Jonathan answered, creating his own picture of what Darryl looked like.

"He went against Harold and Evelyn to help me. Evelyn didn't want me to leave, because I did her work, and I believe Harold wanted me for himself."

Jonathan hid his fisted hands behind Ginny's back.

"Darryl took me to Williamsburg and left me. I'm sure the wrath of Harold and Evelyn was only slightly mollified by the money Patrick gave him."

"I wish there was some way I could repay Darryl for his care of you. But his brother would benefit, and I wouldn't do anything to improve his lot in life."

"Harold would drink it up. That's all he cares about."

"Put them from your mind, Ginny. We have more important things in our life than the likes of them." Before she could move away, he kissed her quickly on the lips.

"I must finish my arrangements before the flowers wilt. I don't think your father would relish traipsing through the fields again any time soon."

"My father would sprout wings and fly, if you asked him. He has become quite attached to you."

"The feeling is mutual, I assure you."

32

Ginny couldn't get comfortable. She'd twisted and turned at the dinner table like a worm in hot ashes. Earlier in the day a slow, nagging pain had settled low in the small of her back, and nothing she did had diminished the pain. Now she paced the room in her slow gait, while Jonathan and Lord Oliver watched her curiously, until she would glance their way. Then they would jerk their heads away, and pretend interest in any number of things. She became confused by Lord Oliver's interest in the fireplace utensils and Jonathan's interest in the window dressing, until it dawned on her what they were doing. Rather than worry them any longer, she bid them good night and excused herself.

As she began the laborious task of mounting the stairs, Jonathan appeared at her side. "I thought my lady might like a lift."

Before she could object, he scooped her up in his arms.

"You'll break your back. Now put me down," she scolded, clasping his neck.

"I had this overwhelming desire to carry my babe tonight. And the only way I can accomplish that is to carry his mother, also. Would you deny me that pleasure?"

"Thank you. I really dreaded trying to get up the stairs. I do all right on flat ground, but since I can't see my own feet, it makes it difficult to see each step. Evelyn sure hit the nail on the head, when she said I'd lost my skinny figure."

"Maybe so, but your condition is temporary. Her bulk is permanent."

When they reached the top of the stairs, Ginny gasped and a gush of water left her body, soaking her gown and Jonathan's pants. Fear encompassed her face. "Oh, Jonathan, what is it? Am I losing the baby?" she cried.

"No, my love, you're not losing the baby, you're going to have the baby." He didn't set her down, but carried her to their bed. After he settled her in the bed, he rushed to the door and bellowed for Bertha.

Bertha came hurrying into the room.

"Send for Mrs. Wagner, the baby's coming."

Ginny's cry of pain sent the color draining from Jonathan's face, and Bertha flying from the room on silent feet.

Within moments, the pounding of hoofs and Willis's shouted commands drifted through the second-story window.

Ginny's pain had subsided for the moment, and she cocked a brow at Jonathan. "Do you ever remember Willis riding a horse before?" Jonathan shook his head in amazement. "Lord, I hope he doesn't break his neck."

"But where shall he put Mrs. Wagner?"

"Oh my God, I didn't think of that." Jonathan didn't have long to ponder the dilemma, when a breathless Bertha entered the room, loaded down with fresh linens and a length of rope.

"If Willis makes it back in one piece with Mrs. Wagner, he'll be a hero. I ain't never seen such a sight in all my born days. He looked like a spraddle-legged corpse astride dat horse. His hat flew off before he got out of the yard, and the wind caught his coattails and waved them out behind him like sails. I'll be surprised if he can sit comfortably for a week, the way he was bouncin' in that saddle. He went out of sight with the reins pulled up under his chin, and his arms bowed like pullet wings."

Ginny and Jonathan shared a moment of laughter before another pain consumed her. He held her hand and offered what comfort he could. And after each contraction, he looked worse than she did by far. His face was ashen and his hands trembled, as he mopped the perspiration from her face and fluffed the pillows behind her head.

After the pain subsided, Ginny tried to take Jonathan's mind off the hours ahead, by talking about the first thing that popped into her head. "I never knew Willis was fond of horses."

"He's about as partial to horses as a dog is to fleas," Bertha quipped. "Still, he was determined to fetch the midwife, 'cause he didn't trust anyone else with such an important mission."

"That was very kind of him."

Downstairs, Lord Oliver poured himself a stiff drink and continued pacing the floor, waiting for word of Ginny's condition. As Bertha made her way up and down the stairs, she informed him of the latest news. The servant's devotion to their mistress amazed Lord Oliver, although he didn't know why it should surprise him. He, too, adored Ginny.

In record time Willis returned, the most disheveled butler anyone had ever seen. He had Mrs. Wagner in tow. Fearing he would pull her arm completely out of its socket, she dared not slow her pace. But it didn't hamper the velocity of her mouth.

Lord Oliver stepped from the drawing room when he heard the racket. As Willis hustled Mrs. Wagner up the stairs, she craned her head over her shoulder and shouted her complaints. "I've never had such ill treatment in my life. This . . . this barrel-headed man had the audacity to sit me atop that four-legged beast, and race us through the night like a couple of criminals. If I don't have a nose bleed from all this excitement, it will surprise me."

"Oh shut up, will you? You've belly-ached since I laid eyes on you. Mrs. Cross is havin' a baby, and I'll not stand for you upsettin' her . . . do you understand?"

"Humph," she snorted.

Willis jerked her to a halt. "Do you understand?"

"Yes." She jerked her arm from his grasp. Smoothing her hair and her rumpled dress, she took her carpetbag from Willis. With one parting shot, and her bony finger taking a bead on him, she warned, "You just stay out of my way, understand?" With that, she entered the birthing chamber.

Willis looked sheepish and downed his head. He'd never behaved in such a manner in his life. It truly embarrassed him when he recalled his ungracious behavior, but then it couldn't be helped. His mistress was having a baby. And he'd done what he had to do to insure her health.

Lord Oliver patted the frazzled servant on the back and handed him a snifter of brandy. "You look like you could use this."

"Thank you, sir."

Mrs. Wagner whirled around the room like a small tornado, issuing orders. If looks were any indication, she looked like she'd just survived a tornado. But no one dared to mention her appearance. They'd all heard the exchange between her and Willis. Only when she started to bind Ginny's arms to the bedpost, did Jonathan speak up. "What are you doing?"

331

"I'm giving her something to pull on. She'll need it before this is over."

"I'll help Ginny. She can use my hands."

The midwife looked at him in shock. "You plan to remain in here, while your wife gives birth?"

"I'll help her any way I can. Do you have a problem with that?"

"No . . . no, it's just that I've never heard of such a thing in my life."

"I am the father. It's my responsibility to stay by her side."

A small smile tugged the midwife's mouth "You are a rare man indeed, Mr. Cross."

"I don't know about that, Mrs. Wagner. We'll see."

Ginny watched her husband with something akin to worship. She would have sworn it was love gleaming from his eyes, when he attended her so gently. And the suffering that encompassed his face when she was having a contraction, was almost more than she could bear.

As the night wore on, the pains intensified as they became more frequent. Jonathan whispered words of encouragement, wiped her face with cool cloths, and held her hands.

Lord Oliver paced the carpet with Nat and Blue close on his heels. The other servants lingered in the hallway, waiting for word of their mistress.

Just as dawn was breaking across the horizon, Ginny's scream filled the manor. Lord Oliver's knees buckled, and he slid weakly into a chair. In a matter of moments, an angry squall pierced the stillness. New life surged through Lord Oliver, and he bounded from his chair with a zest that belied his years. He took the stairs two at a time and reached the master bedroom in record time. He waited anxiously in the hallway, his pacing renewed.

"It's a healthy boy," Mrs. Wagner announced proudly, handing the squalling infant to Bertha. Ginny lay exhausted against her pillows, but the smile that spanned her face would have brightened the darkest chamber. Jonathan lowered himself to the edge of the bed, exhausted. Bertha placed the bundle in Ginny's arms, and watched with pride as the parents took their first look at the babe.

"He's beautiful," Jonathan vowed, as he touched a wrinkled finger.

"Yes, he is beautiful," Ginny agreed, before another pain shot through her weakened body. A whimper escaped her, and fear washed over her face.

"What's wrong?" Jonathan whispered frantically.

"I reckon she ain't done yet," Mrs. Wagner offered, as she rinsed her hands and resumed her position at the foot of the bed.

"Well, glory be," Bertha said, glowing from ear to ear as she took the bundle from Ginny and stepped into the hallway.

The glow on Lord Oliver's face matched Bertha's, as they oohed and aahed over the squirming baby.

"He looks like he's been in the sun too long, doesn't he?" Blue teased, as he leaned over Bertha's shoulder to see the babe.

"He don't look no such way. He looks just like he's supposed to."

"Is Ginny all right?" Lord Oliver asked. "When can I see her?"

Bertha smiled secretly. "Mrs. Wagner says she ain't through yet."

"What do you mean?" he asked, just as Ginny screamed. "Oh my God, what's wrong?" The blood running through his body suddenly chilled, and he leaned against the wall for support.

Another angry squall came from the master suite.

Lord Oliver arched his brow in disbelief, and held up two trembling fingers in question.

Bertha nodded proudly, and stepped back inside the room with her bundle. Nat rushed to get Lord Oliver a chair.

Mrs. Wagner kept shaking her head in disbelief as she cleaned Ginny and removed the soiled linens. Jonathan and Ginny couldn't take their eyes off the matching bundles. Two beautiful, healthy boys squirmed and fretted, their tiny arms flailing the air. There was no way to describe Ginny's happiness, yet she couldn't keep her eyes open. Her exhausted body needed rest. After Mrs. Wagner finished instructing Jonathan, Bertha showed her to a room for a much-earned rest.

When Lord Oliver entered the master bedroom, Jonathan and Ginny were leaning head to head sound asleep, the babies between them. The tender smile that spanned Lord Oliver's face would have melted the meanest of hearts. And he himself was humbled by the scene before him. He touched each baby in turn and marveled over their beauty. Oh, how very proud he was of his son. He'd outdone himself in the selection of a wife. Jonathan had indeed found himself a mate with rich red blood.

The only cloud on Ginny's horizon, was her fear that Jonathan might believe the lies Harold had told him. Still, she wouldn't let herself dwell on it. Jonathan never once voiced a moment's doubt about his sons. He was proud, and his pride gleamed from his eyes like a bright light.

Maureen Sutton did all the things that new grandmothers do. She couldn't take her eyes off the boys, and she and Lord Oliver behaved as though they themselves were responsible for the births. It eased Ginny's mind when her mother mentioned that her own mother had been a twin. No one else seemed bothered that Ginny had had twins. They were all relieved to realize why Ginny had gotten so big. Now it was perfectly clear.

Patrick was the only one who didn't make a complete fool of himself. Still, he came close. It was hard for him to imagine that Ginny had indeed given birth at all, not his little sister.

The manor became a thoroughfare of visitors. Everyone from far and wide came to see the babies. Lord Oliver was the official welcomer, and he relished the chore, extolling each characteristic of his grandchildren. He had a way about him that charmed each individual, until they felt a very special bond with the family.

For some it was a little confusing when the babies were named. All were not privy to the circumstances of Jonathan's birth. But Lord Oliver lied so smoothly with his explanation. His story was that when Jonathan set out for America, he wanted to make it on his own, without the Summerfield name to open doors for him. This information only enhanced the respect they had for Jonathan. Everyone had heard the Summerfield name, and knew of the wealth it denoted. But now the picture had changed dramatically with the birth of the twins, and Lord Oliver insisted that his son claim the Summerfield name. So it was, they named the boys Oliver Eugene Summerfield and Cross Sutton Summerfield.

As the weeks passed, it was harder than ever for Jonathan to go about his daily chores. He loved helping with the babies in any way that he could. And as before, when he seemed to know when Ginny bathed, now he seemed to sense when it was time for her to nurse the babies. He was never faraway.

As had become their habit, they brought the children

downstairs to the drawing room in the evening, as they discussed their daily activities. It became a routine sight to see Lord Oliver with one baby in his arms and the other in Jonathan's. Lord Oliver's return to England was never mentioned. He was in his element, and he planned to make the most of it. He knew well how fast children grew up, and he didn't want to miss anything. He'd posted a letter to Geoffrey, telling him of the births and of his plans for an extended visit.

Ginny's new figure played havoc with Jonathan's peace of mind. His wife was the most beautiful creature he'd ever seen, and he was hard-pressed to keep his hands to himself. Still, he vowed he wouldn't touch her until she wanted him. Daily, he prayed that she would want him soon.

One evening, as they sat in the drawing room completely at peace with each other, Willis informed them they had a visitor. Christine Iverson.

The time Ginny had dreaded was before her. Jonathan didn't miss the look of fear that skirted across her face. When she would have risen from her place beside him, he put his hand on her arm to stay her and shook his head. "You have nothing to fear from her, Ginny. Don't you know that?"

She sighed deeply and settled against the cushions.

Christine whirled into the room as though she still owned the place. She was dressed in the height of fashion, yet nothing she would ever do would make her as beautiful as the new mother. It seemed as though Christine realized that when she saw Ginny sitting comfortably next to Jonathan. Lord Oliver had settled himself on the floor next to the pallet the babies shared. Christine took in the cozy scene with a frown marring her brow.

"Well, well, Jonathan, it looks like you've settled into

family life comfortably." A perfectly arched brow winged upward, as though what she'd just said was an absurd lie.

"Did you ever think that I wouldn't?" he asked coldly.

"I had my moments," she admitted. Christine's gaze wandered to the babies for a moment, before shifting to Ginny.

"Ginny Sutton, you've got it all now, haven't you?"

"I'm afraid I don't know what you mean," Ginny answered softly.

"It's Ginny Summerfield," Lord Oliver was quick to correct.

"How confusing, Sutton, Cross, Summerfield. Your name changes as fast as the seasons, Ginny. What will it be the next time I see you? Marlow, perhaps?"

Jonathan came to his feet in a fury. "What's that suppose to mean?"

Ginny grabbed his arm. He turned to his wife and saw the tears sparkling in her eyes, and the barely perceptible shake of her head. He dropped beside her and put his arm around her, drawing her close.

"You remember the twin Marlows, don't you, Ginny? From what I've heard, you and Darryl Marlow became very close, while you were staying with them—very close."

"Darryl saved my life, if that's what you mean."

"I heard that, but I also heard you were so grateful to him that the two of you became lovers." She turned toward the babies and pointed her finger. "That, in fact, those are his babies you're trying to pawn off on Jonathan."

Lord Oliver and Jonathan came to their feet in a rush. "That's a bald-faced lie, and if ever I hear you repeat the lie, I'll personally wring your scrawny neck," Jonathan shouted.

"If it's a lie, why are you getting so upset? I don't have to say anything to anyone. Everyone already knows it's the truth . . . except you."

"Young lady, and I use the term for lack of a better word, I suggest you make yourself scarce around here. You've worn out your welcome, and I'll not stand by idly while you besmirch the character of my daughter-in-law. If you don't get a move on, I'll personally see you out."

"Humph. I can't believe you are so blind."

"Out!" The men shouted.

The babies began to cry, and Ginny scooped them from their pallet and rushed from the room, her tears blending with her babies'.

Willis slammed the door behind Christine with a resounding thud, as soon as she marched through it. He would have spat, but then he would have had to clean it up, and Christine Iverson, the bitch, wasn't worth it.

Jonathan wanted to follow Ginny, but first he needed to explain to his father what had happened to her that night so long ago—and to thank him for his unyielding support.

33

Ginny quieted the babies, and helped Bertha get them ready for bed. She tried not to cry, but it was a struggle she lost as soon as she left the nursery. Were Jonathan and his father deciding the fate of her and the babies? There was no way she could prove that Christine was lying. The lies were stacked against her, first Harold and Evelyn, now Christine. She'd tried to explain about Darryl, but Christine's lies made it sound like they'd been lovers. Gentle, kind Darryl—how good he'd been to her. Now she knew for certain it was Christine who had found the Marlows, and told them where she lived. But why? Was she so desperately in love with Jonathan that she would do anything to have him?

Ginny had grieved over the love she thought Jonathan had for Christine. But to her pleasure and profound relief, Jonathan hadn't acted as though he was in love with Christine. He was a perfect husband and father. He couldn't possibly be pretending all the time . . . could he? Even before his father had arrived at Crossroads, he'd appeared content with his lot in life. Unless Ginny was completely blinded by her love for him, his tender regard seemed real.

Ginny heard the door open and knew the confrontation was at hand. What had Jonathan decided to do with her? She wiped the tears from her face and turned to her husband.

Anger flashed across Jonathan's face. He hated Christine even more, just knowing she still had the power to hurt his beloved Ginny.

Ginny saw his anger and steeled herself for the worst.

"If you'll let me stay the night, I'll leave tomorrow," she said quietly.

"What are you talking about?"

"I thought you would want me to leave. I have no way of proving that Christine is lying." She lifted her hands and shrugged her body helplessly.

"Don't you know, Ginny?" he asked softly.

"What?"

"Christine could spout her lies until hell freezes over, and I wouldn't believe her."

Amazement flooded her face. "You wouldn't?"

"I don't care if she had the whole Marlow clan in attendance. She's a liar. Don't you think I know you, Ginny? I know what kind of person you are. I could never love someone like Christine described."

"Love?" Ginny croaked.

"Do you doubt it?"

She nodded her head, then changed her mind, and quickly shook her head, as hot blood rushed to every part of her body. Love! He loved her. "Then why were you angry when you came in here?"

"Because she can still hurt you."

"Don't you love her?" she asked bravely.

He laughed. "Love her? Are you kidding? I can barely tolerate her presence."

"But all those times when I was working for you, and she came by and you left with her, I thought you—"

"You thought what? That I loved her?"

Ginny nodded.

"Oh Ginny, don't you know I only wanted to protect you from her wicked tongue? The only way I could do

340

that was to get her out of the house. Those were some of the most miserable times of my life."

Ginny laughed softly. "And all this time, I thought you were grieving for Christine."

"Did I act like I was grieving?"

"Well, no," she admitted.

"Trust me, the only time I grieved about her, was when I thought I would have to spend time in her company."

"Oh, I've been such a fool. I thought when you married me, that it was really Christine that you wanted."

"What did I ever do that would make you think something like that?"

"That day in the stables, I thought I had interrupted the two of you while you were making love."

"Why?"

"Because when she turned around to face me, her bodice was unbuttoned. Now I believe she planned it that way, to make me to think exactly what I thought."

"Well, I for damn sure didn't touch her. I wanted her out of there." He lifted his hand and cupped her face. "You're the only one I've ever wanted."

She turned from him and walked to the window. She didn't see the star-studded sky that lit the sweeping lawn, or notice the sweet-smelling breeze that caressed her face and teased her hair. She was remembering *that* love-filled night and the aftermath of pain she'd suffered. When she could control the trembling of her voice, she whispered, "You called me Christine."

"When?" he asked in disbelief.

"That . . . that night . . ." she stumbled over her words.

He knew instinctively which night she was referring to. "In my mind, I've gone over everything that happened *that night* a thousand times, and I would have remem-

341

bered something that important."

"But you did. I heard you," she said sadly.

"I'll admit I'd had a lot to drink that night, but Christine was the last thing on my mind. Tell me what I said?"

"I can't, I just can't."

He placed his hands on her shoulders and turned her to face him. "Please, I can't stand this barrier between us."

"Oh Christine . . . you're good," she blurted out, and buried her face in his shirt front.

"Are you sure that's what I said?"

"Yes."

"I'm sorry, I would never cause you pain. Maybe that's what I said. I was so frustrated with her that I was ready to wring her neck. She made a complete fool of herself at Milly's party, then made up some farfetched excuse to get me to take her home. I will admit that when I first discovered you in my bed, I thought it was her." He skimmed his knuckles across her face and nuzzled his chin in her hair. "Will you forgive me?"

She nodded against his chest.

He held her tightly, savoring the feel of her.

"Can I ask you something?"

"Anything your heart desires. Like I said, I don't want any barriers between us."

"I know you married me because of the babies. But I overheard Christine and Denby talking, and they said you married me so your father would deed you this property."

"Here, sit down, and I'll tell you what happened." He led her to the bed, where they sat side by side. He took her hand in his, and drew tiny little circles around her palm as he pondered where to begin.

"First of all, let me assure you that I would have married you anyway I could get you. That you were going to have a baby—" he laughed—"*babies,* only hastened my intention."

She smiled and squeezed his hand.

"Ginny, being labeled a bastard is a terrible thing. Even if your father happens to be a very wealthy man, the stigma never goes away, no matter how hard you try to prove your worth. But truly I had a good life, and I made my way. Several years ago, I thought I was madly in love. The girl was from a very wealthy, aristocratic family. But that didn't matter. I thought she loved me. When her family found out about us, it mortified them. It didn't matter that my father came from a distinguished aristocratic background, with a lineage as long as my leg and wealth that far surpassed anything they would ever have. I was still a bastard, and I wasn't good enough for her. She pointed this out to me in colorful phrases." He paused and lifted her hand to his lips. "It hurt me deeply, not because of the love I thought I had for her, but because she didn't believe in me as a person."

"I'm sorry that it happened, but if it hadn't, I would never have met you."

"Me too, now. Anyway, I don't know how Lord Oliver got wind of the situation, but he did. Probably from Blue. And truly, he never mentioned the affair. But he sent for me. He'd come up with this idea. He bought this plantation, and he wanted me to run it, to be the master of my own destiny."

"That sounds like your father. He loves you very much."

"At first, I thought he was ashamed of me, but I realized quickly that wasn't the case. Then I decided he was in ill health, and I would do it to please him. But I'm convinced he used a little deceit to get his way. He wanted me to think he was in bad health. Since his venture

343

to America, I've watched him closely. He's as healthy as a horse, thank God."

She traced the length of his fingers as he talked, listening intently.

"Ginny, it's true my father wanted me to find a wife and have children. It's also true that he told me if I married, he would deed the plantation to me. But that's not why I married you. Try to look at it my way for a moment. If Christine Iverson had been the only available wife material, I would not have married her, no matter what my father offered. I didn't marry you to gain a plantation. I married you because I love you."

She collapsed in his arms. "Oh Jonathan, I love you so, but I was afraid. I couldn't imagine that you could ever love someone like me."

"Ginny, my love, you've brought me peace and happiness I never dreamed possible. You turned this house into a home for me, and everyone else who lives here." He laughed. "Look at Willis. You turned a crotchety old man into a vibrant, caring member of this family. He risked life and limb for you the night the boys were born. And Bertha is in her element with her new position. And our table has never boasted such tempting, delicious food."

"Or desserts?" she added, rubbing her hand over his stomach.

"Or desserts," he admitted with a smile. "And that's another thing. Do you think, for one moment, anyone else would have cared about my penchant for sweets the way you do?"

She cupped his face in her hands, so she could see his eyes as she asked, "What about the boys? Did you ever think they might not be yours? Especially since they were twins."

"Not for one second was there ever any question in my

344

mind. Still, I bet Christine gloated to high heaven when she heard we had twins. I'm sure she thought that was her trump card. I don't know how she found out where you were when you disappeared, but she's the very one who sent Harold here."

"How could she be so cruel? Does she love you so very much?"

He laughed bitterly. "Christine doesn't love anyone but herself. She wanted *this house*. It was always the house she wanted, not me."

"I would want you, if we had to live in a shack," Ginny admitted softly.

"Even if you didn't have anything to wear but my shirts?" he teased, a leer encompassing his face.

"Most assuredly," she answered pertly. "But would you love me, if we had no cakes, and pies, or sweet tarts to whet your appetite?"

"I don't know. I'd have to think about that," he offered in a deeply serious vein, just before he toppled her to her back and his mouth claimed hers.

They became lost in sensation, as she welcomed his invasion. Long, hot, wet kisses blended with quick, urgent biting, licking kisses. They became consumed with their need for each other. Hands and arms, legs and feet became tangled and twined as they sought to draw closer. Clothes loosened and cast aside were quickly forgotten. At one breathless point, Jonathan lifted his head and questioned hopefully, "Can we do this? I mean, is it all right?"

She nodded and wrapped her arms around his neck. It didn't take much urging to draw his mouth to hers.

For Jonathan, it was like returning home after a long absence. That first surge of excitement, when one first glimpses it, and the increasing fervor as one draws nearer. Ginny was home — she was the light in his existence, the warmth of a glowing fire, the foundation of his being. And he loved her with a love that was strong and binding and filled with giving and receiving.

Ginny needed this wonderful, strong man in her life, to make her complete. She relished his warm touch and coaxing smile, his eyes gleaming with laughter and pride. There was no longer any doubt of his love. He was hers completely. He'd given her that assurance.

The lovers played until they were breathless with anticipation. Her breasts were full and tempting, and he stroked them tenderly with a skill that left her panting.

Ginny, secure in the new confidence that he wanted no other, took his breath away with her boldness.

He twined his hands in her coppery hair and slid his hand the length of her gleaming body, taking the time to delve into temptation as he mounted a taut nipple, kissed her belly, and tongued her perfectly shaped navel.

In the past long, lonely weeks, Jonathan had had his memories of Ginny to comfort him when she'd refused his lovemaking. But even before that, when they had made love, Ginny had held something back, and he'd known she was never completely his. Only on that night so long ago had she truly belonged to him. In this, his darkest hour, that memory alone had become the seed that had given him hope. Now his Ginny was back. She teased and tormented him with her own play, until he thought he could not bear it an instant longer. She mounted him and rocked her hips against him. He moaned and raked his hands over her legs, meeting her thrust. The shimmering moonlight that cast its glow into the room lit her hair with a fiery radiance, and the look on her face bespoke a woman deeply in love.

They moved together with an urgency and need born of their affirmation of love. She strained against him, her fingers twining in the mat of curls that spanned his chest. He thrust deeply and rapidly again and again, sending her into the splendor of ecstasy where he joined her in exploding release.

A gentle breeze cooled their damp bodies, as they lay replete in each other's arms, their hearts overflowing with love and happiness. Jonathan traced the fullness of her kiss-swollen mouth, as he whispered softly, "I love you, Ginny."

"And I you," she purred.

"I've been thinking about something," he admitted, rising to his elbow.

"It sounds serious."

"It's important to me. I'd like to give a dinner party." He felt Ginny stiffen beside him. "A small dinner party," he amended.

"Why?"

"To put to rest any gossip Christine might have spread. I don't want any trace of her evilness to stain our marriage or our children. Our future is right here on this plantation, and we are secure in our love — granted it's taken a while to bear out that truth. But what of others? Friends and acquaintances? If they're around us and the boys, don't you think the truth will win out? Without any substance to back up her claim, Christine's gossip would wither and die."

"This means a lot to you?"

He lifted her hand and kissed her palm. "Yes, it does."

"Then a dinner party it shall be." Ginny knew in her heart it was the remnant of his past — that echoed of rejection and pain — that caused him to want to snuff out the rumors. He didn't owe anyone anything, or any kind of explanation. But he loved her and his children, and he would do anything to protect them. Ginny vowed she would be the perfect hostess for her perfect husband.

347

The dinner party was quickly approaching, and Ginny was driving them all crazy. She'd checked and rechecked the menu, until Laine decided she would hide if Ginny entered her domain again. She'd worn the guest list out going over it, and the seating arrangement had caused her nightmares. She'd questioned Lord Oliver about the affair until his voice was hoarse from answering her questions. And to beat it all, she vowed she'd discovered a gray hair from fretting about what to wear.

Jonathan assured her repeatedly that everything was running as smoothly as a well-oiled clock. Finally, the day before the dinner, he'd taken her aside and convinced her a visit to Milly was what she needed to calm her nerves. Nat volunteered to accompany her, and Jonathan and his father assured her they would be home all day to help Bertha with the babies. After an improper amount of hugs and kisses, Ginny left for her visit.

The routine at the manor followed a leisurely pace throughout the day, until Bertha developed a headache and took to her bed.

Jonathan tried to work on the books, his attention easily distracted as he listened for Ginny to return. Giving up the tedious task, he instructed Blue to prepare his bath. So it was that Jonathan was up to his chin in bathwater, when Lord Oliver entered the bedchamber with two squalling babies straining angrily in each arm.

"I can't figure out why they are so unhappy. When I get one quieted, the other starts bellowing and upsets the other, and the whole process starts all over again."

"Here, I'll take one."

Lord Oliver, relieved for any assistance, quickly handed Cross to his father. Jonathan slipped off the baby's clothes and propped him on his knees. Cross instantly quieted. The water lapped over his toes, and he began slapping his fist into the depths. Jonathan laughed at his son's antics, and soon droplets of water clung to their hair and from their eyelashes. Jonathan soaped the baby and lowered him into the water to rinse. Cross laughed. Jonathan lifted him above his head and nuzzled his neck and his belly, then he kissed his toes. The baby giggled and drooled into his father's face.

Lord Oliver had laid his bundle on the bed, and was hurriedly dispatching Oliver's diaper and gown.

No one was at the door to greet Ginny when she returned. She wondered if something might have happened. She hurried up the stairs and checked the nursery. The babies were not in their cribs. She ran pell-mell into the master suite. The scene that met her startled gaze melted her heart.

Jonathan was handing one laughing, drenched little boy to his father, while Lord Oliver gave him the other child. Water puddled around the tub, but noone seemed to care. Lord Oliver took the wet bundle against himself, soaking the front of his shirt, and carried him to the bed. Ginny watched as Jonathan cooed and gooed and soaped and rinsed his son. He scooped Oliver into the air and nuzzled his neck and his belly and kissed his toes. This baby also giggled and drooled into his father's face. As she watched the play, she soon understood why water puddled the floor. Her heart swelled with such love that she didn't think she could contain it.

Lord Oliver tried repeatedly to diaper the wiggling Cross. Ginny couldn't control her laughter. Instead of embarrassment at being in the room with her father-in-law, while her husband lolled naked in his bath, she dismissed the thought with a shrug and entered the room. She leaned over the tub and gave Jonathan a quick kiss, and patted Oliver's bare buttocks. "You look like you're having fun," she said to Jonathan.

349

"I am," he admitted readily.

"And you, Lord Oliver, are you having fun?"

"I would be, if I could get this diaper to fit properly. I'm making the baby angry with my fumbling."

"You need to turn him over on his back. It will be easier."

"Not for me, it's not. I had him on his back."

She laughed and reached for the baby.

"Wait," Lord Oliver shouted. "Let me see something." He studied the baby's bottom for a moment before he turned to Jonathan. "Let me have Oliver." Lord Oliver stepped to the tub and took the child. He placed him beside his brother on his stomach. He studied the babies' bottoms for several seconds.

"What is it?" Jonathan questioned, stepping from the tub and wrapping his robe around him.

"Look at this. They both have it."

"What?" Ginny and Jonathan asked in alarm.

"A backward *S*. It's a mark that all the Summerfield males carry."

"If we all have one, where's mine?" Jonathan asked, draping an arm around Ginny's shoulder as they peered at the wiggling babies.

"On your hip, just like the boys, just like mine," Lord Oliver informed him.

"Why have I never known this?" Jonathan questioned.

"I don't know. It just never came up."

Ginny studied Lord Oliver with amusement marking her features. Wasn't love a mystery? This powerful member of the realm was standing in her bedroom with his finely tailored clothes soaked with bath water, happily trying to diaper a naked squirming baby. Ginny laughed and volunteered to do the task.

"I'll get better," Lord Oliver assured her. "It just takes practice."

350

Freshly diapered, the boys were content with all the attention. To the adults' delight, they rewarded them with toothless grins, kicking the air and cooing with delight.

Later, when the boys grew hungry, Lord Oliver excused himself, and Ginny saw to nourishment of her children. Jonathan sat on the bed and watched, his eyes bright with love and pride. What had he ever done to deserve such happiness?

34

Shortly before the party, Ginny checked with Laine in the kitchen to see how the young cook was faring. Since this was Laine's first time cooking for a group this size, Ginny worried that she might not be running on schedule. Much to her relief, Laine was not one bit nervous, and assured her mistress that everything was going smoothly.

Ginny *was* nervous. For the third time that day, she went into the dining room and viewed it with a critical eye. Yes, the silverware and serving pieces were *still* free of tarnish, the tablecloth *still* didn't have a wrinkle or stain on it, and there were *still* fresh candles in the candelabrum. Nothing must be amiss this night. After instructing the servants on their duties and complimenting them on their attire, she went upstairs to the nursery to check on Bertha and the twins. Mrs. Wagner had suggested they acquire a wet nurse, but Ginny had refused for the time being. Her babies would let her know when she wasn't providing them with enough nourishment.

Afterwards, she entered the bedroom to change into her gown. Jonathan had just removed himself from the tub and was briskly drying off. He looked over at her as he tossed the towel on the chair, smiling devilishly as he watched her watching him. He donned his robe, not bothering to tie it.

"It's about time you got here," he said with a lusty gleam in his eyes.

"There were so many things to tend to."

"Now you can tend to me, right?" As he walked her way, his robe parted, giving her a complete view of his magnificent body.

"We don't have time," she protested, as he hauled her against him.

"We have an hour," he said lazily as his mouth teased her neck, then moved up to nibble the delicate shell of her ear.

"But I've already had my bath and fixed my hair." Even as she made the remark, his hands had already started unfastening the multitude of buttons scaling her back.

"I'll help you with your hair, my love, and gladly assist you with your bath."

"But—"

He drowned her protests with his mouth, his tongue sliding between her parted lips. Her tongue entwined with his, and she melted against him. As he kissed her deeply and thoroughly, he moved slightly away from her and pulled her bodice from her shoulders and over her arms, until it rested on her hips. She was not even aware he had removed her chemise, until she felt the crisp hairs on his chest tickling her breasts.

In the next instant, the rest of her clothing and Jonathan's robe pooled around their feet.

An hour later, Jonathan, Ginny, Lord Oliver, Mrs. Sutton, and Patrick waited in the parlor for the arrival of their guests. Jonathan had issued invitations to only five families and their older children. There was a purpose behind each invitation. The Bradens and their son, William, arrived first, followed by the Harbisons and their daughter, Caroline. They hoped to show the parents of William and Caroline that the pair were in love. The lawyer, Edward Colburn and his wife, arrived next. Jonathan had hired him to handle his legal action against Denby. The Vincents and Milly, and the Talbots along with their daughter

Edna, arrived last. Edna Talbot was the most important guest of all. Through her, Christine would learn that the rumors she had started were all in vain.

Jonathan introduced everyone to his father. Lord Oliver immediately began boasting about his twin grandchildren.

"They look just like my son, and of course," he added slyly, "they must look like me, too, since Jonathan and I favor."

Milly leaned in toward Edna. "They have the thickest black hair you've ever seen, Edna. Someday, I vow, they will be breaking a lot of hearts."

Edna didn't utter a word. Christine had told her that Harold and Darryl were blonds.

Lord Oliver had set the mood for the party. Everyone was in festive spirits, which helped Ginny feel at ease with her new role as mistress. Jonathan watched her admiringly, as she entertained their guests with delightful stories about the joys and problems of twins.

"They have their days and nights reversed. I dare say, there isn't a person in this household who's had a full night's sleep, since they were born."

"Ginny, why don't you bring them down now, so we can introduce them to our guests before we dine?" Jonathan asked.

"I'll help you," Maureen volunteered.

A few minutes later, they returned, each holding a baby in her arms.

Maureen handed Lord Oliver one of his grandsons, and Ginny handed Jonathan the other one. Everyone gathered around them.

Lord Oliver beamed as he announced, "Now, this one's named Oliver Eugene Summerfield . . . after me and Ginny's father. He arrived about five minutes after his brother."

"And this is Cross Sutton Summerfield," Jonathan said,

his long brown finger caressing the baby's cheek.

"How can you tell them apart?" Mrs. Vincent asked. "They look just alike to me."

"It was difficult at first," Ginny said, "until I found a curl at the nape of Cross's neck that Oliver doesn't have."

Edna moved in closer to get a good look at the babies.

"Would you like to hold him, Edna?" Jonathan asked, glancing slyly at Ginny.

"Oh no, I couldn't," she said, jumping back as though the idea terrified her.

"Go ahead, dear. You've never held a baby, and one day you'll be a mother, too," Mrs. Talbot said with a hopeful expression on her face.

Reluctantly, Edna held out her arms, and Jonathan placed the bundle into them. Edna stood stiffly, staring down into the infant's cherub face. His coloring, his dark eyes, his black hair, everything about him resembled Jonathan. Christine had to be mistaken. Also, if Jonathan had any doubt that they weren't his, he and his father would never dote over them as they were doing now. And Ginny? Edna looked over at her. She certainly didn't behave as though she were deceiving her husband. She and her husband were very obviously in love with one another.

The infant turned his head towards Edna's plump breast and began nuzzling it. Again Edna jumped. The baby mewled softly. Oliver, hearing his brother, let out a loud cry.

Ginny could not help replying, "Oh, and that's another way I can tell them apart. Oliver cries louder, and Cross is always hungry."

Edna's face flamed a brilliant red as the guests burst into laughter.

Afraid she'd drop his child, Jonathan immediately took him from Edna's arms and handed him over to Ginny. Lord Oliver gave the crying Oliver to Maureen.

"If you'll excuse us," Ginny said, "I think it's time we put them down."

After a while, Maureen returned, telling them Ginny would be down shortly.

Upstairs she and Bertha diapered the babies. As Ginny leaned down to place Oliver in his crib, she heard a *thunk* and turned to see Bertha fall across the bed next to little Cross. Next, she saw Denby, his hand raised and drawn into a tight fist.

"Mr. Denby?" she asked surprised. "What have you done?"

As Ginny straightened, an icy voice coming from behind her froze her in her tracks.

"Stay where you are, Ginny, and keep your mouth shut. Richard, tie up the maid and drag her into the wardrobe."

Ginny stared at Bertha's still body. "My God, did . . . did you kill her?"

"No," Denby said. "She'll come around in a while."

Ginny turned, noting the gun in Christine's hand aimed at her. Fear surged through her.

"How did you get in here, Christine?"

Christine laughed low in her throat as she moved backwards to the nursery door, locking it. "Oh, you didn't know about the secret passage?"

"Secret passage?"

"Yes, the one my grandfather incorporated into the plans, when he built this house. He wanted an escape route from the classroom, should Indians attack his family. I'm not surprised your father never told you. My father didn't even tell us, because he thought my brothers and I would use it to hide from our nanny. We discovered it quite by accident when we were older." She moved to the bookcase at the corner of the room and pushed one end of it. The bookcase swung back like a door. "Wasn't my grandfather a brilliant man?"

Ginny watched Denby open the wardrobe, then shove Bertha's crumpled body inside it.

She shifted her attention back to Christine. "What are your plans?" Ginny asked, dreading the answer.

Christine brought out a pencil and paper from her coat pocket, and handed them to Ginny. "First, you're going to write a letter to Jonathan, and tell him you can no longer live with your lie. You are going to live with the twins' real father. He mustn't follow you."

Ginny walked to the bureau and hastily scrawled the note. "He won't believe this rubbish," she said, leaving the paper beneath the candlelight. "Bertha will tell him someone hit her."

"And who's to say it wasn't you?"

Ginny could not believe it. "Christine, you *are* out of your mind!"

"I don't care what you think," she hissed. "At least you'll be gone from my house. *My* house, you hear! Denby, you carry one baby, and Ginny can carry the other one. Let's get out of here, before Jonathan comes to check on them."

As Ginny leaned down to pick up Oliver, she broke the chain on her necklace before she lifted her baby from the crib. As Denby lifted Cross, she asked, "Have you lost your mind, too, Mr. Denby? Jonathan will kill you for this."

"How? He can't prove I had a thing to do with it."

"Don't be so sure of that. He and his father have proof you have stolen from them."

Denby's face tightened.

"My baby needs another blanket," she demanded, holding back her tears.

Denby grabbed a blanket and wrapped it around the infant.

"Hurry," Christine ordered.

When Denby and Ginny reached the secret door, Christine unlocked the door leading into the nursery. "That should really frustrate Jonathan. He'll wonder how on earth his wife and children left without someone seeing them."

With Christine close on her heels, Ginny dropped one of her blankets. She bent down to retrieve it, leaving the chain behind, hoping Christine's skirt tail wouldn't rake it inside the passage.

As Ginny went through the door, the damp musky smell assailed her senses. Christine picked up a lighted torch and closed the door behind them. Ginny held little Oliver tightly in her arms, and followed Denby down the steep stairway. *Oh Jonathan,* she cried inside, *she did come back. I told you she would.*

Wondering why Ginny was taking so long to join them, Jonathan excused himself and went upstairs to check on her.

When he entered the nursery, he didn't see Ginny or Bertha. Thinking they'd probably put the babies down for the night and Bertha was taking a break, he walked quietly over to the cradles. The cradles were empty. *That's strange,* he pondered with a puzzled frown, as he left the nursery and went to check the master suite. No one.

A chill swept through his body. Something was wrong, damned wrong. He raced down the hall and entered the nursery again, his heart pounding in his chest. He heard a muffled groan and a thumping sound coming from the wardrobe. Jerking the door open, he found Bertha bound and gagged, lying in a heap on the floor.

"Oh God," he cried out, helping the poor woman to a sitting position. Kneeling, he untied the cloth from her mouth. Her eyes were wide and dazed. "Bertha, where's Ginny and the twins?"

Her answer was unclear, then he noticed the side of her face was swollen, and blood was oozing from her mouth.

Bertha, for God's sake, tell me what's happened?"

"Sumpin hit me, Mistah Cross. Dat's all I know."

Jonathan bounded to his feet. "I'll be back, Bertha."

He ran downstairs and into the parlor. "Ginny and the babies," he said breathlessly, "someone's kidnapped them."

Lord Oliver turned as white as his hair. "Wha-a-at?"

Maureen gripped Patrick's arm. "But . . . I just left them."

"They knocked Bertha out and put her in the wardrobe in the nursery. Men, I need your help in conducting a complete search of the grounds. Whoever took them can't be far away. Willis, ask the servants if they saw anything strange going on. Ladies, please stay inside."

Willis set the wine decanter on the table and darted from the room, while all the men went outside. As Jonathan reached the door, he called back. "Mrs. Sutton, Bertha's hurt. Will you take care of her?"

"I'll see to her," Maureen replied, and quickly made her way to the nursery. As she untied Bertha, tears overflowed her eyes. "Who could have done this, Bertha? And why?"

Bertha was crying, too. "Oh, I wish I could help, but I don't know nothin'."

Maureen helped Bertha to her feet and onto the bed. "I'll get some cold cloths for your head. You lie down."

As she turned to leave, she glimpsed something shiny on the floor at the corner of the room. Walking over, she bent down and saw it was a thin silver chain. She tried to pick it up, but it was caught beneath the baseboard. She recognized it as the necklace that Patrick had given Ginny, but where was the locket? She remembered telling Ginny how pleased Patrick would be when he saw her wearing it. She looked around on the floor for the locket.

"Bertha, I found Ginny's necklace. Do you remember her wearing it, when we came upstairs earlier?"

"Yes'm, 'cause it got caught in the baby's fingers while

359

she was changin' his diaper."

"Did she take it off?"

"Not dat I remember."

Maureen sat back on her heels and looked up at the bookcase above it. Then something her husband told her years ago leaped to her mind. *The bookcase in the classroom hides a secret passage I'm supposed to use, if there's an emergency. The children don't know about it, because it leads to the river. Mr. Lyndal's afraid they could drown if they ever learned about it.*

Maureen stood up and began running her hand along the edge of the molding. She felt a notch behind it, and pulled until the bookcase opened halfway. Looking down, she saw the heart-shaped locket still attached to the chain just inside the passage. She worked it to the edge of the case and picked it up.

Running to the window, she raised it. "Jonathan! Come to the nursery, and hurry!"

She heard someone's voice in the distance calling Jonathan, and knew he'd be there shortly. She turned to Bertha who was staring dumbly at the secret door. "Ginny didn't know about it, did she?"

"No, ma'am, or I'm sure she woulda said sumpin', while we was gittin' the nursery ready."

Maureen went to the bureau to get the candle. It was then she saw the letter.

"Maureen!"

As Jonathan rushed into the room, Maureen thrust the note into his hands.

As he read it, she watched a black fury encompass his face, and the muscles working furiously in his jaw. He scowled darkly and tossed it on the bureau. "She's insane to think I'd believe this!"

"Who?"

"Christine. This is her handiwork."

"I know how she got in here."

360

He followed his mother-in-law into the nursery, where she showed him the secret passage.

"Christine had to have help to carry this off, and I'd bet my last dollar that it's Denby. They have Ginny and the twins, Maureen."

"I don't understand. Why would she want to kidnap them?"

"It's a long story, and I don't have time to explain. Do you know where this leads?"

"Yes, it leads to the river. When my husband tutored the Lyndal children, he told me about it. It wasn't until I found Ginny's necklace caught beneath the case that I remembered."

"I'm going to get my pistol, and I'll take this passageway. Blue's at the stable. Please have someone tell him to saddle Beowulf and a horse for himself, and meet me at the river. I'll bring a torch, and he'll see my light." As he rushed toward the door, he said, "Pray, Maureen, that I reach them in time. Christine is insane."

Maureen sent the message to Blue, and called the rest of the men together and told them what had happened. When she returned to the nursery, Bertha was crying. "Does your head hurt?" she asked.

"No, it ain't dat, ma'am," she said, wiping her eyes with her apron. "I'm hurtin' over Miz Ginny and my babies. Dat woman's plumb crazy, jest like Mistah Jonathan said she was."

"I know," Maureen agreed.

Bertha knew about Harold and his wife coming to Crossroads, and told her the story. "Now, I weren't eavesdroppin', mind you. Things got a bit heated and voices carry. But I knowed everythin' between Miz Ginny and Mistah Jonathan was all right, 'cause they 'came real close after dat. Why, you couldn't break 'em apart if you'd had to."

361

Maureen forced the next question from her mouth. "Bertha, would Christine hurt my daughter and grandchildren?"

"Oh, Miz Sutton, I don't know. For her to go and pull sumpin' like this, there ain't no tellin' what she might do."

When Maureen started crying, Bertha scolded herself for saying such a thing. She stood up and enfolded Maureen in her arms. "Now, Mistah Jonathan ain't gonna let nothin' happen to her or those chillun of his'n. He'll find him, you ken bet on it. And Mr. Lord Oliver, he'll help 'em, too. Yes'm, he will."

Downstairs, Edna was pacing the parlor, while the other ladies watched her.

"Dear, don't worry. Jonathan will find them."

Edna burst into tears. "It's all my fault."

"Your fault?"

"Yes. I helped Christine do this horrible thing, but honestly, I didn't know it. I told her about the party tonight and . . . and even repeated the gossip that the children weren't Jonathan's." She gulped. "I believed Christine. But after tonight, I know how very wrong I was in abetting her. If something happens to them, I'll never forgive myself."

35

The current carried the boat swiftly downriver, the full moon the only source of light. Ginny held Oliver, while Christine held Cross . . . and the gun. What did the woman think she'd do? Jump from the boat and swim for her life, leaving her children behind? Denby was obviously not a boatman, and Ginny prayed they would reach their destination, wherever that might be, without capsizing the boat and drowning her children. Several times they had hit debris in the river, and the boat had tilted precariously.

The babies had not uttered a sound, the swaying of the boat rocking them to sleep. Knowing sound carried clearly over water, Ginny was tempted to pinch Oliver and hope her husband was near enough to hear his loud cry. But insane as Christine was, she feared the woman would toss her baby into the river to silence him.

Had Jonathan found her locket, or had it disappeared on the other side of the passage? Poor Bertha would not have been able to help him at all. The *what ifs* whirled through her mind, plucking madly at any straw of hope. She knew Jonathan would never believe the contents of the letter Christine had forced her to write. He would see it as the workings of an evil, twisted mind, and that in itself would give him a clue to the kidnapper's identity. Her worst fear was that he would not be able to find them before it was too late. She could feel his fears and his anger at not knowing where to begin his search, or what he might find at the end.

In the distance, Ginny saw a light from a torch, swinging to and fro in the woods along the bank. When Denby started rowing toward it, she wondered who else was a party to this horrendous crime.

When the boat neared the bank, Ginny's heart slammed against her chest. Now she could clearly see the man and woman awaiting them — Harold and Evelyn Marlow. Harold waded ankle-deep into the water and dragged the boat ashore, while Evelyn held the torch.

Christine stepped from the boat first and ordered, "Harold, you take the torch so Evelyn can take this baby. He's spit up all over me."

Ginny would have laughed, if there wasn't the chance that Christine would throttle her. Cautiously balancing herself, she held tightly onto Oliver as she put one foot over the side. Harold's fingers bit into her arm as he assisted her. His leering eyes moved over her and a lewd grin curved his mouth. "This time you ain't gittin' away from me," he whispered.

Ginny's stomach churned at the idea of his touch. She would never let him touch her. She would kill him first.

"Let's go," Christine said, shoving Ginny ahead of her. Her voice startling little Oliver, he cried out. "Shut him up."

"If you want him to shut up, Christine," Ginny snapped, "then shut up yourself. You're scaring him."

"What do you want me to do with the boat?" Denby called.

"Push it from the shore and let it drift downstream," Christine answered. "That way no one can trace us."

A wagon was parked nearby, and two horses tethered behind it. Christine took the baby. "Get in, Ginny."

Again Harold came to her assistance. His hands gripped her waist and lingered. He hoisted her into the wagon bed. They handed both babies to her over the side. Ginny

364

prayed they would let her keep them with her. Noticing no one watching her, Ginny drew one of the blankets off Oliver and put it behind her, pushing it through the lower slat. After Evelyn joined her, Harold took the driver's seat and Christine climbed in and sat beside him. Denby untethered one of the horses and mounted.

As the wagon lurched forward, Ginny held her children protectively, watching Christine cautiously, waiting for Christine's taunts. She didn't have a long wait.

Christine turned on the bench. "With you and those twins gone, I expect that in a few short months, Crossroads will be mine again."

"Jonathan will never marry you, Christine, not in a million years."

"Of course he will . . . I'd be an asset to any man," she said casually.

Ginny laughed ironically. "If you think Jonathan will forget his children, just because you wish it, then you are sadly mistaken."

Christine caught her breath. "I see Jonathan really has pulled the wool over your eyes," Christine retorted. "I suppose you also won't believe that he's the mastermind behind our kidnapping you and the twins tonight."

"No, I don't. Nothing you say or do, will ever convince me my husband doesn't love me and the children."

"They won't be his children long," Evelyn put in gleefully. "They'll be ours. Darryl's lookin' forward to carryin' out his fatherly duties."

Now Ginny knew where they were headed, but she could not bring herself to believe Darryl was part of this nightmare. "Oh? Does he also expect me to carry out my wifely duties?"

"No, he won't be bothering you at all," Christine said, a wicked gleam in her eye. "You see, you'll be dead."

Ginny only shivered. *Don't let her sense your fear,* her inner voice warned. With a twin in each arm, she lowered her gaze to their sweet, sleeping faces, then she raised her eyes to the full moon over her. *Jonathan, I know you are looking at this same moon, feeling the same fears I am. Please listen, my love, and hear me. I love you . . . know that I love you more than life itself.*

Ginny hugged her babies, trying to keep her fear at bay. They needed her. For a fleeting moment, she wondered if she would live to see them grow up into the handsome men she knew they would become, but she quickly dispelled the thought.

The wagon stopped abruptly, as it collapsed on one side.

"Damn," Harold swore, "we just lost the axle."

"What's an axle?" Christine asked sharply.

Ginny grinned. "It's that little bar that runs beneath the wagon that turns the wheels, Christine. Without it, we won't be going anywhere."

Crushing fear guided Jonathan and Blue, as they scoured the riverbank searching for clues. They had quickly decided that Christine had taken Ginny and the babies by boat. They knew she would want to travel fast, so she would choose to go the direction of the current. The more he and Blue discussed the kidnapping, they decided that Christine had not worked alone. No doubt Richard Denby was her accomplice.

Jonathan looked at the moon, fading beneath a passing cloud cover. He prayed Ginny was still alive. He knew she would do anything to protect her children. Their lives depended on him, and God, he hoped he could save her. If he lost them, he didn't think he could go on living.

He feared the workings of Christine's demented mind. Her obsession was Crossroads. Ginny and his children were obstacles in her path to attain it, so she was removing them. He was the next obstacle. She would have to get him to marry her to gain it. Was she crazy enough to believe such a thing would ever happen? Yes, or she would never have gone through with this plot to begin with. But he would have given Denby more credit than to ever believe his partner could get away with it, unless . . .

He turned to Blue. "I've figured out what Denby expects to gain in all this."

"What's that, boss?"

"Christine's told him I'll marry her, and probably promised him she'll see that I drop the charges against him. Who knows, as crazy as she is, she might have even told him she'll do away with me after we're married, and marry him."

Blue sighed. "Bloody hell, neither of 'em have both oars in the water."

"Speaking of oars, I wonder just how far downriver they'd go. I doubt they know enough about boats to risk going very far at night. That thought scares the hell out of me, Blue. If the boat capsized, Ginny could save herself and perhaps one of the boys, but not both."

There were only a few clear shorelines along the river, that a boat could put in conveniently. They checked them all. Nothing. In the moonlight, Blue thought he saw the outline of a small boat caught in broken branches along the bank. They dismounted and studied it.

"Yep, that's a boat all right," Blue said jubilantly.

"If it *is* their boat, they wouldn't have put in here, that's for damned sure. The bank's too high. I'd say they got out at one of those places we've already checked, and left the boat to drift. But if it *isn't* their boat, we'll lose time if we backtrack. What do you think we should do?"

"Follow our instincts . . . backtrack, boss."

Jonathan's fears mounted with each passing moment. What if Christine had killed Ginny during the boat trip and thrown her body in the river? *Please God, please don't let us be too late.*

Arriving at the next clearing, he and Blue dismounted. Blue lit the torch. They walked the area and listened, but all was quiet.

Going deeper into the woods, they found what they were looking for, wheel tracks cutting into the soft carpet of pine mulch. Nearby, Jonathan saw something lying on the ground. "Bring the light over here, Blue."

He picked it up and knew what is was before the light ever shone over it. He rubbed the soft flannel over his face, and breathed in the scent of his baby. Blue stood beside him, and saw the tears swimming in Jonathan's eyes, as he lifted his head.

"Ginny's leaving us clues. We'd better hurry. I don't trust Christine at all."

Mounting again, they followed the wheel tracks through the woods. Several times along the way they'd stop and listen, then move on again.

"Fix it," Christine ordered.

"I can't fix it in the dark," Harold said, damned tired of having the woman order him around like a pet dog. "It's not long until daylight."

"We can't wait until daylight, you stupid fool."

"He ain't stupid," Evelyn hissed. "Darryl's the stupid one. Ain't he, Harold?" she asked, as though she was beginning to doubt his intelligence.

"You're all stupid to think you can get away with this," Ginny put in.

"You shut up, Ginny Sutton," Christine shouted.

"Ginny Summerfield," she corrected.

"A dead Ginny Summerfield, if you don't shut up," Christine snapped.

Denby pulled his mount in beside the wagon. "We don't have time to argue. If we can't fix the wagon, then I suggest we leave it here and walk."

"Walk!" Evelyn shouted. "That's fine for you to say. You two have horses. All we have is that swaybacked, good-for-nothing excuse for a horse."

"It's not the horse's fault," Christine said. "Harold should have made sure the wagon was in good condition, before you two met us."

"Now, don't go blamin' it all on me," Harold said. "I checked that wagon over real good."

"Then why did that axle thing break, you idiot?"

Harold leaped to his feet, as angry as he had ever been in his life. "There you go agin, callin' me an idiot. Well, I've had it up to here," he said, slicing a dirty finger across his throat. "You could've brought that fancy carriage of yorn's, and nothin' like this would've happened."

"What! And let you foul it with your unwashed bodies!" Now Evelyn bounded to her feet. "Why, you bitch, I wash regularly."

"When? Once a year?" Christine countered acidly. "And I doubt Harold knows what a bar of soap even looks like."

Their tirade had awakened both babies. Along with the adults' screaming, Oliver joined in, screaming at the top of his lungs. Cross, frightened by the commotion bellowed his displeasure. Ginny felt better than she had since the beginning of her dangerous journey. If Jonathan was anywhere nearby, the babies would let him know their location.

"Stop shouting," Denby shouted himself, trying to raise his voice above the mad chorus. "Do you want to lead them right to us?"

All mouths slammed tighter than clams, all except the twins. Never had Ginny heard them cry like this. Their tiny fists and feet were flailing the air, and she knew their faces would be blood red. Wet, hungry, sleepy, and angry, they wanted the whole world to know about their discomfort. Ginny smiled. She only needed Jonathan to hear, and then everything would be all right.

Christine climbed over the bench and growled between clenched teeth, "God, I can't stand this. Can't you make them shut up?"

"How? No one could sleep through your caterwauling."

Ginny saw Christine's hand coming toward her, but with the babies in her arms, she couldn't protect herself. Her head almost snapped from her shoulders, as Christine's hand slammed against her cheek. If she cried out, she didn't know it, her children were crying so intensely.

"I'll shut him up." Christine snatched Oliver from Ginny's arms, and clasped her hand over his mouth.

Ginny's heart raced as she heard his muffled cry. If she didn't do something quick, she feared Christine would smother him.

"They're hungry and wet, Christine." Ginny's breasts were throbbing, and the front of her gown was wet with milk. "If you'll let me feed them, they'll stop crying."

"We don't have time."

"Then I guess you'll just have to put up with their crying, for the duration of the journey."

"I agree with Harold, Christine. We wait until daylight and get the wagon fixed. We wouldn't make good time walking anyway, having to fool with these babies. Let her feed them," Denby insisted. "If you don't, Jonathan will find us for sure."

"Oh, then feed the little nuisances." The moment her hand left Oliver's mouth, he let out a yowl. She thrust him into the crook of Ginny's arm. "This will be the last time you ever nurse your babies." Her icy words crystallized everything Ginny had feared.

36

Dawn was breaking, when Jonathan and Blue reined their horses in and removed their flasks from their saddles. As they were quenching their thirst, they suddenly straightened in their saddles and looked at one another.

"Are you hearin' what I'm hearin', Boss?" Blue asked, cocking his head toward the sounds.

"You bet I am, and it isn't the sounds of wild cats either." Turning in his saddle, a broad smile broke across his face. "It's the twins, Blue, and they must be madder than hell right now. But damn, I've never heard a more wonderful sound."

"Yeah, me either, and I never thought I'd ever say that, after they've waked me up in the dead of night more times than I can count."

"Let's go get them, Blue," Jonathan said, clucking his tongue and gently nudging Beowulf.

Hardly anytime had passed when they heard voices. Dismounting, they tethered their horses and walked quietly toward the sound. They crouched behind a fallen tree. The towering trees allowed only a scant amount of light to break through their full, leafy tops, but there was enough light for them to see the wagon and the people clearly— Christine, Denby, Evelyn, and Harold. Sitting in the wagon was Ginny and the babies. She was nursing one of the twins. His body started shaking with blinding rage when he noticed Harold, his arms crossed over the side of the wagon, leering at his Ginny. Evelyn sat on the ground and leaned against the tree, her beefy jaws working voraciously on a drumstick. She tossed it aside, and pulled out another one from the sack laying in her lap. An agitated Christine was pacing back and forth, beating her fists together in front of Denby, who sat on a stump watching her, his hands folded between his spread legs.

Jonathan turned toward Blue and whispered, "Four against two, not very good odds when they're holding my family hostage."

"What's taking you so damned long?" Christine snapped, drawing Jonathan's and Blue's attention.

"I can't nurse but one baby at a time, Christine," Ginny countered angrily. She tried to turn her body from Harold's view.

"Well, hurry, will you?"

Harold switched a wad of tobacco from one cheek to another. "Settle down, Christine, we ain't but about five miles from the farm anyhow."

"Why didn't you tell me that before?" she hissed between clenched teeth.

" 'Cause you didn't ask," he said, spitting tobacco juice at her feet.

She threw her head up wildly and laughed, her lip curling contemptuously. "In that case, I see no sense in waiting. We'll kill her now and dump her body in the river."

Jonathan thought his heart had stopped beating, and his whole body went numb as coldness claimed him. He thought he had prepared himself for this moment, but her threat had taken him by surprise. Then his numbness passed, leaving in its place a flaming fury. He had to put a stop to this madness.

"Now wait just a gol-dern minute," Harold exclaimed. "I thought you was just tryin' to scare her back there. You told us we was gonna take her with us when we leave the farm. We told Ma about catchin' her and Darryl breedin'

the barn, and even got her convinced these youngens
re Darryl's."

"You'll still have the twins and the money, Harold, so
hat's the difference? And remember, when I marry Jonaan Cross—or Jonathan Summerfield, whatever his name
—there'll be a bonus for you. But this time, upon my
ord, I'm going to make sure Ginny doesn't return and
ul up my plans."

"This time, Christine?" Ginny asked, her heart in her
roat. "What are you talking about?"

"Will you please hold your tongue, Christine?" Denby
rdered.

"Why? She won't be around to tell on you, Richard. He
t fire to your house, Ginny—on my orders, of course.
nfortunately, you managed to survive, and then returned
 take from me what was mine. I'll see to it you'll never
ep a foot on Lyndal property again."

Jonathan's body tightened as rigid as a bowstring, and
is eyes kindled with a dangerous light as he turned to
lue. "So help me God, Blue, I'm going to kill her. I have
. Stay here while I go get Beowulf. I want her to think
ve just come in on the scene."

Blue grabbed his arm and whispered. "You can't go ri-
in' in there like that! They'll kill you on the spot."

"I'm not going to sit here and watch her murder my
ife." Jonathan crawled back from him, and once out of
ght, took off in a dead run.

Ginny would not beg Christine for her life. That would
e the final humiliation.

"Wait a minute," Harold said. "We don't have to kill her.
ll make sure she never escapes."

"Yeah, so you can bed her," Evelyn drawled. "I've seen
e way you look at her. No way I'm livin' in the same
ouse with that bitch."

"We can't shoot her," Denby said. "Someone might hear
e shots."

"We don't need to shoot her," Christine said. "There's other ways. Put down the babies and come here Ginny."

A rush of nausea left Ginny limp and cold. She laid Oliver and Cross side by side. This time, her bravado failed her. The tears sparkled in her eyes and splashed on her childrens' faces, as she leaned down and kissed each baby's cheek. *Where is Jonathan? He can't let them kill me.* Then a strange calm washed over her. She rose slowly to her feet and looked deep into the forest. *He's here . . . I feel his presence. Yes, I do.*

Jonathan rode past Blue on Beowulf and carefully controlled the tension roiling inside him, as he called out "Somebody here?"

Christine ordered, "Yes, but whoever you are, turn back."

Ignoring her, Jonathan slowed Beowulf to a trot and broke into the clearing, continuing toward the wagon. He glimpsed at Ginny and nodded discreetly. "No, Christine, won't turn back."

Her plans thwarted, Christine's eyes turned wild. "I have a gun, Jonathan. Don't come any closer."

"If you kill me, Christine, you'll never live in Crossroad . . . unless, of course, you can seduce my father into marrying you. He owns it, not me."

Christine whirled toward Denby. "You said he was to get the deed after he married and had children."

"He was, but they dismissed me, so I never saw it through to its completion."

Jonathan swung his long leg partially over the saddle and sat casually atop Beowulf. "It could still happen, if you'd let Ginny and the babies go."

"I'm not that big a fool, Jonathan. How can I marry you, when you're still married to her?"

"I'll have the marriage annulled. Ginny said in her note that the children weren't mine. At last I believe her. He

374

other broke down and told me the truth. She felt guilty
r allowing the marriage to take place, but they knew no
ay out of their dilemma." Jonathan didn't risk looking at
s wife again, afraid that Christine would see his love for
r. "Ginny refused to marry Darryl, and planned to raise
e child without a father. I foolishly thought the child—or
ildren as it turned out—belonged to me, and married
r."

"But you said, you were already married when she got
rself with child."

"I had to lie to protect my child's future. I didn't want
yone to know about his illegitimacy. You see, Christine,
n a bastard, and I know the pain of growing up without
y father's name. That was one reason I couldn't marry
u, though I wanted to. You're a lady, and I felt I wasn't
rthy of you," he lied.

"Wasn't worthy of me!" she exclaimed. "I've known about
ur illegitimacy before you ever arrived at Crossroads.
enby told me. I would've married you regardless."

"Then you should have told me, and we wouldn't have
d to go through all this misery."

"You loved her, you grieved over her death, and now
u're telling me all that was a lie, too?"

"Yes. She was just like me, an outcast. In marrying her,
could live with my lie. As it is now, I'm going to have to
ar the humiliation of having my marriage annulled. Af-
rwards, I doubt even *you* would want to marry me."

Christine ran toward him. She placed her hand on his
igh. "No, you're wrong, I would marry you this instant,
I could."

"Don't believe him, Christine," Denby cautioned. "He's
icking you."

"No, Denby, he isn't," Ginny called. "I'm sorry, Jonaan, for the pain I've caused you. I would have married
arryl, if I'd known I wouldn't have to live in the same
use with his family. He was such a sweet, sensitive man,

375

whereas these two I couldn't tolerate. Quite frankly, I'
rather die now than to live through such torture again."

The word *torture* pounded and echoed in Christine'
mind. She turned toward Ginny. "No, Ginny, you'll live
Knowing you're living in hell would suit my purpose bet
ter."

"Like hell she'll live. Cross won't either," Denby shouted
aiming his pistol at Jonathan.

Pistol in hand, Jonathan leaped to the ground, as Chris
tine screamed and jumped in front of him. "No, Richard!

Denby fired. A split second later, another gunsho
pierced the air, and Denby fell face forward to the ground
Christine turned and staggered toward Jonathan, one han
clutching her chest, the other holding the gun loosely a
her side. Blood gushed through her fingers, as she fell t
her knees in front of him.

When she looked up at him with glazed eyes, Jonatha
couldn't believe the remarkable change in her face. Gon
was the cynical curve of her mouth and the hatred in he
eyes. In its place was peace and . . . yes . . . happiness.

"We'll have the biggest wedding Virginia's ever seen. I'
wear blue . . ." she smiled softly, "yes, blue . . . blue is m
best . . . color . . ." Her voice faded into nothingness
Christine Lyndal Iverson fell against Jonathan's legs, the
crumpled to the ground.

Jonathan looked toward Ginny. She was standing at th
edge of the wagon and sobbing. He never noticed Blu
standing beside him, aiming his gun toward Evelyn an
Harold. Jonathan broke into a run and leaped upon th
wagon. His arm reached out and went around her waist
drawing her into his arms.

"I knew you'd find us," she cried, her voice a thick whis
per as she wrapped her arms around his neck.

She tipped back her head to meet his mouth, an
wrapped her arms around him. They kissed urgently, hun
grily, their thighs pressed hard together and their bodie

straining. Slowly he loosened his hold on her, breaking the kiss, he gazed down at her face. He pushed back the wisps of hair from her face, and saw her busted lip and swollen cheek. "She hit you."

"But I'm alive . . . and she . . . and she isn't."

Then he looked over her shoulder toward the twins. "She didn't hurt the boys, did she?" he asked anxiously.

"No, they've only stopped crying." She smiled softly, her voice choked with emotion. "They know their father's here."

He hugged her to him, his heart just now slowing to its normal pace. Releasing her, he walked slowly to the back of the wagon and knelt beside his sleeping children. Ginny followed and knelt beside him, resting her head against his shoulder.

He took hold of each baby's hand and raised them to his mouth, brushing his lips softly over them. "They saved your life, did you know that?" he asked, turning his head to kiss her forehead. "Blue and I found the baby blanket I assume you dropped purposely, and then later heard them crying."

"Did you find my locket?"

"No, your mother did. Then she recalled your father telling her about the secret passage. It left no doubt in my mind then who'd taken my family."

She placed her hand on his cheek. "We could have both died, you know, pulling that trick."

"I had to take the chance, or lose you. If you hadn't believed I was lying and helped me, we—"

She pressed her fingertips over his lips. "I never doubted for one moment your love for me, Jonathan. And when I wrote that horrible letter to you, I knew in my heart you wouldn't believe those lies. I knew you'd come for me and our children."

"What're we going to do with Harold and Evelyn?" Blue asked.

377

"I forgot all about them," Jonathan muttered and stood up.

He turned and saw Blue standing with one hand on his hip, the other holding a gun. His eyes followed the direction of its aim and came to rest on Evelyn and Harold, as they stood beside the wagon.

"Good question. Thanks for looking after them, Blue."

"Sure, boss," he said with a grin. "Hey, that was some shot you popped off at Denby."

Jonathan frowned. "I didn't shoot him. I thought you did."

"No, everything happened so fast, it caught me by surprise."

"Maybe Christine got him. She still had her gun."

"No," Ginny said, "I was watching her. She never had a chance."

"Then who did?" they all asked in unison. They looked at Harold and Evelyn.

"All right, drop your gun," Blue ordered.

"I didn't do it, and Evelyn couldn't shoot anything if it was standing smack-dab in front of her," Harold said insultingly, receiving a hard jab in his ribs from his wife's elbow.

"Well, bloody hell," Blue cursed, "then I guess one of the twins did it, huh?"

"Sh-h, I hear something," Ginny said.

They all heard it—deep, heart-wrenching sobs, coming from somewhere nearby. Ginny broke from Jonathan's arms, sat down on the end of the wagon, then slid to the ground. Following the sound, she leaned over and looked under the wagon. Darryl was lying on his stomach, his head buried beneath his arms. Beside him laid a pistol.

Kneeling, she said softly, "Darryl, it's all right."

"I did bad."

"No, Darryl, you saved our lives, just like I remember you saving the lives of the little animals." She looked up

378

nd saw Jonathan standing beside her. She smiled up at im sadly.

"I ain't never kilt nothin, Ginny," he said, lifting his tear-reaked face.

Ginny sat down and leaned under the wagon, gently aking her fingers through his hair. "Denby was a bad per-on, Darryl. If you hadn't shot him, he would have killed s, even your brother and Evelyn."

"They won't put me in a cage, will they?"

Ginny knew he meant prison. "No, Jonathan and I vould never let anyone do that to you."

"What about Harold and Evelyn? They didn't kill no-ody, but they was bad to you. When that fancy woman ome to the house the first time, she just wanted them to ay a visit to your new husband. Then she come back gain. I hid and listened. I heared her talkin' about all the noney she'd give Harold and Evelyn, if they'd help her teal you and the babies. That's why I sawed the axle, so it vould break."

A lump grew in her throat. "You did that?"

"Yeah, I had to stop 'em." He leaned up on his elbow. They didn't say nuthin' about killin' you, Ginny, honest hey didn't, or I woulda tole Ma about it. Are you goin' to ell her?"

"Do you want us to?"

"No, it'll kill her. Then I won't have nobody, when they ut Harold and Evelyn in a cage."

After hearing this, Jonathan knelt beside Ginny. "Dar-yl, we won't say anything, I promise," he said in a loud oice, so Harold and Evelyn would hear him. "But if they ver threaten my wife or children again, I won't be able to eep that promise." Jonathan reached his hand beneath the vagon and clasped Darryl's hand. "For you, I'll do this. If t wasn't for you, I might have never seen my wife and hildren again."

"You love her a whole lot, don't ya, Mr. Cross?"

"Yes, a whole lot." He gazed at his wife and drank in her loveliness. Removing his hand from atop Darryl's, he softly stroked her cheek.

"I love her, too. She's the best friend I've ever had."

"She's my best friend, too, Darryl," he said, his eyes filled with loving tenderness as they met and held with his wife's. "Yes, mine, too," he repeated softly from the bottom of his heart.

Epilogue

The sweeping lawn was bedecked with baskets, overflowg with sweet-smelling flowers. Long tables covered with e finest of linens and set with crystal vases of fresh-cut ses dotted the grounds. The cream of Virginia society ngregated on the lawn, awaiting their host and hostess.

They were gathered to witness the reaffirmation of Jonaan and Ginny's wedding vows. It was an unusual occurnce, and not one with which they were familiar. Yet it d a nice ring to it, and fit the peculiarities of the upper ass.

Everyone knew the young couple adored each other, and is act only confirmed their devotion.

Lord Oliver Summerfield was a delight to behold, as he untered through the crowd, greeting everyone by name d exchanging pleasantries. Like his son, he had taken irginia by storm. And to the dismay of the widowed men and the delight of others, he paid an uncommon nount of attention to Maureen Sutton.

Bertha had her hands full with the twins. Still she rived on the care of her charges. She was aglow with ide, as one then another complimented her on the chilen.

Patrick and Milly Sutton wandered arm and arm rough the crowd. Milly's father had agreed to their mar-

riage, and was of a mind to claim all the credit for th
match.

Christine Iverson's death had shocked the communit
but she was not grieved for. No one had escaped the bit
of her tongue or the vindictiveness of her schemes. In th
light of her death, Milly's father discovered Christine ha
been feeding him untruths about Patrick. When Mr. Vin
cent took it upon himself to get to know Patrick, ther
were no longer any doubts that Patrick would make a fin
husband for his youngest daughter. Also, Patrick's future a
the silversmith shop was secure. The owner had told hir
that because he had no children to inherit his lifelong bus
ness, he wanted Patrick to have it.

Edna Talbot had also changed. It had been hard for he
to admit that Christine had used their friendship to fee
her hatred of Ginny by spreading lies. Taking the lesson t
heart, Edna now lent herself to true friendship with he
former acquaintances.

Suddenly a hush settled over the gathering, as th
strains of a melody floated through the air, and Jonatha
and Ginny walked toward the minister. He stood framed i
a lattice arbor draped in red and white roses, the gentl
smile on his face warming all that looked upon it. H
voice rang loud and clear, as he instructed Ginny and Jon
athan on the vows they had exchanged so long ago.

Ginny was breathtaking in pure, delicate white. He
long hair, coiled atop her head and braided with tiny ye
low rosebuds, picked up the light and glistened in the sur
Jonathan stood proudly beside her attired in black, excep
a white shirt with perfect ruffles scaling his chest. H
looked at his beloved wife. She looked at her husband
They spoke solely to one another, as they reaffirmed thei
vows. *Till death do we part,* they whispered at last. And eac
remembered.

The pain and sorrow they'd suffered could not over
shadow the joy and happiness they were sharing now.

382

She squeezed Jonathan's hand and looked deeply into warm gray eyes. How she loved this wonderful man. was indeed her Prince Charming. Yes, fairy tales did ne true. She was living proof that they did.

HEARTFIRE ROMANCES

SWEET TEXAS NIGHTS   (2610, $3.7
by Vivian Vaughan
Meg Britton grew up on the railroads, working proudly at h
father's side. Nothing was going to stop them from setting t
rails clear to Silver Creek, Texas—certainly not some crazy pro
pector. As Meg set out to confront the old coot, she planned h
strategy with cool precision. But soon she was speechless wi
shock. For instead of a harmless geezer, she found a boldly han
some stranger whose determination matched her own.

CAPTIVE DESIRE   (2612, $3.7
by Jane Archer
Victoria Malone fancied herself a great adventuress, but bei
kidnapped was too much excitement for even Victoria! Especia
when her arrogant kidnapper thought she was part of Red Duke
outlaw gang. Trying to convince the overbearing, handson
stranger that she had been an innocent bystander when the stag
coach was robbed, proved futile. But when he thought he cou
maker her confess by crushing her to his warm, broad chest, b
caressing her with his strong, capable hands, Victoria was willi
to admit to anything. . . .

LAWLESS ECSTASY   (2613, $3.7
by Susan Sackett
Abra Beaumont could spot a thief a mile away. After all, h
father was once one of the best. But he'd been on the right side
the law for years now, and she wasn't about to let a man like Das
Thorne lead him astray with some wild plan for stealing the Te
of Allah, the world's most fabulous ruby. Dash was just the so
of man she most distrusted—sophisticated, handsome, and alt
gether too sure of his considerable charm. Abra shivered at t
devilish gleam in his blue eyes and swore he would need mo
than smooth kisses and skilled caresses to rob her of her virt
. . . and much more than sweet promises to steal her heart!